"A truly unforgettable world of spirits and magical men. Guillory's community is like the richest of cultural maps, peopled by some of the most memorable characters I have ever encountered."

—Dolen Perkins-Valdez, *New York Times*
bestselling author of *Wench*

"Literary Zydeco: rolling, captivating, filled with sweet joy yet informed by sorrow. This is everything a debut novel should be: the call of a distinctive new voice staking claim to undiscovered territory. Marcus Guillory has created a heartfelt tribute to the beauty of Creole culture."

—Mat Johnson, author of *PYM*

red now and laters

a novel

Marcus J. Guillory

ATRIA PAPERBACK

New York   London   Toronto   Sydney   New Delhi

ATRIA PAPERBACK
An Imprint of Simon & Schuster, Inc.
1230 Avenue of the Americas
New York, NY 10020

First Atria paperback edition March 2015

ATRIA PAPERBACK and colophon are trademarks of Simon & Schuster, Inc.

For information about special discounts for bulk purchases, please contact Simon & Schuster Special Sales at 1-866-506-1949 or business@simonandschuster.com.

The Simon & Schuster Speakers Bureau can bring authors to your live event. For more information or to book an event contact the Simon & Schuster Speakers Bureau at 1-866-248-3049 or visit our website at www.simonspeakers.com.

Designed by Kyoko Watanabe
Cover artwork by Angelbert Metoyer

Manufactured in the United States of America

10 9 8 7 6 5 4 3 2 1

The Library of Congress has cataloged the hardcover edition as follows:

Guillory, Marcus J.
    Red Now and Laters / Marcus J. Guillory.
        pages cm
    1. African American healers—Fiction. 2. African American rodeo performers—Fiction. 3. Houston (Tex.)—Fiction. 4. Domestic fiction. I. Title.
    PS3607.U48555R43 2013
    813'.6—dc23
                                            2013000901

ISBN 978-1-4516-9911-1
ISBN 978-1-4767-7685-9 (pbk)
ISBN 978-1-4516-9912-8 (ebook)

For Marguerite, a free Negrisse

&

For my sister, Letitia R. Guillory

Contents

part three

confirmation and its burdens

Author's Note

The term *Creole* means many things to many people. The word *Creole* comes from the Portuguese *crioullo,* meaning "native to this place." In eighteenth-century Louisiana, *Creole* referred to native-born Spaniards, French, and enslaved people who were the issue of African slaves, Native Americans, and Europeans. With the arrival of the United States in 1803, *Creole* was used to distinguish between the natives and the Americans. Consequently, many French-speaking whites from Louisiana were considered "Creole," not to be confused with *Acadiens* or *Cajuns,* who were the descendants of French-speaking Acadians banished by the British from the Acadia region of Canada and settled in the Attakapas region of Louisiana.

But prior to 1803, there existed a peculiar class of people called *"les gens du couleur libres."* Free people of color. They were descendants of the enslaved Africans, Native Americans, and French and Spanish settlers who developed their own indigenous culture that was a mixture of French, Spanish, African, and Native American cultures.

Today, the term *Creole* typically refers to the descendants of these free people of color and their culture. This novel concerns the agrarian-based communities of southwestern Louisiana Creoles. As a matter of full disclosure, the author proudly acknowledges that he is a member of this unique American culture.

Also, the author has taken the liberty of referring to the language deemed "Louisiana Creole" by many academics as *Creole,* as it is called colloquially. While there are variances on the language, the author put forth a diligent effort to make the language accurate in the context of the time and speaker.

Finally, the author represents that this is a work of fiction although drawn from historical and factual events, both public and private, and does not seek to disparage any known persons, places, or events, but merely used them as inspiration for a fictitious story.

À la censure, hélas! qui nous surveille,
Vite en passant ôtons notre chapeau,
À ses discours ouvrons bien notre oreille
Pour n'être pas nommé poètereau—
De francs amis.

—Nicol Riquet, public domain, published in
Les Cenelles in 1845 from "Rondeau Redoublé"

As for the censors, dour and unbenign,
Alas! let's tip our cap at them as we
Pass by, and lend an ear, lest they opine
A wretched rhymester shares your company—
My loyal band.

PART I

roux

Tell them when they ask,
tell them that wasn't no nigger
hanging from that tree.
Tell them it was a Frenchman,
a free man of color.
Tell them it was Marguerite's kin
that they hung
on his own gotdamn property.
Tell them.
And if you don't,
then ta hell with all y'all.

—Translated from Creole as Jules Saint-Pierre
Sonnier was about to be hung by Klansmen,
January 5, 1953, in Basile, Louisiana, after
successfully working a powerful gris-gris on
Leon Richard, then mayor of Eunice, Louisiana

growin' up wet

Houston, Texas, c. 1977

God's tears are brown. At least, that's what it looks like in Houston when it floods. Not blue nor translucent but dark brown and murky like gumbo with dark roux amassing in His eyes, waiting to drop and cleanse, waiting to kill, waiting to replenish the depleted or fatten the sated. Glorious roux made of grain and grease then poured into the sweat of the body, the stock water, that holy abandoned fluid, then boiled to make one. Hours later, when it smells familiar and tastes appropriate, it falls onto the land of the living with no apologies nor remorse.

And on this particular day we got proof. God was crying—actually, having a fuckin' fit. The sky was painted gunpowder gray by men in white coveralls with journeymen cards. Intrepid seagulls brave enough for flight resembled chalk glyphs on a blackboard against the pregnant sky, soaring high enough to witness yet confused, not knowing exactly where the docks of Kemah or League City laid anchor. Where was the sun?

Flash floods had laid siege to the city of Houston, holding its residents hostage. Every street, ditch, parking lot, bayou, all of it had been inundated with brown toxic rainwater, taking extreme advantage of the numerous low-lying areas throughout Harris County. Potholes and gullies became urban booby traps camouflaged by brown murky murk that darkened once it hit the ground. Surely those poor seagulls must have been convinced that the bountiful Gulf of Mexico had made land, lending its drunk temper to the Bayou City. Mother Nature's wager gone awry, the age-old fight between land and sea with the odds stacked against resilient land and its foolish, man-made spectacles built on doughty dirt. Yet the land stands resolute, hosting temples to honor the sun, so the sea fights back to remind outflanked land that the house always wins. Neptune can get pushy when he's shooting dice with Olokun on the dirty sea floor. Just ask the Vietnamese shrimpers on Galveston Island.

Schools were closed. Those with four-wheel-drive trucks were conscripted into pulling out low-riding Oldsmobiles, curb-hugging Caddies, and the occasional Toyota from the clutches of the brown murky murk.

Then there were the bayous, four in all, emissaries of the mighty Gulf, running through the city like shit through a goose. Each with its own ailments and reputation, giving the Bayou City a constant runny nose.

Decades before the Civil War, Americans had settled along Buffalo Bayou to create an outpost for trade, a new place to be white and free. Fuck Santa Anna, they said. They named the bayou settlement after Sam Houston, a drunk who could shoot. Thus, the bayous were important to the identity of the city. But matched up against the massive and mercurial Gulf of Mexico, the bayous weren't much but a few creeks moving about like wayward children left unattended.

Father and I had been wading in it for half an hour by now. I sat on his forearm, my tiny arms wrapped around his neck. The water came just below his chest. Too high for me. I was just four years old.

By now I had stopped crying. An hour earlier, Father had arrived at my preschool. I was in the back room huddled with other kids eating PB&J sandwiches in the dark. Kids don't cry with a mouth full of peanut butter.

The rising waters had made pickups a perilous task reserved for the worthy and the fearless, and most of the kids' parents hadn't arrived yet, but Father was there. I knew he'd show. He was a cowboy. A real one.

I recognized his voice at the front door of the converted house on South Park Boulevard. That voice that I first heard when he spoke to Mother's womb—high and hopeful, announcing plans and wishes with repetition and delight. Now at the rainy hour, it was deep and hurried with politeness making way for urgency. It sounded mirific just the same.

Ms. Fisher led me by the hand to the front door, where Father waited in full yellow rubbers with the hat to match like the Gorton's fisherman. He took a knee and helped me button up my raincoat.

"Come on, Sonny. We gotta go get your momma," he said.

I was moving too slow. He avoided my eyes, focused on the process of buttoning with quick, accurate hand movements like a bank teller or cashier. Automaton excelsior with wet face and long hair sprawled across his back. Creole Jesus in motion. No time for the customary ponytail that we both wore on occasion. No time for vanity.

Finally, he looked at me, worried and protective, gently placing his palms against my doughy cheeks.

"Come on, Ti' John. I'ma carry you, okay?" he offered.

I didn't argue. I liked it when he'd scoop me up. He wasn't big. Lean stature, average height. But big fuckin' hands. Big and swollen and scarred. Darker than mine. Father didn't take any mess from anybody and his hands were a testament to that fact. He hoisted me into his arms and suddenly I was six feet tall, just like when I'd stand on the kitchen counter while Mother wasn't looking, even though I was afraid of heights.

The door opened and you could smell it. Noxious air blended with gasoline, liquor, blood, shit, shame, and fear with a quiet hint of desperate courage. My neighborhood—South Park—was underwater.

Heads and shoulders eased through the brown murky murk like brown ducks in a public pond. Trying to find higher ground. Looking for loved ones. Searching for relief. Vigorous brown water crested at the welcome mat before the front door—the little mat with embroidered balloons, smiling rabbits, and cuddly bears that assured parents that their children would be safe. The sloping driveway of the preschool was all brown water that stretched across South Park Boulevard with no way of determining where the street began from the driveway.

Neptune laughed and rolled the dice again, his rapacious eyes set on those unfortunates bedridden in the soaked soil. Homes and structures fronting the boulevard sat lonely and bewildered, lifelike, waiting for their masters' return as small waves washed upon them, leaving wet dirt to mock their sheathing. Vehicles sat stalled on roadways, allowing only their roofs and cabs reprieve from the brown murky murk—mechanical schoolchildren confined to watery desks raising their hands for attendance, insisting that they were present. But nobody was taking roll this day. Nobody cared if you were tardy or absent. The only thing that mattered was staying alive.

"I don't wanna go out there, Daddy," I pleaded, but he was resolute.

"C'mon, boy. Ain't got time for none of that," he said as he took the first step into the gumbo.

A seagull shat on an old black man's head as he waded by us. He smiled at me and started whistling "Nearer, My God, to Thee"—the only melody heard on the streets, competing with splashing water and the mumbles and groans of those wading.

Strange to see things in distress, natural distress like floods. But South Park was no stranger to distress, all but too familiar. South Park. My hood.

South Park occupied the largest swath of land in Southeast Houston, Texas. Developed in the late 1940s and 1950s, the area was filled with starter homes for young white couples reeling from Houston's oil boom and servicemen reeling from the G.I. Bill. The city fathers saw to it that each of those veterans could quantify his victory with a three-bedroom house complete with a front and backyard. Half of the streets in the new development called South Park were named after World War II battles, locations, and personalities: Bataan Road, Chennault Road, Doolittle Boulevard, Southseas Street, Dunmore Drive, St. Lo Road, et cetera. A promise kept and a street sign to remind you, Uncle Sam figured.

By the time these young white urbanites were cutting their yards for the first time, the Negroes were mainly collected in First, Fourth, and Fifth Wards on the outskirts of Downtown Houston waiting on ole Uncle Jim Crow to retire, but he wasn't going anywhere. Yet the law of supply and demand opened the doors for employment and black men from the Gulf Coast found gainful employ in various industries supported by the oil industry, NASA, the Houston Ship Channel, and the burgeoning medical industry. Consequently, the blacks moved into South Park, the whites moved out. My parents were one of the first black families to move in.

Then the oil bubble burst, leaving many in South Park to fend for themselves. But the city fathers hadn't planned on South Park becoming a black neighborhood. There were no street signs related to the American black experience, only nomenclature proudly hoisted on corners typifying Americana at its best—World War II—the good war, the good white American, the good war fought by good white Americans for the salvation of the entire free world. As a result of the black arrival, improvements and funding in the area ceased with the exception of increased law enforcment. South Park became economically depressed, devoid of the optimism it once held in its well-planned hands. But it was well-planned under then-modern notions of urban design so misery was dispersed evenly.

As the 1970s approached and the political landscape began to shift emphasis to housing and education, Uncle Sam decided to throw South Park a bone: one new post office and newly minted government-subsidized apartments that resembled cardboard boxes. Liquor stores and small churches competed neck and neck for claims of cheap dirt sold by woeful white veterans who signed quick claim deeds on the backs of bingo cards at the Elks Lodge with laments that "nigras stole my piece of the American dream." Public schools were neglected, and I mean both buildings and students. Roadways became patchworks of asphalt fill-ins and forgotten cement. Gas stations offering cheap beer and barbeque sandwiches chaperoned each corner. And the only new developments that kept popping up were neon-lit liquor stores and gleaming new gas stations to replace ratty old liquor stores and the forlorn old gas stations.

By the late seventies, South Park had slammed its brakes and skidded violently into a telephone pole called "progress." The hood was totaled and what remained was only suitable for a scrap yard, its potential spent and discarded to the side like aluminum cans and balding tires, with vicious guard dogs barking at its borders, guarding junk like jewels, foaming at the mouth because its master feeds it scraps and beats it with an ax handle. But the dogs guard the fence with misplaced courage, goading outsiders to try to enter. Thus, South Park became a "ghetto."

Its inhabitants were, as they say, good people with better memories of an unforgotten past. Mostly first- and second-generation city folk wired into an urban matrix, sustained by unhealthy food and hearty rustic resilience. Hand-painted signs with poor grammar announced black-owned businesses that serviced the wants and needs of the community. We were survivors and accepted ownership of our happiness and sorrow because we knew that nobody gave a damn, which is exactly why we were floating around South Park Boulevard trying to find our way home.

But nobody complained about the government too much since HPD had sniped People's Party II revolutionary Carl Hampton from the roof of St. John Missionary Baptist Church on Dowling Street in Third Ward years earlier. So we weren't expecting the National Guard to rush in on outboards with life preservers and Caridade's blessing. Not for us. Not for South Park.

What I remember most about that stormy afternoon wading down South Park Boulevard was the deathly silence of the once bustling boulevard. Weeks earlier cars had cruised down South Park Boulevard blasting Funkadelic or Bobby Blue Bland, pausing in front of beauty salons as the foxy ladies stepped out into the world like brand-new money. Tight double knits, polyester stretched across their curves, and afros shaped and sheened, headed to JB's Entertainment Center, the Groovey Grill, the Thunderbird Lounge, or the Continental for a Scotch and soda and a question about their zodiac sign. This was the tail end of the seventies. Black was still beautiful, baby.

But now, you only heard the splash of water, the reluctant seagulls, and desperate murmurs and prayers said under bated breath. Until a scream rent the thick, fetid air.

A young black woman had lost her grip and dropped her infant into a fast-moving current that she soon learned was a five-foot-deep gully. She dipped frantically into the brown murky murk, feeling around broken glass, aluminum cans, and balding tires for her child. Opening her eyes was impossible, and she wouldn't have been able to see anything anyway. Others came to her assistance immediately, mimicking her routine of drop and feel, but it was no use.

The gully took her child.

Law enforcement would find the dead infant three days later at a backed-up drainage ditch resting peacefully, with South Park's debris as a blanket, never to know the sting of the ax handle or the bitterness of scraps. The police report would list his name as Russell Davis.

Father took long but careful steps toward his green Ford parked against the grassy rise of the overpass at the 610 Loop. I was quiet and held on. By now we were both drenched.

* * *

"We almost there, Sonny," he offered, comforting his child, the piercing wails of the young childless mother waning, felt by all who heard or witnessed, causing most to grip their own children tighter. Holding on to life. We'll get through this, man. The floods'll go down, watch. Ain't nuthin' but a thang. These things we grew up saying. And grew up believing.

Yet the real dangers were the things that bite. Water moccasins hove into view, their eely undulations guided by the buzz of hungry mosquitoes and horseflies. Raccoons and possums could be seen performing the breaststroke with nests of foraging red ants camped out on their backs saving room for dessert and sherry. I had ten bites already and that's only because that was as high as I could count at the time. I scratched.

"Don't scratch. You gonna make it worse," my protector barked. Worse than this? I thought.

One time I fell into an ant bed and Father picked me up and turned the water hose on me after stripping off all of my clothes. I was too busy crying to notice that I was in the front yard, and damn near everybody on Clearway Drive was watching. I spent the next two hours soaking in the tub and sobbing while Mother sat on the bathroom floor next to the tub. She cried with me. *Cher bon Dieu!* Then she spotted me with calamine lotion like cheetah spots. Naturally, I ran around the house for the next hour playing jungle boy, butt-naked. Somehow the bites didn't hurt anymore.

As we neared his truck, I noticed that the afternoon had suddenly grown dark purple—the effect of lights reflecting a bloated, toxic sky. The brown murky murk had transformed into a black oil slick that reflected light from faulty, blinking streetlights and neon bulbs of storefronts. People were now more restless. Murmurs and prayers gently recited in the daylight became loud, exacerbated curses and fevered threats in the evening's shadow. Gunshots rang out sporadically. Sirens howled, echoing off the black water into the purple sky. Night had arrived. And niggas act up at night.

I peeked at Father's chest where the raincoat opened—a leather holster with a gun. He wasn't taking any chances and didn't have time for threats, real or imagined. I felt safer.

The rain halted but the thick air remained. Fuckin' humidity. Houston was a sauna on a cold day. Low pressure and warm Gulf waters equaled humidity most days of the year. AC was a must as humidity lay in wait on every corner.

We sweat in Houston. And when we're not sweating, it's raining. Water. Water. All the time, fuckin' water. Needless to say, growing up in Houston meant growing up wet. Sweat stains. Wet shirts. Hand towels tucked in your shorts like a football player to keep your face dry. AC. Window units. Bank loans taken out for a central air unit with as much collateral as the mortgage. Fans in the windows. Box fans. Rotating fans. Ceiling fans. All of this in a futile attempt to stay dry, stay smelling like cologne, soap, or baby powder. And it never worked unless you stayed locked in the house with the AC at full blast.

So we accept it. The wetness.

We accept the humidity. We accept the rain. We accept the floods and the hurricanes. We accept the infant called by the gully, figuring that's what the Lord wanted. It didn't matter if we liked it. We had to accept it in order to get through it. Father knew that. I was learning.

We reached his truck and I learned that the adventure was about to begin. Mother was stuck in Fifth Ward, on the other side of town, and we had to go get her. Water had crested at the top of the bench seat that I was standing on. I started crying again as more black water seeped in around the crevices of the doorframe. The water was coming to get me. Gunshots. Two gunshots nearby. Gunshots louder than the small siren timidly whistling in the distance, scared away by the big bad gunshots, scared away from black water and black people. Where are the cops? Where is Superman? Where is the bathroom? I peed on myself, warm urine salving my little legs, and I was comforted by this for some reason. It felt familiar.

"Daddy. I pee-peed," I reported.

"Quiet down, I'm tryin' to hear this engine," he said.

Father struggled to get the wet engine to turn over. Water in the truck? Somehow I felt safer outside. Father said he had to get under the hood and take off the fan belt. I didn't want him to leave so I protested. He ignored me and quickly opened the door. More water rushed in.

I screamed.

The hood rose, blocking my view of Father, leaving me alone with the black water. I quieted and listened. He was talking to someone but I didn't remember anybody wading over to help us before the hood went up. I listened. He was arguing.

"Who you talkin' to, Daddy?"

"Quiet down, Sonny."

Then I heard him for the first time, but it would be years before we met. A strange voice slightly deeper than Father's—

"Ça c'est ton garçon?"* the voice asked.

"Yeah," Father gruffed, then returned quickly behind the steering wheel. He took a deep breath, then looked at me.

"Who was that?" I insisted.

His eyes glazed with purpose. He looked in the rearview mirror. My eyes followed him. Here was a man who set out to get his family.

He turned the ignition.

The green Ford yelled defiantly and Father winked at me without changing his expression, then—

"It ain't nuthin' but water, Ti' John."

He must've forgotten that I couldn't swim. And with the excitement and relief of a roaring engine and the possibility of making it home to watch *The Electric Company,* I forgot about my question. I forgot to ask him who he was talking to. I forgot to ask him what language was spoken. He probably wouldn't have told me anyway, and besides, I wasn't ready for the answer.

---

* "Is that your son?" In Creole, we use *garçon* or *fil* for "son."

Weeks later, after the water subsided and the dead were counted in various high school gymnasiums, the city fathers made amends for poor drainage and renamed South Park Boulevard to Martin Luther King Jr. Boulevard, acknowledging that South Park was indeed a black community. That would arguably be the last time the city of Houston would ever give a fuck about South Park, Houston, Texas. We were officially on our own.

two

ricky street and other known dangers

Four years after the Great Flood of 1977 and I still couldn't swim. Mother signed me up for classes in the nice, white part of town with the indoor pool. The classes were small. The instructors were nice and gentle. I never missed a class but gotdammit I couldn't figure it out. Rumor has it that at some point I was actually swimming. I don't remember swimming but I've been told that I did. Then I stopped for no apparent reason. And I wasn't scared. I just wasn't able. Fuck! Years later, I would rake my memory trying to find that moment where the water and I were one. Never could find it. And Mother didn't really press it because she couldn't swim either, although her inability was based more on fear.

Patrice Boudreaux (née Malveaux). Mother. It would be kind to say she was a cautious woman. She maintained a very intimate relationship with fear and my entire childhood would be littered with her speeches on safety and danger. Certainly that's what most mothers do. But me? John Paul Boudreaux, Jr.? Danger had recently started hanging around me like funk. I could either ignore it or embrace it. And at eight years old I would have to make a decision about fear because I was really starting to understand the concept of being away from home. School. Playing outside. Sleepovers with friends. None of this under the supervision of Mother. Danger would present itself sooner or later. Her magical protection spell wouldn't last long, but her immediate fear was the very neighborhood we lived in. Too much going on. And me? I had to stay on Clearway Drive. One fuckin' block. That was her rule. One block for all of my imagination. Well, I soon decided that I'd have to change that. Third graders don't normally piss on themselves. Not normally. But Anthony Goodey wasn't normal. In fact, for the longest time we thought he was retarded, realizing only later that he was just spastic as hell. But this particular morning he had deposited a huge wet patch in his all-too-noticeable green Toughskins. Of course, we all laughed. And now we were in line.

There were sixteen other third graders in front of me but I wasn't scared. We formed a line against the wall of the classroom, right along the blackboard next to pictures of famous explorers and the Founding Fathers. The windows were raised, allowing humidity to circulate around the room by way of a noisy industrial fan hoisted next to the Stars and Stripes, which sent the flag into stately, perpetual undulation like when a TV channel signs off.

The room had its time-honored rancid Pine-Sol aroma with a subtle hint of Goodey's piss—the aromatic blend promoted by the fan. The whole place stunk. A few girls were crying. Others said they were going to tell their parents. But Albert Thibodeaux and I had our eyes dead set on Goodey, who sat at his desk, in piss, still sobbing quietly. What a crybaby. After school, his ass was going to be grass.

This was St. Philip Neri Catholic Church and School, a predominately black parish in South Park where Louisiana expatriates and proud black Texans came to worship and send their little ones for learning. My teacher, Sister Marie Thérèse, was the same nun whom Father had cursed out decades before at St. Paul's in Lafayette. Now, she had been magically transferred by the diocese educational wizard to continue her passion for harassing Boudreaux boys. A kind, gentle woman with a heart of gold, she'd come from rural Mamou, Louisiana, to the convent after arguing with her parents about their chosen identity. White. Or more accurately, *passé blanche*. She couldn't accept it. She was a black woman of lighter hue with deep Creole roots. Not wanting to disrupt the social order her family assumed, she was sent to the convent in Lafayette with hopes that God would convince her that she was white.

After several years in meditation and the habit, it didn't work. She knew God meant for her to be a black woman and, consequently, was assigned to the black-only St. Paul Catholic Church and School in Lafayette to teach little black Catholic faces.

She was harsh, adhering to strict discipline and sacrifice as a means to salvation. She believed that education was the only way for secular blacks to progress in the Jim Crow South and imposed her philosophy on her students. But she was also a bit of an elitist with affinities for city folks. Consider this was the 1940s in Lafayette, Louisiana. Many of the students were children of farmers, people of the earth. And although she genuinely meant well, she couldn't help but chastise Father for speaking Creole rather than English. Nor could she get him to sit down and learn his lessons. Nor would she stop other students from teasing him, particularly regarding his clothes. See, Father shared his clothes with two of his brothers, Alfred and Pa-June, both of whom attended St. Paul's as well. Kids would tease them and Sister Marie Thérèse wouldn't say a thing. Besides, Father would rather be chasing fireflies or riding horses than discovering the mysteries of geometry. So one rather unexceptional day in 1949 after a particular ribbing from Sister Marie Thérèse, he stood up, cursed her out in Creole, and walked out. He never returned to any school again.

And lucky me. Thirty years later I was standing in line in Sister Marie Thérèse's classroom awaiting her fury.

The sound of aged wood against clothed bottoms didn't echo but hovered, floated, moved around the humid room, keeping time in between the shuffle of children's reluctant feet on dirty

Catholic school linoleum. The whole class was lined up for pops from Sister Marie Thérèse's paddle because we'd laughed at Anthony Goodey for pissing on himself. I wasn't the least bit scared for some reason. I just wanted it to be over.

So when my turn came, I looked at old Sister Marie Thérèse with her loving gray eyes and thought, What a fuckin' hypocrite. In CCE class she talked of Jesus' capacity for forgiveness, turn the other cheek, let he who is without sin and all that shit, but we're getting a spanking for laughing. Not cursing or drawing naked pictures, which was fast becoming my forte, no, we were getting a spanking for finding humor in Goodey's lack of toilet training at age eight. If anything, he should've been getting a spanking. And given the events of the past few weeks, I thought it fairly reasonable to allow a group of third graders some fuckin' comic relief to lighten the mood. But damn if Sister Marie Thérèse saw it that way. So I had an attitude.

"John Boudreaux, Junior."

"Yes, ma'am."

"Your turn."

"I don't want to."

"Everybody has to."

"So? I don't want to."

"Come on, boy, you're holding up the line and we got to get back to our lessons."

"It ain't right."

"Ti' John. Watch your mouth."

"It's *not* right."

"John Boudreaux, Junior."

"Jesus wouldn't spank us."

Some of the kids agreed. Sister Marie Thérèse took quick note and winced, sensing that she was losing control, but she was clever.

"Jesus wouldn't have laughed at Anthony. Would he?"

She had a point but I had eaten candy all morning and I was alert.

"Jesus woulda gave Anthony a bathroom pass."

"JOHN BOUDREAUX, JUNIOR! DON'T YOU SASS!"

"I'm not sassin'. It's true."

Some of the kids started laughing. I was in big trouble, but Anthony had asked for a bathroom pass. He always asked for a bathroom pass, every hour.

"What am I supposed to do with you?" she asked, pursing her lips, gripping the wooden paddle. She was pissed off. I had to think on my feet.

"We should pray for Anthony so that he won't pee-pee on himself no mo'," I offered.

I even smiled a bit as the class guffawed. Oh, I thought I was clever. And an hour later, when everybody's knees had turned to Silly Putty after a hundred billion Rosaries on hard linoleum, I realized that the smart move would have been just to take the two pops. But who gave a shit? Half of the time we mumbled the prayers until each of us had developed a nice Catholic hum like Buddhist chants. And Sister Marie Thérèse didn't even say them with us. She just walked around the room correcting us and announcing the different parts of the Rosary. She didn't care to pray for young Anthony and his bladder. I told you she was a hypocrite.

Yet despite the eventual paddle pops from Sister Marie Thérèse and the brutal Rosary session on the floor, no amount of dread could measure up to everything that had happened in the past few weeks.

·

Weeks Before . . .

"Ti' John. If I come home and see you playing on Ricky Street, I'ma get out my car and whip your ass back home to Clearway. You can't go on Ricky Street," Mother warned.

"Why?" I asked.

"They got different type of people over there. Hoodlums!"

Hoodlums. What exactly was a hoodlum? I wasn't sure. My

routine had worn down Mother like the dirty, hand-stained section of the living room curtains that I'd pull back to watch kids my age rushing jubilantly to Ricky Street—smiling, shouting, carrying balls or toys, carefully handling cool cups or snow cones while sprinting to the great festivities that awaited on the next block. I didn't have to peek to know that something special was happening around the corner. I could hear it in my house. It was a loud street. Residents sat on the porch drinking from plastic cups and bottles, blasting music and talking loud. You could hear them. Laughing. Cursing. Crying. Yelling. Signifying. Testifying. Lying. Heeeey, Darrell! Boo! Get me an ice cream sandwich! Nigga, where my money! Say, Dwayne, you saw that game last night! Ta-sha, your momma say you need to come home! All of this was yelled, of course. Faircroft and Clearway Drives got to participate in the goings-on of Ricky Street by mere earshot. I mean, they yelled everything. There were no secrets on Ricky Street. Or so I thought. And my only interaction had been when riding with my parents, turning off MLK Boulevard and driving down Ricky Street to witness. We had to go past Ricky Street to get to my house. And every time we'd pass, the kids would stop, clear the street and stare at me. I didn't really know them because they never played on Clearway Drive, even though some of them lived there. I had heard some of the names: Joe Boy, Pork Chop, Booger, Raymond Earl, Maurice, Ronnie, Boobie, Dwayne, Curtis. But I knew none of them personally. Only stares. An occasional wave. What were they thinking? Was I too good to play with them? Did they have the cooties? Did I have the cooties?

"Leave them hoodlums alone, Ti' John," Mother reaffirmed as she spirited me away from the soiled living room curtains. It wasn't supposed to be like this, she thought. They had saved enough money for the down payment on the house on North MacGregor Drive, the one right across the street from the black state senator, the one with the big yard that sat on Braes Bayou for all to admire. She returned to her dishes. Make it clean to be dirtied. No more pretty bubbles. No more lemon scent. Brackish water and wrinkled skin remained. A prayer denied.

After shuffling between apartments in Third Ward, my parents settled on a small, three-bedroom house in South Park on Clearway Drive. It wasn't across the street from a state senator but it was theirs. Front yard. Backyard. Trees to climb. Bugs to smush. Birds and wood rats to shoot with pellet guns and slingshots. Yeah, wood rats. Behind our street was a large, undeveloped forest owned by Henry Taub, who maintained cattle and every imaginable kind of wildlife, but that wasn't uncommon in Houston.

As a city, its oddity was its lack of zoning laws coupled with farm-oriented residents. Horse pastures stood next to grocery stores and minimalls. So while Houston was definitely a modern city, remnants of its rustic past clung to its identity like the famed Texas drawl. And everybody loved horses. In fact, the city of Houston pauses for horses (that should be its motto). You're driving along a major city street and lo and behold, somebody is riding a horse down the median as natural as the streetlight turning from red to green. Amateur rodeos on Sundays found every highway speckled with pickup trucks carrying horses in trailers. And in late February every year, the entire city celebrated the Houston Livestock Show and Rodeo in the Astrodome by costuming at work and school with Western attire. Various factions of trail riders moseyed into the city in a well-planned, well-televised parade that went right to the heart of Downtown Houston for all to see because, of course, school and work were canceled for the horse parade. Again, Houston pauses for horses.

Yet the entire display went well beyond cowboy hats and boots in Houston, and all of Texas for that matter. It's no secret—Texas is a cocky state. For eleven months out of the year, a Houstonian might be a doctor or dishwasher or ditchdigger with no affiliation with, experience of, or knowledge about horses, cattle, or cowboying, but the minute February

28 (or that awkward, insistent twenty-ninth) turns to March, everybody, and I mean everybody, turns into an insta–Calamity Jane or Wyatt Earp with full rights and privileges, a monthlong masking of sorts. Now I would argue that that was more of a Texan thing because Texans have a tendency to make a big deal out of everything. But in all fairness, cowboying was part of the state's identity, giving its residents absolute, unencumbered entitlement to cowboy hats and boots. If you're a Texan, you can wear them and nobody has any right to ask you a damn thing, whether you own a horse or not.

But Houston was far from a Mayberry. This was, and still is, the biggest Southern city in the country. And the expected tropes followed with it. Crime. Racism. Factionalism. Limited resources for unlimited problems. White folks still ran the state of Texas, and Houston was no exception. They had their part of town and we had ours. That simple. And although Jim Crow laws had long been abolished, their fumes hovered over the city with the humidity and smog. Sometimes obvious but most times subtle. But in the safety of South Park, I wouldn't be exposed to that harsh reality. Well, not yet.

With no opportunity for merriment on Ricky Street with the other boys my age, I ventured to my old faithful backyard with my Hot Wheels and G.I. Joe action figures. Hours and hours in that backyard, smelling Father's hunting dogs' feces, on the ground fulfilling my fantasies. Demolition derbies. Stunt jumps. High-flying acrobatics. And every boy's favorite: war.

Action figures warred with each other constantly, never a moment of peace, even when Mother bought me the Princess Leia action figure. Mother had no idea that the poor princess was about to get gangbanged by everybody, including two Hot Wheels cars. She had read somewhere that little boys should have female-gendered toys to develop sensitivity toward women or some shit like that. The only thing they developed was the idea that you could get booty with your clothes on. At least with plastic clothes. And for all that fucking, the fair princess was a bad Catholic because she must have been on birth control. Not one pregnancy since she arrived at Christmas. By March, I started to understand Smurfette a little better.

As Chewbacca and Lando argued about who got to go first, I could hear the kids yelling on Ricky Street. Fuck! What were they doing? Probably something more exciting than playing with toys by yourself. And one song was playing over and over. Heavy bass line and a simple chant—"She's a Bad Mama Jama." I could hear that song playing all over the house, in the bathroom playing the pee-pee game, in the backyard climbing trees, eating cereal, watching cartoons. *Just as fine as she can be.* Princess Leia's favorite.

Mother opened the window blinds in the kitchen with "Ti' John. Time to come in."

The sky turned burnt orange just as Chewbacca and Lando decided to double-team the princess for a quickie before they returned to my shoe box. And the voices on Ricky Street got louder. Damn! They don't even have to come in. But tomorrow was school with Sister Marie Thérèse, who constantly reminded me that I looked like Father. No shit.

three

anointed

The following Monday morning at St. Philip while Albert Thibodeaux and I were pouring salt on morning snails in front of the church, we heard a loud screech followed by a very pronounced yet muted thump right across the street on MLK. Cookie Green got smashed in between a car and a Metro bus. That's what it sounds like when somebody gets hit by a car. A thump. Not a smash like broken glass. Not a splat like a bursting water balloon. Just a thump.

We didn't know what had happened. People ran toward the rear of the bus. Two or three were yelling and waving their arms at the school for assistance.

"Somebody musta hit a dog or something," Albert conjectured.

"They sho' makin' a lot of noise about it," I responded as we stood and watched a crowd gather at the rear of the bus.

She was on the ground with a large crowd circling her. Sister Marie Thérèse rushed us into the hallway of the school and told us to sit against the wall. Adults moved fast, some crying, others with low, hurried murmurs. Something wasn't right and whatever got hit wasn't a dog. Then it was overheard. Cookie got hit by a car after she ran off the bus and decided to head across the street from the rear of the bus to get in the classroom and finish her homework before school started. The guy driving the car wasn't paying attention and slammed into the rear of the bus with Cookie acting as a bumper. Thump.

But this was still conjecture amongst us elementary school kids until the ambulance arrived. Most of the girls started crying, which I found odd since none of them really liked Cookie. She wasn't the cutest and was a bit of a tattletale, but, being good Catholics, the girls found room for remorse and bawled their hypocritical eyes out.

Some of the boys in first and second grades started crying too, probably an automatic response to the general mood. Kids will do that. If adults are crying, kids will cry without knowing why they're crying. It's an obligation. But the third-grade boys were too busy discussing what had happened. Cookie always running across the street without looking. She shouldna' been on the bus anyway. Why was she on the bus? Her uncle stole her momma's car and wrecked it. Boy, I bet he feel bad right now. Her momma be drunk. She mighta been born drunk 'cause she always fallin' down. Various theories were tossed about as most of the staff rushed across the street for a closer look. Was she dead? Would she be in a wheelchair? Remember that witch in *The Wizard of Oz* who got smushed by Dorothy's house? I bet that's how her legs look. Oooh, that's nasty. We were horrible, but I guess we had to process the event in our own way and we sure as hell weren't going to cry.

After about thirty minutes of saying a Rosary in our classroom with Sister Marie Thérèse, we heard the ambulance whine away. The teachers returned to their classes. The janitors returned to their mops and brooms. The priests returned to their rectory. Even Monday returned back to the week. But Cookie Green did not return to homeroom. She was in an ambulance, coughing up blood in between her pleas—

"I was prayin', Momma. Promise I was."

The principal decided to have an emergency assembly to explain the situation and caution us against running out into the street without looking. No shit, Sherlock.

The assembly took almost an hour. The cafeteria ladies

handed out brownies and punch like a party. Cookie should get hit more often, I thought.

The girls were speaking of her as though she had died, recalling memories of playing jacks or jumping rope with Cookie, which I thought was some bullshit because they had never played with Cookie. Cookie played with us—the boys. Ashy legs and all like baking soda under a cookie. She had the perfect name. A skinny, little chocolate girl with a playful attitude whose skin was always ashy. But she'd share her Funyuns with you and if you promised to be her friend for a week she would give you a Now and Later candy. A red one.

By the time the assembly was over, lunch began, followed by an impromptu special-circumstances recess that would remain in effect until school ended. Damn. Cookie needs to get hit more often.

The good thing about going to a Catholic school filled with Louisiana expats is that lunch was the bomb. Red beans and rice with fried chicken. Shrimp po'boys. Jambalaya. Gumbo. Praline candy for dessert. All of this for school lunch. Today we had crawfish étouffée, *cher bon Dieu*.

After lunch, we all headed out to the dusty, ant-bed-laden playground for a game of kickball. Third grade versus fourth grade, a bitter rivalry monitored by the lofty fifth graders, who were too busy kissing on each other.

By the time we figured out the kicking order on the playground, Cookie Green was dead. She had died, we would be solemnly told, at St. Joseph Hospital emergency room. Police investigators found a half-eaten bag of Funyuns in her school bag. Upon closer examination of her bag, they also discovered that she hadn't done her homework for the past two weeks.

She had recently replaced homework with Hail Marys in quick succession. That's what her momma told her to do to get the voices to stop. Her mother had a demon.

Needless to say, it was an uncomfortable topic at church.

Mrs. Green had been sequestered in her home to receive the sacrament—her very own home-delivery Mass complete with a homily, Communion, incense on a chain, robed altar boys, the whole thing—because after Saturday six o'clock Mass, altar boys drew lots to see who would attend the Saturday activities with Father Murdoch and his special attaché, Father Ignacios Hernandez, who was, at the time, the only priest in the Houston-Galveston archdiocese who was authorized to conduct an exorcism. Of course, the altar boys were sworn to secrecy about the exorcism with threats that if they were to speak of the ritual, the exorcised demon would find and possess them. It worked.

However, after two months, Hernandez's special prayers had no effect on Mrs. Green, who chose to sing Chaka Khan's "Once You Get Started" over and over while dangling and swaying her free limbs to the funky sounds of the little Rufus band in her head despite Hernandez's aggressive and committed incantations in Latin with a Mexican accent (which rather sounded like Brazilian Portuguese). She may or may not have been possessed, but her distraught husband was sure of one thing. She was in love and it wasn't with him.

It would take the death of Cookie to make those voices and the band stop. But maybe Mrs. Green should've let her little girl do her homework and deal with the voices her damn self. Of course, nobody but Mrs. Green knew about the voices.

We didn't find out about Cookie's death until the next morning.

Nobody talked at lunch. Not a sound. Nobody from our homeroom, Cookie's homeroom. We knew her more than the other kids and I think that many of us were feeling guilty for mistreating her. No one admitted it, but when does a third grader admit anything if they're not going to get in trouble? Plus the fifth graders were watching and yelling at us for treating Cookie poorly. She ain't do nuthin' to yawl. She just wanted to be yawl friend. She usedta give away chips and Now and

Laters. They were right. Absolutely fuckin' right. Some people want a friend, but Cookie wanted to *be* a friend. I think most of my homeroom made that rather mature evaluation and felt a general sense of guilt. We were extra polite to each other for the remainder of the school day.

I was uncharacteristically quiet in the car ride home that afternoon. We stopped at the corner of Bellfort Street and MLK. I giggled and pointed at him, the Median Man, who stood in the grassy median waiting on the light.

The Median Man was fast becoming a fixture on MLK. Forty or fifty or sixty years old with an afro beard and a physique that belonged either on a chain gang or in a comic book. He always wore gray gym sweats with a bath towel tightly wrapped around his neck. A red, black, and green headband parted his huge afro, separating his furry brows from his crown. He moved with high steps—even, measured, deliberate, exact—never breaking stride as he jogged a steady pace along MLK. He looked forward, focused, and didn't speak to nor acknowledge anyone. If he had family nearby, nobody ever knew, and I doubt that he would speak to them if he passed them on the street. He only yielded for the traffic light and treated errant vehicles as mere annoyances like bothersome butterflies. Other than that, he looked straight ahead.

Simple enough, right? Wrong—this was South Park, where the ordinary required poetry. As he jogged he always carried a four-foot-long iron fence post with a large cement block at one end. Damn, that had to be heavy, I thought, yet he jogged with the post over his shoulder, block to his back, every day, rain, sleet, or heat, only pausing for the occasional flood or hurricane and only when the floodwaters were well above ankle level. Weather didn't matter. He had somewhere to go, his only route the median that divided MLK. From MacGregor Park to the dead end and back again. The clock carrying the pendulum.

"Ti' John, it's not polite to stare," Mother warned as the light changed and we continued along MLK headed home.

I didn't even notice who was playing on Ricky Street. Mother didn't say a thing. It was better that way. When we got home I told Mother that I would be in the front yard. I sat on the curb and pushed a Hot Wheels along a muddy gutter, clogging the plastic wheels until they couldn't turn. Then I pushed the little car against the clean part of the concrete, making tracks.

Mrs. Ballard, who lived up the block, waved as she passed by in a green Cutlass Supreme, windows down, stereo blasting gospel, and smoking a funny-smelling cigarette with fat brown fingers. I looked at her bumper sticker—"Jesus Saves." But not Cookie Green.

"They say some girl at your school died. Did you see it?"

I hadn't noticed him walk up. I peered upward and saw Raymond Earl standing before me, holding a football. We were about the same height but he was a bit stout—thick legs and arms. He had a block head, square with thick, tight, dark curls, but his distinguishing feature was his thick, bushy eyebrows that prompted others to call him Eddie Munster when he wasn't around. But his reputation preceded him. He wasn't a bully but he wasn't a punk. He was fearless and fair with more courage than most of the kids in the hood, even many who were older. At ten years old, he had garnered respect from kids as old as sixteen, which was quite a feat.

"I ain't see it," I responded. He started throwing the ball in the air, then offered, "Wanna play catch?"

Short routes. Long routes. Bombs. He threw it all. He was strong for his age. He was in public school like most of the kids in my neighborhood and he lived on Rue Street around the corner, but he traveled everywhere. Walking. All the time by himself. On busy MLK Boulevard. At the light, eating candy. Raymond Earl.

Mother came to the door and told me I had to come in. I returned the ball to Raymond Earl. He didn't say anything, just a nod. He wasn't going home. Peeking from the living room curtains, I marveled at his calm paseo to Ricky Street. Part bravado, part nonchalance, he resembled the infamous Corduroy

Brothers further up the block, who pushed nickel bags from ten-speeds and a dilapidated Lincoln sitting on blocks in their grandmomma's front yard. But the only time Raymond Earl would run was during competition or immediate danger. That was it. I envied his stroll to Ricky Street, where he was accepted and approved. No slouching nor leaning, just appointed steps, one foot in front of the other, with purpose and direction. He walked like a man.

Mother cooked tripe and lima beans. Yuck! Father watched J. R. Richard pitch a no-hitter against the Padres on TV. I was in my room tracing Conan the Barbarian's muscular arms and thinking about Cookie. I wondered if she was in Heaven. Or did she turn into a ghost? What would her parents do with her clothes and toys? The big Salvation Army truck made runs through the hood twice a year, but most times there was more giving than receiving. Saw a couch in the back that you liked, then you asked for it. You paid the delivery guy a small fee to put it in your house. More than a few families in the hood had their entire homes decorated by Salvation Army. It wasn't a big deal since everybody in the neighborhood had achieved some level of manageable poverty. Status was only a matter of your vehicle and new paint on your house. And if you had saved a few extra bucks, you installed vinyl siding. That was about it.

I wondered if Mrs. Green would give all of Cookie's stuff to Salvation Army for some other little girl to use. What if that little girl got hit by a car too? Would she die? Would Cookie's stuff be cursed? I had read in the encyclopedia that some white guy had opened King Tut's tomb and died. They said it was a curse. I guess you should leave dead people's shit alone.

I hoped that Cookie found somebody to play with in Heaven. Somebody who would be her friend regardless of what she gave them. Somebody to twirl the rope and let her jump. Somebody to play jacks with and tell secrets to. And before I jumped in bed, I went to a knee and asked God to be kind to Cookie.

I turned off the light and listened to the train along Mykawa

Road humming from a distance. I liked to think that I was Cookie's friend and now I had lost her. But I had also gained a new friend in Raymond Earl, a worthy friend, a friend with connections on Ricky Street. I wasn't really one to be a follower but if I had to follow somebody I thought Raymond Earl would be a good choice because for some reason, at least on Ricky Street and in my hood, he was important—he mattered.

Four o'clock in the morning. Benson & Hedges Regular Light. He was awake. Father always started his mornings with a cigarette while he sat at the edge of the bed, thinking about God knows what. He had to go to work, and for a longshoreman that usually meant leaving the house well before dawn. Mother would get up too, put on a pot of coffee, fry a few eggs, stir some grits, and feed her man before he went to work. Then she'd go back to bed for an hour and start all over with me. I'd watch her from the dining room table while glancing at Deputy Dawg on the small TV set that sat next to a huge pile of bills.

"Did you do your homework, Ti' John?" she asked.

"Yep," I replied with a smile.

"Keep doin' your lessons, Ti' John. Do that for Momma?" she said, eyes fixated on breakfast, heart and mind torn by a restless man. She saw salvation in me. I was her chance. Things would be different for me. She'd see to that. A parent's wish.

The next day at school turned into a detective story. Some lady from Child Welfare asked each student in our class about Cookie. It seems that an investigation was begun after detectives interviewed Mrs. Green and learned of her voices. I guess someone had to pay for the Metro bus getting dented and stained, accidental or not. The lady wanted to know if Cookie appeared distraught or abused in any way. We didn't notice. She was ashy, if that was the question, not sure if dry skin constitutes abuse. But the Child Welfare lady hung around the school for a week, prompting more theories about Cookie's mother and Cookie's death. By the end of the week, things got weird. Mrs. Green showed up at the school campus. Butt-naked.

* * *

Someone once said that too much Jesus could be a bad thing. In the case of cults and fanatics, that's certainly true. But Adelai Green never for once believed such a thing. She was admittedly a bad Catholic, relegating her faith to the holiday services when her mother came to visit from Port Arthur. She liked music, gospel music in particular, and found herself coasting through Baptist services in South Park, Sunnyside, and Third Ward every Sunday looking for good music. But she was never invited to stay at any particular congregation because she hadn't renounced her Catholic faith—at least that's what the church directors said. The real reason was her dancing. She loved to dance. It drew her to Martin Luther's children and their foot-stomping, tambourine-shaking gospel music. And she'd get the Holy Ghost and take that ghost for a spin. She'd dance. And not shake or jump around with familiar spastic "holy" movements, oh no. She'd slow-dance. And grind. And do the hustle or the bus stop or the dog or the mashed potato or the camel walk or whatever she saw on *Soul Train* the Saturday before church. Vulgar, yes. She'd shake her ass in church, preferably at the front so the entire congregation could see. Church ladies wrote her off as a coquette, a temptress who intended to lure their dear pastor and upright deacons to the fiery gates of Hell with her suggestive moves. So naturally, she had to move from church to church until finally word had spread and she was banned. When asked who she was dancing with, she'd respond, "The Holy Ghost." And she believed that.

The Holy Ghost. Mister Holy Ghost, yes, it was a "he," stood about six feet tall, smooth brown skin, permed and pressed wavy hair lying on his strong shoulders, wearing a yellow leisure suit that zipped up from the crotch to the neck and white platform shoes. And, baby, he could dance. Adelai first saw him at Mt. Calvary Missionary Baptist Church on Cullen Boulevard, sitting in the back pew looking like a dark-skinned Ron O'Neal who'd found Jesus. Initially, Adelai paid him no mind. Then she started dancing and carrying on. Pretty soon she felt someone or something grab her waist. She opened her eyes and saw this Holy Ghost spinning her around and taking the lead with some wild mambo move. She was in Heaven, or so she thought. A week later at another church, he showed up again.

Eventually, she started giving Mister Holy Ghost a ride to church with her. He even picked some of the churches they would visit. At first, she worried that her husband would find out because Mister Holy Ghost wore too much cologne and her mister might smell it in the car. Hai Karate. She mentioned it one time to Mister Holy Ghost, and he laughed. "Aah, girl. You know a nigga gotta have on some smell-good."

It never struck her as odd that she always picked him up at the Exxon station on MLK and Reed Road or that he always wore the same inappropriate thing to church or that he cursed an awful lot for being the Holy Ghost or that he never ever broke a sweat or that sometimes he'd rub on her thigh while she was driving or that his breath smelled like liquor or that he never used a condom. He only asked her one thing: *Do you believe in me? 'Cause if you stop believin' in me, baby, I will surely die.* But you're the Holy Ghost, she argued while pulling up her panties. Then he grinned and said, "I'm whatever you want me to be." Right then she knew that she had been giving up pussy to Satan and, baby, she freaked out.

She practically ran to confession and told Father Murdoch the whole thing. Adultery. Blasphemy. All of it. And just as she left the church, good ole Mister Holy Ghost was leaning on her car toking Panama Red while humming a Bobby Womack tune. He asked her for a ride to Harlon's Bar-B-Que for a rib-tip sandwich. She screamed but he didn't go anywhere. Hell was busy on Sundays and Heaven was by appointment only. *When it's cold outside, who are you holding?*

As time went by, she found him everywhere, asking the same question with a pimp's grin, "You wanna dance?" She ignored it but he kept asking. *If you think you're lonely now, wait until tonight, girl.* He became a downright nuisance, but because of him she returned to her faith. She prayed harder, made Rosary after Rosary until her index finger and thumb had permanent bead-shaped indentions, became a faithful and active member of St. Philip Neri Church to the letter. Ladies Auxiliary of the Knights of Peter Claver. Bingo helper. CCE instructor. She even asked Father Murdoch if she could get baptized again. He said no. First Communion again? No. Confirmation? No. Father Murdoch told her that she had already accepted God and the Catholic faith into her life and didn't need to go through those rituals again. It was at this point that Father Murdoch called upon Father Hernandez and made a certain request to the archbishop. She was indifferent when Father Murdoch informed her that the exorcism had been approved. She wanted more. She wanted to be closer to God, which is understandable considering she was probably fucking Satan.

INGREDIENTS FOR A BLACK EXORCISM

1 qt. Pink Hair Lotion

2 qt. Caucasian blood, Type O

9 rusty nails

1 black Barbie doll

1 white seven-day candle

1 lb. cornmeal

2 roosters

5 cantaloupes

10 yards of burlap

1 gal. afterbirth from black twins

½ gal. Tanqueray gin

7 horseshoes (used)

1 VHS copy of Melvin Van Peebles's *Sweet Sweetback Baadasssss Song*

1 vinyl LP from Son House

1 pork roast (at least 3 lbs.)
1 no. 3 tin washtub
1 large brown paper sack
2 lbs. ground black pepper
5 lbs. saltpeter

Mister Holy Ghost eventually stopped his visits, but he stayed in her head.

Wanna dance?

Believe in me, Adelai. Believe or I'll die.

Her husband believed she was having a religious awakening, but she was starting to become very annoying. Jesus was in everything. The TV set. The traffic. The food. The clothes. Jesus was alive in everything, she'd say. And she prayed constantly, even when she was having sex with her husband. But the voices remained. She needed help, so she enlisted Cookie to pray with her. Hour-long regimens at the dining room table on their knees. She and her daughter recited Hail Marys over and over with the hope that the Blessed Virgin would quiet her head and forgive her transgressions. She prayed with an open heart and mind, the way she was taught to pray, but it didn't help 'cause that Holy Ghost cat was a slick, persistent dude.

Wanna dance?

One time in a fit of rage and an attempted affront to Mister Holy Ghost, she grabbed her husband and made him dance with her all sexy-like to Marvin Gaye's "I Want You." Cookie watched from the dining room table, still on her knees praying and with a smile big as day because she had never seen her parents dance together. And for good measure later that evening, Adelai fucked her husband like it was their wedding night. And for a few weeks, both daughter and husband found a new joy in Adelai, a new burst of life as a family. Adelai was glowing with energy directed toward her husband and Cookie's prayers. Jesus saves.

But where she succeeded as a wife and lover, she failed as a

mother. Cookie just plain forgot to do her homework and Adelai didn't have the presence of mind to remind her.

At the funeral, Mister Holy Ghost made a surprise appearance and slow-danced with Adelai while the choir sang "Precious Lord." He palmed her ass the whole time.

And now, a week later, Mrs. Green was standing in front of
the church, naked as a jaybird's whistle with her panties on her
head and saluting with a duck-like head movement. I'm not sure
how long she was out there or who she was saluting to, but she
didn't move. Soon, our entire class was watching her out of the
window. Then the cops showed up and grabbed her just as her
bewildered husband arrived. She didn't acknowledge him as he
stormed into the church, where Father Murdoch and two altar
boys were doing a walk-through of the Stations of the Cross.

The church was empty but for Father Murdoch and his two
altar boys, Tommy Babineaux and Louis Price, eighth graders.
In slow, deliberate succession they stopped in front of a small,
wooden icon hanging on the wall. They were at No. 6, Veronica
wipes the face of Jesus.

"We adore you, O Christ, and we praise you," Father Murdoch recited.

"Because by Your holy cross You have redeemed the world,"
the altar boys responded.

Father Murdoch turned to the empty pews. He liked it when
the church was empty because he could hear his voice echo. He
coughed, then—

*Jesus, suddenly a woman comes out of the crowd. Her name is
Veronica. You can see how she cares for you as she takes a cloth and
begins to wipe the blood and sweat from your face. She can't do
much, but she offers what little help she can . . .*

A stacatto fusillade rattled off in the chapel. We thought it
was fireworks, but the Fourth of July was months away. Next
thing you know, the entire school was surrounded by police and
barricades. Nobody could leave their classroom.

As a child, sometimes I know someone could use a little help and understanding. They may be picked on or teased by others, or just sad or lonely. Sometimes I feel bad that others don't step in to help, but I don't help either.

That's right, a fuckin' hostage situation at the church. Sister Marie Thérèse immediately went into sixties civil rights protest tactics. We all had to sit on the floor, nobody could stand in order to stay out of any errant line of fire because the church was right across the hallway. Police negotiated through a bullhorn. SWAT shuffled along the hallway taking positions.

As an adult, I notice the needs around me. Sometimes my own family members crave my attention, and I don't even seem to notice. Sometimes a co-worker, friend, or family member could use help or understanding, but I don't reach out to help lest I be criticized, or they demand more of me than I'd like to give. My tender Jesus, who didst deign to print Thy sacred face upon the cloth with which Veronica wiped the sweat from off Thy brow, print in my soul deep, I pray Thee, the lasting memory of Thy bitter pains.

Our Father, who art in Heaven . . .

And we were saying a Rosary, then—

One more gunshot for good measure.

It was over. One to the head and the bewildered husband dropped, leaving a splat of blood on the wooden icon of the Sixth Station. Right on Jesus' already bloody brow.

May the souls of the faithful departed, through the mercy of God, rest in peace. Amen.

Later, Adelai was questioned about her husband and his motive. She told them that she'd explained her relationship with Mister Holy Ghost to her husband and he got jealous. Fuckin' Hai Karate. Be careful how you use it.

We didn't see the body get taken out. Detectives and SWAT moved quickly, not noticing the small children all around enamored by their shiny guns and shields. School was immediately closed and parents rushed to the scene with fears that their child had been shot. Louis Price took a bullet to the leg. Father Murdoch was skinned on his shoulder. Jesus wept.

We were curtained off in our classroom, and by the time Mother arrived, old Mr. Cecil was pushing the mop bucket to the church to clean up the blood.

Mother was hysterical. I was genuinely freaked-out. When we arrived home I went straight to my room, ignoring the Mickey D's Happy Meal Mother got for me. I wasn't hungry. I heard the shots. I knew someone had died, violently. Like the time Bo Duke and Han Solo fought in my tree because Han Solo was making eyes at Princess Leia. She and Bo were dating at the time, hot and heavy. But Han Solo was at a disadvantage because his arms didn't bend like Bo's. His knees didn't bend either, so he couldn't stoop. Man, Bo beat the shit out of Han Solo and kicked him out of the tree. And sorry-ass Han had to just lie on the ground and watch Bo whisper sweet nothings in Leia's ear. In fact, he had to stay there all night because I forgot he was on the ground when Mother told me to come in. He must've been paralyzed because he was still there the next day.

I sat on the floor drawing pictures of robots and spaceships while my parents argued about keeping me at St. Philip's. Mother wanted to do something to keep me safe. Two deaths in one week at a church was a bit much. And although those deaths weren't really connected to any apparent negligence by the school, Mother felt that moving me away would be a good idea. But where? She wanted me in private school but couldn't afford to send me to any other private school in a safer, affluent neighborhood. Father wasn't really interested in the conversation nor any increase in tuition. The conversation was over.

"Ti' John. You okay?" Mother asked at my door, eyes wet from pleading with Father, eyes thankful that I wasn't shot, eyes angry because we just didn't make enough money for me to be in a safer environment. She really wanted better for me. And at eight years old I recognized that fact.

"I'm okay, Momma," I answered with a big smile. That was my thing. Smiles. Always did it and they seemed to warm everybody up.

She closed the door and I went back to drawing, still wishing that I could go on Ricky Street and not really understanding why she hated where we lived.

Father stuck his nose in the door. He was holding his old shoeshine box.

"Ti' John?"

"Yep."

"I'll be back later."

And he left. He was going to shine shoes again.

Sunday morning came quick enough. Mother had decided that it would be a good idea not to go to church. I learned later that attendance was pretty low that Sunday after the killing. So I laid in bed until Father opened the door.

"Get your jeans and boots on. They ropin' in Angleton," he said, and it wasn't a question.

four

a reckoning

We were going to the rodeo. Despite all the rigmarole with loading up the horses, saddles, and ice chests in preparation for the trip, the entire experience was exhilarating. During the week he may have spent his days loading shipping containers at the Houston Ship Channel until he was exhausted or chanced his paycheck on the roll of the dice on Stassen Street or the dexterity of his pool cue at Jewel's Lounge or listened to Mother's harangues while trying to watch the Astros game, but none of that mattered on Sunday because on Sunday, Father was a bona fide rock star in the black rodeo circuit and nobody questioned that.

We loaded up a palomino named TJ. A beautiful, cream-colored horse that Father had been training for calf roping. Then we loaded in a jumpy quarter horse called Black Jack. That was my horse and part of Father's blatant attempt to make me a horseman. Black Jack had come off the racetrack and was a bit skittish, prone to take off without any warning. And although I protested about Black Jack being my horse, wanting a kinder, gentler ride, Father was adamant. If he rares up on ya, grab them reins and jerk 'em and tell him to cut it out, he said. Take control of the animal is what he meant. Take control. Don't get used or run over. Grab the reins. But it didn't matter. I got thrown off that horse more than I care to mention. And every time I was thrown off, Father would run to me with worry and concern like that day in the flood when I was little. And he'd help me up and tell me not to cry.

"Crying never solved anything, Ti' John. It only makes you

focus on your failure and bad shit. Don't cry. Focus on how to do things right the next time so that you don't have to cry. Do you understand what I'm tryin' to tell ya?" he said.

We rode in his brown Chevy pickup pulling a horse trailer down FM 521 South headed to Angleton, Texas. Cold Schlitz rested in the coffee holder next to my Big Red. Charley Pride crooned on the eight-track asking if anybody was going to San Anton' or Phoenix, Arizona. The AC was on full blast. Driver's-side window cracked slightly so that my middle name wouldn't change to Benson & Hedges. A CB radio crackled under the ashtray with random gibberish, a foreign language understood by men who spent long hours on the white line. Father had been a member of that fraternity from time to time, privy to its secret codes and rituals.

"Daddy, you think they gonna let Cookie stay in Heaven?" I asked.

"Who's Cookie?"

"The girl that got hit by the bus."

"I imagine."

"But she ain't get baptized. Sister Marie Thérèse said you gotta be baptized to go to Heaven."

He took his time with that one.

"Everybody don't go to Heaven, Ti' John," he answered.

"They go to the hot place?" I asked.

He lit a cigarette.

"I'ma tell you something and you better not repeat it. Understand?"

I nodded.

"Ain't no such thing as Hell, Ti' John. That's just some bullshit them white folks came up with to get people scared," he answered.

"What about in the Bible?"

"White folks wrote the Bible." He grabbed the CB receiver. "Breaker one-nine, pushing down 521 South, who got their ears on?"

He joined the precursor of online chat rooms—the CB chat room—effectively ending our discussion on the afterlife.

I stared at passing crops. Green. Brown. Tan. Brown. Green.

"Daddy, look at that," I said, but he stared straight ahead while getting reports on Smokey in between lurid jokes. He didn't see it, I thought.

About a hundred feet off FM 521 in a barren field of dirt I noticed a figure on its knees, hunched over. As we got closer I could see it was a man, a dark man in dark clothes wearing a large hat. He saw me staring. I think. I knew it. Just as we passed by, the man stood up, facing my curious eyes, took off his hat, and leaned forward with a deep ceremonious bow. It was friendly, respectful, even regal.

"Daddy, did you see that man?" I asked more urgently, but Father ignored me.

I peeked through the side view and the man was still there watching. I think he waved.

"That's peas over there. See? Look at that. Boy, I usedta pick some peas back in Basile," Father said fondly after hanging up the CB.

It didn't matter which crop it was, he always would say he used to pick, cut, or dig that particular crop when he was growing up. Field peas. Mustard greens. Sugarcane. Potatoes. Rice. Turnips. Watermelons. And cotton. Cotton. Even Mother admitted to picking cotton back in the day. Now, when I first heard this cotton admission I recalled the TV movie *Roots,* with slaves picking cotton. It didn't make sense to me. How could they have picked cotton? Response? Somebody or the other had a cotton farm and the cotton had to be picked. In Father's case, it was part of his upbringing as sharecroppers if that's what was growing. But Mother, she took a more noble explanation, saying that all of her cousins had to go to their grandparents' house and toil under the sun to make the load as a rite of passage but, more important, as a lesson in hard work and how far black people had come.

Now, all of this was true. No exaggerations. And later I would discover that many people my parents' age from Texas and Louisiana shared a similar plight. Some by necessity, like Father. Others as an excessive summer camp hosted by family members who still practiced the ancient art of cotton farming. Something about saying that you picked cotton carried a sense of history, strength, and perseverance. And these people from that generation downright bragged about that shit. I had to pick cotton. I had to pick cotton every summer. I had to pick cotton every summer or my uncle wouldna' gave us nuthin' to eat.

Since I associated picking cotton with slavery, I'd ask, "Did they whip you real hard?"

"What?" Father would ask.

"The white guy on the horse with the whip. Did he hit you real hard?" I'd inquire innocently, lamenting poor Kunta Kinte trying to escape a color twenty-inch Zenith plantation with foil paper on the antennas. Mother made me watch it, but Father wasn't interested in reliving the past. I mean he really had a problem with *Roots,* which was really a show for white folks anyway. Why we gotta keep reminding ourselves about that shit? he'd say in his nonpolitical way. But keep in mind, Mother was the one who bragged about picking cotton, so a TV show that highlighted the labor was right up her child-rearing alley.

"If you was lazy out there, my uncle would get that belt," both of them would say. Always an uncle who whips your ass extra special.

I continued with the questions about the crops, and Father was more than happy to identify them. In some ways, it was a reminder of Basile and the toils of being a sharecropper, but what I didn't know was that he was an expert at things that grew from the ground.

He grinned and hummed Charley Pride in between sips of beer, puffs of tobacco, and my questions. But as we got closer to Angleton his mood began to shift and he quieted. It would soon be time for him to perform and he had to get in the zone.

We turned off FM 521 onto a gravel road that led into a desolate rough. Trucks and cars lined the sides of the road leading to an aluminum gate where an elderly black man in cowboy attire sold tickets for entry. Six dollars for adults. Three dollars for kids. Small, rectangular tickets were exchanged and we'd put those tickets in our hatbands. The rodeo arenas all looked the same, some larger or smaller than others. But always the same design, very functional and only the necessities.

A dirt road would lead to a large, usually one hundred yards, clearing in the middle of nowhere with a small arena built of rotting wood. Wooden bleachers sided the arena. Rotting wood, of course, with chutes and a wooden tower, where the announcer rambled from a scratchy PA system. Outside the arena, wooden, yes, rotting, outhouses were placed. And a shack with a huge barbeque pit in the rear served food and refreshments, and almost always hosted a jukebox and pool table.

This was the black rodeo circuit in Texas during the early 1980s. No sponsors. No telecast. Just hard-living rural black folks, mostly, who wagered their entrance fees on their ability to lasso or ride a large animal. Dangerous? Hell yes. Both the event and the people.

We waited in a line of trucks pulling horse trailers. Father scanned the large crowd. Some recognized his truck and would hoop and holler. Father casually nodded at his fans, hiding his glee. It took so long to become somebody. But he earned it—the good and the bad.

"John Frenchy!"

That's what they called him after he returned to the South following the incident in Los Angeles, but he would say that he preferred the pseudonym rather than his given name because "them cowboy niggas is a rough bunch. They don't need to know nothing about me." But they did. They knew where he lived, where he kept his horses, where he worked, all the info. But then again, they admired him because he was deadly accurate with the lasso, the bullwhip, knives, pistols, arrows, spit, and every other thing he learned from those years in Basile, Louisiana, and from film sets in Agua Dulce Canyon, California. A regular Wild Bill Hickok with the charm and grace of a screen actor. He was smooth, a fact that didn't go unnoticed by the women in attendance, married or unmarried.

But they also knew that he was tough and would fight at the drop of a dime. Nobody fucked with John Frenchy. Nobody.

Our horses snorted as they shuffled backward out of the trailer. TJ, carved from cream marble with a golden mane, made a stately exit. A proud animal indeed. Father grabbed the reins and huffed a command. The golden horse extended his front hooves, then dipped into a bow. Many looked at the spectacle as Father mounted the prostrating animal. Show-off. I put one foot in the stirrup of my skittish bastard, Black Jack, and he started moving, avoiding my mount, denying my glory.

"Yank the reins, Ti' John."

I did, but Black Jack kept moving so I had to mount in motion. Bastard.

Father lit a cigarette, then made a clicking sound. We headed out. He liked to take a spin around the arena when he'd first arrive to see his friends and let everybody know he was there. An impresario of the highest caliber. And off we'd go for our presentation lap. John Frenchy and Lil' Frenchy. That's what they called me, and I can't say that I minded it much. It carried some weight with the rough kids of these rough people, because you sure as hell didn't fuck with John Frenchy's son.

Now imagine a black carnival where the smells of barbeque, cigarette smoke, and manure mixed into a delightful rustic aroma and nobody held their nose. All around us, black people of all ages in cowboy attire. Hats and boots. If your clothes were too clean then they'd assume you weren't a real cowboy. As we moved slowly through the crowd on high atop our steeds, smiles and waves and whispers and nods confirmed Father's status. He was a rock star and I was his son.

In the 1970s and early '80s, Father competed in "breakaway"

calf roping, where the roper flies out of the chute after a calf that's given a bit of a lead. The roper must rope the calf, jump off the horse, slam the calf on its side, then quickly tie down all four legs with a smaller rope called a "pinky string." The roper who can manage that in the shortest amount of time wins. That was Father's money event. He was going to win that.

But he'd also compete in "team roping," which involves two ropers who chase a steer out of a chute. One roper must lasso the steer's horns (called "head"), and the other must lasso both back feet (called "tails") for time. This required a different type of finesse because the head roper must swing the steer to make the back legs more available. This was John Frenchy's big question as we rode around the arena. Who was going to be his partner for team roping?

Grown men would tease and pander to get Father to partner with them. They wanted the money and a chance for the buckle. Father enjoyed the attention and admiration with gibes and good humor, a subtle coaxing for side bets and lofty wagers. And while rodeoing is about athletic prowess and skill with the animal, it was also an occasion for good ole signifying, drinking, and gambling. This was outlaw business, and those who attended knew very well that only one or two constables might be present and, if so, probably drunk. So you had to watch your mouth and your stuff because anything could happen inside or outside the arena.

Father spotted his close friend, the bull rider Arthur Duncan, who would later become the first black man inducted into the Professional Bull Riding Hall of Fame.

"Eh, John Frenchy, who ya team-roping with?" Arthur Duncan said while helping me off the horse.

"Awh, none of these niggas can rope. Hell, I might have to carry me two ropes and work that steer by my damn self," Father boasted as Arthur Duncan handed him a bottle of Wild Turkey for a hearty swig.

Father turned the bottle up, then chased it back with a

Schlitz. A few slutty-looking rodeo bunnies eyed him from afar with suggestive gestures—batting fake eyelashes with over-applied eye shadow and nail-matching lipstick wet as water, exaggerated leans and bends to highlight skintight Gloria Vanderbilt jeans and danty snakeskin boots, and a "Hey, John Frenchy," or a "You ropin' today?" and almost always a "Where's Mrs. Frenchy?" Answer? Mrs. Frenchy was at home asking the Blessed Mother to watch over her child and make certain Mr. Frenchy didn't bring home anything she couldn't wash out with Tide.

Of course, these rodeo bunnies found me absolutely ador-able as it was Father's habit to dress me in the same clothes that he wore when we'd go to rodeos. Strangely, only a few knew of John Frenchy's affinity for dolls. I was a miniature version of him, I guess. And what greater trophy for a man than an actual living and breathing doll that looks just like you.

But these women fawned over Father incessantly, which only emboldened his hubris as we circulated around the arena before his events.

For his part, Arthur Duncan was the perfect colleague-in-recreation for Father. Duncan was a pure country boy from Brenham, Texas, who'd fine-tuned his championship bull-riding mastery in the Texas Prison Rodeo, where he served seven years for cracking his first wife's skull after she commented on his complexion. Duncan was dark, very dark, and didn't take too kindly to disparaging remarks about what the good Lord gave him. You didn't talk about Arthur Duncan's complexion or his pride and joy—his signature white cowboy boots.

When Duncan walked out of the Huntsville prison, in 1969, he became a black revolutionary but not with black berets, leather jackets, and propoganda. He carried his protest to the rodeo arenas. The white rodeo arenas. Besides his entrance fee, he typically had to pay much more to enter the events, which were basically white-only affairs in huge arenas constructed of steel and tin. Normally after he'd win an event he'd either have to fight envious cowboys or hightail it back to Brenham, usually both, in that order. But as the years passed and the number of championship buckles and subsequent fights grew, the white pro rodeo circuit accepted him—the man who fought for civil rights on the back of a bull with glowing lily-white cowboy boots.

Arthur Duncan and John Frenchy—the dangerous men— wrapped in a titan aura, a glow that gave them an air of nobility among derelicts, pleasure seekers, and good ole country boys—were royalty on the black rodeo circuit. And for two country boys that was a mighty fine accomplishment. Mighty fine, indeed.

Blues and country music blasted from the scratchy PA in between events. A fight broke out here and there. Somebody had a knife. Another had a gun. Men and women would make eyes and lurid whispers in ears for romps later, when it got dark.

Some were ex-cons like Father's friend Butterfield, who was a known rapist and car thief. Others were educators like Dr. Poindexter, the veterinarian who taught at Prairie View A&M. He'd give discounted horse vaccinations to these cowboys, most of whom were cowboying on a budget. The Fifth Ward golden boy Mickey Leland kissed babies and provided photo ops for his next bid for Congress. Ntozake Shange sat sidesaddle on a Tennessee walker conjuring verses about a crowd that really didn't know who the hell she was. Father seemed pleased with all of this as he nursed the beer with a familiar grin. Then he handed me five dollars and told me to be careful. That was it. Off I'd go into this den of thieves, playwrights, politicians, rapists, and veterinarians.

I took off for the refreshment area for a Frito pie and a strawberry soda. A few older kids had commandeered the pool table and were betting on shots, imitating the adults with wagers. Stevie Wonder professed from the jukebox—"that girl thinks that she's so fine." And I just tried to stay out of anybody's way, but my presence wouldn't go unnoticed. Girls my age were milling about, giggling, writing letters and notes on barbeque-stained napkins to the older boys around the pool table. This had been going on before I arrived. Then I entered and the focus shifted. The back of my neck got hot as a toaster, and it wasn't because I was John Frenchy's son, oh no, although that did have its benefits. I was the light-skinned dude in the room and, brother, the letters and notes started coming like I was the postman.

Since kindergarten, I had been well aware of the premium of being light-complexioned among black folks, particularly girls. I hadn't spent much time around white folks, and when I visited family in Louisiana my skin tone really wasn't a big deal because there were a lot of people who looked like me. But in Texas, this complexion thing was carrying some weight, both good and bad. I didn't think too much of it, still working with a developing ego that only sought acceptance inasmuch as it would provide playmates and defense against bullies. At eight, that was my main emotional concern, but I did notice that for the past three years I had gained unearned favor with girls because of my looks. And riding the wall near a pool table in a shanty during a rodeo was no exception. There was a general excitement in their eyes when they saw me. Hell if I knew why. I couldn't swim. I couldn't fight. I couldn't pop a wheelie. I could barely throw a football. All of this because Mother wouldn't let me go on Ricky Street, of course. But somehow none of that mattered and I wondered, if these girls knew all my shortcomings, would their eyes still dance? Or would I be the inadequate fly on the shanty wall that stood before them?

This attention didn't go unnoticed by the older boys, who were plotting to get their fingers stanky or pull a little tongue. I inadvertently thwarted their plans and would soon become a victim if I didn't figure something out. One of them, a little closer to my age, noticed what was going on and decided to befriend me, maybe thinking that some of this female attention would rub off on him. It kind of worked. His name was Harold and his father used to fuck him.

Harold was ten years old and was missing his front teeth. Big brown eyes and complexion with a dusty red afro. He had a lot of energy, but most of the boys didn't play with him because the rumor about him and his father had circulated around the rodeo circuit for some time although no one dared to investigate.

After conferencing with the girls by the jukebox, Harold proudly came over to me and announced that two of the girls wanted to get booty. He pointed at the young vixens, who blushed. Hell, I blushed too. I hadn't got booty, didn't really know how except with my action figures, and that didn't count. Harold then started to chide me about being scared of girls. This went on for hours until Arthur Duncan stepped into the refreshment shack with two young bunnies on his arms, saying, "Lil' Frenchy! Ya daddy 'bout to rope."

"You Frenchy's son?" Harold asked as the older boys gathered around me with looks of astonishment. I told you he was a legend.

"Yeah," I answered as humbly as I could, then left with Arthur Duncan and his foxy escorts.

Father won both events and left me under the care of a hideously obese woman who sold catfish sandwiches from an Igloo cooler so that he could flip his winnings with a throw of the dice. But I didn't mind because the main event was coming as the sky darkened and the stolen stadium lights illuminated the dusty arena. It was time for the bull riding.

There are only two rules when you're a youngster watching bull riding. Don't put your fingers in the fence and don't sit on the fence. Usually, when you become a teenager, you show your courage by sitting on the fence but only after you have stopped shooting duck water. Bull riding is grown men's business and deadly, as I would soon learn. After Arthur Duncan locked in a competitive time on his bull, a flurry of challengers came and went, most thrown off and some with rides too pathetic to garner any respect or score.

Then a gracile, pecan-colored man with a reddish brown "shag" (black folks' answer to a mullet) confidently hopped the fence into the arena and headed for the chutes. His Wranglers looked as brand-new as his floral-print Western shirt, both of which looked heavily starched. I smirked, remembering Father once saying, "Cain't trust no redheaded nigga 'cause a nigga like that grow up mad at hisself, mad at how his hair turned out."

"That's my daddy," Harold said as he joined me next to the catfish sandwich woman.

"Oh yeah?" I responded, rather impressed that his red-headed, pedophile father was a bull rider.

Harold didn't show up empty-handed either. Three prepubescent girls sat with us, smelling like candy, barbeque, cigarette smoke, and the all-too-familiar manure. They started pinching me.

Harold's daddy climbed onto the beast with hurried confidence, staring down at the animal's head with occasional nods to the chute boss and cowboys who strapped his right hand into the bull's collar. He nodded quickly and the chute opened.

The animal charged out of the chute with angry bucks. Up and down. Twist to the left, then the right. And Harold's father held on. You could hear Harold's heart racing as his father reached the eighth second.

BUZZZZ.

The crowd roared. It was a fine ride indeed, worthy of a champion's score if only he could dismount. He was stuck, locked to an angry animal that only sought to get the damn tickling rope off its hinds. But Harold's father wouldn't let go. In fact, he couldn't. He was tied down to a series of ropes that extended to the bull's hinds, behind the ribs. This is a sensitive area for many animals that arguably may tickle if touched. The bull hates this feeling just as most people do when tickled. Then there's the cowbell that's strapped to the animal for dramatic effect but also confuses it with every ring. So this half-ton beast is getting tickled and a bell is mocking it. No wonder they kick like hell.

Cowboys rushed in on horses trying to side the bull so that the trapped man could grab a saddle and escape, but it was impossible because the bull was turning violently, scaring the horses away. Some clowns, the unsung heroes of bull riding, danced and gallivanted around the bull while others attempted to reach the strap to free the man, only to be gored by the animal, which still had sharp horns. One clown took a horn in the thigh and was thrown into the stands. A young girl screamed. Another clown took a horn to the back and quickly decided to permanently commit to a life in the church, jumping quickly out of the arena and dashing for his sister's rusted LTD along the dirt road. Better to be in church on Sunday, he thought as he headed back to Acres Homes while staining the faux velour seats with his bloody wound and singing spirituals.

Yet Harold's father tried desperately to be freed from the animal until he was dangling on its side, arm hyperextended like that of a rag doll. Cowboys on horses quickened their pace. Arthur Duncan jumped into the arena on foot to save his fraternity brother, but it was no use.

The bull tossed Harold's father into the air about eight feet, sending the man crashing onto his back. The crowd, boisterous only seconds ago, now hushed. And rather than embrace the distractions of the sidemen and clowns who fought for its attention to get Harold's father out of harm's way, the bull stopped and looked at Harold, who was basically in a state of shock. For one, maybe two seconds, the bull and Harold made eye contact, a knowing contact. I quickly turned to Harold, whose eyes were locked on the animal, and heard him whisper, "Kill him."

The bull was obedient to a wounded child's plea and sent its horns into the man's guts at a vengeful speed, opening him up like a watermelon, entrails and blood flying to and fro. What horror.

A careful ear could hear the punctures and churning by the horns. The bull huffed and snarled like it was blowing its nose. The crowd gasped. Some cried, mostly women. Others screamed and yelled. Get him outta there! Somebody save him!

Call the police! Yet none of them were willing to step one foot into that arena besides the cowboys and clowns.

The catfish woman grabbed Harold and pushed his face into her supple breast. He wasn't crying. "Lil' Frenchy, turn yer head," she instructed me, but I didn't. I couldn't. My eyes were fixated on the brilliant, fresh red fount from the man's belly. It didn't look real. It looked like cherry Kool-Aid—the flavor used to make red cool cups.

Then two cutting rifle reports cracked the air. The bull stopped abruptly and fell on its side. All heads turned to Father, who was sitting on the fence, chambering another round into a rifle to kill the vengeful beast.

Now there was silence but for the click of Father's bolt action. He jumped into the arena with the rifle aimed at the snarling beast, which remained on its side, breathing heavy, white froth dangling from its nose, eyes half opened—big eyes, big brown eyes. Cowboys and clowns alike moved back as Father cautiously approached with the rifle trained on the animal's head.

"He dead, John," Arthur Duncan assured Father as the men rushed to the dying man's aid. Arthur Duncan was correct, both man and beast were dead. Harold finally started to cry as someone quickly swept him away so that he wouldn't have to witness the mess. *Kill him.*

Suddenly my feet started to itch, both of them, on the soles. I had on clean socks, Mother had made sure of that. Then I smelled something burning.

"You smell something burning?" I asked the catfish woman as I took off my boots and scratched, but she was too busy praying to Jesus.

Dr. Poindexter rushed into the arena and took a knee at the body, yelling for hot water and clean rags. He felt for a pulse at the neck and wrist even though there was a huge, gaping hole in the man's stomach that no longer spouted blood. Harold's father was dead and there wasn't a damn thing the good doctor could do about it but cover the body.

You could hear a mouse piss on cotton as everyone reverently took off their hats and placed them over their hearts while the announcer led them in the Lord's Prayer.

And while Father argued with other men about who'd get pieces of the bull's butchered parts, I put my boots back on and joined him in the arena.

I tugged at Father's shirt and told him, "I don't wanna eat none of that bull."

He laughed and picked me up, then turned to the testy men with "Well, I don't want none of that cursed bull either. Yawl niggas eat up. But you step in one of them arenas with that bull in your belly and you can bet that this here bull's kinfolk gonna tear your ass up."

Louisiana black people, like most black people, are superstitious. Maybe because we are so aware of the real world, having been denied so much of it for so long, that we accept what's just past it, the other side of reality. That understanding gives us access to magic. Father meant what he said. Half of those rough and tough cowboys swore off beef after that night.

Maybe it was the Wild Turkey or the fact that he flipped his winnings three times with the dice or that he got to shoot the bull in front of everybody, but Father was talkative on the way back home. Hero status reaffirmed.

"You all right?" he asked.

"Yeah," I said, a bit remorseful.

"You gotta remember not to be by the fence when they ridin' them bulls. Them niggas be half drunk and not payin' attention and anything can happen. You understand?" he asked.

"Yeah, Daddy."

He popped open another Schlitz and handed it to me.

"Here. That one's for you. Don't tell your momma. Matter fact, don't tell her about none of this tonight 'cause you know how she likes to worry," he said.

"I know, Daddy," I said and took a sip of my very first beer.

That night I lay in bed, tipsy, listening to the distant train on

Mykawa Road and the busy mouse gnawing on the Sheetrock wall trying to get me. He was determined and steady, chipping away inside the wall, plotting his meal. My toes, then my legs to prevent me from running away. He sounded small, innocuous, but his gnawing reverberated, hummed and vibrated the worn wooden floor. I could feel it from my metal trundle bed. The mouse was coming for me. And my only solace was the reluctant glimmer of light peeking from the Star Wars curtains. *Use the Force, Ti' John.* Not enough to muster courage. Not enough to foster hope that the avid mouse would retire for the evening or get lockjaw. Maybe if I could look into his eyes and make contact, like Harold with the bull, he could be convinced.

Despite three killings in one week, I was holding up pretty well. School continued the next morning without a word about Cookie or her father. Adelai had been in psychiatric custody of some sort and there was no blood in the church, but we all knew what happened at Station 6. Gunshots and buzzers and screeching tires, alarms signaling danger, yet I managed to stay safe. And for that I felt stronger, more able to handle what the world was preparing to throw my way. I was gaining a sense of daring. Maybe I could go on Ricky Street now without fear. Maybe. Mother had to be busy or gone. I had no idea what awaited me on Ricky Street, but those other incidents didn't offer warning either. I committed to disobeying Mother. I committed to daring. I'd have to pick a good day for play, because if I got caught there was a good chance that I wouldn't be leaving the house for a while. I needed a day when everybody, young and old, would be outside. I didn't want to miss a thing or person. I wanted to know everything happening on Ricky Street, which could only mean one day out of all seven. Saturday. The official weekly holiday for all black folks in good standing. With God's blessing, Mother would have to be properly distracted for a good eight hours. I had a day appointed. Now I had to wait.

The next day, Saturday, Mother decided that she'd spend the entire day cooking a pot of gumbo. Have mercy! Making gumbo is an event that requires the cook to stay on the pot for most of the day, a sacrifice with the promise of a worthy meal. It requires commitment, attention to detail, and very limited distractions. Excellent. Thank you, God.

I grabbed a few toys and headed for the door.

"I'm gonna play out in the front," I told Mother.

"Be careful. Come in and use the bathroom. Ms. Johnson say she saw you peein' on the side of the house," Mother responded.

"Okay, Momma."

I didn't bother to take up the accusation because it was true and Ms. Johnson didn't have any business looking at an eight-year-old pee anyway. She lived next door and I did pee. On her house. Right under the bathroom window. She saw me peeing and I saw her slamming a syringe in her arm. We made eye contact and she looked surprised. I guess she was doing something bad. If she was a kid she wouldn't have said anything, let bygones be bygones. Fuckin' adults.

Before I opened the front door, I smelled it again—burning wood. But the house could burn down for all I cared. I was headed to Ricky Street to see what all the damn noise was about.

five

red now and laters

I stepped out my front door just about the time Mother poured the roux into the stock water. I didn't run nor pussyfoot but walked steady like a postman, not daring to turn around and see if Mother was watching or else be turned to salt. I had accepted her eventual discovery and the consequences involved. It was the longest fifty yards of my eight years, and no sooner had I turned onto Ricky Street than Raymond Earl yelled, "Ti' John! Catch!"

He was halfway up the block and threw a bomb. A large group of boys watched as the football soared in the air in a perfect spiral, above the tree line, holy and ordained with the blessings of Apollo, Chango, and Dan Pastorini. It was a beautiful throw, but now it was making its descent toward me. I had to catch this ball, but I knew the minute he threw it that I was going to drop it. Oh God, please let me catch the ball. It can hurt, I won't mind. This was my litmus test among the guys.

I dropped it.

The boys burst into laughter.

"That lil' nigga cain't catch," spat an older kid called Pork Chop. The others agreed.

I grudgingly picked up the ball and started walking toward them while taking stock of this famed street. Very similar to my street, but I noticed there were more cars, some on the street, some in driveways, and even some in yards. Nobody parked their car in the yard on Clearway. Old Man Price sat on his porch drinking a bottle of wine and listening to the Astros game on a small transistor. He waved.

As I got closer to the guys, I noticed they were having an argument. Their ages ranged from the youngest, Lil' Ant, all of six, to Charles Henry's sixteen-year-old ass who was too big to be playing with young kids.

Raymond Earl spotted me with a smile and motioned for the ball. I launched a pathetic throw that caused more humor. Damn, this was not how I'd pictured my Ricky Street excursion.

"Them light-skinned niggas cain't throw. Told ya. You ain't never seen no light-skinned quarterback," Pork Chop continued while digging his drawers out of his butt then sniffing his fingers. Nobody said a thing—guess that was Pork Chop's thing.

"What about in baseball? They got all kinda yella niggas playin' outfield and throwin' the ball," offered Booger with his big Frankenstein's monster head and snotty nose. His name was no accident nor misnomer. Dried snot remained around his nostrils at all times, but he never picked his nose. Nor cleaned it.

"Them wetbacks. Mexicans and Puerto Ricans and Dominicans. Them ain't niggas," Charles Henry blurted while rubbing his hairy belly and goatee at the same time. He had taken a recent liking to the popular tight-fitting net shirts cut off at the midriff. Charles Henry grabbed the ball from Raymond Earl and drilled it into my chest. I coughed.

"See. He might be a wetback 'cause they can't catch a football," said Charles Henry, proud of himself for further humiliating me.

"He just a white boy. Ain't you?" spat Pork Chop, walking near as I tried to catch my breath.

"Leave him alone, Pork Chop. He live around the corner," said Raymond Earl.

"I don't give a fuck. Fuck him and his momma."

"Ooooh," the boys sang.

The gauntlet had been thrown and I hadn't been there more than five minutes. I was old enough to know that momma talk had to get answered, but I wasn't sure what to do. All eyes on me. The only way to avoid physical confrontation was a well-placed comeback.

"At least my momma don't be stealin' grocery carts at Rice, talkin' 'bout she wanna be a truck driver."

That was the best I could come up with, but something was very wrong. All the boys hushed. Pork Chop started breathing heavy. He headed toward me quickly, then punched me in the mouth. I fell backward, hitting the hard cement of Ricky Street.

Charles Henry started laughing. "Shouldna' been talkin' 'bout his momma, white boy."

Pork Chop moved closer and pulled his leg back to kick me until Raymond Earl swiped his foot, sending him to the ground next to me. The boys burst into laughter. Both Pork Chop and I were on the ground staring at each other.

Maurice, Charles Henry's younger brother, was more amped to see the fight and chided Raymond Earl. "Why you stop him? That nigga shouldna' been talkin' 'bout that boy's momma."

"Fuck him. He always pickin' on niggas smaller than him," Raymond Earl responded, then took off his shirt.

"Awh, shit. Here this nigga go. Say, Raymond, that lil' red nigga yo' wife or something?" continued Charles Henry.

Raymond Earl ignored him and started bouncing around like a boxer, challenging Pork Chop to get up and fight. But Pork Chop just stayed on the ground, conflicted between anger and fear. He knew he couldn't beat Raymond Earl in anything. Then Raymond Earl started singing—

"Ain't yo' momma pretty / She got meatballs on her titties."

"Shut up an' quit talkin' 'bout my momma," said Pork Chop.

"Here," said Raymond Earl, handing me a red Now and Later candy.

He had a whole pack of them. Red. Or "cherry" as the label said, but we all knew it as "red" like many little black boys around the country. Red. Our flavor. Sometimes called "strawberry" or "raspberry" or "fruit punch." Yet none of those labels

mattered with us; the flavor was red. Red. The official color
and flavor of all little black boys. Red made that noise. Red
the sweetest. Red the king. Red the blood. Red as black. Red
as the black savior. Red as truth; truth that a red shag carpet
leads the way to Little Black Boy Heaven, where red angels answer
the promise and keep the secrets. If God ain't black, then He's
red, brother. Red the Danger. Red the Death, bleeding out on
concrete, asphalt, and dirt roads where little black boys learn
the mysteries of niggadom, whether they want to or not. Red
the Life that pumps through our little veins, flowing through the
body of He-Who-Will-Make-A-Choice or assume niggadom
until Red the Life calls it quits. Sure, there was apple and grape,
but none of those flavors ever mattered. The choice would always be red, not cherry, strawberry, raspberry, or fruit punch.
Just red.

"You need to quit pickin' on people," Raymond Earl advised
as he leaned over and helped me up.

Then he looked at Pork Chop. This wasn't the first time Raymond Earl had intervened on another's behalf because of Pork
Chop's aggression. But they were friends. He extended a hand
to Pork Chop and pulled him up with "You gonna fuck around
and mess with the wrong nigga one day."

Silence agreed.

Hours passed with an intense game of touch in the street/
tackle in the grass, stopping play only to allow passing cars by
and occasional water breaks at Mr. Price's water hose. I have to
admit that my presence on Ricky Street was pretty bold. My
neighbors drove by and waved to me. They knew my parents.
It would only take one phone call or passing conversation to
say that they saw me playing with the hoodlums. But like I
said, I had already accepted the consequences, and for all that
Mother had said about Ricky Street, it seemed pretty cool and
safe. Mother was wrong. There was absolutely nothing to worry
about on Ricky Street, I thought. Yet hubris is a reckless and
dangerous attitude to develop at eight years old, and just after

we huddled up and Raymond Earl decided to send me on a short route for a few yards, I heard his truck. Absolutely could not mistake the sound of his brown Chevy, particularly as it pushed up Ricky Street headed my way. Damn. Father. But we had a secret together; maybe this could be another one.

He spotted me with no expression, slowed down, and motioned for me to come to the truck.

"Your momma know you out here?" he asked sotto voce.

I kept my head low. "No."

"Well, you better not stay out here too long or she gonna have a fit."

Then he drove off. That simple. I mean, he gave me five dollars to survive around a village of criminals and risk takers; playing football on Ricky Street was minor league compared to the rodeo. At least I hoped he had made the same deduction.

"You Mr. Frenchy's son?" Charles Henry asked, a little excited.

I nodded.

"Shiiited, Mr. Frenchy's crazy. He got all them horses and shit. You be ridin' horses?" Charles Henry furthered.

I found my opening. I shared with them the death of Harold's father and the general atmosphere of the rodeo. They had never been, so were intrigued by the wantonness and danger of the rodeo circuit, hanging on to my words as I described every detail. The rodeo had everything they were looking for. Danger. Sex. Alcohol. Gambling. An AstroWorld for adults.

At dusk, I excused myself to head home. I took a look at the guys. I had made a few friends and allies, but I had also made a few enemies. Pork Chop was still pissed that Raymond Earl came to my aid, but probably more pissed that his mother had left him. Joe Boy was his normal, disagreeable self. He was quiet the whole day. He lived across the street from me, but he didn't have anything to say and nobody asked him.

"Lil' Frenchy. What yo' momma cookin' for supper?" Charles Henry asked, rubbing his belly.

"Gumbo."

"Daaaamn."

"They from Louisiana, they be cooking that shit," Charles Henry explained, then added, "Tell her I'll be around there after I wash my nuts. I still got that soap she gave me."

The guys laughed. I did too. It was funny. Charles Henry always had jokes, meant not with malice but with pure humor.

Booger looked at Raymond Earl and said softly, "Man, they havin' gumbo. I want some."

Raymond Earl fidgeted with the football, then blurted, "Me too."

I would love to report that Father and I kept a new secret, that we had developed a bond from the rodeo that was enduring by witnessing death together and sharing a Schlitz. But that would be some bullshit. Mother tore my ass up and then went into Father for letting me drink beer at the rodeo, arguing that I was picking up bad habits from his cowboy friends.

Back and forth it went all night as I sat on the bed making Darth Vader pistol-whip Han Solo. And Father just took it, telling her to calm down and not to get excited. No decent rebuttal whatsoever.

It was good to hear Mother having her way in an argument with Father for a change. Normally, he'd curse her out, slap her a few times, then storm out of the house for friendlier company. But it's kind of hard to leave the house with a belly full of gumbo and in bad spirits.

Gumbo has a magical quality and is not to be confused with the satiated "itis" found in many black dishes. Gumbo is about being together, community and love. Gumbo is meant to be shared with no judgment. Your bowl or spoon is never too big. Your napkin is never too greasy. You can spill a little on the table or TV tray without criticism. And you can usually bring some home in a container if you're visiting. The idea of greediness doesn't exist when talking about eating gumbo. As long as there's rice in the cooker and gumbo in the pot, anyone is welcome to as many bowls of the intoxicating ambrosia as their gastro mechanics will allow. Believe that.

The following morning a Cajun ballad jingled from a radio in the backyard. Tee Pee's Cajun music show on 90.1 KPRC. Father sat on a patio chair methodically shining a worn pair of oxblood cap toes, which, judging by the size of the shoes, didn't belong to him. He mumbled to himself as he shined the shoes. I joined him.

"Hey, Daddy. Whose shoes?" I asked.

He stopped mumbling.

"Grab a chair," he ordered.

I pulled up a chair. He handed me the shoe and a rag. An old half-empty whiskey bottle rested next to his shoeshine box with a faded label reading "Dixie Boy."

"See that part where it's dull? Buff that part," he said.

Since I was five he had been teaching me how to shine. Mother said that all men should know how to shine their shoes, but with Father it was different. It was an art, a serious act.

"Now, I want you to keep shining, clear your mind, don't think about nothing, and repeat after me," he said.

> *Notre Père qui es aux cieux;*
> *que ton nom soit sanctifié;*
> *que ton règne vienne;*
> *que ta volonté soit faite*
> *sur la terre comme au ciel.*
> *Donne-nous aujourd'hui notre pain quotidien;*
> *et pardonne-nous nos offenses,*
> *comme nous pardonnons à ceux qui nous ont offensés;*
> *et ne nous induis point en tentation,*
> *mais délivre-nous du mal.*
> *Amen.*

Mother had already taught me the Our Father in French, the Creole way, but Father wanted to be certain that I enunciated it perfectly. He watched my lips while I repeated after him. His eyes appeared anticipant—showing the same bated joy one has while opening a wrapped present. What was in the box?

Thirty minutes later, he and I pulled up to an old shotgun house off Collingsworth Street in Frenchtown (a Creole neighborhood in Fifth Ward on the north side of town). An old man moved an orange pylon that had been placed to save a parking spot for Father. On the porch, several old Creole folk watched as Father and I exited his truck. He had the shined shoes in his hands. We approached the porch. They greeted Father in Creole. I didn't know any of these people, although they looked like they could be family. They smiled profusely with a strange hint of deference. They were happy that he'd arrived, and the slight nervousness of some of their grins suggested that they hadn't been sure he was going to come.

At the front door, they made way, leaving the door closed. I smelled burning wood again and looked at the people staring at us with this strange, nervous grin. Father handed me the shoes, then said—

"Open the door, Ti' John."

I opened the door and stepped in. Father followed behind. Inside the humble living room-den, several older women watched a TV evangelist and drank coffee but quickly made a sign of the cross when they saw Father. The matriarch of the house emerged from the kitchen in an old work skirt and apron. Her olive skin was aged, with liver spots and moles, juxtaposing crystal blue eyes and white hair plaited to her waist. She took hurried, short steps to Father, holding up her coarse, ankle-length skirt.

"Eh, Coon. Ki ça dit?" she said and gave Father a deep hug.

She was overjoyed, and I noticed tears in her eyes.

She led us to a back bedroom. The door was closed. She stepped aside.

"Ouvri la porte," Father said, pointing at the doorknob.

I opened the door.

We entered a stuffy, messy bedroom. An old man rested in a large bed with posts; antiques, both man and bed frame. The old man was sick. You could smell it, along with the undeniable scent of burning wood.

"Presentez les chaussures," Father said while motioning for me to bring the shined shoes to the sick man.

I was nervous and had no idea what was going on. I took timid steps toward the bed, then held out the shoes. The sick man raised trembling, wrinkled hands and took the shoes. I stepped back toward the door as Father approached the man.

"Comme ça-va, Monsieur Rideau?" Father asked gently.

"Mal. Très mal," he responded in a raspy voice.

I stuck my nose in the hallway. All of the people had gathered on their knees in the living room–den—saying a Rosary in French.

"Ferme la porte, Ti' John," Father asked.

So I closed the door.

Who is my father?

judgment of the pecan

Basile, Louisiana, c. 1941

"Where's Coon?" Paul Boudreaux asked his teenage son, Evariste, as he approached his cypress-planked house nestled deep in the woods of Basile.

"He probably playin' by the creek," Evariste answered. "And Mama mad 'cause the blackberry dumpling is missing."

Paul winced. He loved his wife's blackberry dumplings. Coon was in hot water.

John Paul Boudreaux, or Coon as he was called in the 1940s, was by all estimations a peculiar rascal—elusive, secretive, and completely engaged in his own world. A world where he either couldn't or wouldn't make distinctions between humans and animals, animate and inanimate objects, spending both public and private moments engaging chairs and birds with similar expectations, asking questions of squirrels and plant life, oftentimes getting back a response, or so he'd say. His mother, Clarice, paid no mind to his behavior, figuring, "That's just his way. Long as he don't hurt nobody or hisself."

Most in the area turned a blind eye to Coon's behavior since he was a Boudreaux, a family that had a certain penchant for mischief and scandal that dated back to the night of "La Grande Promesse," in 1877. They were by all accounts a quintessential anomaly in Evangeline Parish. Rice farmers who didn't care much for farming even though their rice was celebrated throughout southwestern Louisiana. Catholics who didn't regularly attend Mass even though they provided the stolen bricks and timber used to construct the local church. Moonshiners who didn't grow corn or sugar yet their stills had run nonstop for over eighty years. And a family that usually operated as a loose-knit collection of single-minded individuals who shared a name, land, and a bad reputation, but not much else.

But not every Boudreaux was a misfit. In fact, many were God-honest farmers. Yet it was the few bad apples that sullied the name with exceptional success that cast the entire lot of them into infamy. This bad reputation, well earned by a few, placed a veil on the family, burdening each generation with unearned contempt and constant gossip. However, it wasn't the family's less than pious behavior or nonchalant attitude that promoted the pattern of less than glamorous events that plagued the Boudreauxs; rather, it was the rumored presence of their blood relation in the woods of Evangeline Parish that prompted the scuttlebutt. A relation who was part legend and part fact—the legendary *traiteur**, Jules Saint-Pierre "Nonc" Sonnier. And it was Paul's suspicion that young Coon had been in contact with ole Nonc Sonnier.

So with both Coon and the blackberry dumpling missing, Paul decided to personally investigate the matter. Grabbing his coveted gunnysack by the fireplace, he headed out to the woods to find his young son.

Minutes later he spotted little Coon, face covered in blackberry juice, sitting on a log with a tattered white baby doll. He moved closer, careful not to make a noise. The young child was talking to the doll, his small voice carrying into autumn's wind with moaning dried leaves clinging defiantly to spry spring branches and chatty chickadees. Paul listened as Coon suddenly began to sing—

---

* A *traiteur* in Creole and Cajun traditions is a "treater" who practices healing with self-procured medicines found in the environment and/or with prayer.

O kwa, o jibile
Ou pa we m'inosan?*

Paul panicked. He had heard this strange song before.
"Coon! Ça suffit! Veniz ici!"† he yelled at the boy as he rushed
to the log by the creek and picked up his child.
"Who taught you that? Dis-moi!‡" Paul barked.
Now most children at any age would become frightened by
such a display by their father, but not Coon. Instead, he smiled
generously at his angry father and kissed him on the nose. What
could Paul do? He forgot that his young son did not speak a
word of English even though his sister, Catiche, had been trying
to teach him for the past two years after she graduated from the
nearby Eunice School for Colored Girls.
"Qui!" he yelled.
But Coon just giggled and pointed at the scruffy doll on the
ground and replied, "Bébé blanc."
Paul relented and put the young jokester down.
"Aiye, mon garçon. What am I going to do with you? Huh?"
Coon yanked at the gunnysack, then sang—

J'ai fait tout le tour du pays
Avec ma jogue sur la plombeau.
Et j'ai demandé à ton père
Pour dix-huit piastres, chérie.
Il m'a donné que cinq piastres.§

---

* *O kwa, o jibile* / *Ou pa we m'inosan?* means "O cross, o jubilee / don't you see I'm
innocent?"—a Haitian vodou invocation for Bawon Samedi, lord of the cemetery
and guardian of ancestral knowledge.
† "Coon! Stop it! Come here!"
‡ "Tell me!"
§ "I went all round the land / With my jug on the pommel. / And I asked your father / For eighteen dollars, dear. / He only gave me five dollars." A stanza from the
famed *juré* song *"J'ai Fait Tout le Tour du Pays,"* which many consider the source song
for the music genre termed *zydeco.* Zydeco is a unique music created by Creoles of
Louisiana, which mixes old French Acadian folk music with African American blues.

Paul couldn't resist. He quickly put the boy on his shoulders and headed home, singing the refrain—

O mam, mais donnez-moi les haricots.
O yé yaie, les haricots sont pas salés. *

Coon left Bébé Blanc by the creek.

Weeks laters, Coon convinced his siblings Alfred and Belle to take him to the picture show in nearby Eunice even though he hadn't taken his morning bath. Coon fancied the shoot-'em-ups on the silver screen as much as his mother's blackberry dumplings and counted the days before he could see Hopalong Cassidy, the Scarlet Horseman, Gene Autry, Roy Rogers, or the local favorite, native-born Cajun Lash LaRue and his famed bullwhip. Six cents for the colored section. Cowboys versus Indians. Coon was in high cotton.

Walking back home after the show along a dirt road, he spotted a herd of horses grazing. Alfred didn't stop him and Belle cheered him on. In a flash, Coon was atop a palomino, holding its mane as reins, kicking the horse's ribs and flying across a burnt-out sugarcane field into the sunset. He knew God wouldn't let him fall off. Nobody ever fell off their horse in the movies unless they got shot or hit by a tree branch. At least not the Indians, and they had good hair too.

Just hold on and you'll get there, he thought.

You'll get there, nigger boy, the horse agreed.

He released one hand and formed a six-shooter. He pointed at the tree line and shot the bandits. One by one.

Coon got his six cents' worth. Nothing mattered more than the rush of wind through his dirty long hair as he rode the horse in every imaginable direction. The wind irritated his long eyelashes, causing his eyes to tear as he descried Alfred and Belle

---

* "Oh mama, give me the beans. / Oh yeah yah, the beans aren't salty," chorus to *"J'ai Fait Tout le Tour du Pays."*

waving and hollering from afar, but he refused to succumb, willing to steer the animal with closed eyes if he had to. Willing to be led but more willing to lead. His teary eyes remained open. Nothing mattered more than that moment. Nothing nor nobody. Not even the fact that today was his fifth birthday and nobody remembered except for Bébé Blanc and, of course, Nonc Sonnier.

Coon's love for horses was undying and unflinching throughout his childhood. He possessed a natural gift and command with horses that surpassed physical ability and leaped well into the ordained. Soon enough, nobody really looked for Coon when he went missing. "He in the woods," they'd say, or "I saw Coon riding bareback on a wild mare by the bayou." No one questioned what Coon was up to and, since he was a middle child in a family of thirteen children, no one really noticed his absence.

How Coon actually became a *traiteur* was a mystery to most. Perhaps it was the extensive amount of time he spent alone with Bébé Blanc—trekking the woods of Basile listening to leaves while his siblings shucked rice and picked peas. But it was when Arnaud Papillon (Old Man Papillon's brother), from a neighboring farm, took ill that everyone soon learned what Coon had been doing in the woods.

M. Papillon had been suffering from a horrible stomach virus for a week, not able to hold down any food. Various *traiteurs* in the area had visited him, making teas and *baumes* to relieve his troubles, but to no avail. By the second week, Mme. Papillon had enlisted a regiment of devout Rosary sayers to make a nine-day Novena—no effect. Yet on the last day of the Novena, as weary women rose from the cedar floor with beads in hand, one of the women caught Coon peeking from the window. The woman was his mother, Clarice, now widowed. She brought her curious son inside to reprimand him, but he wasn't present, as some would say. He immediately entered M. Papillon's bedroom and placed his hands on the sickly man's belly . . . and mumbled underneath his breath. No one had told

Coon that the man was having stomach problems. And no one understood the language that Coon mumbled with intentions. It wasn't French or Creole or even Haitian Kreyol, which some of the old-timers in the area spoke on rare occasions. Whatever Coon spoke was older, ancient and powerful. Arnaud Papillon made a full recovery by the cock's next crow, and Evangeline Parish had a new *traiteur*, skilled in the mysteries of secret prayers and barely seven years old.

By 1949, months after being kicked out of St. Paul's Catholic School for cursing out a young nun from Mamou, Sister Marie Thérèse, Coon spent his days treating the area's sick with secret prayers, shining shoes for nickels at the train depot in Lafayette, and smoking Chesterfields. Coon's older siblings had moved to larger towns for work as severe drought pummeled the Boudreaux farm. Coon moved in with an aunt in Lafayette who didn't care much for him but took a liking to his monetary contributions every week. He saved money, coins mostly, in an old sock that he secreted under his mattress.

One day his uncle found the money and bought a gray Stetson and a bottle of white lightning. When Coon returned and learned what had happened to his savings, he found his uncle passed out under a pecan tree with the new Stetson resting on his brow. His aunt said that he had no right to protest because they were housing him regardless of his rent payments. But Coon didn't give a damn about what they thought was right. *Couillon* stole my money, he said. His aunt slapped him in the mouth for calling his uncle an idiot, then returned to her dishes. Coon, being Coon, quietly walked to the backyard and sat down right under the tree in front of his inebriated uncle. He didn't look at the man—au contraire, he cracked a pecan and carefully extracted its meat with the expertise and guile of a surgeon, then chewed the sweet meat with brown, neglected teeth. He looked around the backyard. Not much there. A half-empty bottle of white lightning rested in his uncle's lap.

If Coon was pissed, nobody knew, not even the blue jay

that sang sweetly above in the pecan tree. Coon looked up and smiled at the bird, then whistled, trying to mimic the bird's melody. But the bird didn't fly away—rather it smiled with appreciation that this little black boy with long hair like an Indian thought enough of its song. He grabbed more pecans in his right hand, then crushed them. Some of the pecan meat clung to the hard shell. Other pieces rested naked and alone, out of the shell, exposed to the world and its secrets. And the birthed pecan meat revealed its own mysteries too, presenting itself to the sun. Why did the pecan hide? The baby bird breaks from the shell. The butterfly emerges from the cocoon. All leaving behind the dirty, harsh carapace, the dried teat of the jilted mother who curses her young with a warm smile. Several rotted pecans lay on the ground around him, never able to kiss the sun, parched after the teat gave all it could.

Suddenly, he dropped the pecans. Something caught his attention in the yard.

"Go on, get away. You ain't supposed ta be here," Coon said low but forceful and angry.

Anyone watching would tell you that no one was in that backyard with Coon and his uncle. Of course, the warbling blue jay sure wasn't gonna say anything.

Coon looked at his tattered clothes and small, delicate hands smudged with Shinola. His mother used to say that his hands were soft like a girl's and he didn't like that too much, but it made his mother smile when she said it. And that, he did like. But now his hands were getting dirty. He picked at a few recently formed calluses with dirty fingernails. He was too young to have regrets, but it seemed that he just wasn't getting to where he was trying to go. And he wasn't quite sure where that was. He reflected on his situation as he peeled off the painful calluses, then lit a Chesterfield.

He looked at his uncle again, then noticed the old sock dangling out of his pocket. Two months of savings down the drain. And what was he saving up for? A horse, of course. His very own. A horse that he could name and feed. A horse that would come when he called. A horse that wouldn't throw him off or rear up on him. A horse that could take him away. A horse that he could love and be loved back by.

The blue jay continued to sing but Coon had stopped his chorus because it's hard to whistle when you're crying. But the blue jay continued, hoping to end Coon's need for solace, to comfort him in the shade of the big pecan tree. Yet that beautiful melody was interrupted by his uncle's phlegm-lined snoring. Intrusive. Vulgar. Drunk snore. An affront. A teasing. Coon looked at the bottle and the hat, then his dirty hands.

There are moments in life, incidents, that define who we are for the remainder of the roller-coaster ride. Some call them "epiphanies," but epiphanies have a tendency not to be singular but rather a series of realizations. No, it's that other moment where one discovers one's personal truth. A tao of one's self. The part in life where you actually get a peek at your personalized and monogrammed user manual. For Coon, his moment had arrived at the age of twelve.

He carefully removed the gray Stetson from his uncle's head and tried it on. A little big, but he figured his head would grow into it. He took the bottle of white lightning and emptied it over his uncle's chest and legs, then threw the Chesterfield in the drunkard's lap. The blue jay changed its tune and flew away. Coon waved at the bird and sauntered away just as his aunt burst through the screen door screaming.

Days later, Coon sat proudly in the colored section of the Argonaut as it pushed along the tracks loaded with rural folks headed west to Los Angeles. He kept the brim of the gray Stetson low over his eyes and pulled slowly on a Chesterfield like the white guys in the detective movies. He was ecstatic even though it was stifling on the train and the fried chicken Catiche had packed for him was starting to smell. Jubilee. Bodies sitting together, moving in segregated steel to the next chapter, the next reality. There's gold up in dem hills. There's gold.

Coon didn't smile until he crossed the state line into Texas, although he had to remind himself that he wasn't nervous, just fidgety.

There was still daylight when they reached Houston. A long stop. Noisy. Barbeque. Somebody brought a lot of barbeque. And rotgut wine. Smelled like Saturday nights at Mouton's nightclub in Mallet. They poured into Coon's colored car, loud and overdressed—the Texas Negroes.

"You'se hungry, young man?" asked a dark doddery dough-boy in pressed uniform, carrying a basket of barbeque sandwiches wrapped in wax paper, nickel bottles of RC cola, and memories of the front where nigger blood was just as red as European—mixed on the muddy floors of the trenches, it could easily be mistaken for barbeque sauce.

"No, suh," Coon answered.

The old veteran continued on. Coon had eighty-three cents nestled in a handkerchief he stole from his father's body while it lay in state during the wake. Coon was supposed to be praying, but he stood on the kneeler at the casket so he could see his father one last time. He poked Paul's pale cheek. Nothing. He poked it again. Still nothing. A yellow silk handkerchief with burgundy stitching was professionally tucked in the gray suit pocket. Nobody was looking so Coon swiped it, which didn't bother Coon the least bit, particularly after he learned that his older brother Pa-June got the fiddle.

The yellow handkerchief with burgundy stitching was the only thing he had of his father. And now, eight years later, it held all of the money that Coon had in the world—eighty-three cents—tucked away next to three pieces of fried chicken and two slices of homemade bread, all secreted in an empty half-gallon Steen's pure cane syrup tin.

The wooden benches were packed. Many stood in the aisles holding the rail, some sleeping, others chatting with tales of home, tales of racism and violence. Tales of love left behind. Tales of Momma's cookin' and Poppa's belt. All told in the extreme past tense as though it had happened lifetimes ago yet they hadn't been on the train for twenty-four hours.

Most had never left their county or parish, like the young woman from Beaumont who sat across from Coon with ambitions of being the next Lena Horne. A few were fugitives, usually fleeing a vengeful white sheriff or a cuckolded husband, like the sinewy umber-colored man standing next to Coon's bench with a pistol in his waistband and a pensive frown, still figuring out what to say in case he got picked up at the next stop. And it's a wonder that Coon noticed any of this because his eyes hadn't left the window since he jumped on the train in Lafayette.

The train finally jerked, huffed, then slowly stretched its rotund legs against the steel tracks as the sun limped westerly. Coon pressed his face against the glass looking for the sun that seemed to have run away with orange smoke at its back. Outside the window, the buildings passed quickly. No time to wave at fuzzy faces and blurry buildings. There's gold up in dem hills.

The window went black. Night was official. A few lights shone in the distance, bemoaning their labor, jealous of their celestial cousins who manage a twinkle for all to see. Coon looked at the blank sky littered with stars, big and small. That's all he could see.

A fat man ate a barbeque sandwich next to him. He smelled like good soap.

"Dey shakin' dem ivories in da back," he informed the pistol-packing man, but he wasn't interested.

Coon looked at his hands. Small, stubborn deposits of Shinola still clung to a few cuticles. He stood up quickly and moved to the aisle, syrup-tin lunch pail under his arm. He nudged the pistol-packing man, offering his seat, thinking, He probably do some better figurin' starin' out tha winda'. The man nodded a thank-you and sat as Coon moved toward the rattle of shaking dice.

"Five. I'm bettin' five."

Three days later, Coon stepped off the Argonaut on Central

Avenue in Los Angeles, California. He arrived with more than he left with, and I'm not talking about the six bucks or so he made with the dice. Twelve-year-old Coon made a startling discovery the night of that dice game, a discovery that would change the rest of his life. Some might call it "luck," but he knew it was much more than that.

A white porter eyed the young lad emerging from the train.

"You Willie Leders?" he asked.

"No, suh."

"What's your name, boy?"

The twelve-year-old looked around. Strange faces. Palm trees. Streetcars. Sunshine.

"John Boudreaux, suh."

Nobody in the Golden State, save his sister whom he was to live with, would ever know about "Coon."

seven

catechism

Houston, Texas, c. 1981

One autumn morning at St. Philip's, most of the kids stood under the basketball hoop watching a navy blue Lincoln Continental idle in front of the rectory. The door opened. Otis Redding was playing in the car. Three brothers stepped out of the Lincoln like Shaft, surveying the campus with a cool grin. One had a well-manicured afro and lamb chops. They all wore Florsheim ankle boots and dark sunglasses. And the collar. Enter the Vatican's late response to James Brown—the black Benedictine monks from St. Louis, Missouri. Apparently Father Murdoch didn't have enough prayers or health insurance for St. Philip's, so the bishop sent in the soul brothers: Father Jerome, Brother Al, and Brother Barry.

We were floored. Most of us had never seen a black priest before. But here they were, coming out of hiding with a bit of a militant-hustler swagger. Father Jerome had the most presence, standing at six feet, three inches, with the Isaac Hayes haircut and a gold crucifix pinkie ring. The brother was smooth. His sidekicks, a little younger, were Brother Al, an overweight, red dude with the fro and chops, and Brother Barry, a chain-smoking man of the cloth with bad razor bumps who looked like an ex-con from Chicago because he was.

Father Jerome looked at us, then waved with "Hey, lil' brothers and sisters!"

He didn't sound like a priest but rather a Black Panther or some other revolutionary you might run into at S.H.A.P.E. Community Center in Third Ward. We didn't know what to think, but we knew the homilies at Mass would probably change.

"Watch, they gonna start hollerin' and jumpin' around like them Baptist preachers," I said to Albert.

"They don't do that kinda stuff in Catholic church. It's against the law," he responded.

"What law?"

"Them laws that the pope makes."

But if their arrival and demeanor were any indication of what was to come on Sunday, the Benedictines knew damn well how they were coming off. The entire week at school we only saw them in passing, moving their stuff into the rectory and having countless meetings with the principal, Sister Benedict. No special assembly. No altar boy meetings. Nothing.

Every day when I'd return home from school, Mother anxiously awaited reports on the black Benedictines at St. Philip's, but I had none to share. The rumor mill was red-hot and some of the facts began to leak, not all of them good. Brother Al had an eating and drinking problem. Brother Barry was sent to jail when he was young for killing a man over a dice game. And Father Jerome was a former navy man turned numbers runner turned janitor who found God. But those particulars were not the subjects of the queries among parishioners. Everyone was really interested to see how Father Jerome would conduct Mass. Even the choir director didn't get any information nor visits from Father Jerome. Everyone was kept in the dark until Sunday.

That Sunday there were more people at St. Philip Neri Catholic Church than there had ever been, even on Easter and at Christmas midnight Mass. In fact, most in attendance didn't go to St. Philip's but rather had floated over from St. Francis Xavier's and St. Mary's. Everyone in the black Catholic community on the south side of Houston wanted to check these brothers out. And as luck would have it, that Sunday was my day to serve as an altar boy.

Mother and I parked in the almost full lot.

"Do your best today, Ti' John. Don't make the new priest look bad," Mother advised.

"I won't, Momma," I returned with a kiss on the cheek.

I got out of the car and dashed for the sacristy, running the litany and ritual through my head. I had only been doing altar service for a few months.

When I reached the door to the holy secret room, I saw Albert Thibodeaux's momma waiting outside like a groupie. Only altar boys, priests, brothers, and the occasional woman who serviced the robes were allowed in the sacristy.

"Hey, Ti' John," she said.

"Hey, Mrs. Thibodeaux."

Her eyes were dancing.

I opened the door and entered. Albert was dressed and stood against the wall like a statue. Brother Al was shining his shoes, and Brother Barry was in a corner on his knees in prayer. I guess he was on punishment. And Father Jerome methodically adjusted his vestments in the mirror.

"Hey, lil' brother. What's your name?" boomed Father Jerome in a smooth, deep voice.

"Aah, John Boudreaux, Junior. They call me Ti' John," I answered somewhat timidly.

He turned with a fantastic smile and extended a hand that smelled like cologne.

"Ti' John. Petit John. Little John, huh?" he asked. "Your people from Louisiana?"

"Yep. Basile and Opelousas."

"Opelousas. They got that church down there, Holy Ghost with Father McKnight. You ever met Father McKnight?"*

"Nawh, but I heard of him."

---

* Every black Catholic had heard of Father McKnight, the Caribbean-born civil rights activist who raised more than his fair share of hell with the diocese. Some thought he was a radical, but what can you expect from a black man whose vocation is to lead?

"Well, this is gonna be fun today. Whatcha think?" he asked.

"Fun?"

The Catholic Moors laughed. I had never heard of church being fun. Mother always said that you shouldn't laugh in church because it was a serious matter, and here was this bald-headed guy talking about fun. But, hey, he was the new boss, so I guessed fun was in order.

The first part of Mass was nothing exceptional. All the normal procedures of the litany, on cue with bells and incense, et cetera. Then the choir began to sing before Father Jerome's homily and he stopped them. A general hush filled the room because Mass was something of an autopilot experience, efficient, planned out, and hardly any room for improvisation. The Holy See wouldn't allow jazz interpretations of Catholicism—ask Martin Luther.

He rose and walked toward the choir director and took the mic.

"When I was a boy in Philadelphia, I used to live across the street from this Baptist church. And I remember a song they used to sing, talkin' 'bout 'Take Me Back.' No matter where I'm at, if I hear that song then I feel like I'm home," he confessed.

He glanced at the choir director, then the choir. "You know that song?" he asked.

The choir director started playing the famed gospel song on the organ, leaving the choir clueless since they'd never heard blue notes from that organ. But Father Jerome was back home in Philly, eyes closed and body swaying like the pendulum of a grandfather clock. And when his momma walked in the icy vestibule in tears and told him Poppa wasn't coming home, he began to sing.

Take me back, take me back, dear Lord,
To the place where I first received you.

His voice was aged and seasoned. Sorrow. Tragedy. Reaffirmation. All of those things you hear from blues singers, their entire lives on audio display, wrapped in a melodic mea culpa, testifying to realizations. That's what gospel and blues had in common. Truth. Testaments to the human spirit and personal realizations. Epiphanies. My woman don't want me. God works in mysterious ways. I got a no-good woman but I'm a no-good man. Ain't no love like sweet Jesus. The thangs that I used ta do, Lord, I don't do them anymo'. We come this far by faith. I got a sweet little angel, I love the way she spreads her wings. All of this, professed as truth, sung with conviction and certainty, felt like divine power preordained. Adelai Green missed out.

This was the place that Father Jerome decided to go on his inaugural Mass. And his rendition of "Take Me Back" was nothing short of a full confessional to a congregation of strangers. He sang the first stanza solo with heart and soul. The choir took the cue and joined in. They had never sung like that at St. Philip Neri before, and everyone in the congregation knew that things were about to change at church.

Needless to say, his homily was more aligned with the black Baptist traditions, sans telling the congregation to turn to certain pages in the Bible. Shouting, jumping, call and response, the whole package. Some in the congregation didn't know what to make of it. Others felt released and freed from the constraints of past Catholic Mass behavior. And after Mass, sides were being chosen—those who liked the direction that Father Jerome was heading and those who felt that it conflicted with the standards and practices of Catholic Mass. Bottom line: it was too black, too common. Father Jerome even mentioned that in his homily but said that how we worship should not call into question our sincerity and belief in the Holy Trinity.

The next Sunday, some parishioners left, vowing not to return until the tall, bald black heretic was sent packing. But a lot more new members joined quickly. Father Jerome was a hit.

Later that day, Mother came to my bedroom door and told me that I had visitors. She was pissed. The visitors were two of my new friends, Booger and Raymond Earl.

"You can't bring them in the house or the backyard. Play in the front so Momma can see you, and don't bring out your new toys," she instructed as I grabbed a Crown Royal bag full of plastic army men. She was serious and definitely pissed that I had found some playmates from the neighborhood.

This marked the beginning of my rebellion, my personal *cause du jour* into the risky unknowns of South Park. As I passed her in the hallway, I knew Mother was angry and frustrated. I had taken a stand. Gotdamn Ricky Street, she must have thought as I cheerfully bounced past her for the front door.

We sat on the curb and lined up the army men. Three nations. Each a general and king of his troops. I had enough of the plastic men to give each a fair war. The kneeling guy with the M16. The kneeling guy with the bazooka. The standing guy with the M16. And my favorite, the guy sprawled out on his stomach with his rifle. The least favorite, of course, was the communications guy carrying the radio with the antenna. He didn't even have a gun in his hand. Nobody wanted that guy. But I bet dollars to doughnut holes he was happy as hell to be the communications specialist, avoiding M16 gunfire, bazooka rounds, and grenades. You always kept the communications guy off the line, snuggled behind the Jeep or behind a log. Fuck him. He's a pussy, which is exactly why I kept his scary ass in the Crown Royal bag. Who wanted that dude?

"Your momma don't want us in yawl house?" Booger asked.

"She cleaning the floor right now," I lied, sparing his little snotty-nose heart. Raymond Earl watched me when I answered. He knew I was lying.

"You went to church today?" Booger continued.

"Yep," I answered.

"Where you go?" Booger asked.

"St. Philip's."

"You'se a Catholic?" Booger asked with innocent eyes. I had no idea what the answer meant.

"Yeah, he's Catholic, ole stupid nigga. Why else would he go to church there?" chimed in Raymond Earl.

"They food might be good over there," Booger responded with his best logic.

"They don't give us food," I said.

"Then why you go? You gotta spend all that time up in there, they could at least have some food. Them Baptists be havin' food," Booger continued.

"They don't be in there all day. Them Catholics be in there for a minute, then they go home," Raymond Earl explained.

"Yawl don't have to come back to church for evening service?" Booger asked.

"Nawh, you just gotta go to one service. It be about an hour," I answered.

"An hour?" they both exclaimed, astonished that Catholics didn't subscribe to the Baptist tradition of most of Sunday spent in church.

"Yep. About an hour. If you go early in the morning or on Saturday, it be shorter," I explained.

"I wanna be Catholic," Booger admitted.

I was on a roll now. I told them about being an altar boy and the vestments.

"The priest wears a cape?" Booger asked.

"Yeah. And he can fly," I answered, pushing it a bit, but I told you I was on a roll.

"Nawh-unh," Raymond Earl chided.

"For real," I said. "Come by and see."

"Ask your momma if we can go to church with you next week," Raymond Earl asked.

"Okay," I said. It seemed simple enough.

Across the street, a screen door slammed against a hate-filled home—

"You think you'se a man?"

Joe Boy flew out of the door, landing in his front yard. His red eyes were wet, but he wasn't crying. His father rushed out of the house carrying a broom and beat the shit out of him. But he didn't cry; rather he curled up on the ground and took it until his drunk father tired and returned inside. Joe Boy waited for a minute, then got up slowly, legs welted from burning straw. We made eye contact. Bad idea. He directed his anger toward me.

"Ti' John, time to come in," Mother yelled from the door.

I dashed inside, escaping Joe Boy's loathsome stare.

Later that night—

"Momma?"

"Yeah, baby?"

"Can Raymond Earl and Booger come to church with us next week?"

"No."

"Why not?"

"I said no."

"Ain't church for everybody?"

She stopped washing dishes and let her hands rest in Palm-olive.

joseph street

Opelousas, Louisiana, c. 1944

Margaret Malveaux liked to sweep the floor. She told herself that the Devil manifested himself in dust particles collected around homes to spy on people, waiting for a moment of weakness. In fact, she even said that witches flew on brooms that they stole from Christian households so that people couldn't sweep the Devil out of their house. And with two small children, Patrice and Herman, plus operating a small grocery store while her husband, Joseph, worked at the oil mill, Margaret found herself in continuous motion around the floors of her home store in Opelousas, Louisiana.

World War II had been going on for some time, and many had speculated that it was coming to a close and soon battle-weary white men would return home to reclaim their jobs. She worried for her brothers, half of whom were on the front line in Europe while the other half were brokering deals between black sharecroppers and black grocery store owners from Lake Charles to Baton Rouge. She prayed that her brothers in uniform would return home in one piece, and for that she hoped that the war would end quickly. But she also prayed that her deal-making brothers were saving their money because the Klan had already gotten news that the Lemelle boys were getting rich and not a white man, Cajun or American, was seeing a penny of it. And for that, she prayed that the war would last long enough for her brothers to save a fortune. So she swept harder while saying a Rosary, the blessed beads rapping against the broom, for she gripped both, creating an echo to her labor.

She glanced out the front door of the store. A big green Buick with a white convertible top rumbled down the gravel road on Joseph Street, leaving a white trail of dust. Joseph Street in the summer. Hot noontime air slowed down everything but the singing cicadas. The gravel road led directly to train tracks that led directly to LouAna Oil Mill, which made cooking oil from cotton seeds.

At noon, the mill sounded its lunchtime horn, competing with the bells of St. Landry's Catholic Church a few miles away, each calling to its faithful, a constant reminder of obligation. She knew her husband wasn't coming home for lunch as usual. He, like other black men in town, had recently volunteered his free time to build a new church for the Holy Ghost Catholic Church parishioners. A new church built of bricks and faith with a tall steeple like St. Landry's, which was only three blocks away. We should have a church that we can be proud of, many thought, because St. Landry's was not an option for Margaret or Joseph or anybody who looked like them, even the discreetly *passé blanche*. Because although St. Landry's was a Catholic church promoting the Holy Trinity, confession, and the forgiveness of sins, it did not welcome its darker brethren with open arms except with a roped-off colored section in the rear pews.

Margaret squinted at the fast-moving Buick. Mr. Tex was always in a hurry. Small shotgun houses in pleasant colors lined the tree-lined street with four-foot runoff ditches along both sides. This was her home.

She rested against the doorframe, hand on her hip, reflective on all she had seen but anxious for all she had left to do. Her long black wavy hair was pulled back, off her shoulders, allowing sweat to collect on her honey-hued neck. At thirty, her face was beginning to round out with supple cheeks, losing the jawline of a vigorous, independent twenty-something for a focused, caring, rotund visage. But it was her magical hazel eyes that delivered her messages like diamond streetlights for those she encountered, accentuating every emotion with two sparkles, leaving everyone with the impression that she meant exactly what she said. An arresting honesty so pure that she never had to say much. But she did have much to say, and for that, she was a powerful woman. This magical allure had caused Joseph Malveaux to chase Margaret Lemelle around three parishes during the Great Depression like Sir Galahad seeking the Holy Grail.

Her truth was her attraction, felt by all who came in contact with her, including the tall blonde who was sauntering masterfully across the gravel road in short shorts, hair in a scarf, and a yellow shirt tied together above her navel to highlight her D cups just as the green Buick turned off Joseph Street. Her working name was Peaches. And, yes, she was a prostitute.

Margaret knew Peaches wanted to use the phone. They had the only phone in the neighborhood, and most of the girls that worked at La Jolie Blanche made their personal calls at Malveaux's Grocery. La Jolie Blanche was a gambling/whorehouse stuck in the black neighborhood called the New Editions yet only serviced white clients. It was run by two mob guys from Chicago, Mr. Tex and his hotheaded, cigar-smoking brother, Frank. Night after night, nice cars would park in the makeshift parking lot of La Jolie Blanche. Business usually started around the time Margaret finished teaching catechism on her porch. And even though La Jolie Blanche was planted smack-dab in the middle of a black neighborhood, the only black person allowed on the premises was the old cook from Leonville, Miss Helen. One may wonder how an upstanding, Catholic woman like Margaret may have felt about a whorehouse across the street from her home and children, but then again, La Jolie Blanche was their biggest customer. Moreover, Margaret couldn't find the grounds to judge, being a follower of the mighty J.C. and all.

She thought about this while watching Peaches tell more lies to her family in Florida with Hollywood flair and false pleasantrics. Margaret eyed the tall, well-built woman from head to toe, then slowly took a few steps toward the front door with her very own special gait. She had a limp.

It had only been a few months since she'd started walking without those painful wooden crutches. Years before when her brothers were running shine with the Fontenot Brothers, she'd agreed to secrete a large box of rifle bullets. But new inventory and scarce ration books forced her to move the heavy box to the rear of the store by herself. Fearing that the bullets would explode if dropped, she fell with the box in hand. She was paralyzed from the neck down, staring at the hole in the tin roof as her infant, Patrice, and young son, Herman, cried, not knowing what to do.

The doctor said she'd never walk again.

As she lay in bed on her back, her thoughts weren't governed by her disability but the care of her children. They needed her. In the late hours as weary Joseph snored away the day's toil at the mill, she offered a bargain with God:

If you let me walk so that I can take care of my babies, I promise, Lord, I will forever bring souls to your church.

She said this aloud with her diamond eyes open so God could attest to her truth. He believed her, and one year later her feet touched the familiar cypress floors of her home. And even though dust had collected after a year of neglect, she knew that the Devil would find no weakness, for she was now in the service of God.

Ten minutes later, Peaches finished broadcasting her lies, then returned to La Jolie Blanche with a loaf of Evangeline Maid bread, so good and wholesome, soft and white. Margaret dutifully cleaned the phone receiver with Lysol because being Catholic didn't make you immune to syphilis.

Margaret kept her promise with God from the very moment she stood on her own two feet. She worked at Holy Ghost, tending the linens, and taught catechism on her porch. Her emphasis was baptism, believing that one can only get to Heaven if one has been baptized. Day after day she began a slow and methodical mission of converting people to Catholicism. She wasn't pushy but was effective. She formed the Home Circle Club, an informal group of black Catholic women who sold crawfish étouffée and played Pokeno on Fridays to raise money for the new church that was under construction. She was committed. The entire town of Opelousas watched as these black folks put the new church together. Some white folks shook their heads and laughed. Klansmen theorized on who sold them niggers red bricks. But nothing was going to stop them. Not World War II or racism. And Margaret continued teaching children about the Trinity even as a small, elderly black man took careful steps up her driveway while she told the story of David and the giant Goliath.

"Good day, sir. Can I help you?" she asked the elderly man.

"No, ma'am. I just wanna listen," he responded in a weary voice.

The kids made room for him on the porch steps, amused by their ancient guest. Margaret offered him a glass of water, but he declined, so she continued with the story. And after class was over and the kids went home, the old man remained on the porch. Margaret approached.

"That's all for today, sir."

"Mrs. Malveaux, my name is Ezekiel Williams but everybody calls me Pops," he said and extended his old black hands, both of them, the way you shake when you really mean it or you're really grateful. He was all of five feet tall with a slight hunch. Jet-black skin offset by snow-white hair. His eyes were red, pupils discolored to unnatural gray. He'd seen some things, Margaret thought. She'd seen the old man walk around the neighborhood, mostly along the train tracks.

"I wanted to know if you could teach me about God," he said with a pure heart, eyebrows raised with the utmost sincerity.

"Have you been baptized?" Margaret inquired, as she had done initially with many of her converts.

"No, ma'am. Cain't say I have."

"Well, how old are you?" she asked.

"Don't know. I'm right from slavery time, ma'am. Don't know much about God, but I reckon I should, bein' that I hope to see Him one day," Pops said with a gentle smile. "Reckon I gotta get right with God."

Margaret agreed to teach Pops privately in her home in the evenings. She was able to track down a birth certificate issued by the Freedmen's Bureau stating that Ezekiel "Squirrel" Williams was born on October 28, 1844, in Greenville, Mississippi, making him one hundred years old. In his early years, he'd had a reputation for climbing trees and freeing slaves with the help of the Appaloosa tribe, the Black Legs. After the Civil War, he made a name for himself ferrying people and goods through the network of bayous that webbed Louisiana. Who would've guessed that Pops had already lived an entire century; he was playful and excited all of the time. He had most of his faculties and seemed to be managing quite well by himself. He especially enjoyed playing with Herman and baby Patrice, making game of her toes and fingers while teasing Herman with his false teeth.

For Margaret, Pops had become a cause célèbre. She even managed to get him registered to vote although he couldn't write his own name. And Pops was willing to do whatever she asked because she was preparing him for the glory of God, as he would say.

On the evening of his baptism he stood in Margaret's dining room with a sullen look. "I don't have no clothes for church. And I know church is a special place," he said, head hanging low.

"Don't worry. I'll give you some clothes. It'll be your baptism present," Margaret offered.

He slowly raised his white head; rivulets of tears shone against his black skin, glistening like snail juice on hot asphalt. But salt wouldn't kill his joy knowing that a better life waited for him behind the pearly gates. Mary would be there. And all of his children. Two ex-wives. And one granddaughter. All waiting on Squirrel, waiting to reclaim love, to rejoin family, to live forever in peace.

He felt young again and excused himself to the Malveaux backyard, where he found a small ladder next to the chicken coop and placed it against a low-hanging pear tree. He gazed at the tree, surveying its branches and limbs until he spotted a sufficient branch. With quick feet, Squirrel the Amazing Tree Nigger, as he was called by Masta Williams before the Civil War, was back on a branch eight feet off the ground, one hand holding the trunk and the other hand reaching out to God, figuring soon enough God would grab his hand and help him climb higher.

News of Pops's baptism spread throughout St. Landry Parish and the diocese of Lafayette. Soon Margaret received news that the archbishop was coming to town to honor her for her missionary work. She had brought 112 converts to the Catholic Church, a remarkable achievement. But there was only one rub. She was to be honored not at her church, Holy Ghost, but three blocks away at St. Landry's. Segregated.

The idea of a segregated church didn't really cause much commotion in Opelousas or many other Southern towns in the Jim Crow South. Most facilities drew the line anyway; why should church be different? But Margaret was aware of the extreme contradiction between faith and practice. If God didn't see differences, then why should His children? She was being honored at a church that saw differences, a complete offense to the Gospel considering the differences were but a fiction in the eyes of God but were a fact at St. Landry's. But she was as much an activist as a Catholic, participating in voter registration with as much vigor as she taught CCE classes. If she took a stand against segregation and declined the invitation, she would offend the diocese and, arguably, the Catholic Church. Yet if she accepted the invitation, she might feel the sting of hypocrisy, contradicting her civil rights activities. She desired to do neither, and after she put Patrice and Herman to bed, she made a Rosary and asked the Blessed Mother for guidance.

The day she was to be honored by the archbishop, Margaret had been on a nonstop Novena. And although she had dressed herself and her children for church, she hadn't made up her mind about attending the service at St. Landry's. Everyone in town knew about the honor. The *Daily World* had published a front-page story on Margaret's accomplishment complete with a photo, which was noteworthy considering the newspaper, at that time, didn't make a habit of posting photos of Negroes unless they committed a crime or were performing nearby. All of the town was talking about it, assuming she would gratefully accept the honor. But she still had reservations. Faith versus Race. That was the question. Herman came to the door in a cute suit with short pants.

"Momma? We goin' to church?" he asked.

She was still on her knees, leaning against the bed where Patrice was lying, hands clasped with Rosary beads. The children don't understand this race thing, Lord, she thought. It's hard being colored. The world expecting so little from you and you expecting so much from yourself, she pondered. We're remembered for what we do, particularly making the hard choice rather than taking the easy, convenient path. This was her philosophy, and she made a choice. She turned to her child and said—

"No."

"What about all them people?" Herman asked.

Margaret stood up slowly, took painful steps to the front door, and opened it.

About a hundred or so black folks had gathered in front of her house and cheered when she opened the door. Pops was in front in his baptismal suit and bowed deeply, honoring the queen of Catholicism. Margaret was at a loss for words, touched by the outpouring of love from the crowd, mostly children. After a second look, she noticed that many were people whom she'd brought to the Catholic faith. Her very own apostles.

Church was for everybody, Margaret thought as she stood before the white parishioners of St. Landry's, eyeing her children, who sat on Pops's lap in the colored section. When Patrice was old enough, Margaret would tell her about the incident and the honor. She would tell Patrice that the community expected her to receive the honor, not only for herself and her missionary work but to highlight the fact that anybody can be worthy in the eyes of God regardless of how they look, light-skinned or not.

nine

the cape

Houston, Texas, c. 1981

"She said no."

"Why?" Booger asked, his little feelings stepped on like dog shit in deep grass. He didn't see it coming.

Raymond Earl continued popping wheelies on his stolen BMX, ignoring the whole conversation. His little feelings may have been hurt too, but he wasn't going to cry about it. Not Raymond Earl. He didn't need permission for anything, so he offered:

"What time?"

"What time what?" I asked.

"What time that preacher start flyin'?" he answered.

"Right before Communion. Right after the bell rings," I lied.

"We'll be there," he said with authority.

Booger lit up.

"But my momma said you can't come with us."

"I know where it is. We'll be there."

I was excited. My new friends would get to see me on the altar in the robe.

"That nigga better fly or I'ma tell Pork Chop you was talkin' about his momma," Raymond Earl added as he jumped off the curb.

Awh, shit, I thought. He wasn't smiling. He meant it. I'd promised him the miracle of flight and he was willing to walk about a mile to witness it. What would happen when Father Jerome didn't fly, but, hold up, I didn't know if Father Jerome could fly. I worried. I finally got some friends in my neighborhood and now they were gonna kick my ass for lying.

That night as I listened to that hardworking mouse gnawing away on the wall, I hoped that Father Jerome could fly. The black verb guy on *Schoolhouse Rock!* could fly. Surely the pope had taught Father Jerome how to fly. Why else would he wear a cape? Dracula had a cape and he could fly. Superman. Underdog. Mighty Mouse. All of them blessed with the miracle of flight. But then there was Batman and goofy-ass Hong Kong Phooey. They mustn't have been Catholic. I realized that I needed a plan B in case Father Jerome wasn't so endowed.

The fire department showed up first, then an ambulance, and finally a cop car. Nobody rang the doorbell, and half of Clearway Drive was collected in the street watching me. I figured if Father Jerome couldn't fly, then I should fly so that Raymond Earl and Booger wouldn't get mad at me, but I needed practice. And, of course, a miracle.

So there I stood with a bedspread tied around my neck, hands stretched out like Superman, on the roof of my house saying an Our Father. I had been doing this for about twenty minutes, waiting for the sign from God that I could take flight. I didn't know what the sign would be. Locusts. Eclipse. Talking snake. Burning bush. So I waited and listened for instructions. A voice saying take flight or something. I heard the train on Mykawa Road, but that wasn't new. A gunshot rang in the distance. Nothing new. Somebody was yelling nearby. Metro bus brakes squeeled to a stop on MLK. All the same recognizable things, but I stayed there and waited. Father was at work and Mother was vacuuming the floor, probably why she didn't hear all the hoopla.

The fireman told me to come down, but he wasn't God. I knew that God was going to give me a sign, so I stared straight ahead, ignoring everybody until—

"Ti' John! Git yo' ass off that roof, now!" Mother yelled.

But I ignored her too. The ladder was still leaning against the house, but somehow the fireman deemed this a suicide attempt from a one-story roof about ten feet from the soft Gulf Coast ground. So they cautioned Mother against sudden moves, fearing I might make an attempt. It was a standoff, and now Mother was pissed and embarrassed. Hell, I had to fly now because I'd need that miracle later when she'd pull out that extension cord. So I just stood there with my arms extended. Waiting on God.

"Nigga, you crazy. What you doin' up here?" said Raymond Earl as he and Booger walked over to me from the other side of the roof. They must've snuck in the backyard, climbed a tree, and jumped on the roof.

"I'm tryin' to fly," I answered honestly.

"Man, you ain't no preacher," Booger said.

"Shiiited, look at all them people. Your momma mad," said Raymond Earl. "You better get down before your daddy show up."

I put my arms down and sat on my hinds, a bit defeated. They sat down too. I was in no hurry to get off that roof.

"I thought God was gonna show me how to fly in case Father Jerome didn't tomorrow," I explained.

"We know he can't fly, fool," Raymond Earl chided.

"You wasn't gonna be mad?"

"Nawh," Raymond Earl responded.

"Shit, here comes the ice cream man," Booger exclaimed.

I followed them quickly off the roof to applause by the curious crowd in the street. Mother asked me what the hell I was doing on the roof.

"Waiting on God."

Later that evening when Father returned home, Mother gave him a full report while he watched the news.

"Sonny!" he barked.

"Huh?"

"Come here!"

I ran to the den. I could smell his feet, conveniently propped up in his reclining chair.

"You had the firemen out here today?"

"I didn't call 'em, Daddy."

"Tha hell you was doin' on the roof?"

"I was trying to fly. I had a cape and everything."

Then something clicked with him. He jumped up quickly and took off his belt.

"Who told you to get on that roof?"

"Nobody, Daddy. I justed wanted to fly."

"Don't lie to me. Who told you to get on that roof?"

"Probably them lil' badass boys he's been hanging around with on Ricky Street," Mother added.

"One of them boys told you to get on that roof?"

"No, Daddy."

He grabbed my arm tightly and raised his belt.

"Don't lie to me! Who told you to get on that roof!" he yelled, but something was different than when he normally scolded me. I looked at the hand with the belt, poised behind his body for the maximum swing—his hand was trembling.

"Nobody, Daddy. I promise," I pleaded as tears fell because of his increasing grip. He dropped the belt and stormed out the front door. Mother sent me to my room.

Later in bed, I listened to the train on Mykawa Road, then I heard something outside. Father never returned inside after he walked out, but he didn't leave. I snuck out of my bedroom and felt my way through the dark house to the front living room and peeked through the curtains. Father sat on the back of his truck talking to himself. He wasn't speaking English, and he was pointing to the sky, moving his finger in different directions real quickly. Then he stopped and turned to me. I fled to my room.

The next morning in the car headed to church, Mother didn't say one word. I had embarrassed her in front of the entire block. I didn't mean to but that's just how it worked out. But what bothered me most was Father's stolen moment alone outside. He was really talking and pointing at the sky. The only people that did that were— Oh no, Father is crazy. And the more I thought about it, the more little incidents started rushing into my head—Father alone and yapping. I wondered if Mother knew he was crazy. And if she did, then what a saint, taking care of the mentally ill, even having his baby. But if she had his baby and that baby is me, then, oh no. I don't feel crazy. I looked at my hands. Did I have crazy people's hands? I placed my right hand over my face but remembered that was for cancer. Maybe Mother knew that both of us, Father and I, were crazy and she got money from the church to feed and clothe us. What a saint. Saint Patrice, Holy Mother of Lunatics.

She looked pretty that morning in baby blue double knit and white heels, hair falling off her shoulders. Isaac Hayes played on the eight-track telling his love to walk on by. I stared at MLK Boulevard, looking at faces, wondering if they saw me on the roof, wondering if they admired my foolish courage.

In the sacristy while slipping on the robe, I asked him a question—

"Can you fly, Father Jerome?"

Father Jerome turned away from the mirror and squatted at eye level with me, eyes warm, heart pure.

"I'm flyin' right now, lil' brother," he said.

"No ya not. You right here on the ground," I answered, more innocently than sarcastic.

He smiled and took my small hands into his.

"My mind can fly as high as my imagination. My heart can fly as far as my love for God is willing to go, which is infinite. My soul can take my heart and mind wherever they want to go with the grace of God," he offered.

"So can you fly today? Before Communion?" I asked, not fully appreciating his poetry.

He laughed.

"Quit bein' stupid," Albert Thibodeaux chimed in.

"Oh, he's not being stupid. Brother Boudreaux is asking

the practical question. Will my feet leave the ground? That's his question. I've given him a philosophical answer. Yawl know what *philosophical* means?" he asked his altar boys.

We shrugged. *Philosophical?* Sounded like medicine, I thought.

"Ti' John, it has to do with your thinking. It's like your imagination, when you're playing with your toys. Some of your toys can fly, right?" he asked.

"If I let 'em, but I gotta hold 'em up or they'll fall," I answered.

"But in your mind, in your imagination, they're flying by themselves, right?" he continued.

This I understood and got a little excited.

"Yeah. They always flyin', even when I put 'em up, and when I go to sleep, sometimes, they fly around my room without me, like they wanna play by themselves, then my momma gives me a spankin' 'cause my toys are all over the floor. And I told her I didn't put them toys on the floor, they did it by theyself. And she spanked me for lyin'," I blurted.

"Well, God doesn't want you to lie," he said.

I leaned in closer to whisper—

"But I wasn't lyin'. One time, I opened my eyes just a little bit and I saw all of them flyin' all over the room by theyself. I got scared and hid under the covers till Momma came to wake me up," I confided.

I was telling the truth. Maybe I am crazy.

"I just thought you could do the same thing 'cause you got a cape. That's why I got on the roof yesterday with my cape, 'cause I wanted to see if God would let me fly. And Momma gave me a spankin' and God didn't stop her. And it hurt. Did I do something wrong?" I asked.

His cape hung on a clothes hanger against the closet. It was long, green velour with gold brocade and embroidery. An elegant garment fit for a king or knight or superhero.

A small, secret tear fell from Father Jerome's eye as he turned to look at the magnificent green cape against the closet while the organ began, signaling the opening processional. The cape was only for the priest, head priest, the boss. Neither Brother Al nor Brother Barry got to wear one. Must've been one of those pope rules.

Minutes later—

All heads turned to the center aisle as we slowly trudged toward the altar. I noticed the nuns first—some were covering their mouths in shock. Mother squinted, confused and shaking her head in disbelief. Surely I was going to get a spanking for this. Some in the choir chuckled, pissing off the choir director for missing cues. Sister Benedict smiled wide and proud, as did Father Jerome while I led the processional holding the wooden crucifix and wearing the magnificent green cape.

Father Jerome opted not to wear the cape, encouraging me to fly, encouraging my crazy. Even though my ass still burned from the spanking the day before, I felt strong and powerful. At that moment I turned on the imagination button, shifted the crazy gear, and took flight right there in the church. The first place I flew to was the candy store and filled my pockets with red Now and Laters, telling the cashier that God was going to pay for them. I'd need some energy because I had places to go and I'd have to be quick because Mass was only an hour.

An hour later, I had made it through Mass and, in that time, I had traveled to AstroWorld, ridden to the Americas with Columbus, fought dragons with King Arthur, destroyed the Death Star twice without Obi-Wan Kenobi or Luke Skywalker, eaten a giant pizza, jumped a dump truck over the Grand Canyon, and played quarterback for the Oilers in the Super Bowl. I was busy. And just as Father Jerome was announcing the fall bazaar, the back door swung open—

"Ti' John! He fly yet?" Booger yelled as he and Raymond Earl entered, dirty, sweaty, and wearing play clothes. Booger was barefoot.

Father Jerome stopped abruptly as I waved to my friends.

"Nawh, but I did! You missed it!" I yelled back.

Mother's jaw dropped.

"Can I hold on to the cape till tomorrow? I ain't gonna get it dirty," I whispered to Father Jerome.

Nothing like lying in church. But Father Jerome was a jewel. He needed to show the congregation what he was made of—

"I want these young brothers right here. Come on. Right up here with me and Jesus," said Father Jerome.

Booger and Raymond Earl sat on the floor next to me on the altar. They were ecstatic.

Church is for everybody, Margaret Malveaux would say if she was sitting in the car with us, which is why Mother didn't say a thing on the way home. And I didn't get a spanking either. Margaret Malveaux, my grandmother, wouldn't have had a problem with Raymond Earl and Booger showing up for Mass. And Mother knew that she shouldn't either.

When I returned home, Father was in the backyard with his calf rope, lassoing a plastic bucket.

"They ropin' in McBeth. Wanna go?" he asked.

I shrugged. Anything to get out of the house in case Mother changed her mind.

I sat on a dirty ice chest and studied Father. He twirled the lasso over his head with ease, flicks of the wrist, then let it go. In the bat of an eye the lasso was snug around the plastic bucket. Effortless. I ran over to the bucket and loosened the rope. He snapped it back, quickly recoiling the rope for another throw.

"Daddy? Who was you talkin' to the other night?" I asked.

He knew what I was talking about, but he ignored the question and threw the lasso again. I unloosened it, then went around the side of the house to Ms. Johnson's bathroom window and took a piss.

ten

them your people

Part One: Black Gal, 1981

"He ain't ready yet, Patrice," Father said.

"He seem to be ready on Saturday mornings with you," Mother answered.

I heard them in the kitchen while I was supposed to be asleep. All I knew was Mother took a phone call in the bedroom an hour earlier. She talked for a while, then returned to the den, where Father and I were watching *The Jeffersons*. Mother had a strange, sickly look on her face as though she'd found out someone had died. Father inquired, and Mother immediately put me to bed. And no sooner had I fallen asleep than she was waking me again with a packed bag and Father's Chevy idling in the driveway.

"Wake up, Ti' John. We gotta go to Louisiana," she said soft but urgent.

"Why?" I asked.

"We need you to do something," she answered.

It had to be four in the morning. I went back to sleep and barely remembered Father carrying me to the truck.

Three hours later I smelled Benson & Hedges. Mother stared out the window, lips moving quietly as she made a Rosary with worn beads. Father looked straight ahead, hand on the wheel. I looked out the window and saw nothing but sugarcane.

"Daddy, where we at?" I asked.

"We home. Basile," he answered.

What the hell were we doing in Basile? There wasn't a family reunion scheduled. Maybe somebody had died.

"Somebody died?" I asked.

They didn't answer, but something was afoot.

We cruised along U.S. 190, then turned onto a dirt road that cut directly through a young cane field.

"Why are we turning here?" Mother asked, breaking a decade.

"Gotta make a stop if you want him to do this," he replied.

"Do what?" I asked.

"Your father is gonna tell you," she said.

"Why don't *you* tell him? Them your people," Father remarked.

Mother quieted and returned to the Hail Mary.

At the end of the road, the cane fields abruptly turned to forest. Father pulled the truck over and opened the door.

"Come on, Sonny. Let's get out. And bring that thermos. Patrice, stay here. We won't be long," Father ordered.

I grabbed my Star Wars thermos that was filled with Kool-Aid—red Kool-Aid. Father scanned the great forest before us, then started walking directly into it. I followed.

"This used to be a rice field when I was a little younger than you," he said.

"Is this where you grew up, Daddy?" I asked.

"Nawh. We was on the other side of the cane, but I used to play back here when I was little. This is where I'd used to hide when they was looking for me," he said.

He stopped.

"All of this used to be ours," he said proudly.

"What happened?" I asked.

"Them white folks took most of it. Your uncle Pa-June gambled away the rest. But it's still ours. You'll see," he said, then continued walking.

We stopped at a large cypress tree with a huge trunk.

The bottom of the tree looked like several small tree trunks were bound together then merged into one sturdy trunk that stretched endlessly to the sky.

Father took a knee at the tree, one hand leaning against the trunk, then he spoke to the tree—

"Eh, Couzain. This my boy, John Paul Boudreaux the Second. We call him Ti' John. He's a good boy. And he's one of us. Ti' John, put your hand on the trunk and say hello," Father asked.

It seemed fun. Make-believe, I guess.

"Hello, Mister Tree," I said.

"Tell him your name and how old you is."

"My name is John Paul Boudreaux the Second and I'm eight years old."

"Na'. Empty out that thermos."

"Uh-unh, I got Kool-Aid in there."

"Boy, empty that thing out."

I poured out the sweet water. He dried the thermos with a handkerchief, then gave it back.

"Na', grab you a handful of that dirt."

I did.

"Smell it."

No smell, really.

"Na' put it to your ear and listen."

"Listen to what?" I asked.

"Listen to your people. They in that dirt."

Honestly, I didn't hear a damn thing but, since we were playing make-believe, I went along.

"Na' put that dirt in that thermos and tighten the cap."

I poured the dark soil into the Star Wars thermos, then twisted it shut.

"Bon," he said, then put me on his shoulders.

"Nonc Manuel brought us here after the Civil War. You learned about the Civil War yet?"

"Kinda."

"In those days, we was all farmers. It was just us and Indians and the slaves and half of them was our cousins. We took to the land real quick, made use of it. Had to. Wasn't no grocery stores or hardware stores. Nothing. Just land. This is what we had to work with and become something. This land. Louisiana. This is where we were supposed to be. Nous sommes La Louisiane."

"Huh?"

"We are Louisiana, Sonny. Always will be. Never forget that," he said.

With dirt stored in my thermos, we headed back to Mother and the truck.

"You gonna have to treat on your cousin today. You momma's people. You remember what I did with my hands?"

"Yeah."

"All right, then. I'm gonna whisper in your ear what you need to say in your mind, but don't say it aloud, not even a whisper, 'cause then it ain't gonna work. Can you do that?" he asked.

"I think so," I said.

"Either you can do it or you can't. Can you do it?" he asked again.

"Yep. I can do it, Daddy. If you show me," I answered.

We continued along U.S. 190 to State Highway 13 northbound until we reached the outskirts of a small town called Mamou. We moved from asphalt to gravel to dirt back to asphalt until we stopped at a large white house in an area called Pin Claire. Father parked the truck behind an old station wagon, then looked at Mother. Her recitations of the Rosary became jumpy and forced, confusing lines between prayers to yield to her own secret prayers. She was terrified.

"You sure you wanna do this? 'Cause we can turn around right now," Father asked.

"Yes. We here," she said.

This was her aunt's house, Tante Sy-belle Gagnier. Apparently, Tante Sy-belle's daughter, Cozette Augustine, was gravely ill and the doctors at Lourdes Hospital and Opelousas General had given up hope. Somehow it was suggested that Father and I treat her, so here we were.

The white house sat on three-foot cinder blocks with a worn tin roof that covered a massive front porch that creaked as we followed Mother to the front door. She stood at the door for the longest seconds until Father finally knocked. Small talk inside chirped like chickadees until the door slowly opened and a little blond, blue-eyed girl about my age peeked around, then turned back inside with "Nenaine! They here!"

The door opened wider. I began to take a step forward until Mother threw her arm in front of me.

"Wait right here," she ordered.

From the dark room, an old gray-eyed woman in a wheelchair rolled to the front door and looked at Mother with a smile.

"Well, glory be. Lil' 'Trice. Well, come on in, chère. Come see your people," said the old woman.

But Mother was stuck. She couldn't move. This was the first time she'd been invited in.

Opelousas, Louisiana, c. 1955

Little Patrice Malveaux, all of eleven, was having a fit near the playground at Holy Ghost Catholic School. Her older brother, Herman, and their cousin Paul Gagnier had been entertaining three teen girls for nearly fifteen minutes in the sultry afternoon heat of Opelousas, Louisiana.

"Herman, hurry up," she protested, finding a cool breeze under an aged cypress. And although cool breezes were a hot commodity in the summer months, she wasn't seeking relief from the heat but cover from the sun. It was her new habit, confining her afternoon strolls to shaded areas, prisoner of eaves, trees, carports, overhangs, canopies, and the like. And for added measure, she had adopted a dainty new habit of carrying a little pink parasol at all times, whether or not rain was in the forecast. Her mother thought it was cute and her father thought it was silly, but she was resolute. She couldn't stand for her skin to darken.

Herman rejoined his sister with Paul in tow. Paul had long since ditched school for work at the oil mill and high-stakes dice games in Lafayette. Patrice's parents normally didn't approve of Paul hanging around Herman, but he was family. Plus, the corner of Church Street and Railroad Avenue often required backup for any black kids walking by.

"What you doin' Friday night?" she asked Herman.

"I don't know, why?" he responded while eyeing a brand-new, candy apple red Bel Air that drove past.

"Can you take me to Cozette's birthday party?"

"Nope," Herman said matter-of-factly.

"Why not?" she protested, but she knew the answer.

"Momma ain't gonna let you."

"But I wanna go . . ."

" 'Trice!" Herman stopped and faced his little sister, who stood holding her pink parasol with anxious eyes. He didn't want to say it, but she knew the answer and she knew why. He didn't want to hurt her feelings but protect her from the evils of the world, the abuses that would be directed toward her. One day she'd have to face it alone, but for now, he was her protector. And somehow she'd decided that she wanted to attend Cozette's party knowing that she couldn't. Sure she was well behaved and made good marks. Margaret would sometimes say that she was a perfect child as mothers do and it may have been true. But none of that mattered.

"You know you cain't go."

"Why?"

" 'Cause you too dark."

Ma Negrisse.

"Young ladies do not attend parties uninvited, Patrice," Margaret told her daughter at the dinner table.

Patrice pouted and refused to eat. Joseph Malveaux put down his fork and stared at his daughter, warmed by her predicament. It was his darker skin that cast her with a caramel hue. And it was his wife's family, the Lemelles, who didn't really accept her nor him. When he married Margaret only half of her family showed. He was a darker Creole with a hint of Native American blood. And despite the good name and the large landholdings, Joseph Malveaux's skin was a pebble in the Lemelles' shoe.

"We eatin' at this table, not poutin'. So you can go 'head and 'scuse yourself," Joseph said, although he wanted to give her a hug.

Patrice excused herself from the table and went to the front yard to count fireflies. Five.

The next afternoon, Joseph took Patrice for a long drive in the country. Maybe a drive out of the city would calm the anxious preteen, he thought, a short break from Chuck Berry, picture shows, and malt shops. Both were quiet in the car. His favorite song came on the radio. He turned up the volume, laughing along as Louis Jordan signified. Patrice wasn't amused, rather bored and hoping that Cousin Cozette may have realized that she'd erred and forgot to invite her little cousin. She imagined the phone ringing and Cousin Cozette telling her mother that she couldn't imagine having a party without Patrice in attendance.

"When we going home, Daddy?" she asked politely.

"Aah, black gal. You don't wanna ride with your daddy?"

Black gal. That was his nickname for her; a moniker that highlighted their special bond. Herman favored his mother's creamy beige that reddened with exposure to the sun. But Patrice had a darker, olive tone that browned under the sun's rays. Of course Joseph was aware of his daughter's insecurities about her complexion, but he only meant the benign sobriquet in jest. Either way, Patrice hated that name. Every time he said it, the hair on her arms stood up and her stomach knotted even when he said it while embracing her. She didn't love him less for the name and he never used it in anger or reprimand. But she wasn't too young to know that there wasn't any decent place in the world for a black gal, any black gal. She gripped the parasol tighter, staring blankly out the window.

She turned to Joseph, whose smile had faded as he bit off the end of a cigar and flipped out a flame from a brass Zippo. He took off work to spend the day with her, his only daughter, yet she was still resolute to pout.

"Daddy?"

"Yes, baby."

"I'm sorry."

"I know, baby. Tell ya what. We'll stop and get some ice cream before we go home," he said as he slowed his brown Ford on the empty country road and made a U-turn.

"Oooh, Daddy! Pull the car over," she exclaimed.

A field of dandelion seed heads resembled a white blanket along the road. She jumped out of the car, pink parasol in hand, and took off into the field. Joseph eased out of the car and leaned against the fender enjoying the cigar, relieved that his troubled daughter had found a small moment of joy. This wasn't a paid sick day at the oil mill but damn money, he thought, my little girl is smiling again.

She plucked the perfect dandelion, closed her eyes, and held the seed head up to God as she made a wish, then said, "Amen."

She blew the fluff into white, dancing fibers that fell at her feet. Joseph watched from afar as she grabbed her parasol and headed back to the car. He quickly wiped tears with his sleeve that smelled of LouAna cooking oil. He knew her wish.

Meanwhile, Herman and Paul had gotten themselves into a bit of a pickle with the Ribodeaux Brothers on the corner of Church Street and Railroad Avenue. And even though the Ribodeaux family were Cajuns who could easily be mistaken for fair-complexioned Creoles, they hated niggers, light or dark, which Herman thought was a bit ironic as the Ribodeaux Brothers surrounded him and Paul. White folks passing by pulled their cars over to watch the two negra boys get beaten. Chuck Berry rattled from car radios. The manager at the nearby Piggly Wiggly passed out cold Pabst.

"Get 'em! Get them niggers!"

Paul pulled out a straight razor to even the odds. Swinging wildly, he managed to literally carve out an opening for him and Herman to escape, but not without giving little Aubère Ribodeaux a parting gift across his cheek. Poor cher. Lil' Aubère was traumatized and sent to New Orleans the next day where he later became an internationally renowned chef.

Herman and Paul hightailed it along Duson's railroad tracks until they reached the New Editions. They fell onto the grass in Herman's front yard on Joseph Street—spent, bruised, and dirty.

"As soon as I get old enough, I'm goin' up North," Herman said.

"You don't know nobody up there," Paul countered.

"Don't matter none. I know damn near everybody here and look what just happened," said Herman.

Joseph and Patrice pulled into the driveway. Patrice skipped out of the car holding a messy ice cream cone and dashed into the house. Joseph approached the boys.

"You gotta leave them white boys alone," he advised, but the boys were oblivious. Joseph understood.

"Eh, Malveaux! Dem boys been cuttin' up?" Doris Chenier* yelled from across the street as he loaded ice into his café.

"He don't know. I'm gonna send him to the country to pick peas," Joseph said with a laugh.

Herman wasn't amused. Damn the country, I'm going North, he thought.

Hours later, after supper, Herman sat alone in the front yard

---

* His nephew Clifton Chenier had recently gained notoriety as a first-class zydeco artist, mixing blues with the standard fare developed by Amédé Ardoin. His first hit single, *"Ay, 'Tit Fille,"* was blaring across St. Landry Parish at that time.

by the ditch watching lively colored people going to Chenier's café across the street. He was still angry.

"I saw the prettiest sweater today at Abdalla's, Herman," Patrice said as she sat next to him, trying her darndest to sound like a movie star or at least one of the girls from La Jolie Blanche. He ignored her.

"It would be perfect for Cozette's party."

He turned to his sister.

" 'Trice, why you wanna go to that party? They don't want you over there."

"Ain't you ever wanted to be somewhere you wasn't supposed to be?"

He put an arm around her.

"What color you think Slim gonna be tonight?" Herman asked.

She thought about it.

"Hmmmm. Pink."

"Pink?"

"Okay. Orange."

"Maybe."

They waited. Forty minutes later, a yellow Cadillac pulled up to the café as the band started thumping a heavy blues stride.

"Now, ladies and gentlemen, from New Orleans, put your hands together for Guitar Slim!"

On cue, the Cadillac door opened and he stepped out. Lime green. Suit, shoes, and conked hair—all lime green.

"He looks like a Popsicle," Patrice said and laughed, watching the famed blues man step into the packed club.

The next morning, the whistle at the LouAna Oil Mill blew. No one heard it. Yet the day began anyway. Cotton don't wait on nobody, the whistle said. The Jolie Blanche girls giggled, cackled, behind silk curtains filtering the wholesome scent of ham and eggs. Breakfast for hookers. Still, the LouAna whistle competed with prayers for the dead and bedridden petitioned by the distant church bells' Catholic lament tuned in B flat at Holy

Ghost where black folks make their sacraments. By afternoon, the bells will rejoice off-tune and lazily, and the mill whistle will sound, strong and certain, minding time, minding obligation. Elvis Presley will replace the morning mirth of the working girls' afternoon hour. And downtown Opelousas will find two of its children wandering about, ignoring all of it.

"That's it right there," Patrice exclaimed.

The mannequin in the window at Abdalla's department store sported a gray wool pleated skirt complete with a stiff cancan slip, a red three-quarter-length wool sweater with collar, and a black four-inch-wide elastic belt. This was her outfit, she thought, and this is what she pointed out to Herman with a little note listing her sizes.

Later that day the men's section of Abdalla's department store mysteriously caught fire, and magically Patrice had her outfit, tucked deep in the bottom of a Piggly Wiggly grocery bag underneath a package of bologna and a loaf of Evangeline Maid bread. Paul had called in the threat five minutes before, giving his best impression of a St. Landry Parish Klansman—protesting Abdalla's forward-thinking policy of servicing coloreds. It was Herman's idea—a perfect opportunity to strike out against Jim Crow and nearby Klansmen who had left a burning cross in Joseph Malvcaux's front lawn to discourage customers, particularly the girls from La Jolie Blanche. With blame securely laid on the KKK, Herman had no problem committing larceny.

Hot thick bayou air.

They caught a ride with Mr. Prejean to Pin Claire. Paul came along in case things got testy and, also, he was invited—Cozette was his sister.

Patrice rode in the front cab of the truck so as not to dirty her new outfit. Herman and Paul sat in the back payload finishing off a pint of rye. As they turned off the blacktop for gravel, they could hear the music—boogie-woogie. Cars lined the gravel road. The truck stopped at the driveway and they got out. Paul passed Mr. Prejean a few coins with "Come back in two hours." Mr. Prejean tipped his hat and drove off.

Patrice was nervous, still clutching her parasol.

"You ready?" Herman asked her.

She wasn't sure.

"Aah, come on, 'Trice. We're here now."

"Yeah, 'Trice. Don't you worry 'bout nuthin'. Them your people," Paul added.

Herman took her hand. "Let's go."

They approached the front door, where a group of older Lemelle and Gagnier women sat in chairs cutting okra—her aunts.

"Paul, cher. You done come see your maman," Tante Sy-belle said with a warm smile. Paul gave his mother a hug and a kiss. She hadn't seen him in two months.

"Hey, Auntie," Patrice managed.

"Eh?" Tante Sy-belle responded with a questioning look. "Your mama know you here?"

"She came for her cousin's party," Paul interrupted.

Tante Sy-belle looked at the other women, then focused on the pile of okra in her apron.

"This party not for you," Tante Sy-belle said, avoiding her niece's eyes.

"Maman, this is Cozette's cousin, your niece," Paul argued.

"I know who she is. This party not for her," the ornery gray-eyed old woman spouted.

The door opened. Laughter and music spilled out. Cesaire and Louis, Paul's older brothers, came to the door.

"Well, look who showed up. You forgot about your baby sister's birthday, Paul?" said Cesaire. He hated Paul.

"You see me here now," Paul chided and took a few steps toward the stairs leading into the house with Patrice and Herman in tow.

"Eh, na'! She ain't invited," Cesaire asserted with a defiant

arm blocking the door. Paul took another step up the stairs, but
Cesaire pushed him back, sending his brother to the ground.

"Eh! Fais pas ça!" Tante Sy-belle yelled.

Paul let off a little laugh to himself, then slowly stood up. A
small crowd of beige teenagers gathered by the door. Patrice held
Herman's hand tighter.

" 'Trice. Go wait over there," Paul ordered as he started
taking off his shirt. Herman followed suit. This fight had been
brewing for years.

"Don't fight with your brother, Cesaire, you know he's
crazy," Tante Sy-belle advised.

"Nawh, Maman. He been had this coming," Cesaire responded, walking down the stairs rolling up his sleeves. A few
other boys rallied behind him.

"No black gal in here tonight, Paul. You know that," Tante
Sy-belle reminded her son, but it didn't matter.

Paul threw his shirt on the ground. The crowd hushed. Some
made a sign of the cross in disbelief.

"Cher bon Dieu! What you done let them do to you in Lafayette, Paul?" his mother bemoaned.

Paul Gagnier's body was littered with scars, mostly old stab
and cut wounds. The sight of his battle scars cautioned a few of
the approaching boys, but not Cesaire.

"Blessed Mother, don't let my babies fight," Tante Sy-belle
petitioned.

"Yawl ain't gonna let your lil' cousin in the party 'cause she
darker than yawl?" Paul asked.

No one said a word.

The Same Porch, 1981

My little blond, blue-eyed cousin, Daphne, led me to her
mother's bedroom. Tante Sy-belle, partially senile, partially
performing, unloaded pleasantry after pleasantry while Mother

waited in the living room with plastic-covered furniture, thick, cheap carpet, and pictures everywhere of the Lemelle and Gagnier clans. Mother chose not to look at the pictures, knowing there wasn't a picture of her anywhere on the wall or faux mantel or in the whole damn house, for that matter.

Cousin Cozette was around Mother's age and bedridden. Father walked in behind me. Daphne stood by the door. Cozette looked at me for a long while, then said, "Thank you for coming to see me, Cousin."

"Close the door behind you," Father told Daphne.

Daphne left us alone with her mother.

"Ti' John. We gonna go real slow. Take your time," Father said.

What I would learn later is that the treatment would be more effective if the treater carried the patient's blood, which was why I was treating and not Father.

He looked at me and nodded. We both made a sign of the cross and began.

About two hours later, we walked out of the bedroom to a huge crowd of beige relatives. Me. Father. And Cousin Cozette. The crowd applauded and yelped as Cozette took sickly but certain steps toward Mother and gave her a desperate, long hug.

"Cousin Patrice. Please forgive me, Cousin. I know we ain't never treated you right, but please forgive me," Cozette pleaded.

Mother nodded slowly, then bent down and kissed her aged aunt, who at this point was crying aloud. Fuckin' family.

Cesaire showed up late but quickly hugged Mother—all smiles—asking questions like he ever really gave a damn about Mother. And Mother? She took it all in stride, but she added one punch for good measure—

"You know, I'm sure Ti' John is tuckered out. I was thinking we'd sleep here tonight," Mother announced.

Father and most of the room did a double take. It was a

known fact that we had relatives within five miles in any direction, but Mother had planned this all along. I was sure of that. She was going to milk this situation down to the bone. Guess she was having a reckoning.

"That's fine, chère. You stay right here. Cesaire, go light the pit and cook some rice," Tante Sy-belle ordered.

None of these relatives spoke directly to me. They just stood back, maybe in awe, eyes trained on me with quick-moving lips. I was one of the youngest treaters many of them had ever seen.

I looked around for Father, but he had disappeared.

"Yo' daddy outside," Daphne told me.

I went to the porch looking for him. Father was speaking with a worried man next to an orange truck on the gravel road. Inside the truck, a young girl, maybe twelve or so, was crying and gripping the seat belt across her chest. We made eye contact. *You better not tell nobody.* That's what I heard when I looked at her, but it was a man's voice.

It appeared as though Father and the worried man were making plans, then Father spat on the ground. Suddenly the worried man appeared gracious and relieved as he returned to his truck and drove off. Father watched the truck drive away, then turned to me. He wasn't smiling.

The tip-tap of the tin roof sent me to sleep quicker than Cesaire's dirty rice and Tante Sy-belle's peach cobbler. I was tired, which was why I didn't notice that Father was nudging me while I slept on a pallet on the living room floor.

"Sonny. Be quiet and come with me," Father whispered.

Together, we slipped out of the house in the rain.

"Where we going?" I asked.

"Goin' to work," he responded.

We drove to Ville Platte. Father didn't say a word. At Ville Platte, we pulled into a closed gas station where the orange truck waited for us.

"Stay in the truck but don't go to sleep. Just watch," Father advised.

The worried man got out of the orange truck carrying a brown grocery bag. Father got out and met him at the hood of our truck. The man gave the bag to Father, who then poured its contents onto the hood—silverware, jewelry, coins. They had a brief conversation as Father put the items in a large purple half-gallon Crown Royal bag, then returned to the truck.

"Don't tell Momma, right?" I asked.

Face dripping wet, excited eyes, he tucked the purple bag under the seat quickly and said "You gotdamn right" like he was talking to a grown-ass man. I had barely turned eight. And I damn sure wasn't sleepy anymore.

eleven

good luck

Winter in Anahuac, Texas, on White Folks' Property, 1982

Trees talk. No bullshit. All you have to do is listen. The leaves act as vocal cords. Soprano in the spring. Baritone in the fall. The wind pushes through, forcing the trees to tell the truth. Cold, crisp air gets the most testimonies. Damp air makes them lie. And when you hear nothing, that's when you should get worried. That's what Father told me as we carefully walked through waist-high briar following the occasional yelps of rabbit dogs. They caught a scent, so we followed.

Forty-eight degrees Fahrenheit. Dressed in layers with rubber boots. Single-shot .410 with No. 4 shells. Arthur Duncan, Cleatis Mitchell, and Father's other hunting buddies were thirty yards to our back. We led.

Father listened closely as he carefully planted feet through thorn-filled thickets, making a way for me to follow. He listened with his entire body, shotgun pointing in the air across his chest. I imitated every move, the swagger, the pauses, the listening.

The dogs yelped louder near a creek that carved through this heavily wooded property that we were hunting on with white folks' permission. Father motioned for me to fan out to his left, far left. He knew where the rabbits would jump. Something small scampered toward us. Father motioned for me to move further left near a clearing for a clean shot. I followed his direction and pushed the safety off the trigger. He raised his hand for me to wait, then took a stick and started beating the bushes. He was sending the rabbit to the clearing. Clean shot.

About twenty yards ahead, a small brown rabbit sprung out of the thickets. I squeezed the trigger. The stock slammed against my shoulder. Gotdamn it was loud.

"You get 'im?" Father yelled.

"I think so," I answered.

The small brown bunny was crippled, desperately using its front paws to get away. I aimed the rifle at its head.

"Put that gun down. You gonna waste shells," Father ordered as he joined me.

"What'm I supposed to do?" I asked.

"Kill it. Run it against that tree," he said, more excited than me.

More shots in the distance. More rabbits. Less time to kill in privacy. His friends were moving closer, but I couldn't kill the brown bunny. I could shoot it, but I couldn't commit to savagely bashing the animal. I hesitated.

"Sonny, come on. Put it out its misery," Father barked.

I was frozen.

He winced, grabbed the bunny by its hind legs, and slammed its head into the tree trunk. Thump. That's what it sounds like when a rabbit's head is smashed into a tree.

"Now. Put that in your bag. Your first kill," he said proudly as he helped me slide the warm body into the bag of my hunting vest. The bunny's body was hot against my lower back. And for a minute or two, I could feel its little heart thumping.

"Next time don't hesitate and don't waste shells. They cost money," he said.

He was proud that I shot the animal but could tell that I didn't want to resort to bashing, complete the kill.

"Ti' John. When you hurt an animal real bad, you gotta kill it. Put it out its misery or else it's a sin," he explained. "Don't let me see you hesitate like that again."

I was ashamed and he knew it. I'd let him down. The bunny's heart was fading.

"Pick up your face 'cause you gonna have to skin your kill later and I don't want you makin' no faces," he said.

"Daddy, I don't wanna skin it," I pleaded.

"You ain't got no choice. That's your kill," he said, then took the rabbit out of the bag and handed it to me but I wouldn't touch it.

"Grab it," he said.

I reluctantly took the bunny. Brain matter oozed onto my hands. I dropped it quickly.

"Gotdammit ta hell, Sonny. Pick it up," he ordered.

I squatted down and carefully picked up the animal.

"Na' put it in your bag. That one's yours."

Hours later I skinned and gutted the animal with the men-folks, amusing them with my disgust. Father watched me closely with a Benson & Hedges dangling between his lips, hiding a smug grin.

"Can I keep the foot for good luck?" I asked.

"You don't want that, Sonny. It's gonna stink up," he answered.

"For good luck?" I continued.

"Ain't no such thing as good luck, Son. Not for niggas. White folks get good luck. But us colored folks, we either get bad luck or no luck at all," he explained.

"Like hell, John," Cleatis interrupted. " 'Cause I saw you roll five sevens in a row at Jewel's last Friday."

The men laughed, but Father was serious.

"Hell, that ain't luck. I know them dice. I'm tryin' to teach my boy a lesson. A colored boy go out in that world looking for luck, he gonna end up on his ass," Father explained, then looked at me and the dead rabbit on the tailgate. Its feet were still attached.

"Arthur, give Ti' John your knife," he told Arthur Duncan, who produced a large, shiny Buck knife from a leather sheath attached at his belt like a fuckin' sword. He handed it to me.

"Now. Cut off them feet," Father said.

I cut off the feet, through the tendons, flesh, and bone. All the men watched. When I finished, I looked at Father, waiting to see if he'd change his mind and let me keep a foot for a key chain or something.

"Lucky rabbit's foot, huh?" Father commented. "Look at that rabbit, Son."

The pink carcass with large brown eyes stared at me.

"That rabbit's dead, right?" Father asked.

"Yeah."

"Then na're one of them feets is lucky."

He collected the severed feet and threw them deep into the woods. I wanted to cry.

"And wipe that frown off your face. You'se a colored boy. You gotta learn how to make your own gotdamn luck. You understand me?" he asked.

"Yes, Daddy," I answered.

He was right. I just needed to learn how. How does one *make* good luck? Is it like making gumbo? Start small, finish big. Or is it like boiling crawfish? Throw it all in a pot of boiling water, add seasoning, corncobs, and potatoes, then wait for it to happen.

I thought about that first kill while I urinated on the side of the rectory during recess.

Sister Benedict caught me.

An hour later, I was expelled.

Mother cried all night. She was too distraught to spank me. I watched Benny Hill on channel 39 and fell asleep just as the blonde removed her brassiere.

I can't tell you why I did it. It felt good. It felt free.

Black Jesus wept.

* * *

The next day Mother took off work so she could focus on finding me another school. Some of the teachers at St. Philip's said I
was a bad kid. Mother cursed them out. Not Ti' John.

Around noon, the doorbell rang. It was Father Jerome. He
wanted to take me to lunch.

Mother was befuddled but trusted that Father Jerome was up
to something. Some form of punishment.

Father Jerome and I cruised down MLK headed to Frenchy's
Creole Fried Chicken (no relation to Father, unfortunately)
listening to Sun Ra.

"How do you dance to this music?" I asked.

"You don't. You just sit still and listen. Kinda like reading.
You like to read?" he asked.

"If the book got pictures for me to trace," I answered.

He didn't say anything about the incident the entire ride.

He ordered a whole box of spicy and a bag of fries with
plenty of ketchup. I was too anxious to eat to notice that something was afoot, but fuck it. I liked fried chicken.

Fifteen minutes later, my lips were covered in grease and
ketchup. Father Jerome sat quietly, watching me eat and smoking a Kool.

"You don't like chicken?" I asked.

"Fried food is bad for my heart," he answered while Kools
bellowed from his nostrils.

The day manager motioned for him, and he excused himself
rather politely like I was a grown-up. They talked outside for a
while, sharing cigs, long pauses. It looked like Father Jerome
was telling him a story, occasionally pointing at me. They both
returned to the table with fixed looks.

Penance.

I had to scrub the men's restroom at Frenchy's Fried Chicken
while reciting the Act of Contrition. In Latin. And when I finished at the chicken joint, we continued my penance at all the
boys' restrooms at St. Philip's, which was in session, by the way.
Anthony Goodey saw me in the hallway and stuck out his tongue.

Finally, Father Jerome walked me to the rectory to complete my command performance on the rectory walls.

Amen.

Later that evening, as Father Jerome drove me home, he asked why I did it. I didn't answer. I didn't know.

Silence.

He stared straight ahead, both hands on the wheel. I stared at the gold Jesus on his pinkie until it winked at me. Swear to God.

In the name of the Father, the Son, and Fried Chicken.

In bed that night listening to the train on Mykawa Road and that persistent mouse, I armed myself with a bat and slept without the covers. If that mouse managed to get through the Sheetrock, I was gonna kill that muthafucka.

twelve

the woods

It didn't take long for Mother to find another school for me. This time I would leave the soiled hands of South Park and head to another part of town that I had only heard about. Third Ward.

That first morning I looked out the window quietly, passing familiar streets down MLK headed toward MacGregor Park. Mother gave a UN worthy speech on the importance of education and respecting people's property, particularly not urinating on people's property. I was more enamored by the change in scenery as we approached Third Ward. It was the trees that made the announcement.

The trees changed. South Park was loaded with an ill-planned hodgepodge of misshapen, misguided trees, awkward chinaberry trees, confused ferns, nestled in loitering St. Augustine grass and ant beds. But as we passed under the 610 Loop the trees grew dense and tall, more proud. More leaves. Darker green. We passed the King's Flea Market across Old Spanish Trail to MacGregor Park, the visiting center of Third Ward. Suddenly the haphazard tree-planning of South Park transformed into the stately uniformity of pine. Tall pine trees as far as the eye could see. Welcome to the proud and historic Third Ward, the pines said to me as I watched from Mother's Buick.

Third Ward was an older black neighborhood in Houston that displayed a peculiar socioeconomic dichotomy. Affluent blacks occupied many large homes in the area, remnant swag after the Jews fled in the 1950s, and had managed to establish this piece of Houston as their very own buppie utopia. Churches, colleges, frat houses, golf courses, and massive homes lined a twisting waterway called Braes Bayou, shared with the privileged whites further along the trail. Mercedes-Benzes ushered kids to tennis practice and Cub Scout meetings. High tea on Saturdays promoted highbrow black activism with constant reassurances that their bourgeois status was preserved. Many of these houses had been passed down from the black professionals of the civil rights era, whose kids, adults in the eighties, seemed only to care about accumulating and displaying wealth and status. And their neighbors? Mostly victims of the dream deferred and the working poor, managing day to day on cheap gratification and genuine love. Since major thruways carved up the neighborhood, crackheads and hookers pervaded this black Walden with pomp for profit and pleasure, giving the privileged residents real meaning to car alarms and Brink's. This audacious display of wealth locked hand in hand with desperate poverty heightened the sense of danger in Third Ward, reminiscent of disparity seen in Third World countries. No wonder it was called Third Ward; the thinly transparent line of demarcation between the haves and the have-nots was its greatest obscenity.

We cruised along North MacGregor Way, winding along Braes Bayou sided by huge, palatial estates with Mercedes, Jaguars, Cadillacs, and Corvettes parked in driveways or driving past us. Black people were driving these cars—men with neckties, occasional cravats, women with silk scarves and well-appointed brooches. We continued on to Scott Street then Southmore Boulevard near Texas Southern University, where students moved quickly between dorms and classrooms. Black fraternity houses sat off the street, proud and nonchalant. Even Debbie Allen's father kept a medical office along the street. We slowed down and turned in to a long driveway at my new school. St. Andrew's Episcopal.

I was excited, warm and tingly as if I was crossing the bridge to AstroWorld with a Coke can on a June day. Mother gave me a big hug and a kiss. I stepped out the car and could smell it. Pine needles. It smelled clean. Smelled like something better.

What was the vibe at St. Andrew's? More than white folks doing good. Post-hippie, Thoreauesque, kindhearted white Christians determined to educate the predominately affluent, little black minds with an almost nondenominational Christian framework. John Denver as Black Jesus. It was an open-concept curriculum designed to allow each student to learn at his or her own pace. No more desks. We sat on the floor. No more uniforms. No more Rosaries. And no more fuckin' paddles. Granola bars and Christian folk songs on acoustic guitar cushioned the academic program at St. Andrew's. *Free to Be . . . You and Me.* Roberta Flack and Michael Jackson with Carole King on tambourine. Save the whales and don't bash the baby seals. Scavenger hunts at Camp Allen. Songs from the Americana songbook. *This land is your land. Good morning to you. They'll know we are Christians by our love.* Hippie songs. No gospel. Not at St. Andrew's.

And when I got out of Mother's Buick, it didn't feel like the dreaded first day of school. It felt like vacation.

The principal showed me to my new homeroom, Miss Madison's room. The kids were sitting on the floor with Miss Madison in a rocking chair reading to the class. *The Lion, the Witch and the Wardrobe.* They stared at me as I found a seat on the floor, then returned their attention to Narnia. Two minutes into Aslan's Jesus talk, a little, pudgy, light-skinned boy started kicking me in the back and giggling. The kid next to him dared him to do it. He was kinda pudgy too. I turned around quickly and they held their smirks, faces reddening.

"Stop," I whispered.

"Pussy," the kicker retorted.

Later, at lunch, the two boys approached with other kids.

"What school you came from?" Mike Braddock, pudgy kid who kicked me, asked.

Mike, the apparent leader, was a bit cocky for a pudgy kid,

maybe because his father was running for reelection to city council. He broadcast jokes and insults loud enough for everybody to hear, then looked around to make sure everybody was laughing. A complete asshole.

"St. Philip's," I answered.

"Where's that? I ain't heard of it."

"South Park, off MLK."

"That's where you live? South Park?"

"Yeah."

"Damn. That's the ghetto. You ain't supposed to be in Third Ward."

"Why not?"

" 'Cause you might steal something."

The kids laughed. I laughed too, even though it was at my expense, which only made them laugh harder. What was "ghetto"?

Five minutes later, Mike had gathered a crowd and was making fun of my clothes, which I didn't understand because my clothes were clean and pressed. Mother had spent almost thirty minutes ironing my green Toughskins. We didn't have time nor money to buy new school clothes, so I had to mix and match with my St. Philip's uniform—green and white. From head to toe, Mike found an insult for every item of clothing, typically referring to it as cheap or stolen from Goodwill. Most of the crowd laughed with Mike, but I just smiled. Figured I'd smile my way out of it; smiling worked before.

But the smile didn't work this time. Mike continued lampooning me until finally he pushed me and told me to go back to South Park. I couldn't resist.

"I am going back. After school is over."

The crowd hushed from my sarcasm. Mike interpreted my answer as a challenge, so he hit me. It didn't hurt, but I didn't hit him back. I couldn't. I didn't want to get kicked out of another school, and I sort of liked St. Andrew's. But I wouldn't fight back. The kids taunted, but I didn't move. And Mike's fat ass took great delight in such an easy target. The school bell ended the fight, if you want to call it that, and for the remainder of the day nobody talked to me.

At school's end, most of the kids lined up near the driveway for their parents to pick them up. This was an opportunity to see who had a nice car or fine sister or sexy mother. I watched most of the luxury cars from the public bus stop near the driveway's edge. Mike gathered a group of boys to stare and laugh at me for riding the ghetto bus, but Mother had an appointment so I was on Metro. Mercedes, Lincolns, Cadillacs passed me with professional parents at the wheel on the ingress, then returned with their professional kids, some pointing and sticking out their tongues as they passed again on egress. It felt like the whole school got a chance to stare at me one by one in their nice cars with the delightful smell of pine needles all around. A few of them mouthed the word *ghetto,* and I started to get a hot pain in the back of my neck. These kids had nice things: Levi's, KangaROOS, Trapper Keepers, and Polo shirts. And half of the boys had small video games in their backpacks.

Mike drove by in a brown Seville and shot the finger at me. Then it hit me. I'm poor.

Riding on the Metro back home, I saw Mike's father's campaign posters everywhere, and dammit if little Mike wasn't the spitting image of big Mike with that same fucked-up grin. After the fourth sign, I tried avoiding the placards, but no use. Every time I saw one I swear big Mike was saying "ghetto" and laughing at me, continuing the bullshit that his son started. Corner after corner, ghetto. I replayed the day in my head to see where I went wrong. The whole day actually went wrong. Mike saw to it that I was excluded from everything while bragging about some trip to Six Flags that many of the kids had gone on with a group called Jack and Jill. It sounded fun, so I asked Mike if I could join.

"Nope. You gotta be invited and we don't let no ghetto niggas in."

More laughter.

The bus stopped at MLK Boulevard and Ricky Street. I got off and found Joe Boy and Curtis sitting under a tree drinking Blue Bull and smoking cigarettes. Fuck. I got my ass beat again. And Joe Boy wasn't little Mike. His punches hurt.

Minutes later, I trudged into my backyard, nose still bleeding. I jumped into my favorite tree and climbed as high as the branches would allow. I could see my neighbors' roofs. Nobody would get me up here. I leaned against the trunk and pulled out a notebook to draw.

A bloated, dead wood rat was lying upside down in a water bucket in Father's rabbit-dog kennel. I started drawing it.

"Hey, Ti' John!"

"Who's that?"

"Booger."

Booger was tromping through the woods behind my house.

"Whatcha doin'?"

"Drawing."

"I can draw too," he said, then I could see his big smiling eyes emerging from the brush. He was barefoot and shirtless with a necktie as a headband, carrying a makeshift bow and arrow. He liked to play in the woods by himself about as much as he liked to draw.

Delano Tiberius Jackson, or Booger, was eleven years old in the third grade; technically, he was supposed to be in the fifth grade. He had become a burden on Houston Independent School District, a squatter. And with each school year, various teachers would check their rosters and gaze at their classes with hope until they realized that Booger was also in attendance. Teacher after teacher made a little place in the lesson plan to keep Booger busy, usually with crayons, construction paper, and pencils. There would be no silent reading or book reports. His elementary education had been reduced to show-and-tell and drawing, year after year. It wasn't a secret. Booger couldn't read.

His schizophrenic mother, Louella, walked to house after house, day after day, selling imaginary encyclopedias, while his father was pledging a new urban fraternity, the Order of the Crackhead, so Booger pretty much was raising himself. A state check came to the house at the first of every month; he took that check to his next-door neighbor, Ms. Bunky, ensuring that the lights, water, and gas would continue to run. Next, Ms. Bunky would take him to Rice Food Market, where he could buy candy and junk food as well as other household needs. It only cost a case of Schlitz Malt Liquor Bull for Ms. Bunky. Finally, the remainder of the money was buried in the backyard in a pickle jar so his father, Julius, wouldn't find it. That was Booger's routine.

"I bet Mrs. Randolph got Mr. Randolph's drawers hanging on a line. Bet they still got doo-doo stains too. Let's go see," said Booger.

Peeking in people's backyards can be as intrusive as watching them change clothes or use the toilet. People normally treat backyards in one of two ways. Some treat the backyard as an extension of the front yard, an ordered, idyllic presentation with trimmed hedges and manicured lawn complete with sprinklers. Others treat the backyard like a workshop or junkyard suitable for anything that's been banished from the home, the glorious excommunicated, broken appliances, laundry on lines, card tables, dirty folding chairs, forgotten or outgrown amusements, and anything else that couldn't fit or shouldn't fit in the house. From the tree branches, Booger and I had a clear view for half a block.

Booger had been trekking around the woods all day, following cattle paths and deer trails along Sims Bayou, the forgotten little brother of Buffalo Bayou, nearing the prison, or P farm, to Mykawa Road and its moaning tracks.

The "woods," as we called it, was curtained by MLK to Telephone Road and Bellfort Street and south, well past Adair Park, all of which hosted spotty housing developments randomly placed along main roads in parcels of land used for cattle, junk-yards, city dumps, juke joints, cheap motels, brick churches with gravel parking lots, with no design whatsoever. But in between all of that, there was the woods. Some went hunting in it. Some got booty in it. Some grew marijuana or dumped their large trash in it even if the dump was across the street. It didn't matter because the woods carried the inherent authority of absolution, a duty-free wasteland that served whatever clan-destine purpose sought by those fearless enough to set foot in its indeterminate bowels.

Rampant wildlife roamed these unknowns, prompting un-spoken fear in the community. Possums and coons raided gar-bage cans. Wild, rabid dogs infected squirrels and domesticated canines, leaving them frothy-mouthed and delirious until wiser trigger fingers unloaded shotgun shells into their sick heads. Cottontails and wood rats held court to decide who would offer the sacrifice to the hawks and occasional owls that soared above looking for a good country dinner. Henry Taub's cows and bulls kept the grass low enough to make out trees, brush, and clear-ings. Rumor spoke of a reclusive family who lived in a shack far away from everybody in the woods. Rumor also spoke of escaped prisoners from the nearby P farm who stole clothes off laundry lines and raped children who were reckless enough to venture into the woods. And generally nobody ventured into the woods unless they were in trouble or up to no good. But despite all of the known and unknown dangers of the woods, Booger always played in there. He didn't give a damn, and it wasn't like his parents were going to caution him against it.

I followed him along a cattle trail that reached a small brook. We sat on a fungus-covered log and threw spear grass at frogs.

"Are you poor?" I asked Booger.

He shrugged.

"You?" he asked.

"I don't know. How do you know if you poor?"

"Poor people don't have that much stuff."

Well, that made sense. Those kids at St. Andrew's had a lot of stuff, expensive stuff.

Tadpoles wiggled in brown murky murk knowing that soon enough their tails would be a memory. We don't stay the same. I threw a chinaberry in the water. The tadpoles scattered.

"I think my daddy's crazy," I posited.

" 'Cause he be talkin' to hisself? My momma be doin' that all the time," Booger offered.

"Yeah, but you already know your momma crazy," I responded.

"I know," Booger said, a bit sullen. I didn't mean to embarrass him, but it wasn't a secret.

"It's okay, dawg. It ain't your fault. But my daddy might be crazy 'cause he be talkin' to hisself when nobody lookin' but I be peekin' at him."

"You better not get caught or he gonna beat your ass," Booger advised.

"I'll tell you a secret. My daddy can heal people. Like Jesus," I said.

"Ti' John, you be lyin' too much," Booger said.

"I ain't lyin'," I said.

"Then how come your daddy don't work at the hospital?" Booger asked.

I didn't have an answer, but Booger was right about peeking at Father. Those moments were private, not meant to be shared with the child, like seeing your parent naked—absolutely taboo. Why else would he go to some secluded area for the conversations? Was he talking to God? People did that in church in front of everybody. But Father never went to church, not even on Easter or midnight Mass. When I made First Communion, he was smoking a cigarette outside on the church steps and having his own Communion with Albert Thibodeaux's daddy and a pint of Crown Royal.

We looked in Mr. Cardell's backyard. An aluminum tool-shed. A pristine flower bed underneath the kitchen window. African violets and gazanias.

"How much stuff you supposed ta have if you ain't poor?" I asked. Booger shrugged.

We could see Mrs. Cardell. She always wore rollers and a colorful head scarf, just like the talking fat woman on the syrup bottle.

Booger wasn't interested in the conversation. I looked at his dirty, bare feet. Chicken pox marks, scratched mosquito bites, and dried snot. He reminded me of a cross between Chewbacca and Benji. Today he was Krofft's Bigfoot, roaming the forest and fighting crime while evading capture with his trusty, articulate sidekick, Wildboy.

Later, when I returned home, I counted everything in my room while my parents argued. Mother absolutely refused to wash a shirt with lipstick on it; it was mostly a one-sided argument, and I didn't listen much, more concerned with my inventory. I had to know if I was poor or if Mike was just being mean.

In bed that night, listening to the mouse, I thought about poverty. What constituted being poor? Those African babies on TV with flies on their faces were surely poor, but I never met anyone living like that, although Booger was pulling a close second. Was the mouse poor? Gnawing holes everywhere, no bathroom, stealing. Stealing! Yes, stealing. Poor people steal so they won't appear poor. Yes, I figured it out. If you steal, then you're poor. I wasn't totally sure, but I'd ask Mother the next day.

Next morning, driving to school—

"Are we poor?"

"No," Mother said forcefully. "Who told you that?"

"Nobody."

She was still pissed off from last night.

"Can I join Jack and Jill?"

"Why don't you join Junior Knights at church? I'm sure Father Jerome would like that."

"Not the same thing. I wanna join Jack and Jill. Mike says they go on trips and have parties and stuff."

She was quiet. She knew something.

"Is it 'cause we poor?" I asked.

"We're not poor, Ti' John."

"Then why can't I join?"

"There are different kinds of black people, Ti' John. You know how your cousins in Louisiana are kind of different?"

"Yeah."

"Well, it's the same thing with the black folks in Jack and Jill. They're not like us. We don't celebrate Juneteenth. We from Louisiana."

"What's Juneteenth?"

"Some foolishness these black folks in Texas celebrate. They were freed from slavery for two years and didn't know. And you know them rednecks weren't gonna tell them. Then somebody in Galveston told them and they made it a holiday."

"They were just happy they was free," I posited, noticing Mother's snide manner.

"They were just ignorant, Ti' John. Don't be ignorant 'cause you won't get anywhere. You understand Momma?" she asked, eyes still on the road while we passed the large homes on North MacGregor. These were homes owned by black Texans. Ignorance wasn't holding them back much.

"Momma? Is Daddy crazy? 'Cause he be talkin' to hisself?"

"Don't talk about your father like that."

Later that day when I got off the bus, I saw Arthur Duncan's pickup truck on the corner. He was waiting for me.

Father was in the ICU.

thirteen

penance

Arthur Duncan's truck smelled like candy or maybe it was the air freshener with the naked brunette dangling from the rearview mirror. We drove directly to St. Joseph Hospital. Father's left leg had been crushed when his beautiful, loyal, cream steed, TJ, fell over while he was practicing at a roping pen in Hitchcock, Texas. Arthur assured me that Father would be all right. I mean, that's what you tell a kid, right? He didn't prepare me for what I was about to see, so I focused on the air freshener, naturally.

"She got some big titties, huh, Lil' Frenchy?" said Arthur with a gold-tooth grin.

"Yeah," I said coyly. I wasn't supposed to talk about titties with an adult. I knew that. I looked away, watching wet streets pass like slow-motion butterfly wings drunk off Crown Royal. Ten minutes ago, God cried. But He didn't cry long. Instead, He showed His own gold-tooth grin on the cavity-filled streets and bayous of Houston. Steam rose from the cement, shortening the breath of damp angels, then rays of light cut through gray clouds. Sunshine again. No more tears. Just slow-motion butterfly wings with tipsy syncopation.

A ray of sunshine found its way between the windshield wipers on Arthur Duncan's truck and landed smack-dab on the brunette's breasts. God likes titties too, I thought, particularly titties that smell like candy.

I didn't like hospitals. They smelled dirty, and I feared that I would catch some unknown disease in them. The waiting rooms were always filled with anxious or distraught faces, praying for good news but somehow expecting bad, reading magazines they didn't like, watching TV shows they weren't interested in, waiting for death or a bandage. Mortality as truth onstage, real time, in your face. *If you gotta believe in something, why not believe in me?* I heard something. *Dis-moi.* I looked around. Nothing. Sharp pains prickled my feet, slowing my steps toward the room where Father was tended.

Arthur thought it would be a good idea if I brought Father a pinkie string to cheer him up, but he also gave me a long red string at Father's request. I put the red string in my pocket.

We entered the hospital, Arthur with his bull-rider limp and big buckle. A few nurses smiled his way. I walked alongside him carrying the small rope, looking more like an apprentice cowboy. We entered a steel elevator with bright lights.

"Na', Lil' Frenchy, your daddy kinda messed up. They just put pins in him, so try not to ask him too much 'cause he gonna be tired," Arthur advised.

Arthur's bloodshot eyes seemed removed. He knew something or he'd lost something. Maybe both. Father was his close friend and compatriot in the rodeo circuit. Something wasn't right.

When the elevator opened, I saw Mother leaning against the wall, arms knotted together below her bosom. She turned and looked at me. She was crying. As I approached, she grabbed me and held tightly. The last time she'd been at St. Joseph she was saying good-bye to her brother, Herman.

Then Arthur opened the door, and there he was—Frankenstein's Creole muthafuckin' monster.

He lay in the mechanical bed with plastic tubes stuck all over his body running to bags of various liquids and bleeping machines on stands. He had turned into a video game. Small steel rods ran along his left leg through gauze all the way up to his hip. His eyes were half open, and he was smoking a cigarette.

"Hey, Sonny," he said in a low, weak voice, and he didn't smile but grimace. He was in pain. I stayed by the door.

"Whatcha got there?" he asked.

I slowly walked over to him and held out the worn pinkie string, the kind he clenched in his mouth while roping calves. He truly looked Olympic when he was calf roping, bursting out of the chute, then practically flying off the horse, one hand lightly guided by the lasso tied around the calf's neck, the other hand reaching for the calf itself. Reaching for the buckle, the applause, and the money. He'd grab the young calf and throw it on its side, then grab the pinkie string and wind it around the calf's feet with breathtaking speed and dexterity to the amazement of the crowd. Just after he tied the knot, John Frenchy ceremoniously threw both hands in the air. He was a champion. Since 1965, nobody in the Texas black rodeo circuit had collected as many buckles for calf roping as Father.

But now, in the hospital, he scowled at the rope as he yanked it from my hand with a slight wince. The painkillers weren't really working. He held the rope for a minute, rubbing his thumb against its ridges, then threw it across the room like a hot potato and closed his eyes.

Arthur stood by the door.

"Give us a minute, Arthur," Father requested.

Arthur left the room, closing the door behind him.

Father stared at me, making a calculation, then—

"You got the string?" he asked.

I pulled out the red string. He motioned me over. I held out the string, but he shook his head.

"No. That's for your hands. You gonna make nine knots in that string and I want you to do everything I tell you to do. Can you do that?" he asked.

"Yes, Daddy."

"And you can't never tell nobody what you about to do. Can you do that?" he asked.

"Yes, Daddy."

"This between me and you. Now repeat after me," he said, then sang—

> *O kwa, o jibile*
> *Ou pa we m'inosan?*

I repeated every syllable, every intonation. After the strange song, he instructed me to start the knots with

> *Je vous salue, Marie, pleine de grâce.*
> *Le Seigneur est avec vous.*
> *Vous êtes bénie entre toutes les femmes,*
> *et Jésus, le fruit de vos entrailles, est béni.*
> *Sainte Marie, Mère de Dieu,*
> *priez pour nous, pauvres pécheurs,*
> *maintenant et à l'heure de notre mort.*
> *Amen.* *

When I finished with the knots, he instructed me to tie the knotted string around his waist. I did, then stood back, not sure what I had done.

He placed his right hand over his heart, then extended it out toward me, palm turned upward—

"Merçi beaucoup, Monsieur," he said with strange reverence; a new sound from his lips directed to my ears.

I left the room. Father Jerome was consoling Mother, who quieted when I emerged.

"Father Jerome is gonna take you to the rectory, and I'm gonna pick you up later, so behave," Mother said.

Yeah, the same rectory that I pissed on.

Father Jerome didn't waste any time giving me a speech on God or accidents or pissing on church property—

"How's your new school?"

---

* Hail Mary prayer in French.

"It's fun sometimes. We don't have to wear a uniform, and on Fridays we have hot dogs from Coney Island. They bring 'em in. But some of the kids are mean to me."

"Why?"

" 'Cause I'm poor."

"You're not poor, Ti' John."

"Then how come them other kids say I'm poor? They all got nice stuff and nice cars. I saw a Porsche last week. You ever seen a Porsche?" I asked.

Father Jerome grinned. "Nice sports car. Real fast."

"Real fast. It goes vrrooooom! Shoot! I'ma get me one of those one day when I grow up," I exclaimed. He just focused on the road, even though I wanted him to share in my excitement.

"I started counting stuff at home to see if we poor," I admitted.

"If you can count all you own, then you don't have much," Father Jerome advised.

"Hunh?" I asked again, not understanding his poetry.

"It's not about how much stuff you own, Ti' John. A man can be rich without material things, cars, houses, clothes . . ."

"Video games?"

"Even video games," said Father Jerome with a light chuckle.

I still didn't understand, my mind driving a Porsche down MLK on a Sunday headed to MacGregor Park to hang out. Faces looking, fingers pointing. There go Ti' John. Oooowee, his car is clean. Can I get a ride, Ti' John? How fast that car go? Boy, you must be rich.

We slowed down at the corner of MLK and Bellfort. Mike's daddy stared at me from a placard on a bus stop bench. Ghetto.

"A man like that needs to go to church," said Father Jerome.

At the light, the Median Man jogged in place wearing sweats and a pair of combat boots painted yellow that were so bright they damn near glowed.

Three Months Later . . .

Father was still in the hospital. Mother didn't know what to do. Her entire married life revolved around his schedule, so she worried, not knowing what to do with this temporary freedom. She worried that Father would lose his job. She worried that we wouldn't have enough money for the mortgage, groceries, and utilities. But Father was well-respected in his circles, and soon enough, slick-looking brothers from Local 24 at the ship channel arrived at the house to drop off money and food stamps. We were going to make it.

After several weeks, I learned that Father was going to be in the hospital a little longer. Mother made arrangements for me to stay with Father Jerome and the good brothers at the rectory because she quickly took a night-shift job at Foley's. I think she tired of the Local 24 guys coming on to her when they dropped off money and food stamps. Moreover, I think she had to fill the excess time she'd spent dealing with Father with some form of labor.

Now I'd have to return to the scene of the crime: the rectory. I didn't know what to expect with the priests. What did they do all day when they weren't preaching? I wondered. Read the Bible? I figured they knew the Bible by heart. Maybe they practiced miracles or sewed sequins on their costumes like Mardi Gras Indians. I tried not to think about it while my class sat on the floor watching *The Hobbit*.

I decided to focus my energies on making friends at school, but Mike was countering every move I made. I had no choice but to focus on my lessons because the kids still weren't playing with me. However, in the sand-filled playground, I noticed something. Mike was stealing other kids' Hot Wheels cars by hiding them in the sand right before recess would end. The target kid would search in vain for his toy, Mike even helped him look for it, but soon the teacher would call us in. At some point during the day, Mike would excuse himself for the bathroom and recover the buried treasure. A week later, Mike would magically "find" the trove and claim it. He was such a politician, like his father. He'd actually convince the crying kid that the toy now belonged to him, and those kids bought it. He had money, but he was stealing. My theory about poverty and theft was wrong. At the water fountain, I waited while Mike sucked down most of the cold water.

"I saw what you did," I said. He ignored me, quaffing cold Houston tap like Flavor Aid.

"You been stealin' them cars."

"Nawh-unh," he responded, head still hovering over the fount.

"Yeah, you was. I saw you," I continued. Nobody was around but us.

Without even rising from the fount, he reached in his pocket and handed me a Hot Wheels car. The General Lee.

"Don't tell nobody," he said, then dashed off to play kickball.

While everybody played kickball, I ventured into the wooded area near the train tracks looking for frogs. Low-hanging oaks draped in visiting Spanish moss hugged the fence line, loaded with four-foot-high thickets and brush. Curious St. Andrew's alumni had carved a worn walking trail along the fence line that led to a clearing beneath large, majestic pines near the train tracks. Frogs required water, and I hoped that the awnings provided by tree cover allowed a small collection of water to host tadpoles. But I only found a few wandering wood rats and a dead possum. As I slowly crept toward the clearing, I could see an adult squatting in the center. Vagrants were known to frequent St. Andrew's lot, particularly the wooded area. Transients moving along the tracks, dope fiends seeking sanctuary from cement, urban boogeymen, Bloody Mary, Mad Pierre, all rumored to lurk along the fence. I stopped. Mr. Brooks's whistle sounded at the kickball game far away—too far away.

He slowly stood upright. Tall. My feet tingled again. He turned around slowly to face me, wearing a dirty old suit and hat. I couldn't make out his face, but he stuck out one brown bare foot, took off his hat, and made a deep bow at the waist, long, stringy hair falling before him. This was him—the regal man I'd seen in the field when Father and I were headed to the rodeo in Angleton a while back. He'd followed me.

"Hey! What you doin' back here?" I stopped and yelled, but the figure didn't move.

I glanced over my shoulder. My classmates resembled blurry brown action figures following the ball. Kick it. Catch it. Throw it. Roll it. Dodge it.

"Hey! Why you back here? You gonna get in trouble," I exclaimed with the deepest voice I could muster. He could snatch me and hop the fence; nobody would ever know. Maybe it was that guy who killed those kids in Atlanta—kids who looked like me. Maybe the guy had escaped, jumped on a train, and landed in Third Ward. Wayne Williams. The whole summer he was on the news. Big afro and eyeglasses. Most blacks thought the Klan did it and pinned it on Williams. Black folks just weren't buying the idea of a black serial killer, reasoning that black folks just didn't do those kinds of things. I should have been scared, but he spoke—

"J'ai venue pour te 'oir," he said.

"Argggggh!"

Mike yelled several yards behind me. I whipped around and took off running. Mike was on the ground holding his bloody foot. He'd stepped on a nail. I looked back toward the clearing, but the stranger was gone.

Mike's face reddened, his sarcastic grin reduced to a desperate frown. A blood-covered, rusty nail sticking out of a dry wood panel lay next to him. Tetanus shot. He was crying and weak. I threw his arm around my shoulder and helped him to the office where the nurse was stationed. Mrs. Queen, the kindergarten teacher, filled in for the nurse and treated Mike's wound with bandages, but his mother was called to take him to the hospital for the shot. He was freaked out.

I considered for a moment whether I should help him with my secret prayers but . . . that didn't take long.

Many tales had been spun regarding tetanus shots, shots in the stomach or forty shots in the ass. And if you stepped on a rusty nail, the very thing adults always warned you about, you could get gangrene and have your foot amputated or lockjaw. Mike was hysterical, but I talked him down with summaries of *The Benny Hill Show.* He'd been watching too. Then I heard Mother in the principal's office explaining that she'd be late with tuition. Mike listened too.

"Mrs. Boudreaux, you don't have to worry. We have scholarships for special students."

"I won't accept charity."

Kinda. She wouldn't accept charity from white folks, not Margaret's child.

"It's not charity, Mrs. Boudreaux. We sent a letter out yesterday. John is gifted."

Mike turned to me—

"Nigga, I'm smarter than you."

"Oh yeah? 'Cause they didn't send your momma no letter."

"Well, at least my momma can pay for school."

My eyes darted to the ground. *Ghetto.*

"Hey, Ti' John. I didn't mean it," Mike offered with his right hand.

I stared at him for a minute, then shook his hand with "And I know you been stealin' them lunches too."

"Man, don't tell nobody," he pleaded.

I still held his hand, but I gripped it tighter and offered the deal—

"Then quit fuckin' with me."

He nodded as his mother rushed in and swept him away to Hermann Hospital for the shots.

fourteen

trickin' the dice

Channel 39, Saturday Morning, 11:39, 1983

Paul Boesch announced the main event: Junkyard Dog vs. Butch Reed for the North American wrestling title. *¡Llame Mr. Norman!* Two months I had waited on this match, and I would've seen it if Father hadn't started throwing dishes at Mother at approximately 11:37 A.M. He hadn't been home two hours and had already managed to start some shit. He was arguing with somebody who wasn't in the room. He did that a lot when he was drunk. By 11:00 A.M., he had popped enough Valium and Vicodin to sedate an elephant. And of course, he washed it down with Wild Turkey, no glass, no ice, straight from the bottle. And what was the argument about? Mother didn't bring him a coat hanger quick enough. His left leg was in a full plaster cast that stretched almost to his hip. The bottom of his left foot was itching, and he needed to slide the hanger between his cast and leg as a scratcher. The hanger refused to make a hard turn at his heel, so he suffered, which meant Mother suffered. He grabbed his crutches, got to his feet, and tried to lunge toward her, but she sidestepped. She knew he'd have the cast on for four months. And for four months he wasn't going to lay a hand on her. Not because his infirmity would soften his choler, oh no, but because she knew he wouldn't be able to catch her. Not with that Frankenstein cast. Over fifty steel pins held his bones in place. Metal and muscle living and loving together to mend a good cowboy's leg. But it hurt like hell, and he had begun a comfortable habit of popping painkillers like candy.

Mother told me to play outside. Shattered glass, ceramic, and porcelain covered the kitchen floor. Father returned to his warm seat at the dining room table and stared at the floor. Men like him weren't meant to be physically impaired. They were meant to conquer with action and movement, their intentions executed with the muscle and the soul. Strangely enough, the drugs didn't dampen his desire to commit action. Rather, the drugs made him antsy and the alcohol mocked his immobility, so he resigned himself to staring a hole in the floor.

"Stop laughing at me," he yelled at the gray indoor/outdoor carpet.

"Ain't nobody laughing at you, John," Mother pleaded.

"I told you to quit laughing at me!" he yelled, and that's when the dishes started flying.

And while Mother was certain that Father was aiming the dishes at her, that particular Saturday afternoon had awakened an old-timer that John Frenchy hadn't seen in years.

"Stop throwing dishes at me, John!" I heard Mother yell.

"I ain't throwing no dishes at you, woman! Get outta the way!" he yelled as he hobbled toward the front door.

He stared at me bewildered from the door, then hobbled closer. I was scared.

"Don't hurt him, John!" Mother yelled from the house.

"I ain't gonna hurt him, woman. Clean up the damn house and leave me the hell alone!" he answered.

He moved closer, still staring like this was the first time he'd ever seen me.

"Lemme see your hands," he said gruffly.

I held out my hands, and he examined them closely.

"How old is you now, Sonny?"

"Ten."

"You got you some pussy yet?"

"Don't ask him that, John. He's a little boy," Mother commented from the kitchen.

"He ain't no little boy," Father responded.

By dusk, Father and I were driving around South Park headed absolutely nowhere but one place. He was still high, but his driving didn't show it. He had changed clothes, beige polyester pants with the left leg cut off. A gold chain with a bullhorn pendant dangled around his neck. Strong, deliberate cologne rode shotgun. His eyes were alert. A straightened coat hanger rested between us. Bobby Womack said he wished you didn't trust him so much. I had been there before, the place we were going. The gambling shacks on Stassen Street in a neighboring companion ghetto called Sunnyside.

Stassen Street was something akin to a low-budget Vegas strip hosting houses of various levels of ill repute, but primarily gambling. No neon signs nor valet. Park your car on the narrow street of broken asphalt and find failure or fortune. The street was lined with several quaint run-down homes that had running water and electricity. The Devil paid the mortgage, but the utilities were strictly an affair for the living. Aubrie Manning ran a respectable card game on most nights. His son, Lil' Aubrie, hosted a high-stakes dice game next door, complete with one or two girls from the Butt-Naked Club in Third Ward that serviced the willing on filthy mattresses with clean sheets stolen from the Alphonse Motel. Slow-talking Johnny McAllen kept the felts clean and the racks tight at his pool hall across the street, where nine-ball was going for fifty dollars per ball and absolutely no Amen shots afforded. Over the years, Father had worked that street from corner to corner, depending on who was playing and what kind of money was sitting on the table.

He found a parking spot behind a dirty Mary Kay Cadillac with Arkansas tags. He cut off the engine and quickly pulled out a Texas Commerce Bank envelope filled with money. A steady thumb flipped through the bills, his quiet lips confirming the count. He opened the glove compartment and yanked out a chrome revolver that he stuck in his pocket.

"Stay by me," he said, then slowly opened the door and climbed out on his crutches.

We headed to Lil' Aubrie's, which got me a bit anxious. Lil' Aubrie's place was almost a nightclub, with a younger crowd, full bar, and disco ball over the dice table. Lil' Aubrie always wore a net muscle shirt to show off his prison build, compliments of Huntsville state penitentiary.

"John Frenchy!" someone exclaimed as Father eased into the house. I followed behind him carrying the coat hanger.

The place was packed. Local pimps and drug dealers exchanged crime stories and rumors with low talk and subtle, expressive movements of head and hands. Ghetto slickster pantomime. Working stiffs clung to the dice table waiting on a miracle. A few big-legged gals flirted with the patrons for a free drink and maybe a go-at-it in the back room.

"Hey, Lil' Frenchy. You want a soda?" a scantily clad Rubenesque woman asked me, standing by the doorway to a small kitchen and shaking her hips to gutbucket.

"Yawl niggas ain't shooting no dice in here," Father exclaimed as he found a place at the dice table.

"John Frenchy at the table. John Frenchy shooting," barked Lil' Aubrie.

Father leaned into the table and picked up the dice with a quick, sweeping motion of his right hand, left hand gripping the crutch handle.* His gold horseshoe pinkie ring with a lone diamond blinked its eye as the disco ball revolved above with checkered reflections. Several small, mirrored panels were missing from the ball, survivor of the dead disco era. Father shook the dice near his ear, working out the arrangement, negotiating

---

* Dice Rule 1: Always keep your hands visible to avoid any accusations of mischief; namely, switching dice or pulling a weapon.

the cost for the reward. The gambler's petition. It's a silent arrangement between the gambler and whatever petitioned or nonpetitioned gods are sought for assistance. A few profitable rolls and the gambler is given mystic status. That gambler is considered to be in league with chance, and that's when the real money is wagered with side bets. On any given night, an un-suspecting gambler may receive the blessings of chance during a dice session. Colloquially, they'd say that gambler was "on fire" or "hot." Thirty minutes after arriving at Lil' Aubrie's, Father was officially a four-alarm blaze. He had rolled a four, or Little Joe, twelve consecutive times to make point. Although he'd al-ready garnered a reputation for having an uncanny relationship with dice, this improbable occurrence had catapulted him well beyond mystic status.

Lil' Aubrie stared at the dice emotionless, calling the roll. The half-nude obese woman brought Father a Crown Royal and 7-Up, then blew on the dice. Bad move. There wasn't anything lucky about that woman as far as I could tell.

Some at the table were becoming angry, like Sammy Reed, whose wife of fifteen years had recently left him after he'd been caught having relations with a skittish mare in Pearland on Valentine's Day. After two long hours at Lil' Aubrie's, he'd al-ready lost his child support and alimony payments and was fast approaching mortgage and utilities monies. Next to him stood Bertrand LeBlanc, who worked with Father at the ship channel. He had money to blow, having been a longtime participant in the fencing of stolen goods on the docks. I had him to thank for my Atari 2600. Arthur Duncan stood across from Father, more a spectator than a participant. Father stood there, crutch under his left armpit to support the pins. Granted, he wasn't supposed to stand on that leg at all unless he was going to bed or the bathroom.

When the dice finally came back around to Father, Sammy Reed started calling "no dice" on every roll. Lil' Aubrie warned him, but he continued, frustrating everybody who had money on the table.* Sammy was making bogus calls. Father grabbed the dice, then turned to me—

"Sonny, get that pistol out my pocket," he said casually.

"Unh-unh, Frenchy. None of that in here," warned Lil' Aubrie, but Father could care less.

I reached into his beige polyester pocket and grabbed the heavy revolver.

"Stick it in my waistband. Right there," he said, pointing to his left side, then he stared at Sammy. "Nigga, can we shoot some dice now?"

The dice game continued with Sammy's eyes focused on Father's gun rather than the dice. The obese woman brought Father a barstool to rest on. He gave her a ten-dollar tip. I watched her sashay away to a waiting man in the hallway who'd been staring at me since we entered.

He was a tall, dark-skinned man with straight, wavy hair pulled back into a ponytail. Lesser-informed minds might've called him a "Geechee." The deformed disco ball caught a gold watch and bracelet on his left wrist, which rested comfortably on his crotch. A soft, milky glow hovered around his left pinkie. The woman on his arm wore snakeskin boots. He didn't smile, just watched, then he turned his attention to me. It was him. He stuck out a foot—snakeskin boots—and took a bow, then winked. Who bows? The only people I'd seen bow were priests, altar boys, and the guys in the karate movies, so this time I bowed back. He grinned, then nodded.

"Look who done showed up!" someone yelled; all heads turned to the front door, and for the first time today Father smiled.

---

*Dice Rule 2: Do not call "no dice" if the call is not applicable. Calling "no dice" disqualifies the roll, nullifying the outcome. "No dice" is normally called when the dice roll has been interrupted unnaturally, such as by someone kicking or handling either die as it rolls, or if a die rolls off the table or too far from the center of play.

It was Father's old friend Johnny Guitar Watson, easing into the gambling shack with a flashy entourage, wearing a white suit with matching hat and cape. A cape! Gotdamn, he has a cape! And then he spoke with a voice right out of the seventies pimp films—

"Hell, I must be in the right place if John Frenchy is here," he said, then hugged Father. They hadn't seen each other in over twenty years.

Then Watson turned his red eyes to me, red eyes hidden behind huge designer sunglasses—

"This your son?"

Father nodded.

Watson pulled out a huge roll of money, peeled off a hundred-dollar bill, and handed it to me with "Put that in your pocket." No shit.

Many had said that Watson did try his hand at pimping after John Frenchy dropped him off at his grandfather's church years back, but that was just a rumor. What wasn't a rumor was the company that Watson kept, basically pimps and hustlers. His popular soul-influenced blues music merely reflected the company he kept.

Sammy Reed wasn't at all impressed that Father knew Watson. Pockets empty, he excused himself from the table.

"Make sure that nigga don't come in here with a piece," Father told Lil' Aubrie, but Watson had already motioned for two of his men to follow Sammy. Nobody needed to make an announcement. Men who deal with this type of crowd know that the only words you need fear from a man are the words not spoken.

Sammy Reed returned to the table and dropped a pink slip.*

"How much?" Sammy asked Lil' Aubrie while he inspected the pink slip.

---

*Dice Rule 3: Do not accept wagers of personal property, including, but not limited to, jewelry and pink slips.

"Five grand."

"Bullshit, five grand. That car about fifteen," Sammy protested.

"It's five grand at this table," Lil' Aubrie said. "And I ain't cashing you in."

"I got it," Father interrupted before Sammy could argue. Father counted out five grand on the table and took the pink slip. Sammy glared at Father as he accepted the cash. The game had turned personal. Luck so had it that it was Father's roll.

"Gimme that hanger," Father asked me, then slid the hanger behind his cast to scratch. I reached down to my KangaROOS and scratched my foot as well. Then I smelled it. Burning wood. When I rose, the dark-skinned man was right beside Father, whispering in his ear on the left side.

The Burning Wood Man stepped back from Father with a grin, hand returning triumphantly to his crotch. He had done something special, something proud. Because he was so close, I noticed that the milky glow on his left pinkie was in fact an opal set in gold. I stared at the table, trying to avoid his presence. I could feel his eyes. My feet prickled like there were a thousand straight pins, red-hot, embedded in my bare soles. I didn't want to look at him, fearful that he might ignite me with some preternatural combustion by a mere glance. He felt powerful, at least in presence, like a burly cop with a black gun and strong aftershave. I wanted to say something, but the ranting, music, and rattling of dice in Father's hand, which hadn't stopped since the Burning Wood Man delivered his communiqué, drowned out any idea of an utterance. The other gamblers complained, encouraging Father to roll. He ignored them, then stopped, placed the dice gently on the table, and pushed them toward Sammy Reed. No dice.

"Sammy, I want you to check them dice out," Father signified. " 'Cause tonight, I'm gonna give you winehead niggas a miracle. But first I want this worrisome muthafucka to check these dice out 'cause I got bullets in that gun. And although yawl about to witness a miracle, the good Lord didn't teach me how to bring a dead nigga back to life."

Sammy sucked his teeth, then grabbed the dice.

"Check dice," Lil' Aubrie announced so no wagers would be placed.

Sammy examined the dice, then rolled them a few times. Satisfied, Sammy pushed the dice back to Father, who, in turn, put all of his winnings and the pink slip on the table.

"Now. I bet all of this, mostly yawl money, on this next roll, but I'm gonna change the game if Lil' Aubrie don't mind," he said.

"What's the game, John Frenchy?" asked Lil' Aubrie.

"Trey deuce. I'm 'bout to roll a five," Father answered.

Half of the men laughed, assuming the Crown Royal was talking, but he said it again.

"Five."

And he didn't smile. The room quieted. Some appeared frightened, but nobody said John Frenchy was crazy. That had been firmly established years ago. Watson looked at Father and nodded respectfully.

"Cut that gotdamn music off," Sammy blurted.

Now there was true silence. A passing ambulance blared on Bellfort Street, close enough to scare the mice in the wall that counted the hours until they could come out and do a bit of their own gambling.

Shiny plastic cubes rested on the table with throbbing flashes of light cast from the disco ball above.

Father turned to me with anxious eyes. A familiar look. The same look he always had when he sat on his horse, rope in hand, waiting for the chute to open. Waiting to rope the calf. Waiting to win the buckle. Waiting on God or maybe something else. Whatever it was, he knew the outcome. Victory was in his eyes. Confirmed victory.

"Watch this, Sonny. This is how you trick the dice," he

said directly to me, instructionally, as though we were the only people in the room. That same warm, paternal tone he used whenever he taught me something—passing down the secrets, be it riding a horse, shooting a gun, cutting the lawn, baiting a hook, saying the prayers. This was the first time he announced the left hand, but it wouldn't be the last.

"John Frenchy shootin'. Trey deuce on the hop," Lil' Aubrie announced.

Father grabbed the dice and shook them hard. Five grand and a pink slip lay on the table.

Then I heard it again and I knew damn well I heard it.

"J'ai venu pour te 'oir,"* it said in a loud whisper.

I looked around quickly just as Father let the dice roll out of his left hand.

Bertrand Leblanc made a solemn sign of the cross. Sammy Reed bit his tongue. Lil' Aubrie and most of the room threw hands over mouth and nose. Something was burning. Wood. That's what it smelled like. Burning wood. Two red plastic dice stood still on the table. 2 + 3 = 5.

"Trey deuce," Lil' Aubrie announced between his fingers.

"Fuck that! John Frenchy cheatin'!" Sammy Reed yelled, then reached for the pink slip.† Father stood up quickly while grabbing a leg of the stool, then slammed the stool over Sammy Reed's head. Everyone jumped back from the table as Father hobbled around the table with the crutch and the freed stool leg. He pushed the disoriented man to the ground and started whaling on him with the wooden stool leg. Head shots. I moved closer. Father continued relentlessly, crazed. Sammy Reed was paying for all of Father's anger. Lame limb. Los Angeles. Las Cruces. Lafayette. Life. All forced through every swing. He didn't say a word as he beat the man, just grunts and

---

* "I came to see you."

† Dice Rule 4: Do not touch any money wagered or near the center of play unless it is yours.

gasps between swings from his heavy cowboy hands. Sammy Reed's face was mangled, but Father didn't stop. Maybe he couldn't.

"Eh, John Frenchy! He had enough," said Watson.

Father obliged. Blood dripped off the stool leg, staining the beaten indoor-outdoor carpet. Still angry and panting, Father turned to me but didn't say anything, as though he was trying to figure out who I was. The drugs and alcohol had changed him, and the sudden burst of energy from the fight had spent the remaining opiates in his system. He was coming down. The whole room watched him closely. What would he do next?

"Somebody cut on that fan and open the door. And look around 'cause something's burning," ordered Lil' Aubrie.

I looked for the Burning Wood Man, but he was gone. A few men picked up Sammy Reed.

"Put him in the back and call his old lady," Lil' Aubrie instructed.

Watson looked at Father and said, "Five?"

Father just nodded, then slowly grinned.

"Yeah. Five," Father said, and just like that the night turned back on as the jukebox belted out Buckwheat's version of "Sitting in the La La" on cue.

"You wanna drive my wife's Christmas present home for me?" Father asked Arthur Duncan.

Driving home later, Father sang along with Clifton Chenier. His mood had dramatically shifted, and it had nothing to do with the huge roll of money in his pocket nor the dirty Mary Kay Cadillac with Arkansas tags that followed behind us. There was something very different that made him smile and sing, something removed, maybe a memory. Maybe it was something the Burning Wood Man said.

"Daddy?"

"Yeah, Sonny."

"Who was that man that was talking to you?"

"Which man, Sonny?"

"The tall one that smelled like something burning. Who was that?"

Alcohol tells the truth, and there was just enough alcohol left in Father's blood for him not to realize what he was about to do. Something he should never have done. He gave it a name.

"Oh, that was your kinfolk, Sonnier. Nonc Sonnier," Father said.

"How's he related to us?"

Then it occurred to Father what he had done, so he changed the subject and pulled the car over. He flipped on the dome light.

"Make a fist."

I balled my fist as hard as possible. He took my fist and examined it, then looked at me.

"Don't never let nobody whip on you like that back there. You hear me?"

"Yeah, Daddy."

"If you gotta hit somebody, ball your fist up hard and hit him first. Right between the eyes."

"So I can knock him out, Daddy?"

"So that nigga won't fuck with you."

"Daddy?"

"Yeah."

"How's Nonc related to us?"

"Quit asking me all them gotdamn questions. Sounding like your momma," he snapped as we drove off.

Hours later, before dawn, after we slid into the house without disturbing Mother, after the last train ran down the tracks on Mykawa Road, even after that busy mouse in the wall called it a night, a fireman banged on the front door.

Sammy Reed must've been a sore loser for setting his baby sister's Mary Kay Cadillac on fire, I thought. At least, that's what Father told Arthur Duncan later after the fire truck drove off. But for some reason he didn't tell the police about Sammy.

Mother would never get to drive her early Christmas present, which didn't bother her much. She hated pink, it reminded her of that parasol she carried around shamelessly in the fifties.

He thought Sonnier would never show up again after that scene in Basile some twenty years back. But Nonc Sonnier never says good-bye, not to family.

Father leaned against the tree in the front yard, chain-smoking with shaky hands, staring at the burnt-out Caddy. I watched him.

PART II

the left hand practice

Red nigger moon. Sinner!
Blood-burning moon. Sinner!
Come out that fact'ry door.

—Jean Toomer, *Cane*

fifteen

las cruces

1963

Even on the Sabbath, Satan's torrid breath blows across forgotten deserts, sautéing sediment without butter or grease, a hot pan laying in wait. Behold, the cool breeze from flapping angels' wings—spit on the hot pan. The illusion is born with a sizzle. It all conforms with Satan's plan, tricking the willy-nilly angels into becoming confederates in his humor. And the thoughtful angels only seek to comfort God's creatures from the sun's heat. Yet the mirage appears on the horizon boasting that Mother Earth is flat-chested, shimmering with the promise of a refreshing spring to those most in need. An absolute lie. If only those angels weren't so good-natured and naïve, the trick would never work. The thirsty see the mirage and squeal in delight, double-timing their efforts toward the sparkling hoax, only to be rewarded with a failed promise.

Go west, young man, said Satan, *and when you get there, you'll still be a nigger.*

Shortly after moving in with his older sister in the West Adams district of Los Angeles, John Paul Boudreaux quickly found work as a delivery boy for a pharmacist, Dr. Noel Stein of Hancock Park. But it wasn't until John noticed a man trying to get a wily horse into a trailer that his old love affair was reignited.

The man was delivering the horse to Agua Dulce Canyon,

where they were making a Western film. John quickly grabbed the reins, and five seconds later the crazy horse was secured in the trailer. One thing led to another, and a week later John was donning buckskins and face paint waiting for the director to yell "Action!" John Paul Boudreaux soon became well known in the Western filmmaking fraternity, always ready to take a fall or provide some acrobatic maneuver on the appointed steed and on cue.

But John had rolled the dice a bit too hard, making an error—well, several errors—that he could've avoided. He figured nobody would know or at least hear about it in Louisiana. He knew better, but ta hell with him, he thought. He hadn't seen Sonnier anywhere in Los Angeles County, not even at Shepp's Playhouse on Central Avenue when Louis Jordan came to town. But John wasn't too far gone to know that you didn't try to pull a fast one on the Ole Haitian, not in this lifetime nor the next. There were consequences to his actions, and despite his regular attendance at St. Bernadette Catholic Church in the Crenshaw District, no amount of prayer would cover his bet with the Ole Haitian. Loaded dice can only get you so far. The left hand was a tricky thing, and without Sonnier's guidance, bad karma was bound to befall John. And, of course, having an affair with Dr. Stein's wife didn't help, particularly after they got caught.

John Paul Boudreaux had recently stopped believing in angels since those little girls were killed in that church in Birmingham a few months back, but the angels hadn't stopped believing in him. Nor had Satan, whom John was convinced had an on-again, off-again love affair with the Negro, both rural and modern. Who else would spend so much time making Negro life so cumbersome? God? Hell no, John thought, He was too busy making sure white folks didn't blow each other up with their newfangled atomic bombs.

So by the winter of 1963, the only thing John really concerned himself with was where he was going to sleep, when he was going to eat, how he was to going to make some scratch,

and who he was going to fuck—and not always in that particular order. And now he was leaving Los Angeles very much the
same way he arrived in 1949—running away from some shit.
But this time he was coming back home with something—a
new reputation and a new nickname. Something deserving of
a swashbuckling pirate or a slick-talking politician. Something
with a little flair. Something to be remembered.

It was a young, up-and-coming blues guitarist named John
Watson who gave him the name one night while the two shot
dice behind a ribs joint on Adams Boulevard.

"That nigga speak that French," somebody said on bended
knee as John Boudreaux rolled a seven out the gate.

"John Frenchy knows them dice," Watson responded as
John Paul Boudreaux swiped money off the concrete with the
left hand.

John Paul Boudreaux paused and looked at Watson. John
Frenchy born.

Sand blew in sheets across the road, but John Frenchy knew
damn well that wasn't a Dairy Queen he was looking at several
miles ahead on Interstate 10 due east, having already laughed off
Satan's ploy miles back in Palm Springs as California orchards
tapered into an arid dust bowl. The burgundy '59 Caddy now
resembled a lavender Plymouth covered in dust and insects from
grille to bumper. But John Frenchy didn't mind the dust or the
heat and dropped the convertible top after they crossed the
state line near Blythe. He even removed his ponytail, allowing
his long, black, shoulder-length mane to wave in the wind. Six
years had passed since his last proper haircut, since he'd found
long hair a job requirement as a Comanche stand-in, along with
a clean face. Movie work afforded him a gray sharkskin suit with
matching Florsheims, but the Caddy belonged to Dr. Stein.
Finely manicured fingers gripped the large, white steering wheel
while on the radio Chet Baker lamented that they were writing
songs of love but not for him.

An opal pinkie ring, gold tiepin, wafer-thin Patek Philippe, and gold bracelet were all listed on the police report after John Frenchy left. But Stein couldn't bring himself to admit that the nigger who stole his Caddy was the same nigger who had relations with his wife. I mean, there's only so much a man will admit.

Now twenty-six, John Frenchy had adopted an entirely new attitude, colder and more calculated, optimism disintegrated to disappointment—the unwilling punch line to a bad joke. The world knew him as a "Negro," but he saw himself as John Frenchy. Damn what the world thinks, he reminded himself, I got a gift.

Twelve hours had passed since Watson had jumped into the Caddy with his guitar. Watson figured he'd try his hand at pimping in Houston. Plenty big-leg gals without a pot to piss in over there in Fifth Ward, he told John Frenchy.

"If I had your hair, shiiited. Them white broads would go crazy over me, just crazy," Watson said while running a jeweled hand against his freshly conked pompadour tied down with a floral silk scarf that still smelled of teenage pussy and Chanel No. 5. On the backseat next to Watson's guitar case was a box wrapped in manila paper.

"John Frenchy, you something else. You mean to tell me you got down with that cat's old lady and that cracker didn't kill you?" asked Watson.

John Frenchy just stared at the black road cutting across the desert. He didn't believe in answering rhetorical questions.

"Ain't that a gas, you something else. But what I don't understand is how you made out with this big-ass hog. With the keys and that nice finery you sportin' and whatnot," Watson said.

"She gave me the keys," John Frenchy replied in a low, uninvolved voice. His lanky buddy burst at the seams in a high-pitched cackle with both hands holding the fragrant scarf in place.

They turned off the interstate to fill up at a damn near dilapidated Texaco on the outskirts of Las Cruces, New Mexico.

Watson was still cackling as John Frenchy brought the Caddy

to a stop at the pump. Hot wind blew dust against his face and hair. He didn't like that, so he found a water hose on the side of the building and ran hot water over his head. Hunched over facing the ground, he watched droplets of water fall off the strands of his hair, forming small mud puddles on the New Mexico dirt. He thought of Basile.

Every time somebody in Basile decided they needed a brick fireplace or stove, all of the nearby children gathered pine needles. A pile of wet clay would be dumped near the house and the pine needles thrown into the clay. The children's job was to stomp the clay and needles with their feet until the mixture was appropriate for forming bricks. Their little brown legs would be covered in tan sheaths as abler hands grabbed clumps of the mixture with wooden planks and shaped earthen rectangles. The result would warm someone's home for the winter.

While rinsing his hair, John Frenchy drew a rectangle in the mud before him, then cupped his right hand, collecting warm water in his palm. He doused his face and blew his nostrils. Damn sand. He heard a nearing roar. A westbound passenger train came out of nowhere on tracks hidden by the blowing, sticky dust. Emerging from the tan haze, the massive train pushed by with steam, steel, and hope. If only he could tell them that the air would never be cool, but would stay hot no matter where the damn train stopped. Central Avenue or Timbuktu. It would always be hot. Nigga hot.

No way to make out an anxious face from the blurry windows that passed before him. Everyone rushing to the shimmering pond marooned in unwelcoming blankness.

The tail end of the train rushed by with a young black boy and an old black man leaning against the caboose railing smoking cigars. They waved at John Frenchy as he stood up and watched them pass. He wanted to wave back but he couldn't. He didn't believe in lying to the hopeful.

As the train's roar lowered to a distant hum, he could hear the argument. He walked toward the front of the station and found Watson pinned against the dirty lavender hood by a redneck with time to kill. Watson was scared and eyed John Frenchy as he casually strolled to the disinterested clerk at the register.

"What I owe you for the gas?" he asked the suspicious clerk.

"Two thirty-eight. You need to go see about yer buddy, fella. Jasper don't take too kindly to coloreds," the clerk advised.

John Frenchy laid three dollars on the counter, then watched Watson try to talk himself out of an ass-whipping. The clerk put his change on the counter.

"You got a phone, boss?" John Frenchy said in a voice he'd learned from TV.

The clerk pointed to a small phone mounted on the wall near the front. John Frenchy headed out.

"Yer change?"

"Keep the change," said John Frenchy as he yanked the phone off the wall, disabling the line.

The clerk protested, but John Frenchy walked steadily toward the Caddy.

"Sir, is my friend bothering you?"

The redneck turned around with one hand on Watson's neck.

"Well, lookie here. Tonto done ran off the reservation. I'm teachin' yer lil' nigger buddy some manners," he said.

"Hey, mister, you done taught him enough today."

"Oh, I don't know. I figure this nigger got a few more lessons to learn."

Before the redneck could turn back to Watson, John Frenchy delivered a right cross that sent the man to the ground. John Frenchy jumped on his chest and started pummeling him until he was bloody and unconscious. The clerk ran out with a service revolver pointed at John Frenchy. His hands were shaking.

"Put yer hands up right now or I'll shoot!" said the fearful clerk.

John Frenchy stopped and turned to the clerk. Eyes reduced to hot slits, blood covering his hands—

"Mister, how many bullets you got in that gun?" John Frenchy asked while standing up to look at the clerk eye level.

"I got enough," he said.

"I ain't got no quarrel with you, so put that gun down," John Frenchy told him as he walked slowly toward the clerk with his hands up.

"Stop right now! Stay yer nigger ass put 'fore I blow a hole in yer gotdamn head!"

But he moved closer. The ground was fairly soft, two or three inches of loose dirt and sautéed sand. Then John Frenchy delivered the inveterate Negro compliance statement—

"We don't want no trouble, mister."

"Too late for that," the clerk blurted but—

With the toe of his right Florsheim dug four inches deep into the ground, John Frenchy kicked dust at the clerk's face and disarmed him in a flash. He'd learned this trick on the movie sets. He chucked the gun past the train tracks and headed for the car. The clerk yelled, rubbing his eyes. Watson quickly went through the redneck's pockets, swiping some coins and a few bills, then joined John Frenchy in the car. They drove off.

Several miles later, John Frenchy, staining the white steering wheel with good American redneck blood, grabbed the silk scarf from Watson's head and cleaned his hands. Watson didn't say a word, staring from the passenger seat at hills, sand, and cacti. John Frenchy's expression returned to its earlier quiet resolve.

Being a free-moving black man in those days was something akin to being an outlaw. John Frenchy didn't like rules, especially when they were aimed at him. Watson managed to fall asleep. John Frenchy turned to the backseat and glanced at the manila box.

The next morning, John Frenchy sat in the sparkling, clean '59 Coupe de Ville. He'd gotten the Caddy cleaned in Third Ward after he dropped Watson off at his granddaddy's church. He'd been parked on Washington Street in Lafayette, Louisiana, for about a half an hour, parked in front of his aunt and uncle's home. Much time had passed since he'd set his uncle on fire, and the burnt old drunk was now a widower. John Frenchy eased out of the car and grabbed the manila box. It was around six thirty in the morning. He carefully walked to the porch and placed the box at the front door. He stared at the door for a minute, contemplating an apology for his uncle, but he couldn't find one so he turned and headed back to the car.

"I see you, Coon. I see you. I knew you'd bring your lil' bad ass around here. I see you."

But Coon didn't turn; rather, he moved with intention back to the driver's seat with Lot's discipline, then drove off.

On the porch, his horribly disfigured uncle stood at the open door watching him drive off, then reached down and grabbed the box. He shook it first. No sound. He opened it carefully.

A tattered, gray Stetson hat.

After visits with several relatives in the area, Coon had learned that his younger brother, Alfred, had recently left for Los Angeles to join him. And this worried Coon because Alfred had a hotter temper than him. *That boy gonna get himself killed,* he thought. But even if he had reached Lafayette before Alfred left, Coon knew he wouldn't have been able to talk his brother out of leaving. And what the hell was in Lafayette anyway? Alfred was a Boudreaux too, and Boudreaux men have to learn things on their own. Besides, Coon came back to Louisiana in a Caddy, many of the relatives commented, maybe Alfred'll have some good luck too. But there ain't no such thing as good luck for nigga boys. There just ain't.

By afternoon he was driving down the scenic Highway 190, headed home to Basile. None of his immediate family members lived there anymore, but something was calling him.

When he reached Basile and turned off Bearcat Road, his heart sank. Woods. The entire area was covered in woods, no longer parceled out into farming land. Neglected. Forgotten.

He continued down the road, hoping to find the trail that led to his childhood home. All around him he noticed that other lands had been maintained. The Guillorys' parcels remained portioned for rice. The Fontenots' parcel was mixed between cattle and peas. But the Boudreaux rice fields that were once the pride of the parish had morphed into a thick, overgrown Acadian forest. For two centuries, Boudreaux rice was the standard. Exceptional rice. Long grain. Evangeline pride grown from the ground to the stalk. After the harvest, the rice fields soaked and coveted water, nesting thousands of crawfish, providing steady income with crawfish farms in the off-season, but now only a thick mess of trees and bushes remained.

Where was that road? he asked himself until finally he found it. The town of Basile had recently given it a name. Repast Road.

He pushed along the dirt road until he found an opening. The Caddy idled at the woods' edge. He put the car in gear and floored it through the woods, knocking down lesser branches and brush. But the woods fought back as he plunged deeper into its entrails. Soon the trees started tearing the Caddy apart, side-view mirrors swiped off with grille and bumpers, all yanked from the car by the defiant old woods until he crashed dead center into a huge oak, slamming his head into the big steering wheel. He cut the car off. It was quiet again but for the cold winter breeze singing through the treetops. It was always quiet this time of year. He got out of the car and examined the wreckage for the remission of sins, acknowledging the resurrection of the dead.

He could smell the pine needles in the trees above and under his feet. He stooped and grabbed a handful, then held them to his nose. The scent reminded him of bricks and labor, reminded him of community. And now, all of that seemed gone, replaced by woods and breezes. Then he heard something. The unmistakable chopping of wood. The heavy thunk. Not to be confused with the higher-pitched thunk of cutting sugarcane, no, this was chopping wood, a familiar chopping. A certain cadence and rhythm between chops. It was his father, Paul Boudreaux.

He carefully removed his gray Florsheims and matching

thick-and-thin socks, then dashed through the forest toward the sound of his father.

Coon once again ran through the familiar forest with crunching pine needles under his bare feet. The air chilled, and Coon noticed that he was running on soft ice, yet he continued. The chopping got louder. He could smell his father's pipe. Sweet cavendish with dried mint leaves. He could smell it. The last time Coon had heard the chopping of wood and smelled the cavendish, Paul had told his family that Pearl Harbor had just been bombed. He never saw Paul after that evening, an evening like this one. The last time it all happened just like this.

Coon sprinted now. Ice on the ground. This time he wanted to say good-bye. He leaped over a fallen oak, just missing a massive bull nettle. The chopping got louder. Nearer. Paul usually chopped wood for half an hour. No more, no less. Coon continued running until he approached a clearing. At the clearing's edge, near the rear of where his old home once stood, he could make out a large building. It was his old home built of cypress planks and a tin roof. He stopped. How could that house still be here? he thought. A tin stovepipe jutted out of the side, bellowing white smoke. The chopping sound ceased abruptly. Paul wasn't there, but Coon wasn't alone. He noticed a peculiar tiny white hand jutting from the soil. A familiar hand. Quickly, he dug around the hand and retrieved the body. Bébé Blanc. Then a chorus began from the front of the house—

> *Je vous salue, Marie, pleine de grâce.*
> *Le Seigneur est avec vous.*
> *Vous êtes bénie entre toutes les femmes,*
> *et Jésus, le fruit de vos entrailles, est béni.*
> *Sainte Marie, Mère de Dieu,*
> *priez pour nous, pauvres pécheurs,*
> *maintenant et à l'heure de notre mort.*
> *Amen.*

A dark figure in a tattered gray suit huddled over a small black kettle on the ground in what used to be the backyard. It was the Ole Haitian, his great-uncle, Jules Saint-Pierre Sonnier, or Nonc Sonnier. Coon froze. He feared Nonc Sonnier even though they were blood relations.

But there was no way Nonc Sonnier could be sitting over a black pot in the cold in 1963, Coon thought. Sonnier had been lynched by the Klan in 1953 under the auspices of a McCarthy-type witch hunt for spiritual subversives, or at least that was the official account.

Was it an apparition? A grown *feu follet*? Maybe. Coon studied the man who was busy with his pot.

Coon couldn't make out Sonnier's face, but he knew it was him.

"Qui t'après faire icite?"* Coon asked, wanting to know what Sonnier was doing in the land of the living.

Sonnier kept his head to the pot. Coon knew not to ask a second time. Not with Sonnier. Sonnier was known to hear everything from an ant scratching its feet to tugboats a hundred miles away in the Mississippi. So Coon waited for the answer.

"J'ai venu pour te 'oir,"† Sonnier said in a low, gravelly voice.

"Quoi moi fait?"‡ asked Coon, childlike.

Sonnier laughed but didn't look at his great-nephew.

"You did everything and nothing at the same time. Tout que chose et rien au même temps," Sonnier indicted, but Coon didn't understand.

He took a few steps closer, coming out from the woods into the clearing.

"Fais pas ça!"§ Sonnier ordered.

---

* "What are you doing here?"
† "I came to see you."
‡ "What I do?"
§ "Stop that!"

Coon stopped. Sonnier didn't want to be bothered and Coon wasn't going to push it, John Frenchy or no John Frenchy.

"Donnez-moi c'est montre,"* Sonnier said, raising a bony black finger at the Patek Philippe on Coon's wrist. Coon quickly took off the watch and threw it near Sonnier, but Sonnier did not lower his finger. Coon knew what Sonnier wanted. He took off the gold tiepin, opal ring, and bracelet, and slung it all over to Sonnier.

Sonnier nodded. "Bon."

Coon waited as Sonnier leaned over and grabbed Stein's gold particulars. Sonnier inspected the items with smell, taste, and bite, then threw them in the pot, saving the opal ring for his pinkie.

Sonnier finally stood and faced Coon, eye to eye.

"T'oublié?"† Sonnier asked.

Coon took a bow. Sonnier followed suit, then they clasped hands and began a coordinated vodou salut on the cold forest floor.

There was a problem that needed to be worked out between Sonnier and Coon. And only Bébé Blanc would bear witness to its solution.

Minutes later, Coon took off through the woods and didn't stop until he reached the small jail alongside Highway 190 in Elton, miles away. Winded, he hunched over to catch his breath, then looked up at the small jail and laughed uncontrollably. He could still see his older brother Pa-June sticking his arms out of the jail window trying to grab a knife that the sheriff held out to him for amusement. The small jail was loaded with Atakapas from a nearby reservation who got out of line on Saturday nights. Pa-June regularly went to jail on Saturday nights in the 1940s, and the sheriff always got a kick out of starting a fight between Pa-June and whoever was locked up with him.

---

* "Give me that watch."
† "You forgot?"

Yet Coon just continued laughing hysterically at the empty, abandoned jail as night fell in Jefferson Davis Parish. He didn't even notice that he had pissed on himself—too consumed with nervous laughter and relief to properly weigh the debt.

On that cold night in 1963, John Paul Boudreaux made an error in earnest, seeking the divine for the most selfish of reasons. He was lonely.

sixteen

burn to shine
(le char et la souris)

Houston, Texas, c. 1984

Once during noon Mass, Black Jesus showed up at St. Philip
Neri Catholic Church, reeking of Tanqueray and Aramis cologne. He was shaving in the water fountain behind the sacristy.
I saw him. He had on the robe and sandals just like the pictures,
except his hair was nappy as hell. He asked me to be an altar boy
and told me Santa Claus was a fake. I got a whipping when I
told Mother, not because she thought I was lying. She was pissed
that I said our Lord and Savior's hair was nappy.

Jesus wept, then bought some relaxer.

Years later . . .

Kinda pitch-black.

Aramis cologne.

"Forgive me, Father, for I have sinned."

"Hey, hey. Ti' John."

"Hey, Father Jerome. Can I holla at you for a minute?"

Pitch-black.

I peed in the water fountain at school while the fourth and
fifth graders had assembly at St. Andrew's. *Free to Be . . . You and
Me.* I took the meaning a little too literally. While Rosey Grier
was telling us that it was all right to cry, I stood on a chair and
painted my initials with urine in the fount. Rosey was a bitch or

a liar. I just couldn't see his big ass crying. There's only so much a fifth grader will believe, and after that dice scene with Father and that Sonnier dude at Lil' Aubrie's, I wasn't sure what to believe anymore. At every turn, some grown-up was shattering myths left and right. Easter Bunny. Tooth Fairy. Santa Fraud. The whole lot of them were peddled to kids with promises of candy and toys and coins under a pillow, and I had never seen one of them. Fuckin' frauds. But Black Jesus and Sonnier? They were real, at least to me.

Father Jerome chuckled when I told him about Black Jesus and Sonnier as we walked around the parish hall parking lot for confession while he smoked a cig. By now the parish was his. He owned it. He chain-smoked. He shadowboxed most days at noon, wearing khakis and a white tee until both were drenched. He played music a lot, usually soul and jazz. And he'd jog in the mornings while imagining he was playing a trumpet. Miles Davis on "Gabriel's Horn." "Ave Maria" in B flat with Tony Williams on skins, Ron Carter holding down the bass, and Hancock on the eighty-eights.

"Is there such a thing as spirits?" I asked.

"Of course," Father Jerome answered.

"Do they look like Sonnier?"

"Usually you can't see them."

"But I saw Sonnier, he black and got straight hair like my daddy."

"Well . . ." He shrugged. I think he didn't know the answer or he wasn't saying.

"In the CCE book they show the angels and the angels are white. Is that what spirits look like?" I asked. A fair question.

"Ti' John, I believe spirits come in all colors," he answered.

"Like crayons?"

"Yeah, like crayons."

"So why the CCE book only show the white crayons, I mean angels?" I inquired. "Nobody even uses the white crayons."

"Who knows?" he said.

Apparently not him. He didn't know much that afternoon. Because I was a repeat offender, the Free-for-Me-to-Pee incident cost ten Our Fathers, three Hail Marys, and one Act of Contrition. Not that pricey, considering I wasn't required to tell the teacher or Mother. I told you Father Jerome was cool.

After stopping by Ralston Liquors for a pint of Chivas Regal and smokes, Father Jerome drove me home. I noticed his gold crucifix ring was gone. A light ring circle on his pinkie suggested that the ring had been recently removed. I mean, damn, J.C. has things to do, I thought. Father Jerome must've forgot to put it on. Such piety.

For two weeks I searched for the Burning Wood Man, Sonnier. I wanted to know why he was following me. Father kept a tight lip and claimed ignorance when asked about it. But you said it, Daddy, I protested. Yet he shrugged. I say a lot of things when I'm drinking, Sonny. But he knew. He just wouldn't say.

My circle of friends at St. Andrew's had expanded since that day in the office with Mike. Of course there was Russell, but also Mike's younger cousin, Ricky, and another younger kid named Patrick. We had one semester of elementary school left until middle school. Our interactions were PG, parent-friendly outings like Chuck E. Cheese's and day trips to AstroWorld. Mother saw to it that none of my St. Andrew's friends would ever come to my house to play or spend the night. She never said it, but it was understood. And strangely, I didn't mind.

Mike and Ricky lived in impressive homes in Third Ward with the big trees. Patrick lived in Hiram Clarke, a very quiet, black, middle-class neighborhood that had a lot of pretty girls with curfews. Russell lived in Meyerland with the white folks. There was more to see at their homes. Less danger. Either way, those guys didn't need to come to South Park because shit was about to hit the fan.

Two days after Father told me to ball up my fist after leaving Lil' Aubrie's, I started a war with Joe Boy. He lived across the street and I would be in middle school next school year. Some shit was going to have to change before I'd recite my first sixth-grade Pledge of Allegiance.

Since the first day I stepped on Ricky Street, I'd been a target and even before then. It was the light-skinned thing. And of course, it's not like I had any say in the matter. God puts us in the oven and watches soaps, Mother said. Sometimes He changes the channel or His favorite daytime drama will come on and He forgets what's in the oven, so people come out looking different. Like cookies or corn bread, it all depends on how you like it. That's how she explained it to me after she caught me in the bathtub filled with dirt, brown liquid shoeshine, chocolate milk, and hope, wishing I could get darker so the older boys wouldn't pick on me and call me "white boy." Don't laugh, I was six years old. And you know what I asked Santa Claus for Christmas that year? A return trip to the muthafuckin' oven. Actually, compared to many of my couzains in Louisiana, I was kinda dark, particularly among my Lemelle relations. But it didn't matter. In Texas, I was light-skinned. It wasn't my fault, but explain that to South Park. Sure, the girls would pick me to play house and doctor, but the minute that was over, there'd always be a collection of darker boys waiting in the wings for my ass. So I'd just cover my face and take it.

But middle school was coming and I-be-damn if I was gonna get picked on in middle school. That could be catastrophic. I could be a victim for the rest of my life. So I decided, maybe foolhardily, to take on my number one nemesis, Joe Boy.

Summer Sorties for the Communications Guy with the Antenna

At 2:00 P.M. on a clear summer's day, hot air boiled the bayous, giving St. Augustine's beard a jaundiced hue, maligning spring flowers until they were reduced to hateful peat, and sucking the air from small animals seeking a shady respite. Hell complete. Hell for the living. Alas, the singing cicadas whose bellyaching reports that all is not lost. The adamant cicada, who insists that life goes on in Hell or at least noontime in the summer months of Houston, which is about the same thing if you're outside or your AC is broken. Yet the cicada reminds us that we will survive the fire. Just wiggle your belly and make a prayer.

On the eve of the first battle, Mother fried pork chops for supper. Knowing that the next day I would begin my campaign, I loaded up my plate, figuring I'd need all the energy I could muster for 'morrow. I should've known better.

Pork gives me strange dreams. That night I dreamt that I was a sniper scoping a brown bunny at the beach on Galveston Island. I couldn't get the shot off in time because a storm was moving ashore quickly from the angry Gulf. The bunny was stationed in a lifeguard tower with a bolt-action rifle and scope. The bunny spotted me as dark, low clouds rolled in with rough, high surf. It should have been over. I should have shot the bunny. Lord knows the bunny had cause to shoot me. But the bunny jumped into a golden raft and paddled into the rough sea against the strong waves, then turned around and stared at me as it floated away. I didn't follow. I didn't have the will.

When I awoke the next morning, I felt a warm wet patch in my drawers. I knew damn well I hadn't peed in the bed. Despite my proclivity for public urination, I had long ceased the habit of pissing my bed. Upon further investigation I discovered that I, John Paul Boudreaux, Jr., FMC, had in fact experienced a wet dream. It was official. I was no longer shooting duck water. I ceremoniously slid off my underwear while humming "The Star-Spangled Banner," then secreted my new merit badge in the closet. This had to be a good sign. Right?

Saturday, Holiday

A roach is such a brave, stubborn creature. Reckless but committed. Too committed, maybe. It crawls the inches, pulled by a desire to know. Sometimes they die. Other times they live but move forward nonetheless. A roach does not crawl backward. Maybe it physically has the ability for reverse, but nobody told the roach, so it moves forward, sideways occasionally, but always forward. Come hell or high water.

The corner of Ricky Street and Clearway Drive right by the dead end. Touch in the street, tackle in the grass.

High noon.

The cicadas were loud. High-pitched, monotonous droning like a drumroll at a military execution greeted me as I stepped out of the house. Father sat on the back of his pickup whittling a long branch. He didn't say anything. Captured in an opiate haze from painkillers balanced with a cup of café noir, he was almost comatose or, rather, a volcano waiting to explode. Oro Iná redux. Red-hot cayenne nestled in sauce rouille over rice. Eat it and you need water. Don't eat it and you starve because that's supper and there ain't leftovers.

On the corner, the guys were playing. I approached—

"Can I play?"

"Fuck you, white boy," said Joe Boy before drilling the ball into my chest. My entire upper torso was on fire, but I sucked it up and picked up the ball. I drilled it back at him, but he caught it and walked heavily toward me, then started punching me in the chest. I turned my head quickly. Father was watching. Then Joe Boy slapped me and returned to the game.

I walked home with my head to the ground, trying not to cry. I avoided Father and went straight to the backyard and up a tree. I cried.

"Bring your ass down here," Father yelled as he hobbled into the backyard. I came down quickly, eyes still avoiding him. But it didn't matter, one leg or not. He beat the shit out of me with the long branch.

That night, listening to the train and the mouse, I snuck out my bedroom window and watched Ms. Johnson nod off on the toilet. Nobody came to my aid against Joe Boy, I reflected. Not even Raymond Earl. Yet the cicadas had shifted to their night melody. *Lève-toi,* they sang gently. Sonnier didn't help either. Could he? And why did Father beat me? I didn't have any answers, so I peed under Ms. Johnson's window.

seventeen

dandelions

When blacks folks bow down in labor, we usually acknowledge God's power, but sometimes we try to get a peek into Hell to determine if the grass is greener down below. Few people smile while bent. More people smile when erect and staring at the heavens. Still we prostrate and profess what we see when our backs are bent. Colored backs. Brown backs. Red backs. Copper backs. Black backs. Black backs bent over for peas, potatoes, rice, greens, cotton, and the sharp white rocks on the railroad tracks of Mykawa Road.

Each of us was filling white plastic five-gallon buckets with the *blanche* missiles. It was Raymond Earl's idea. Booger came along because Harris County psychiatric officials were at his house trying to take his momma away.

I looked down the steel tracks, which squiggled from Satan's trick. No one said a word; the only sounds were foot to rock and rock to bucket. We'd been at it for over thirty minutes, quiet, bending, sweating. Not one word. The same way Father described harvesting peas, cotton, and rice when unseasonable frost threatened late-blooming crops in Basile. Not even a song to remove one's mind from the toil of a hard crop and regular visits by watermelon-scented water moccasins. Actually, they smelled more like rotting watermelons, a bizarre fruity musk like an infant's toe cheese or a Bomb Pop napping in day-old dog shit. Yeah, I knew the smell because my bucket was half filled when I noticed one staring at me about six feet away by the gully. La serpent. Raymond Earl threw a rock at it and it slithered away. We continued until a Santa Fe Rail regular interrupted, pulling shipping containers marked "SeaPort" and a few tanks from LouAna Oil Mill.

This was the furthest I had walked from home. Damn Ricky Street. I was at least two miles away from my porch.

"Man, yawl know Ronnie fucked his dog?" Booger said, finally breaking the silence.

"Nawh-unh," Raymond Earl replied, scratching a new mosquito bite.

But Booger was adamant—

"We was at Muscle's house playing basketball and Eddie and dem started fuckin' wit' him about it. But he didn't say nuthin'. Then that nigga's lil' brother, Santana, came by, and Eddie was like 'Say, Ronnie, your brother's the one who told us.' And Ronnie got all mad and shit and started whippin' Santana's ass, talkin' 'bout he be talkin' too much," Booger reported.

"Man, that don't mean nuthin'. Eddie always talkin' shit," Raymond Earl argued.

"Nawh, but that ain't it. Later on, I was smokin' fry* with the Corduroy Brothers—" Booger continued.

"Nigga, quit lyin'!" Raymond Earl barked.

"Let him talk, dawg," I said, handing Raymond Earl a red Now and Later.

"Thank you. I walked by Ronnie's house and I could hear his momma whippin' his ass," Booger offered.

"Whose ass? Ronnie?" I asked.

"Nawh, nigga. Santana. That nigga's momma was on the same shit. 'You be talkin' too much, Santana. That's family business, don't be tellin' our business all over the damn place,' " said Booger.

"Oh shit! It's true," said Raymond Earl.

"That's what I'm tryin' to say," said Booger.

---

* Marijuana cigarettes soaked in embalming fluid laced with PCP.

We fell over laughing. Of course we were repulsed, but we weren't shocked. There was always a nasty rumor or two floating around the hood, most of which were true, but nobody ever did anything about it. Ronnie already had a reputation for molesting little boys younger than him. He'd fool kids into following him into the woods, then threaten them if they didn't give him head. It was always some younger kid who didn't really play outside on Ricky Street, like Donnie Carter or those people who lived by Boobie on Rue Street. Usually a kid who didn't have a big brother or a man in the house. I told you Ronnie was fucked-up, a certified psychopath with a method and a target group. But nobody reported him. Nobody ever called HPD or Child Protective Services. He just fucked little boys and went on his merry way. I guessed he was moving on to canines now.

"Don't he have a German shepherd?" I asked, causing more laughter.

Dandelions littered the drop to the gully. The wishful serpent closes its eyes, makes a wish, then blows the dandelion to bits—a white explosion into stardust carrying Dambala's breath to Bondyè. *Lève toi,* the cicadas reminded us as we lugged our buckets of rocks off the tracks headed home. Headed for some sneaky shit. *Dis-moi.*

We hid behind a truck across the street from Joe Boy's house and waited. Soon Joe Boy emerged and we let him have it. White rocks pummeled him and a few windows. He ran back into his house with a few new shiners.

"Sonny! Bring your ass over here!" Father yelled from the back of his truck.

He saw the whole thing and considered it cowardly. Now he'd have to buy new windows for Joe Boy's house. The windows were already Swiss cheese with a few BB gun holes and two clean .22-caliber wounds, which is why Joe Boy's father didn't raise too much hell after Father hobbled over there to make arrangements and apologies. And of course, all of this was coming out of my meager savings and allowance. Yet that didn't bother me. What bothered me was that Father thought I was a coward.

That night while trying to sleep, I heard the mouse. Then there was a crack like someone had stepped on a pecan with church shoes. Something was in my room. I smelled it. Him. I cautiously opened my eyes, and there he stood, holding the dead mouse by the tail. Jules Saint-Pierre Sonnier, FMC.

"What you doin' in here?" I asked.

"I came to see you," he said.

"What I do?"

He laughed.

"Get on away from here," I said, then hid under the covers. When I mustered enough courage, I looked again and he was gone.

He found me.

The next day I took a personal field trip on the Metro bus and rode all over Houston. I was looking for him, although I had the impression that he was not far away and was watching me the entire time. I could smell it. Burning wood.

Around 3:00 P.M. I got off the bus at Ricky and MLK, where a crowd of kids, old and young, had gathered. They were waiting for me. Waiting with Joe Boy.

The first punch landed on my mouth, splitting my bottom lip against my bottom teeth. That shit hurt. Warm blood seeped from my lip, confusing my ego with the notion that it was only hot spit. The customary oohs and aahs and rants only resembled the train on Mykawa, a low, sonorous constant tucked away on the back burner until it's merely a hum, almost muted. I couldn't hear anything, didn't want to hear anything. My heart was beating so fast that I thought I heard it; senses confusing feeling with hearing. My hands felt heavy, weighted by fear and inexperience, but I kept them up, if not to guard then at least to look like I knew what I was doing. I didn't.

Scott Joplin's ragtime sang. The ice cream truck. Fuck! I wanted a Bomb Pop. Damn this fight, I thought, but the crowd had encircled us and there was no getting out.*

Joe Boy stood back, one foot planted before his body with all of his weight leaning back on the other foot. He wasn't smiling and he wasn't talking shit. He was serious. Some guys would bounce around aping Sugar Ray Leonard with exaggerated punches and self-broadcast in-fight commentary, but not Joe Boy. He came to fight.

I threw a slow left cross, and he countered with a punch in the stomach. I buckled, but he didn't throw me to the ground or wrestle like some guys. No. Joe Boy was only interested in pure pugilistic combat, so naturally, I kicked him against the side of his knee. It didn't do much, but he unloaded on me and the whole thing happened too gotdamn fast for me to keep up.

Several punches later, I was sprawled on the concrete covering my face as he continued whipping my ass. Then he got up. I peered between my fingers and noticed Sonnier in the crowd, yelling—

"Lève! Lève-toi!"

STAND UP!

I had heard Father say it before when I would fall. *Lève-toi*. Stand up, Sonnier was screaming. Nobody noticed him. Joe Boy had taken a few steps back, then I noticed that his fists were covered in blood. My blood.

Fistfights are essentially about openings and opportunity coupled with skill and belief. Joe Boy was a static target who led with his right and planted his right foot forward for balance. God, if I was a lefty. Technically, there was an opening, but he'd literally beat me to the ground, and now he was giving me an opportunity to get up and try again. A second chance at bat. He knew I was inexperienced and really didn't have comparable

---

*Dice Rule 5: When gambling in an enclosed area, always know where the exits are located.

skills, which was why he had to jump back and give me another shot. His pride was on the line too.

The hood, as are many hoods around the world, is always a predatory environment. We, little black boys, learn this early in life. The strong defeat the weak. Advantage is never given. Cowardice is a death knell. These are the rules.

The only thing left was whether I believed I could beat him. And I didn't believe. I wasn't a fool. But I had managed to make a showing. *Don't cry.*

"Lève-toi, Couzain!" Sonnier yelled again.

Stand. Stand up. Stand up for yourself.

So I stood.

The prospect of throwing flurries at Joe Boy seemed as rational as committing to hard jabs dead center against the trunk of an oak tree. But in order to fight with fists, one must commit to the pain of the oak. The pain is part of the process. When you're removed from the fear of pain, then you can hold your own. You may not win the fight, but you won't look like a bitch.

It certainly would've been nice if Sonnier would've tied Joe Boy's shoes together, invisibly of course, but that only happened in cartoons. In fact, by the time I got to my feet, Sonnier was gone. By now, a few older guys had parked their Monte Carlos, Cutlasses, and Regals around the circle and watched from their hoods. Fuck. Graduation in the hood.

I can't tell you I kicked Joe Boy's ass and he cried "uncle," but I can say that he got a bloody nose. After ten minutes, he stopped and stuck out his bloody hand.

Armistice.

The crowd roared above the shrill chorus of approving cicadas. White boy got wit' him. Ti' John put hands on him. That nigga crazy like his daddy. Don't fuck wit' 'dem Creole niggas when they get mad. Ti' John got nuts. Ti' John handled his business. Ti' John got heart. I bet Joe Boy ain't gonna fuck wit' him no mo'. And they were right. Joe Boy and I never fought again.

I walked back home triumphant with Booger and Raymond

Earl by my side giving me the play-by-play. Apparently, I'd connected a few lucky shots. I guess I made my own luck.

"Mr. Frenchy, you shoulda seen it. Ti' John gave Joe Boy a bloody nose," Booger reported to Father as we jumped the fence into my backyard.

Father didn't even say a word, focusing his lasso on the white plastic bucket twenty feet away from him.

His cast was off.

Father didn't give a shit about my fight after he heard the details. He just shrugged with a haughty "That's what you supposed to do." He lit a Benson & Hedges; then I noticed a gold crucifix ring on his pinkie. Yeah, that one.

Later that night as Mother nursed my bruises with ice packs and comforting words, we watched Mike's daddy give a speech on the news about crime prevention in the city of Houston, even though at St. Andrew's, the mystery of urine puddles, stolen Hot Wheels, and missing bag lunches would remain unsolved.

With the mouse dead and Ms. Johnson in Harris County Jail for possession, I climbed onto my roof and listened to the train on Mykawa Road. I thought about the water moccasin beseeching the white dandelions. What did the snake request? Was it granted?

The cicadas sang in spurts. The train's distant roar softened. Under the stars of a hot, humid Houston night and while lying on warm roofing tile, I pulled out my member with scabbed, swollen knuckles and masturbated for the first time.

I didn't consider whether anybody on my street was watching from their window. I mean, I was on the roof full monty. Then I looked on the corner and I saw him again, smoking something, shadowy, still . . . nosy. What the fuck did he want? I thought.

eighteen

le pélican

Louisiana, July 1870

In the mornings after the cock crowed and dawn dampened leaves and fruit, the old women would return from the lagoon with jars of that sweet water on their heads, singing quietly as the village awakened. Singing *that* song. The field hands would move toward the cane fields, dazed but constant, heading toward their obligation to the land. I watched from a cracked window.

Those were different days back then. Flesh could be measured by grain or gold and adjudicated by effort and intentions. We dealt in absolutes. Memories of slavery still lingered, buttressed by a desperate hope to understand what freedom meant. The land and our labor would determine our future, most believed. And the lwa would judge our actions and shape our faith.

We felt the rain, tasted its vitality, witnessed crops grow from sprout to stalk with the generous sun enriching their hopeful leaves. We prayed for the land, asking for its nourishment to feed our bodies so that we could live and honor the lwa and our ancestors. God was not far away, not in the sky or the clouds but right there on land—the dark dirt dampened by our patriots' blood. You could hear it. Taste it. See it. Smell it. God. Everywhere. On wet dirt where cane and fruit sprung forth proudly in this new republic. This is my earliest memory of Haiti.

Je m'appelle Jules Saint-Pierre Sonnier, FMC.

**Aboard the Schooner *Jeannette*, Due Northwest at
Approximately Ten Knots in the Gulf of Mexico**

My uncle Emmanuel Guillory leaned against the railing of the
deck smoking a cheroot and gazing at the Alabama coastline as
the schooner navigated past Dauphin Island. A hundred years
earlier, his grandparents were run off the small island by British
forces, forcing his grandfather Gregoire to petition for a land
grant in the Spanish-held Opelousas Post of the Louisiana Territory. His grandparents' storied love affair was the talk of the
legal community and French aristocracy. Gregoire, the French
landowner, fell in love with his slave Marguerite, birthing a new
family in the Louisiana Territory—the Guillorys, FPC.

In 1859, Nonc Emmanuel took us to Haiti with the promise
of sanctuary and prosperity. What we found was dismal infight-
ing among Saint-Domingue's quarrelsome *affranchi*. P. E. Desdunes had promised a land of freedom and liberty in the Jacobin
tradition, but Nonc Emmanuel didn't give a damn about idealism
or politics, only soil. He was a farmer.

The Civil War had forced many of us, *les gens du couleur
libres,* to pick sides. Some, like my cousin Auguste Donato, had
joined the Confederacy as a way to preserve their property rights.
Others, like my other cousin Martin Guillory, had joined the
Union resistance, forming a special unit of guerrilla Jayhawkers,
the Free Scouts of Bois Mallet. Most knew what both Cousin
Auguste and Cousin Martin were doing—stealing. Under the
auspices of their respective allegiances, they raided farms and
towns throughout southwestern Louisiana, stealing white cotton from white farms. Most of our people stashed their cotton
crops deep in the woods of Bois Mallet under Leon Fontenot's
supervision. Now the war was over and Nonc Emmanuel was
bringing us back to La Louisiane. Land speculation was high,
and the war had left most in St. Landry Parish impoverished.
We weren't sure what we were returning to.

Yet it wasn't the economic turmoil of St. Landry Parish that worried him. It was me—the little boy who had been born in Saint-Marc and was now returning to Louisiana with him. My mama, Mathildé Sonnier, journeyed with the Guillorys to Haiti. She was related to Nonc Emmanuel's grandmother Marguerite, and he didn't believe St. Landry Parish would be safe for her if war broke out between the states—she was four months pregnant. Upon my birth, the villagers of Saint-Marc embraced me as their own and began secretly instructing me in the ways of the Dahomey. While Nonc Emmanuel and my cousins exchanged farming techniques with the locals, I was learning how to draw vévés and call spirits under the guidance of the great *houngan** Etienne Delbeau. Very soon the great *houngans* and *mambos* of the region heard of me—the boy who could divine with knucklebones fashioned from goat ankles. My predictions were gospel, but I couldn't predict that Mama would leave me. She died of yellow fever on my tenth birthday.

And now, two months later, many on the *Jeannette* were whispering of throwing me overboard, not wanting to arrive in the newly reunified United States of America with a voodoo child, but they were thwarted. With scabbard in hand, Nonc Emmanuel threatened the wary, highbrow New Orleanian Creoles who conspired to kill me while reciting verses from *Les Cenelles.*[†] They backed off, leaving the rustic patriarch and his rural brood to their pastoral ruminations on farm life.

For his part, Ozémé Boudreaux, my biological father, stood resolute with Nonc Emmanuel, although most had grown tired

---

*Vodou priest.

† In antebellum New Orleans, a group of well-educated Creoles called Cordon Bleus were gathered by Armand Lanusse for an intellectual exchange. They called themselves Les Cenelles (or the holly berries) and in 1845 published an anthology of Creole poetry also titled *Les Cenelles.* This would be the very first anthology of works by African Americans published in the United States, and it reflected the French Romantic Movement in literature with absolutely no references to the social ills of the time, as such content was banned so as not to create civil unrest. Written in French, it's as popular for what is not said as for what is said.

of his antics, primarily petty theft and adultery. Ozémé was not an honorable man, so Nonc Emmanuel took it upon himself to provide me with an upstanding role model. Mama's husband, Jacques Sonnier, had been killed in the war, but it was no secret that Ozémé was my father.

And now, hours away from reaching the Port of New Orleans, the passengers had grown hostile toward me. Edmund, Emmanuel's teenage son and my best friend, had taken ill. So I took the opportunity to cure him with methods I had learned in Haiti, which caused an uproar with the New Orleanian Creoles. But Nonc Emmanuel didn't have time to worry about them, marshaling his wishes toward his boy's speedy recovery before making port and hoping that his land grant in western St. Landry Parish was still intact.

His cheroot died out from damp air. He lit it again and thanked the British for running his forefathers out of the mosquito-ridden Dauphin Island to St. Landry Parish, where a French-speaking, God-fearing free man of color could own land and make something out of himself. Land was the measure, Nonc Emmanuel used to say, not fancy titles or European educations. Land would determine the fate of his family. And for him, family included me—the young copper-colored boy who practiced cleromancy with knucklebones and spoke the Dahomey and Kongo tongues to the stars.

A large brown pelican circled the mast above, lured by the foreign smell of Nonc Emmanuel's burning cheroot. Distanced from the caucusing highbrow Creoles of New Orleans, he didn't notice that chatter had abruptly ceased as I led a weak Edmund to the deck. Emmanuel looked at his boy and smiled inwardly as Edmund took feeble steps toward the railing.

"Qui c'est ça?"* Edmund murmured, pointing to the shore.

"Ça c'est l'Amerique,"† I answered.

---

* "What's that?"
† "That's America."

Nonc Emmanuel turned and embraced his son, his burning cheroot dropping on the deck.

"Ça c'est nos pays, mon garçon. Nos pays,"* said Emmanuel with joyous wet eyes.

I reached down, picked up the cheroot, and put it in my mouth. I didn't cough but blew a steady stream of grayish white smoke even though this was the first time my young lungs welcomed tobacco. I immediately took a liking to it.

They stared at me, pointed, speculated. "Bastard," they said aloud. "Witch," they said under their breath. Both were true. And there was absolutely nothing I could do about it. They hated me because I was one of them. They hated me because I was born in Haiti like many of their own parents. But they were right about one thing. I *was* different. I *am* different.

It was a familiar tongue that brought us together—La Louisiane and Haiti. Distant cousins banded together by vague revolutionary republicanism masked in new freedom. Africa came along too as the Guinea people made Saint-Domingue their home. Nowhere was this new feeling of discovery and absolute faith more prevalent than Haiti.

The day I was born in Saint-Marc, Etienne knew. He found me. He showed me. He showed me God.

Docks of the Mississippi River, New Orleans, July 1870

God's tears are brown. These tears swell the banks of the Mississippi, carrying higher power to its marshes, tributaries, and bayous—saturating the rich Gulf Coast soil with divine gumption that's readily available to the faithful and the willing. La Louisiane. Its land is predisposed to the making of miracles, the forgiveness of sins, and the realization of dreams because . . . La Louisiane is a land for believers.

---

* "It's our country, son. Our country."

We arrived in New Orleans on a hot night. The docks were busy with cargo and carpetbaggers. Vieux Carré was exceptionally congested for the late hour, with all manner of people crowding the city, but very few awaited our arrival. Nonc Mannie had secured lodging in case the steamer was late. As we approached the docks we looked at each other proudly with weary eyes. We were fatigued, some felt foolish, some felt clever. But we had dodged the War Between the States. P. E. Desdunes, the Haitian consul in New Orleans, had left an attaché to inform him of our arrival. But he never showed.

Before dawn the next morning, we boarded an old Confederate steamer and pushed into the Mississippi headed to Bayou Plaquemine. Early morning fog masked the route with only the sounds of the river to support the notion that life still existed west of Orleans Parish. At Bayou Plaquemine we shifted direction and headed toward Grand Lake, then Grand Bayou. Moss-draped oaks guarded the banks of the still bayou. All on the steamer were silent as we navigated further into the quiet abyss. My father didn't say anything to me since the standoff in the Gulf; rather, he conferenced with Nonc Emmanuel and occasionally looked at me. They were making plans.

By daybreak we reached the Atchafalaya River, where I was introduced to a new type of people called "Acadians." They were French-speaking fishermen and trappers—gruff, hardworking, and suspicious. Nonc Emmanuel told all of us to stay close and not to say anything as our cargo was transferred to a flatboat. Midday we continued along the Atchafalaya headed toward Bayou Courtableau. The heavy foliage along the banks hid the utter destruction of farmlands that we had heard about once we reached New Orleans. It was very clear that the War Between the States had ruined Louisiana, and the general feeling was that everybody would have to start over, including these new dark eyes that were everywhere, watching, hoping, praying—they were the "freedmen."

From Bayou Courtableau, we headed toward a small town

called Washington. This was our last stop. Leon Fontenot, FPC, of Bois Mallet waited for us at the docks along with two stage coaches and five wagons. Nonc Emmanuel stepped off the flat-boat and greeted Fontenot with a great deal of relief. He'd made it back home. He felt safe again.

By the time we reached Washington, Edmund had told all willing ears that I saved his life. He wasn't scared of me, and to him I wasn't a bastard. I was his hero.

In those days, the right hand was fairly common; *traiteurs* were everywhere. Nobody blinked at Edmund's account of events on the *Jeannette*. Nobody whispered "witch" anymore. And by the time we reached Bayou Courtableau, they just left it at "bastard." That's how I was to be presented to my new home—a foreign land—Basile, Louisiana. A bastard. A bastard to be cared for like a mule or hunting dogs.

nineteen

the barn

Houston, Texas, 1984

Busted lip, busted nose, bruised ribs, scabbed knee, and the most ghastly-looking swollen, scabbed knuckles earned Mother's edict: banned from Ricky Street except for going to and from the bus stop, which made no sense whatsoever. Poor thing. It's not like she didn't have enough to deal with already. Reaganomics was kicking our ass. Father was catching hell getting shifts at the Houston Ship Channel. More pills. More whiskey. He forced her to quit the night-shift job at Foley's the minute his cast came off—no way she was going to bring in more money than him.

The night after my fight they kept me up, but there was no yelling, no arguing nor fucking—just calm talking, explaining. He promised her he would figure something out, and not gambling. Gambling was reserved for quick fixes, not long-term financial planning.

The next morning at St. Andrew's the war wounds caused wholesale concern. Everyone felt bad for me but kept their distance—GHETTO—everybody except for Mike.

"Damn, boy. What happened to you?" he asked, handing me a pack of stolen Twinkies from his morning pilfering. I looked at the delightful Twinkies sitting next to each other behaving themselves on the small, white rectangular cardstock and plastic comforter, packed with love and the promise of delicious white cream filling, then I looked at his eyes. No longer the smirk and the suspicion. No longer the hunger for an opportunity to humiliate me. No longer. And I could see this all in Mike's eyes even though his eyes weren't big but rather small, a wink short of beady.

"I had a fight," I said and waved off the cream-filled gift.

He looked at my knuckles—the mark of defiance. I think he was impressed. In fact, the scabbed knuckles threw off most of the kids at school. You normally didn't see an eleven-year-old with scabbed knuckles. Of course, this made sense considering I was *ghetto*. Mother had spoken with the principal before school and told her that I had gotten jumped, which pissed me off because I had a fight, I wasn't jumped. I stood up for myself, dammit, and the only public testament to that fact was my infirm knuckles. And being good, thoughtful Christians, the principal and Mother decided that I should participate in the upcoming school play.

"John Boudreaux. We're gonna try you as the Scarecrow," Miss Patterson said at the small assembly for fourth and fifth graders.

Just great. Mike, Patrick, Russell, and Ricky snickered, then dangled their arms out like marionettes.

"That's Pinocchio, ole stupid muthafuckas," I whispered. Every year there were two plays: the Christmas play and the spring play. Yet none of my friends ever volunteered for lead roles, only supporting chorus and extras lest you get teased during weeks of rehearsal and well after the final curtain call.

"Ah, Miss Patterson. I wanna be one of them Munchkins or something," I countered.

"I don't care. I think you'd be a brilliant Scarecrow. And the Munchkins are for the first and second graders anyway."

"I don't mind."

"C'mon, John. The Scarecrow is a wonderful role. He thinks he doesn't have any brains but he figures everything out. He's the smart one."

"This fool," Mike blurted after sucking his teeth, a bit jealous. Now the whole assembly stared at me; granted, nobody but Mike spoke to me the whole day—scared of my battle-scarred ghetto ass.

"John ain't gonna need no costume 'cause he already look like a hobo," Ricky teased.

"Richard! Enough of that. So will you do it?" Miss Patterson asked. "You're already smart, so it should be easy for you."

And then it happened. We were sitting on the stone floor of an atrium with a glass roof. It was cloudy the whole day. Gray. No rain, just God's threat—holding a wet fist saying, "Act right or I'ma drench yawl no-'count asses." Light—through gray clouds—shone on my hands, which rested on my knees. Light. Sunlight. "You're already smart." My feet were itching, burning. My head felt light, dizzy. I wasn't alone, but I didn't smell anything burning. I looked around for the mysterious Nonc but didn't find him.

"See. And you already have the spotlight," Miss Patterson continued.

Goose bumps on the veins. An electric charge shocked me, but I wasn't dragging my feet on carpet. Something said yes.

"Yes!"

And it wasn't me. It came from my mouth, vibrated off my vocal cords, even sounded like me, but I promise you *I* didn't say a damn thing.

Great. Just fuckin' great. Now I'm the Scarecrow. And I don't even need a costume—just slide on whatever the fuck was at the back-to-school sale at Target last fall.

Riding the bus home that afternoon, I studied my lines. This Scarecrow dude wasn't that bad. The bus slowed. The Median Man trotted along wearing a cowboy hat and a big smile. He never smiled. I waved, but he kept smiling and jogging. As the bus neared the Ricky Street stop, I tensed. Who was waiting for me now? Would it be this strange Sonnier dude? I got off one stop early and walked through the woods to my backyard.

Father was feeding his hunting dogs when I jumped the fence.

"How was school?" he asked.

"Okay. I'm gonna be in a play. *The Wizard of Oz*," I said.

"Wanna take a ride?" he asked. He could give a fuck about a play. Hell, I didn't either.

"Momma said I can't be goin' to them gamblin' houses with you no mo'," I said.

"We ain't goin' there. Put your books up. We'll stop by Popeyes and get some chicken on the way back," he said.

I dashed in the house. Fried chicken.

First off, nobody drives cooler than Father. He doesn't drive slow but doesn't tear ass everywhere either unless he's excited or drunk. When the light changes to green, he hits the accelerator and lunges forward past other cars, then finds a steady pace usually ten miles an hour over the limit. Left hand on the wheel, elbow out the window. Right hand with a cigarette or a beer or a hot coffee or a plastic cup of Crown Royal. Eyes slowly looking around, not fast-wandering like a criminal, but more like a cop—cruising, casually looking around like he's got better shit to do, riding around like he owns everything he sees—entitled.

We turned into the driveway at St. Philip's.

"We goin' to church, Daddy? It ain't Sunday," I queried.

"Nawh. I gotta make a stop. Wait in the truck," he said.

He pulled in front of the rectory and got out quickly before I could ask any more questions.

He left a lit cigarette in the ashtray. The blaring accordion of John Delafose punched out of the ratty truck speakers. *"Joe Pitre a Deux Femmes."** I watched him from the window. He was moving, mailman-ish. Knocked on the door, Brother Al opened, and he went in. No small talk at the door. No sign of the cross. I waited.

I looked at the cigarette. It looked at me. Why not? I quickly

---

* "Joe Pete Has Two Women," the title of a popular zydeco song by John Delafose.

grabbed it and took a careful pull, imitating Father. I coughed then did it again, but this time trying to blow circles like Charles Henry. No circles. I coughed again, but this time my bruised ribs had something to say about all of this smoking business. I put the cigarette out as Father stormed out of the rectory door mumbling to himself in Creole with something in his hand. Father Jerome came to the door with the fear of God all over his face. He didn't even look at me, eyes cemented to Father's back.

Father got in the truck quickly and slammed the door.

"Hey, Father Jerome!" I yelled as I waved at the fearful cleric.

"Put your gotdamn hand down. Don't wave at that shiftless sonofabitch," Father barked. Then I looked at his hands—he was counting a small but respectable roll of twenty-dollar bills.

Jesus would have some questions for Father Jerome, I thought.

"Put that in your pocket and don't tell your momma," he said, handing me sixty dollars.

Ten minutes later, we pulled into an unkempt field of knee-high grass and weeds off Cullen Boulevard. He cut off the truck and got out, walking directly into this field of nothing.

I watched him for a long time, maybe too long. He left the driver's-side door wide open—the way a man does when he has no care in the world but for the thing that pulls him, like jumping off a horse without tying down the reins. Mighty powerful thing, a man's curiosity. The need to discover. The passion to place his own feet on uncharted or unclaimed land. He finds himself in the obscure. Fancier tongues say he learns his *raison d'être* in this unknown—a place where expectations are lost, submitting to the inertia of pure will and intrigue. A vision. A hankering. An itch. Every man has to scratch. Sometimes with a coat hanger. Sometimes with innate desire firm as a proud penis. He took the keys with him when he left, so I got out and joined him in the field of nothing.

Approximately five acres of South Park nothing lay before us, fronted by the straight and narrow Cullen Boulevard, reared by a quiet sub-hood called Cloverland. Father stood tall, survey-ing the entire lot. Various trees and brush straddled the fence line with the rears of Cloverland homes hiding its intimate particulars behind the overgrown foliage, homeowners unaware that John Frenchy was taking account of their idiosyncrasies. I saw nothing—a baneful hinterland littered with foot-high ant beds and contumacious brush, Cloverland's forgotten parcel. Yet Father saw gold.

"I'm gonna bring a box blade in here, clear all this out," he said with plans dancing in the juke joint between his ears.

"You gonna use a tractor?" I asked.

"Nawh. *You* gonna use a tractor," he replied.

A tractor. I was going to drive a tractor, not a go-cart or a green machine but a big, diesel-fueled tractor. I would tame the lot.

"A man should build something once in his life," said Father. "Something he needs."

"Whatta 'bout that birdhouse? 'Member when I built that birdhouse?" I said, wanting to validate my union membership.

"Not like that, Sonny. You didn't need a birdhouse. If you don't need it, it won't mean anything 'less you gettin' paid for it. When you need what you buildin', you take care to do it right. Do it right and you can do it again. For somebody else. Like maybe your own boy one day," he said.

Two weeks later Father and I had built a barn with forty-two horse stalls, each complete with a tack room and trough, going for twenty-five dollars a month per stall, less Father's four stalls, which meant an extra nine hundred fifty dollars per month. It wasn't much, but he'd figured out a way to pay for his cowboying without dipping into the ship channel money, which was getting lighter by the day and strictly for household use. It also gave him a great excuse to get out of the house. This was the Reagan era—a working-class couple was normal to have a few arguments a week about money during television commercials. How was it earned? *I'm watching* Dynasty, *be quiet.* How would it be spent? *Them white folks sho' is sharp. J. R. Ewing is a cold piece of work.* Who was entitled to it? *They got money to burn.* Who paid for what? *Blake Carrington got a phone in his car. You paid the phone bill?*

Slow-ass 1984 was dragging along, and George Orwell wasn't looking, neither was the Gipper, at least not at us. But somehow I was learning my lines and my wounds were healing.

At school, I was quickly becoming a minor celebrity. Sure, Mike and Russell didn't believe that I was driving a tractor or even Father's truck, as he chose the five-acre nothing to teach me how to drive, but it didn't matter. I pranced about and stumbled all over the stage delivering lines and awkwardness. In a strange way that role was designed for me—a kid who already felt awkward. Tanya Strawberry, that really was her name, was transforming into a delightful and endearing Dorothy just as wholesome as toasted Pop-Tarts. Normally she was an irascible lass who would slap you for staring at her barrettes too long. Most of the other little girls feared her, but after weeks of skipping around the cardboard yellow brick road, she made the discovery that life was better if she was pleasant. In fact, she just said "fuck Tanya" and became Dorothy for the remainder of fifth grade. No one complained.

Purvis Bailey, a fourth grader who was small for his age, served as the tenderhearted Lion, which made perfect sense because we all thought he was gay. The reality was that he was really small and the other boys picked on him plenty so he just played with the girls. But when it came time for him to roar, he'd wake up napping first graders, bird chest poking out, standing firm. He may have acted like a punk at recess, but you definitely didn't test his mettle at rehearsal. He'd bite your ass.

And finally there was Johann, the German boy whose parents were Episcopal missionaries who dumped the bewildered blond at St. Andrew's while they saved Africa. He was the Tin Man, German accent and all. Nobody understood what the hell he was saying, but Miss Patterson taught us improv techniques to maneuver around his lines.

So here we were—this motley crew of unfortunates dolled up for the big night when proud parents could snap Polaroids and feel good about paying tuition in a tough economy. All things were quiet at home, even tranquil. Father stayed at the barn collecting money and breaking horses for a fee. Mother started selling Amway and regularly coming home with a smile. And Mike, Russell, Patrick, my cousin James from Dallas (Uncle Herman's son), and I had managed to convince a young couple to purchase us tickets for *Purple Rain*. Apollonia's titties, enough said. And just when it couldn't get any better, I bought my first season pass for AstroWorld.

Opening night, Mother and Father were in attendance in their church clothes. The entire performance went off without a hitch. Standing ovation. Mrs. Strawberry brought little Tanya a bouquet of roses, and we took a bow.

Afterward, Father took Mother and me to Red Lobster despite Mother's complaint that we couldn't afford it. A huge seafood platter, my favorite, rested before me. Father ordered a steak and Mother got the grilled fish platter. They both went on and on about the play and my performance even though I was more focused on the food. The chatter ceased as they ate, then I looked up. They were both happy. Happy with me. Happy with each other. This would be the last time we'd go out to dinner as a family. The last time we'd smile together, attentive to each other's comfort with the fullest detail. The last time I would ever think that they were in love. The last time their love would be considered in the present, not a past memory. Someone should've taken a picture.

twenty

wet prayers of the red cicada

Basile, Louisiana, Winter 1870

The air smelled different here in the bayous near Basile and L'Anse aux Vaches. Faces hid behind the moss, watching, reporting, speculating. They were here before I arrived, I thought, because they seemed to know the landscape. I could hear them clearly, speaking from unusual vantages like they had done in Saint-Marc. They greeted me kindly . . . the lwa. They were alive in Basile, very alive . . . and loud . . . and maybe too familiar. The pine trees hummed like bumblebees, lamenting their woes, celebrating their proud cones and needles. The waters of Bayou des Cannes moaned low, fat with fish and snakes. Brown murky water that preferred to sit still and wait and watch the life that depended on its existence. The bayou knew it was important. It told me. The cool, tall grass was deep purple-green, thick and humble, succumbing only to paths. I noticed that there were more roads here than in Saint-Marc but not many running toward the deep northwestern area of town. After five months in Basile with my father's legitimate children, that's where I found refuge. Near a large cypress tree. This was to be my tree. And my tree wouldn't beat me.

Claude Boudreaux, my half brother, and the two girls, Marie and Cecile, were older than me. They were adults now, managing their rice fields in hiding with the Atakapas and Choctaw near Bayou des Cannes. The Black Legs moved quickly along the bayous with a strange little black man named Squirrel. He saw me by my tree one day. Someone had told him that I could treat, that I had a powerful, heathen African prayer. He was sick, so I fixed him. This activity of treating very slowly became my routine. Edmund would come along, and though he was younger than me, he became my protector because neither Claude nor the girls would touch me if Edmund was around for fear that Nonc Manuel would find out. My father knew that the other children were abusing me, but he didn't pay it any mind. I was invisible to him. But not to Claude Boudreaux.

Claude was twenty-four years old, married to Christina Papillon from Eunice, and he managed half of the Boudreaux rice farms in the area. Starting at thirteen years old, he took over the farm management after our father decided to skip town for Haiti when word reached him that Mme. Sonnier was with child. He hated me because in his eyes I stole his father, so he took advantage of me at every possible turn. And although Nonc Manuel would've put a stop to this abuse, I couldn't bring myself to tell him or Edmund. I honestly believed that I had caused enough trouble and times were difficult. So I retreated to my tree, and it was at my tree where I first saw it—the red cicada.

As the years moved along I sequestered myself in the area near the tree, setting up a small camp where I slept, cooked my meals, and began receiving visits from the ill for treatment. Edmund frequented my camp most days with reports of the goings-on in St. Landry Parish. The Reconstruction efforts were tearing apart Louisiana and *les gens du couleur libres* in particular, but it didn't bother me; I had bigger problems. Although I was far enough away from the Boudreaux house, Claude saw to it to regularly stop by my camp and beat me for his own pleasure. He knew I would make no report of it, which only emboldened him to more heinous grievances against me. Edmund found out, but I made him promise not to tell. I knew that I had to do something about this, then I remembered something from Haiti while I was tending an old man suffering from arthritis. Etienne once told me that there was a time when we didn't have to say a thing, but it was heard. Just by the will alone, we could take action.

I thought about my half brother. I thought evil things that I shouldn't have. And when Edmund was sent for me to treat Claude for some mysterious illness that befell him, I was nowhere to be found. I had burnings to do, burnings at the direction of the red cicada.

Many treaters were called but none could save Claude, and he succumbed after two months of anguish. My father's son was dead. I could have saved him but I didn't. I didn't have the desire plus I was on urgent business with Squirrel, business that was foolhardy but would prompt a secret night and a secret meeting.

La Grande Promesse
Bois Mallet, Louisiana, 4:30 A.M., July 24, 1877

After the war, Les Americains realized that these free people of color had amassed a significant amount of wealth and land in La Louisiane, yet now we had the same political standing as the freedman, which sent the Democratic Party's White Vigilante League into full furor against us. They wanted our land and sought to disenfranchise our vote, so they employed various intimidation tactics that included murder, rape, and theft. I recalled stories from Saint-Domingue—Toussaint, Dessalines, and Christophe. I decided to take action. If they sought to take our land, land that we'd cultivated from dirt and weeds since they were in Europe, then I decided to attack their lands with fire. From 1876 to 1877, Squirrel and I routinely set ablaze the crops of white farmers in St. Landry Parish, particularly those farmers who were part of the secretive White Vigilante League. But I made a serious miscalculation. The more white farms I burnt to the ground, the more aggressively these whites sought to take the plentiful lands of *les gens du couleur libres.* Whereas I thought I was helping my people, I only hurt them, so the leadership of our community gathered to sort things out—a meeting that would remain a secret for over a century.

We knew that times were changing for the worse, changing for our people and for our culture, which meant that our next moves had to be strategic and clandestine. And I wouldn't have been invited to this meeting if the crop burnings weren't my fault. Rumor held that I had caused Claude's demise, which made me a pariah to other treaters in the area as well as both the Boudreaux and Guillory families. I had broken a sacred rule— never harm your blood, because by harming your blood, you harm yourself. With that realization, I began to drink.

At the meeting were Emmanuel and Edmund Guillory, Jean-Philippe Mouton of Plaisance, Rene Metoyer of Cane River, Pierre Chevalier of Frilot Cove, Leon Fontenot of Bois Mallet, and Narcisse Donato of Opelousas. These men were farmers and businessmen of southwestern Louisiana who had everything to lose if the next steps for our survival were not taken in unison. And although I can't tell you the particulars of what they discussed because they wouldn't say anything in front of me when I was dragged in by gunpoint, I can tell you that at that moment I was conscripted into the medicinal services of our community and the assistance of making whiskey with Fontenot and my father in the woods of Bois Mallet. The men were quick with me and quicker after I agreed. Edmund walked me out of Fontenot's parlor to the front yard, where he was joined by Nonc Emmanuel.

"Go inside, Edmund," Emmanuel told his son, who left quickly.

Nonc Emmanuel and I stood in the dark yard, night creatures about reporting concerns. I couldn't tune them out because I was a bit drunk. Nonc Emmanuel was concerned.

"Jules, I'm sorry I didn't protect you from Claude, but . . .

Claude was your blood like me, whether you liked it or not, whether he liked you or not. And what they're saying you did was wrong. Do you understand that?" Nonc Emmanuel asked.

I nodded. I was ashamed.

"Now, the girls will leave you alone, that's true, but I'm sure you heard that your father has had another child. A son. Paul. I'm entrusting you with Paul's safety, do you understand?"

I nodded.

"*No!* Let me hear it. Tu comprends?"

"Oui, monsieur," I answered with my head still down.

"Leve ta tête and look at me," he demanded.

I raised my eyes to his. So much he had seen. So much he had gone through for his family, for his blood.

"You have a gift, Jules. God's given you something special. Do not misuse it. For what can be given, can also be taken away," he said, then returned to the house.

Paul would be my obligation. This I promised to the lwa.

twenty-one

holy week
(easter basket rock)

Houston, Texas, c. 1985
Palm Sunday

Raymond Earl and Pork Chop said that Mr. Harris had a brand-new set of sparkling, chrome valve cover caps on his dualie truck and if I didn't hurry up and get them, they might very well be gone by sundown tomorrow. Those caps were probably the last of their kind in the whole neighborhood because not a single BMX rolled up Clearway Drive without the small but magnificent mark of distinction gleaming from its wheels. I'd have to go in the morning, adhering to the rules of petty ghetto theft. Pork Chop would have to pump me on his sister's bike because, well, I hadn't finished making my bike; I had everything but the handlebars and the seat. And, of course, the deal was he got two caps and a mini pack of red Now and Laters. Transportation cost. Ten o'clock Mass was fast approaching, so I had to move quick.

We set out early on Palm Sunday morning—the beginning of the blessed Holy Week, marking our Lord and Savior's journey to martyrdom. Across the globe, palm fronds would be twisted and contorted into miniature crosses, transforming Death's instrument into the divine light post. Of course, none of that mattered to me. Holy Week signified closure of the Lenten season; candy and cartoons would soon return to my twelve-year-old agenda. No more fish on Fridays or Stations of the Cross. One more week and everything would return to normal. I'd even complete my bike by then.

Pork Chop waited on the corner with Raymond Earl on his sister's bike with the banana seat and sissy bars and a pair of pliers. I jumped on the back, and we rode off. Raymond Earl decided to jog. *Rocky* had been on TV the night before. Funny thing. It was seven thirty in the morning and Pork Chop smelled awful. The roomy banana seat had the distinct but unmistakable stench of ass. But it wasn't unusual; Pork Chop always stunk.

We rode quietly past parked cars, yards, street signs, and the thick morning humidity of Houston. The targets were in sight, implanted on the wheels of this massive pickup truck. He wouldn't miss them. I mean, it wasn't like the tires would deflate. I jumped off the bike and scooted over to the back wheel. I looked around. Pork Chop gave me the thumbs-up.

THOU SHALT NOT STEAL

Father Jerome had gas that morning while putting on his vestments. Bobby Le Det smirked; he was a rookie altar boy. His momma had just been elected president of the Ladies Auxiliary of the Knights of Peter Claver, so getting little giggly Bobby on the altar wasn't a problem. I shot him a glance to cool it.

Being an altar boy was fresh. First, you didn't have to dress up for Mass because you wore the robe. Second, you got to watch the entire congregation from high up. It felt majestic sitting on the altar—a prince monitoring my subjects. The parishioners responded with a subtle air of deference. Such a nice Catholic boy.

Everything was set. The palms were on the altar, the organ chiming "We've Come This Far by Faith." The pungent incense. The stale wafers. The polished crucifix. All ready to welcome the mighty J.C. to Jerusalem.

This year was going to be special, a grand performance.

Father Jerome was going to ride a donkey up the aisle to the altar. Aisle-seated parishioners had been supplied with palm fronds and were instructed to throw the palms in his path as he approached.

Father Jerome was quiet and routine, but I knew he was excited. He avoided my eyes, sensing my awareness, masking his eagerness to ride the donkey before his chocolate flock—God's very own cowboy.

Ushers opened the chapel doors. Parishioners peeked from the pews. The donkey moaned as Father Jerome climbed on and gave the beast a Florsheim three-inch heel to the ribs. Nobody rode donkeys anymore, the poor animal reflected, its eyes saddened, harkening to its ancestor's burden.

"Bobby's gonna carry the cross," said Father Jerome.

What the fuck? Just how far did Momma Le Det's pull go? I handed giggly Bobby the heavy brass crucifix. He could hardly balance it. Father Jerome charged me with making certain that young Bobby didn't drop the crucifix. He could tell I was not taking the demotion lightly and promised that my cross-carrying duties would be restored next Mass.

"Let's go."

And off we went in full majesty. I saw Mother's shining eyes above heads and shoulders. She was proud, almost tearful. I felt the valve covers in my Toughskins pocket, and I beamed bright as any sun on any Sunday morning. Father Jerome piloted the woeful donkey down the aisle with poise and grace in an altered state, consumed with role-playing. Parishioners gazed upon him with hope and wonder, disregarding his now apparent flatulence and the fact that little Bobby wasn't going to make it down the aisle. His little arms were beginning to falter, palms perspiring, betraying his grip. He hadn't yet discovered the therapeutic nor calisthenic wonders of masturbation. With every step, he feigned a smile while sweat collected on his brow, figuring out the running order of each drop. Yeah, Bobby wasn't laughing anymore. And Momma Le Det sat her big ass on the front pew with her Kodak wearing an obnoxious pre-Easter hat, resting on her crown like a bonnet on a sow. Bobby's big fuckin' day.

As we approached the altar, she navigated her torso out of the pew stage left of the altar. Her stocking-draped thighs rubbed together with each movement, providing an accompaniment for the organ.

At the altar, the donkey stopped. Momma Le Det aimed her Kodak. Bobby timidly leaned forward to bow, then . . . the cross fell over as Momma Le Det snapped the photo. The donkey was startled by the flashbulb and began bucking and hee-hawing. The parishioners gasped. Bobby fell to the floor. Father Jerome held on as the donkey bucked and kicked. And I just watched and secretly counted to eight, waiting to see if he could win the buckle.

I AM THE LORD YOUR GOD, THOU SHALT HAVE NO OTHER GOD BUT ME

Mother was quiet on the way home, probably sympathizing with Father Jerome, little Bobby, even the poor donkey. I felt the valve cover caps in my pocket, the light contraband. I had the remainder of the day figured out. First, I'd grab a snack, probably Doritos and a Capri Sun. Then off into the streets in search of handlebars and a seat. I seemed to recall an abandoned bike in Ms. Bunky's backyard. Of course I'd have to explain to her how I knew about things in her backyard, but it wouldn't be a problem. She was sure to be on her porch drinking malt liquor and listening to gospel.

I swear to God, Mother was driving extra slow. Her two palm fronds rested between us, still segregated and awaiting their holy union. Something was bothering her. I didn't ask any questions. I only thought about finishing my bike. I had even chosen a color—black.

We arrived home, and Father's truck was parked in the yard, which was odd. Mother cut off the car and stared at the house.

Stuck. I heard the ice cream man coming, and it was starting to get humid in the car. She still hadn't unlocked the doors.

I wanted some red Now and Laters.

She turned to me with stone gravitas. "When we get inside, go straight to your room."

I walked in behind her, uncertain of any pending threat, and there he was, sitting at the dining room table drunk as hell. Father.

He was barefoot and his feet were dirty. That's what I noticed first. At his feet, the gray indoor-outdoor carpet was littered with folding money and jewelry.

"I'll say it again. It ain't right. None of it. Them the same dice. You looked at them. Quit looking at me, ole winehead nigga. I don't know you, mister. My name is John Paul Boudreaux. Everybody calls me John Frenchy . . ."

He didn't notice us.

"Yeah, like that pope. Nawh, he named after me. What? Is that right? That's Sonnier's fault, not mine. Take that up with him," Father continued.

"John!" Mother yelled, but he kept going while collecting the money and jewelry on the floor.

"No, dammit. That's for him," Father grunted while collecting the shiny things.

I looked in the kitchen. Maybe he was talking to Nonc, but I didn't see the strange Burning Wood Man. My feet itched. He heard voices whispering, many voices. It was obvious. Mother was stone still—standing at the edge of the Grand Canyon on a plastic straw, waiting to fall or fly.

He put the jewelry in a Crown Royal bag.

"Come here, Sonny," he said.

I stepped forward.

He held out the bag.

"This is for you. All this. I'm gonna give it to him for you. 'Cause you just like me," he said.

"Don't say that, John," Mother pleaded.

"Shut up, woman. This don't concern you. Ti' John. This is what you is. You one of us. So I gotta go pay you off. Comprends? I gotta do this for you," he concluded.

I had no idea what he was talking about.

He rambled some gibberish about "gimme five," and I obliged. The purple Crown Royal bag rested by his elbow next to a half-empty Mason jar of whiskey. His bloodshot eyes swayed from his soiled feet to Mother to me with suspicion, that suspicion that hides the drunk's guilt and pain—that helpless suspicion, transparently built on nothing. I took my cue and headed for my room. I loved Father and didn't want to witness him at his lowest. I wasn't supposed to see him like that; the same way a little boy shouldn't see his mother naked. So I darted past my sticker-laden door to my sanctuary. And no sooner had I fully armed my G.I. Joe men for a Palm Sunday battle royale than the yelling commenced.

I couldn't understand what they were saying, but I found it interesting that Mother's tone was explanatory and apologetic. Hell, Father was the one who was drunk on a Sunday afternoon. Then went the dishes crashing against the wall and the heavy steps to the bedroom. Mother burst into my room and grabbed me by the wrist. She was crying and scared as she half-dragged me out of the house and across the street.

We rushed to the house of our neighbor, an elderly woman whose home smelled like mothballs and cats, but Mother beat on that door like her life depended on it, and maybe it did.

Father burst out of the front door brandishing a shotgun, and he was headed straight for us while chambering a shell. Neighborhood kids started hiding behind cars. Everyone was heading for church or just getting back, and Father was on display, acting a damn fool.

After fifteen minutes of him yelling at us to come out, the police finally arrived. Father sat in the back of the squad car crying off his drunk. Mother answered questions and chose not to press charges. And me? I sat under the chinaberry tree in my front yard, admiring my shiny valve cover caps. Pork Chop, Booger, and Raymond Earl passed by on bikes and just nodded. I could've been embarrassed but didn't have to be—not in my neighborhood. Domestic disputes were about as regular as the mail. Sure, I'd get teased about it tomorrow, but Raymond Earl's dad was dead, Pork Chop's dad was in jail, and Booger's dad was the neighborhood's first initiate in, at that time, a new urban cult—the Order of the Crackheads. I watched Father in the squad car. His head was down as he mumbled to himself. What had happened? What was so important, so critical, so outrageous that he would chase his family across the street with a shotgun? And what was all this business about paying me off?

He raised his head shamefully and stared into my eyes. He was weak, defeated. I knew he wanted to apologize. And I would've accepted it. I wanted to embrace him, let him know that I was still his son and that I loved him. Let him know that he wasn't alone and everything was going to be all right. But then—hold up—*couillon came after me with a shotgun. What in the fuck was he thinking?*

HONOR THY FATHER AND THY MOTHER

Mother methodically transformed the palm fronds into a cross while answering the police's questions. She didn't even have to look. Over thirty years of practice with the palm fronds had resulted in mastery in the fine art of cross making. And after Father left with Uncle Pa-June and after the police returned to their beat and after the neighbors went back into their homes, Mother had finished a most excellent palm cross that Jesus Himself would have been proud to hang upon.

Two hours later, I threw the purple bag of particulars in Sims Bayou. Wasn't nobody gonna pay me off. I ain't Chicken George.

Monday

"Man, yo' daddy crazy."

"Shut up, man."

The ribbing was mild considering Father's spectacle the day before. It was after school, and my comrades and I were scouring the neighborhood in search of handlebars and a seat. Old discarded bikes could usually be found in the backyards or at the sides of houses. We focused on homes that housed teens and young adults who'd abandoned the freewheeling freedom of two wheels for the mature sophistication of four. Kids have the habit of becoming bored with things, especially things that identify their youth. It was Father's suggestion that I build the bike. Sure he could've bought me a bike, but he felt that I would care for it more if I built it.

Despite his episodes of menacing, drunk theatrics and the very distinct possibility that he might be an undiagnosed schizophrenic, he was a sensible, hardworking man who understood that nothing in life is free. Manual labor was truth, a testament to tenacity and character. These principles were infused in every minute work detail he assigned to me. Cut the yard. Fix the roof. Change the oil. Lay cement. By the time I'd turn thirteen, my tenure as a preteen journeyman would surely qualify my admission in most labor unions. If he "paid me off," it wasn't from labor. Mother said drunks say all kinds of things when they're drunk. Father didn't mention it the next day, but I looked for Sonnier, figuring he might be able to explain Father. I couldn't find him, though.

"Marianne Williams's little brother, Willie, in jail," Booger reported.

"Well, he won't need that bike seat then," I concluded.

THOU SHALT NOT COVET THY NEIGHBOR'S PROPERTY

Marianne Williams and her brother, Willie, lived in their grandmother's house. Their dear grandmother passed after choking on a chicken bone. The drumstick. Marianne quickly married Thomas Hackford, a truck-driving man. He was forty-three, she was twenty-two. She didn't mind. The bills were paid and Tom only came home twice a month. So despite Tom's bimonthly visits, she was practically alone, easy prey for temptation's talons. And on this Monday afternoon, temptation delivered itself via a hung UPS driver named Derek. We snuck up to the side of her house. The Isley Brothers competed with the staccato ring of Marianne's ceiling fan, all a chorus for her deep-throated moans.

THOU SHALT NOT COMMIT ADULTERY

Derek was wearing her ass out. And we watched. He was a short, stocky man with Herculean definition. Her windows were up for polite ventilation. Booger nervously looked around, Pork Chop was mesmerized, and then I saw it, sitting along the fence—a dusty, Kmart-brand BMX. Perfect seat. Perfect handlebars.

"Man, what are you doing?" whispered Booger.

Pork Chop had already whipped out his johnson and started stroking. He didn't respond, focusing instead on his member and the two lovers.

"What yawl doin'?" yelled a group of girls.

We turned, Pork Chop with his dick still in hand. And there she was—Royal. Thirteen, wearing makeup and developing what would be, years later, a great pair of tits. The girls snickered as Pork Chop reluctantly returned his gun to the holster. He wasn't embarrassed.

"Yawl peekin' at Marianne?"

"No."

"She a ho."

The girls were in agreement about Marianne's virtue. We walked over to them. The girls stared at me, then snickered. They whispered in Royal's ear and giggled. One of the girls called me over privately.

"Royal like you, she wanna get booty with you."

"For real?"

"For real." That was the best my twelve-year-old mind could come up with—"for real." And Royal just stared at me with a look of knowing. She was older, developed, and already wise to the ways of men. She lived about five blocks away with her mother and little sister. Rumor was that she had already fucked Andre Johnson on Ricky Street. Andre told Maurice and Charles Henry that it was good, saying that she learned how to do it by spying on her momma and watching her uncle's porn tapes. I was getting nervous. What would I say? And more important, what would I do? Royal made her way over and offered standard preteen pleasantries. She asked why I never rode down her street. I proudly announced that I hadn't finished building my bike.

"You know how to build a bike?"

"Yep."

"Nawh-unh, yo' daddy helping you."

"I wish."

"Well, you can walk over, it ain't far."

You goddamn right it ain't far. I'd walk a mile just to finger fuck. She had issued the challenge. I was expected to pay Miss Royal a visit, maybe get some booty, but definitely tongue-kiss. Finally. I'd always wanted to tongue-kiss since I saw J. J. Evans do it on *Good Times*. Tongue-kissing was grown-up business; it wasn't a peck on the lips or some strange routine distant relatives indulged in. Tongue-kissing was the real deal and I—

"Here," she said.

She handed me her number and told me to call. Soft brown, dancing eyes, smooth chocolate skin glistening in the afternoon humidity. Hell, her barrettes even matched her shoes. I had a hard-on and I was proud of it.

The girls quickly walked away with giggles and whispers. Booger had the seat in his hand. In all of the flirtatious distraction I didn't even notice that he had hopped the fence and yanked the seat. Pork Chop shot back to Marianne's window to finish what he had started, somewhat inspired by the girls' visit.

Booger handed me the seat with "Here. Didn't have time to get the handlebars, but just wait until Marianne ain't home." Booger. Always a team player. We looked at Pork Chop.

"How long you figure he's gonna do that?"

Booger shrugged with "Dat nigga's nasty."

I returned home with the seat and headed straight for the backyard. Father was there, feeding his hunting dogs. He looked at me for a minute, then blurted, "You done almost finished that bike. Now what you gonna wanna do is spray that chain and them sprockets with some WD-40, you listenin'?" That was his way of saying—*I'm sorry about yesterday. I'm sorry I showed my ass. You know I love you and your momma.* He looked at the seat.

"Got you a seat, huh? Where'd you get it?"

"Booger gave it to me."

"Umm-hmm. You gonna paint that thing?"

"Yep. Black."

"Well, remind me and I'll pick up some sandpaper and spray paint."

He'd offered his olive branch. Translation: *Please accept my apology, Son. You have the whole week to ask me for dumb shit and I'll do it because I showed my ass on Palm Sunday.*

Tuesday

I couldn't wait to call Royal when I got home from school. The entire day, from homeroom to gym to lunch to sixth period, I thought incessantly about what I would say and how I would sound. My voice was starting to crack more regularly; I was unable to harness the man inside the boy. I had begun practicing my deep voice, usually with strangers. Occasionally I would try it out with Mother, preparing her for my grown version, announcing the forthcoming clipping of the umbilical cord. She thought it was cute, like a child proclaiming completion of his potty-training program. If I forced my breath to the bottom of my throat and stomach, the lower registers would emit, though not amplified but soft and whispery, producing an unintended low, smooth talk. Puberty's way of birthing the preteen bedroom voice.

Father had left a can of black spray paint and a pack of sand-paper on the dining room table. I decided to get a head start on the painting with the tedious task of rubbing off the old paint. I wanted this bike to be perfect, comparable to any store-bought cycle. The sanding process required patience and diligence, guiding the paper through every nook and cranny, revealing the bike's naked truth. It was also cathartic; the back-and-forth motion offered ample opportunity to think about Royal. I already knew she liked me, but what would she let me do? The eight-month-old condom in my Velcro wallet was anxious for action, but it didn't come with an instruction manual. Boy, was I pitiful. So I sanded. And sanded. And sanded until the sun rested in the western horizon to the melody of cicadas, loud TV sets, and the train on Mykawa Road. It was time to call her.

"Hey, Royal."

"I knew you was gonna call."

"You did?"

"Umm-hmm. Trecie and them ain't think you would but I knew you would."

"Oh."

"You like me?"

"A little."

"Why just a little?"

"I mean, yeah."

"How you not sure?"

"I'm sure."

"That's better. What you listenin' to?"

"Prince, 'Do Me, Baby.' "

"I like Prince."

"I got all his slow jams on one tape."

"You gonna let me hold it?"

"If you give me some tongue," I bargained.

Where did that come from? I wanted to snatch those words from the air. I didn't mean to. Well, I meant it, but I definitely didn't mean to say it. Blame my puberty-induced alto. Of course, she snickered, but she was happy to oblige. Like I said, I had all of Prince's slow jams on one tape. God bless the dual-cassette recorder.

Plans were made, and there was no way I could get out of it. I was to pay her a visit the next day at 7:30 P.M. It wouldn't be a long visit; my curfew was at 8:00 P.M. She told me not to forget the Prince tape and giggled before she hung up and so did I. Oh yes, another hard-on. Wow, this was happening too frequently. But I thought it was kind of cool, some grown-man shit. It was the subject of jokes among my fellow sixth graders. The woody. On hard. Saluting. My lexicon had become increasingly filled with a never-ending catalog of words and phrases dedicated to the wee-wee. And just to think, sex ed was next year during gym for one month. One month dedicated to the wee-wee and its cohost, the vagina. I really didn't like that word—*vagina*. It sounded like cough syrup or special vitamins. I preferred *pussy hole* or *coochie,* fun words that made you chuckle when uttered. But I always found it interesting that you wouldn't get a spanking for using *vagina,* yet you were sure to get your ass beat for using *pussy hole.* I pondered that oddity with words as I studied my spelling list for the quiz the following day.

Mother gently knocked on my door and entered. She took a seat and asked how my studying was going. Two days had passed since the incident and she hadn't said one thing about it. No explanation. No inquiries of concern regarding my emotional state. No nothing. Instead, she chose this evening to discuss my religious duties as an altar boy during this Holy Week. *Vagina. Coochie.* I was clearly distracted with thoughts of pulling tongue with Royal, but Mother pressed on. She wanted me to think about the sacrifice that Jesus Christ had made for all of our sins. She wanted me to think about God's love for mankind, demonstrated by offering His boy's life on two big-ass Popsicle sticks. And in some way, by some form of reasoning, I was supposed to love Him more for that. Death. Because of Love. *Vagina. Coochie.* Shit can really get complicated when you're twelve years old. *Smack!*

"Listen to me when I am talking to you," she yelled.

She set out the rules. No laughing or smirking. No staring, look solemn. I would be at the altar for three of the next five days acting as God's emissary, so no funny business. Plus, if I committed one malfeasance in front of the parishioners, she told me she would whip my ass like I had said "pussy hole" to a nun. Well, maybe not with those exact words, but she made her point.

Wednesday

I practically ran home when I got off the bus. It was 4:15 P.M., roughly three hours and fifteen minutes until my big fifteen-minute date with Royal. The plan was simple; sand the bike until it was time to go. It made sense. If I sat around and waited for three hours, I would surely go crazy. My preparatory plans had already been executed, and there was no way I could concentrate on homework with the possibility of tongue-kissing only three hours away. I needed to do something to burn the anxiety and regain my composure. I wanted to be smooth when I approached Royal, pretentious alto and all. I had practiced my alto all day at school and realized that, if nothing panned out with Royal, there were certainly one or two seventh-grade girls who would meet me behind the gym. Then it dawned on me that my whispery, weak alto could be a powerful weapon, a charm.

I arrived home out of breath and tried to leap over the backyard fence but fell.

"Boy, quit that runnin' before you hurt yourself."

Father was in the backyard sitting on a stool. He had sanded off the last remnants of the old paint. His clothes, hands, and boots were sprinkled with metallic enamel dust. His shirt and ILA Local 24 mesh cap were soaked in sweat. His shoulders hung like moss, but the bike shone brilliantly from the remaining sunlight percolating through the trees. It was pure, clean metal, a buff away from chrome. It looked magnificent and new. Father adjusted his focus on me with the calmness and serenity of a master craftsman delivering his goods after toiling with resistant materials.

"So what you think?" he asked, needing acceptance for his penance. I offered my gratitude and he accepted. In some way it was understood between both of us that our peace had been made. He slowly rose and stuck out his palm.

"Lay it on me."

And I gave him five. I hadn't noticed the chalky white smoke bellowing from the barbeque pit. Gotdamn! Barbeque.

DO NOT TAKE THE LORD'S NAME IN VAIN

Seven twenty P.M. I pushed off on my skateboard with the Prince slow-jam tape in my pocket and fearless intensity. A few neighbors waved, but I ignored them. I had to get there on schedule because I didn't have a lot of time. I passed Mr. Harris, who was replacing the valve cover caps that I had stolen. He waved, I ignored him. I passed Pork Chop, Maurice, and Booger, who were sitting on the curb listening to Blowfly on a boom box.

"Say, man! Yawl barbequin'?"

I ignored them. They knew damn well I was barbequing, and they knew damn well Father wasn't letting them in the yard. I passed Marianne Williams's house just as Derek was stepping out of his IROC-Z with a confident smile.

" 'Sup, lil' man?"

"What's up?"

I kept going. Groveton Street. Faircroft Drive. And finally, Buena Vista Way. Damn appropriate name for that street, I thought. Nine months of beginning Spanish was paying off. I saw her leaning against a car in her driveway. She had on hot pink stretch pants, a Guess rugby shirt, and jelly sandals. I slowed down a bit so as to not seem as anxious as I really was. I went over my plan. Wait. What plan? I was starting to panic. I began taking long, deep breaths as I coasted to her driveway. She was smiling; she knew I would come. It's funny how girls know those sorts of things. She started with a play-by-play of her day. My math teacher crying in class. Seventh graders fighting at lunch. Tina Henry mad at Shawna Bryson and ain't her friend anymore. *Vagina. Coochie.* My little sister took my Walkman without asking. Momma got a new boyfriend. *Vagina. Coochie.* I want a black leather miniskirt but Momma say it's too expensive. And on and on and on. And I listened, responding with an occasional nod and a "Is that right?" and a "That's messed up." Maybe to catch her breath or maybe there was nothing left to report, but she finally shut the fuck up just as a huge black tractor-trailer passed by. Her eyes warmed up to me. I had passed the "listening test" and was rewarded with a pause. I guess it was my turn to say something. So I spoke.

"My daddy barbequing right now."

"You lucky."

"I could be a lil' more lucky."

"You brought the tape?"

"Yeah, but I don't know, it's my only one and, you know."

She moved closer and ran her fingers through my shag.

"You got good hair," she remarked. A rare spring breeze rushed upon us like Mother Nature was saying, "Now, nigga! Now!"

So I grabbed her and pulled her closer. She leaned her head toward mine, slightly turning forty-five degrees. She closed her eyes. Why was she closing her eyes?

Mother Nature responded with "Kiss her, nigga! Kiss her!" Her mouth was slightly opened, her wet tongue waiting behind her chipped tooth. I leaned downward, placing my lips over hers, and something immediately happened. Quick movement. Her wet tongue was moving at the speed of light around mine. I tried to keep pace, but her tongue's dexterity would've made a lizard blush. It was warm too. It felt good. It felt grown. My eyes were still open, gazing at her eyelids and the young pimple on her nose. She slowly half-raised her lids; two dreamy slits stared back with a look I hadn't seen before. Desire. She increased the tongue speed and closed her eyes. I grabbed her butt and pushed her young womb to my abdomen. This was fucking fantastic. Good-bye, G.I. Joe. So long, Rubik's Cube. I couldn't believe that I'd been missing out on this. I couldn't wait to get behind that gym tomorrow. *Coochie. Pussy hole.*

THOU SHALT NOT KILL

Pistol shots popped like tin pan popcorn on a hot stove.

Startled, we jumped back and peered toward the intrusion from Faircroft Drive. We looked at each other with a new familiarity. She held out her hand. I pulled out the tape and gave it to her. She grabbed it and held it to her face.

Once more gunshots rang, but neither of us gave a damn.

"Thank you, thank you. I love Prince. My cousin can make a copy," she said.

"That's okay, just keep it."

"Oooh, you so sweet."

She kissed me again, thinking I had made the holy sacrifice of the Prince slow-jam tape. It was chivalrous and selfless, deserving of more tongue and maybe some booty. Well, at least that's what she probably thought. Swatch said 7:54. Time to go. I jumped on my skateboard like the cowboy in the Westerns Father watched religiously. She looked on with thankful, desirous eyes as I pushed off into the sunset and the flashing lights of police and paramedics on the corner of Faircroft and Clearway. As I approached the commotion, I saw the black tractor-trailer parked behind Derek's IROC-Z, parked in front of Marianne's house. Neighbors began to gather as police hung crime scene tape. I slowed down to find out what happened.

Ever since Thomas Hackford was a little boy, he loved big trucks. On family trips to East Texas he anxiously stared out the window at passing cars, waiting for the Peterbilt or the Mack. And when a diesel did arrive, he would furiously yank his little arm until the truck driver answered with a "honk, honk." He only hoped that one day he'd be the truck driver answering a child's request on a long, lonely stretch of road. And as soon as he was old enough, he signed up to be a truck driver. A little boy's wish come true. He drove all the great routes that connected goods across America. It was an important job, necessary to the vitality of the national economy. He understood its importance and was proud to be a part of Uncle Sam's great chain of commerce. After years alone on the road he looked for a wife he could love and nurture, someone he could look forward to coming home to. He found Marianne, twenty years his junior. And one night he came home early, having cut time by driving twenty-seven hours straight from Dover to Houston. Unfortunately he didn't tell his precious wife he would be home for *Dynasty*. He found her having sex in his bed with another man. He shot and killed both of them, then gave his wife one last kiss before he blew his own brains out.

When I got home, Pork Chop, Booger, and Maurice were sitting in front of my house eating barbeque with Father. Booger raised his hand holding the handlebars from Willie's bike. He saw the whole thing but didn't tell the police because he was more interested in ribs.

Holy Thursday

Dramatic death as an occurrence has a way of staying with you like chicken pox that no one can see but you definitely can feel. I had never lost anyone close to me. And by "close" I mean someone I saw several times a week. I remembered my grandfather, Mother's dad. I remembered his old house that he built and the constant smell of King Edward cigars and Juicy Fruit gum. His bathroom and body smelled of Old Spice. He was an old man when I knew him, clinging to his final years of vitality with vigor, filling his days with constant laborious movement to show God that he hadn't yet thrown in the towel. I imagined that Father's golden years would be the same way. I did not have such connectedness with Marianne, but I did have her brother's seat and handlebars. A parting gift. A keepsake from the dead.

The school day passed without incident, my mind still reeling from the encounter with Royal. Was she my girlfriend now or just a clever merchant? I had my duplicate copy of the Prince slow-jam tape firmly in my Walkman, and all day I relived that cherished kiss. Maybe Father at one time felt the same way after kissing Mother, I thought. Surely some similar magic had existed between them, some innocent attraction acted upon without pretension or embarrassment but wonder and sincerity. I had heard that couples do have their problems from time to time. I guessed that was grown folks' business.

When I arrived home Mother was waiting; she had left work early. She had ironed a white dress shirt and laid out slacks, a belt, and socks on the bed. She stood by the door as I commenced preparations. Once again she was quiet and pensive. I started to rush but remembered that Holy Thursday Mass didn't begin for another two hours. Where's my Rubik's Cube?

This evening would commemorate the Washing of the Feet, when our gracious J.C. took time out of his busy schedule with numbered days to bathe the feet of his disciples, including

Judas. Father Jerome had already chosen the twelve parishioners who would be seated at the altar, while newly minted Father Al would be performing as J.C. I, and of course Bobby Le Det, were to assist him as, one by one, he knelt and cleaned their feet with a soft rag and a small basin of water. I didn't know who would be seated at the altar, and I can't say that I was pleased to share my throne with so many. Then, there was a knock at the door.

THOU SHALT NOT BEAR FALSE WITNESS AGAINST THY NEIGHBOR

Mr. Harris was pissed about the theft of his chrome valve cover caps, and neighborhood gossip led him right to my front door. Of course this was a big surprise to Mother, and when asked where I got the caps, I had only one choice.

"Booger gave 'em to me."

Booger, the eternal team player, even when he didn't know he was helping out. I knew that there would be no repercussions for Booger; his parenting factor was limited to his mildly schizophrenic mother, who still walked aimlessly from house to house selling imaginary encyclopedias. I woefully returned the caps to Mr. Harris and awaited whatever punishment I could be charged on such a holy evening. Mother's choices were easy. Belt. Extension cord. She chose the belt and began a beating session that would've made Pontius Pilate say "Damn." In fact, she went overboard, and I could tell that her anger with Father had reared its head in her swinging arm. Never mind that I had to assist in the Washing of the Feet that evening or the dreaded Stations of the Cross the following evening, my crucifixion was happening right now. At least for the next half hour.

By the middle of Mass I wasn't sure who was in more pain: me or the porcelain J.C. with the oil-based stigmata hanging on the wall behind me. I turned to get a glimpse of his face to see what type of expression a man makes when he has iron stakes driven through his body, to see the agony that he must feel from terror and pain, to see the ruefulness of betrayal accentuated by barbaric corporal punishment. And you know what I saw? I saw a long-haired white dude who looked as though he had a stomachache after eating a slice of pie. He just hung there doe-eyed, looking at me. And I, of course, squirmed and rocked, trying desperately to find a comfortable position in the chair because my ass was still on fire. He stared at me, mocking my discomfort with so minimal a punishment. And for a quick second I swore I heard our Savior, the mighty J.C., say to me, "Couillon, that ass-whipping ain't hurt."

"What!" I exclaimed aloud, very loud.

Father Jerome abruptly stopped his homily and glared at me. He wasn't doe-eyed, nor was Mother or the rest of the parishioners.

"I said, Jesus knew that his death was nearing; he knew that he'd have to endure great pain for the benefit of all mankind," Father Jerome repeated tartly.

I quickly took a page from my Baptist friends. "Amen!" I retorted, and Father Jerome carried on. Bobby Le Det looked at me and snickered. I shot him the finger. A widespread gasp emitted from the pews. Apparently many of the faithful, including Mother, had witnessed my offense. This was just great. She was certain to use the extension cord this time. I looked back at J.C., to offer an apology, and he appeared as though he was laughing at me behind his glossy cheeks and doe eyes. Something wasn't right. I looked at Father Jerome, a strong, confident black man from Philly. I looked at the parishioners—black people. Then I looked at J.C. hanging above all of us, and I grimaced. At that point I knew there was something wrong, conspiratorial even, about black folks worshiping a white dude with a smile. From the little bit of history I had learned in school, I knew one thing for sure—black folks had no business trusting white folks. Collectively, white folks had mastered their ability and creativity in treating black folks like shit. When we worked for free they treated us like shit, and after the Civil War they continued to treat us like shit. History didn't lie. And here we were worshiping this guy on a Thursday night, knowing damn well *The Cosby Show* was coming on TV in five minutes. I felt betrayed and became suddenly ashamed of myself for donning the altar boy robe. Black Jesus popped up next to me on the altar and whispered, "Quit trippin'." Then he was gone, leaving a hint of Tanqueray in the air.

THOU SHALT NOT COVET ANOTHER MAN'S WIFE

The time had finally arrived to wash the feet. I was just happy to get off the chair. I hadn't noticed before, but Mrs. Humphrey was showing a lot of cleavage. Mr. Humphrey sat proudly next to his beautiful wife with the great tits. You would be proud too if you got to wake up next to those every morning. But Mr. Humphrey was a jealous man, prone to resort to fisticuffs from a mere glance at his wife. He had been involved in many altercations with other men because of those tits and, needless to say, he was the parish champion. Eight KOs, ten wins, and one draw because Father Jerome stepped in just in the nick of time. And on this special night, Mrs. Humphrey wore a dress with a low, revealing top, and lo and behold she was to play one of the disciples. She was number seven. And when we finally reached her, Father Al took his sweet time as he knelt and caressed her bunion-free feet. I stayed focused. On her tits. That dark, inviting crevice between them seemed to call me, and the pain in my ass was gradually becoming a lump in my crotch. I didn't even notice. But just as Fate had decided to show its ass on Thursday, Luck would have it that Mother had picked out extratight polyester slacks for me to wear, which waited until Mass to betray me.

This woody was something to be remembered. Mrs. Humphrey smiled knowingly. Father Al returned the smile, thinking his Aqua Velva aftershave was working until he turned toward me to be greeted by my hard-on. Oh, and Mr. Humphrey wasn't too thrilled either. Years of keeping an eagle eye on his wife had developed his superhuman vision. He saw the whole thing, and his proud smile quickly vanished. And Mother saw too. After my outburst and then shooting the bird, she was conducting intense surveillance from the pew. What could I do? It wasn't like I wanted any of this to happen. Like I said, shit can get really complicated when you're twelve years old.

During the ride back home, Mother didn't say a thing. I knew she was planning my crucifixion.

Good Friday

Fear is a tricky and misleading emotion. It fools you into believing that opportunities for relief exist when rational thinking clearly prescribes certain doom. I couldn't think about anything the entire day but the horrors that awaited me when Mother would return home. My ass had whelped, I'd lied on Booger, and I flunked the spelling quiz. The more I thought about the recent turn of events, the more I realized there wasn't a damn thing good about this particular Good Friday.

I returned to an empty house and passed time with my Rubik's Cube, twisting and turning the plastic cube with commitment, seeking to achieve nothing but the passage of time before my impending death. Death. On Good Friday. I laughed out loud, recognizing the similarity between me and J.C. I only hoped that when it was over I too would be raised from the dead.

Mother came home, went to her bedroom, and retrieved her mother's set of Rosary beads. The judgment? Novena. All night. I went to my room and stared at the hardwood floor. It laughed at me. So there I was. And there I'd be for the next hour. On my knees, saying Rosaries. She went to the kitchen to start dinner. Catfish court bouillon—Father's favorite. I guess they had made up.

Our Father, who art in heaven . . .

What was "art"? Did God finger-paint and draw robots like me?

Hallowed be Thy name . . .

Tap, tap, tap.

Booger was at my window, and I was certain he was going to jump through and whip my ass.

Tap, tap, tap.

If I didn't hurry up and answer, then Mother surely would come in. I stood up, still mumbling prayers, and opened the window. And there he was. Booger. The eternal team player with tears in his eyes. Mr. Harris had called the cops. The cops visited Booger at home. His mother tried to sell them imaginary encyclopedias. They gave him a warning and left. He wasn't angry but hurt. He told me that I was the best friend he ever had because I would play with him and I didn't tease him about his momma. And that I shared my Now and Laters with him. And that I always picked him for my team. Kickball. "I got Booger." Basketball. "I got Booger." Football. "I got Booger." And he had been a good friend too. He helped me fight Joe Boy last summer. He shared his Frito pies and moon cookies with me. He'd let me play with his toys if he had any. He had practically procured every part of my new bike with only one request—to let him ride it once in a while. He only wanted to know why I'd lied on him, and as much as I wished I had the answer, I didn't. He waited with desperation, needing to understand the betrayal. He asked me what he did wrong, how he had failed me as a friend to cause such a deception. As he stood there, I could hear his heavy breath still heaving with sorrow. I remembered the story of the Last Supper and shamefully realized that I was, in fact, Judas. He slowly walked away more saddened, stopping periodically to look over his shoulder with hope that I'd offer some justification for my actions. I offered none.

Saturday

Good Friday had passed and the pain from my ass had relocated to my knees. Nine Rosaries on the hardwood floor. Both Mother and Father were in great spirits, all night praising God as their headboard rapped against our adjoining wall. Mother explained to me that my penance was served and I was to report to altar boy duty bright and early for Easter morning. She mentioned that a girl named Royal had called but I was on phone restriction for a week. That was all that was said and none of it mattered to me. I took leave for the backyard, disgusted with myself. I found my sparkling bike, the bike that Booger helped build, waiting for me. I grabbed the black spray paint, took a painful knee, and began painting. It would take a full day to dry before I could ride it.

There was a garden in the place where Jesus had been put to death, and in it there was a new tomb where no one had ever been buried. Since it was the day before the Sabbath and because the tomb was close by, they placed Jesus' body there.

Easter Morning

For some reason, when I awoke I felt invigorated, born anew. I had decided that I would tell Mr. Harris the truth with Booger by my side. Sure I'd get my ass whipped and maybe have to say a few more Rosaries, but Booger was a real friend and worth it. Mother had bought me an Easter basket filled with chocolate eggs and bunnies wrapped in foil, knowing I had passed the age of such pomp. For her, it was a reminder of my youthful innocence, which was fleeting at every passing moment. The only thing I wanted to do was take my new bike for a spin before Mass. She said no and I begged. Father walked into the disagreement wearing a suit. He was going to church with us. Wow. He never went to church with us, and then it all made sense. The barter. Catfish court bouillon and sex for an Easter Sunday church visit. Prince slow-jam tape for some tongue. How amazingly mercantile the world operates, I marveled. Father convinced Mother to let me take one spin around the block. Plan set. Take a spin, then go to Mass. Come home and straighten out the business with Mr. Harris and Booger, then ride my new black bike to Royal's house to see about an Easter kiss (Side B would certainly guarantee it). My own personal resurrection was occurring right before my eyes. I practically bunny-hopped to the backyard. I'd do a wheelie. An endo (or stoppie). Burn rubber. Jump off the curb. I had made it through the most unholy of Holy Weeks in one piece.

REMEMBER THE SABBATH DAY AND KEEP IT HOLY

But my bike was gone. Stolen. I couldn't move at first, then I trudged to the front yard and sat under the chinaberry tree. I knew he'd take it, but I pretended for a whole week that he wouldn't. He only needed a reason and my dumb ass gave him one. Booger. The eternal team player. I didn't make any noise or groan because I was now a man. *Coochie. Pussy hole.* And when Mother yelled that it was time to go to Mass, I didn't move. I just cried silently and vowed never to attend church on Easter Sunday again.

twenty-two

yanvalou for bad catholics

Basile, Louisiana, c. 1879

At dusk the wind blows gently through fields of cane, singing to Azaka,* reporting to concerned lwa as the red sky begins its journey to dawn. It feels like Heaven, against a back wet from hours of cutting cane.

The first sugarcane plant was brought to Louisiana from Saint-Domingue and stuck deep into the rich Gulf Coast soil. Sunshine, water, and dirt. Triametrically opposed, maybe. Taken for granted, yes. Left to rot or drown. But intention is the greatest architect and prayer becomes the Prime Mover. In 1751, Jesuit priests planted the first cane in New Orleans near Tchoupitoulas Street, but it only produced syrup. Many planters were still struggling with the failure of indigo. A choice would have to be made. Indigo versus sugar. But in 1794, Étienne de Boré cracked the cane code. Sugarcane would flourish in Louisiana, flourish in the remnants of the indigo industry and bring sweetness to the harsh pioneer days of the burgeoning Louisiana Territory. Soon enough, the tall cane rose high in the low-lying parcels west of the Mississippi, competing with cotton and rice, competing for sunshine, water, dirt, intentions, and

---

* lwa of agriculture in Haitian vodou tradition.

prayers. Some would argue that the introduction of sugarcane in les États-Unis was part of the lwa's commitment to protect their followers in foreign lands. With roots literally planted in Louisiana ground, the lwa would also flourish in the tumultuous early days of La Louisiane, allowing Those-That-Understood access to the mysteries of the Dahomey and Kongo, transforming fields of cane into proud *pito mitans** connecting the spirit world of ancient Guinea to the corporeal world of sunshine, water, and dirt.

Thunk, thunk.

I could hear the unmistakable sound of cutting cane on the Fontenot parcel a mile away. The thin blade of the cane cutter sounded like heavy plunks in an empty tin bucket. *Le sucre sacrée.*[†] In the name of the Sun, Water, and Soil.

My coarse cotton shirt was drenched by 11:00 A.M. We, me and other Boudreaux men, my natural kin, had been shucking rice for two weeks—bundling cut rice stalks with twine, then standing them up to dry with a layer of rice stalks, called "caps," spread atop the bundles to keep them in place. We worked from "can see" to "can't see," measuring movement and time to the nearby cadence of cane cutting.

The Boudreaux family grudgingly accepted me more out of fear than love, which was quite all right with me. I held to my agreement with Nonc Manuel and split my days between treating the ill and pulling tall café sauvage or "coffee weeds" in the Boudreaux rice fields in preparation for harvest. Within a few weeks of treating fever, gout, and various circulatory and digestive ailments, I had earned a reputation as a first-class *traiteur* in Rapides, Lafayette, St. Martin, and St. Landry Parishes. My methods may have astonished onlookers, yet I only utilized

---

* Sacred posts in the dancing space of a vodou temple (*ounfò*) through which the lwa arrive among humans.
† Sacred sugar.

cool *Rada*-influenced* treating learned from the wise *houngan* Etienne Delbeau of Léogâne. And despite what I did to my half brother, Claude, this was all I could remember—the right hand. This was light practice. The hot *Petwo*† was a mile away in the cane fields. And it called to me.

Despite numerous warnings of water moccasins cooling off under the rice caps, I preferred to work barefoot, connecting with the damp mud of the rice fields and its cool, invigorating charge of electric impulses tingling my feet that I'd begun to ignore for the past weeks. There wasn't any form of electricity for miles, but I knew something was prickling my feet every time they touched the ground. It was the same prickling I'd felt when I entered the *ounfò* to make amends with Bondyè.

"Eh, Sonnier! Dîner!" my kinsmen yelled as they broke for the noontime meal. I stood tall and watched as they left.

The breeze blew through the fields, whistling between blades of leaves and stalks. When my kinsmen were far enough away to not witness, I squatted on the damp mud and listened. Nothing. I leaned my left ear to the soil and listened again. I was not alone.

> *Azaka gweli-o,*
> *Azake gweli-o,*
> *O minis Azaka Mede,*
> *Na wè sa.*

It sang.

Joy. That's what I felt. The voices of Saint-Marc, silent since I stepped foot on the *Jeannette,* were awakened. Slowly, I began to remember. I had two heads, as they would say. I remembered

---

* The line of "cool" lwa or spirits in Haitian vodou originating from Ginen (West Africa).

† The line of "hot" lwa or spirits in Haitian vodou deriving from the Kongo and Diasporic slave experience, invoked by firing guns, cracking whips, pouring libations, et cetera.

the left hand. I remembered that things could be changed, and I began to hear the voices. And that song. I began to hear the red cicada.

Grabbing two handfuls of Boudreaux soil, I stood erect and held the soil to Bondyè.

"Par pouvoir Azaka Médeh, nègre montagne-la-voûte, nègre coueh-sih mangnan, nègre aroum'bla vodou, nègre Azaka-sih, nègre Azaka-Lah, nègre Azaka-Tonnerre,"* I proclaimed at the top of my lungs.

Later that night, I busied myself in the henhouse, stealing eggs, or rather, eggshells. And with mortar and pestle I ground the eggshells into a fine powder that I collected in a small jar mixed with cornmeal. Without the guidance of a lantern, I traveled into the woods until I found a clearing where moonlight shone upon the ground. *There must be no interference or obstacle from the ground to the sky.* I lit a cigar and poured rum on the wooded floor, then prayed. I had to remember. I must remember. Etienne said I would never forget, so I asked for the door to be opened:

"Papa Legba ouvre baye pou mwen, Ago eh! Papa Legba ouvre baye pou mwen, Ouvre baye pou mwen, Papa. Pou mwen passé. Le'm tounnen map remesi lwa yo!"†

I opened my eyes, and I could see it in the dark sky, littered with glowing baby angels that took form. Lines. Circles. Arcs. Dots. Code. *In the air for emergencies. To the ground for the left. The right is between heaven and earth with mortal man. The right does not touch the ground.* I remembered everything in the span of a breath, and I was overjoyed knowing that I wasn't alone in this strange land.

I cupped a handful of the eggshell and cornmeal powder, then began—

---

* Invocation for Azaka in Haitian vodou tradition.
† Invocation for Legba in Haitian vodou tradition.

When I finished, I looked at the vévé and took a long, satisfying pull from the cigar, thankful that Saint-Domingue's gods had not forgotten me. The door was now open.

A rotting pine branch cracked near the dark edge of the clearing. Edmund was watching.

twenty-three

becoming

Houston, Texas, c. 1985

Our secrets are our strength and our weakness, which is why
our secrets may only be told to those who will honor them,
those who will use them. It must be passed down so that
the lwa may continue to live. *Nan san ou.** It will reside in
all who carry your blood with or without their knowledge.
But if you tell them, then they must act. Their *ti bon anj* is
awoken with responsibility. Once told, they must honor the
lwa or they will offend the lwa. They must not ignore this
obligation, for it is better for those endowed not to know of
their gift than to ignore what Bondyè has given them. You
must not forget this.

—April 12, 1870. Translated from Haitian Creole.
Advice given to the ten-year-old Jules Saint-Pierre
Sonnier, FMC, by the legendary *houngan* Etienne
Delbeau of Léogâne, Saint-Domingue

Easter Sunday. Who needs it? Big hats. Dyed eggs (some rotten)
hidden behind bushes. Streetside vendors sell baby chickens
with dyed feathers as toys—only for them to be trampled or
smothered by clumsy toddlers with Easter chocolate fingertips.

---

* "The lwa live in the blood."

Chocolate bunnies with big brown eyes and no lucky foot. Easter church services—the Hypocrites Ball—where pews are filled with the unfamiliar, making a showing for the big man Himself, piously attending the funeral-rebirth shindig with newfound conviction. *Oba Kosso!* God ain't mad at ya if ya only show on Easta'. 'Least you went fo' Easta'. Who needs it?

Father took my cue and opted for a rodeo in McBeth about a half hour after Mother pulled out of the driveway rolling her eyes at me. Five minutes of yelling at me to go to church didn't work. I leaned against the tree, who told me I should stay my ass put. She eventually stopped after her perspiration started causing her Easter makeup to run, so she left without me.

I found a small magnifying glass in my pocket and started burning ants.

"Ti' John. Booger stole your bike."

I looked up. Little Donnie Carter stood before me awaiting a prize for his report, so I stood up and punched him in the mouth. I shouldn't have done it, but he was only in town for the Easter holiday. He wasn't part of South Park.

He ran off screaming, "I'ma tell Big Momma!"

"Well, you go on and do that! I'll punch her in the mouth too," I yelled.

Ms. Johnson watched me from her porch, taking slow drags on a cig, jonesing on methadone.

It was in that afternoon hour as families returned home from church with Easter guests, lit barbeque pits, music, laughter, families gathered, ice cream truck on duty, in that hour, I was alone under the tree—angry. J.C. came back from the dead and my bike got stolen. How the hell was that connected?

It was too pretty an afternoon. A Sunday. The same kind of Sunday that Father, drunk and high, chased Mother and I out of the house with a shotgun. It smelled the same way, the air.

My neck ached. I hadn't raised my head since I sat down over an hour ago, so I only heard the hooves pounding perfectly against the pavement.

"Get on. We gonna take a ride," he said.

Father returned home on TJ, quiet, pensive—both horse and man. I learned later that he had tried to rope calves at the rodeo but wasn't able to jump off the horse like before. His calf-roping career was over. His glory diminished. But that wasn't why he was quiet.

I climbed on his horse and wrapped my arms around his stomach. He made that clicking sound and we took off into the streets of South Park extremely fast like he'd done before, but this time he didn't smell like alcohol, dodging cars then pushing onto MLK in the median. He stopped.

"First, I want you to know that I appreciate you helping me with the treating and keeping quiet about it. You been askin' 'bout Nonc and I know I've been avoiding it. I know you met him, and I want you to know that you don't have to be scared of him if you don't want to," he said.

"I ain't scared of him, Daddy," I lied.

"I kinda wish you was scared of him, that way I ain't gotta tell you 'bout him. But you just like me. You curious. I was curious too," he said, then turned his shoulder to me. "You sure you wanna know about him?"

"Yeah, if he ain't gonna hurt me," I said.

"Well, Sonny. He might. And what I mean is ole Nonc is like fire. You remember what I told you 'bout fire when you was little?" he asked.

"You said don't touch it."

"Or what?"

"Or I might get burned."

"And what did you do when your momma wasn't lookin'?"

"I touched it. But I didn't touch it after that."

"You remember when we was trail ridin' and you made the fire?"

"Yep."

"You used the fire, right?"

"Yep."

"But you didn't burn yourself, right?"

"Nope."

"Why? Why didn't you burn yourself like before?"

" 'Cause I learned how to use it. Like a gun."

"Exactly. Like a gun. That's how Nonc is. You gotta know how to use him," he advised, then made that clicking sound and gave TJ a heel. We started trotting along the median on MLK.

He told me that I was becoming a man and that I would have to understand Nonc Sonnier, but I had to learn how to communicate with him. I listened.

Every Creole doesn't know voodoo or hoodoo or whatever the hell else they're peddling in New Orleans. In fact, most Creoles are scared to death of the thought of it, as many unfamiliar people are. Many confuse it as pedestrian Devil worship, although I never learned of anything or anyone called the Devil or Satan with Nonc's practice. Academics and ballyhoos in the French Quarter had sold the popular consciousness on the vague idea of New Orleans hoodoo, practiced by spell-casting quadroons who sought revenge or profit—all part of the bullshit associated with my people due to profit-seeking sensationalists in the New Orleans tourist bureau who marketed "Cajun" and "Creole" as basically the same thing and that gumbo is red unless you add filé. Many of those opportunists were Creoles who wrote verse after study after prose constantly explaining themselves, explaining their Americanisms, their Francisms, and even, strangely enough, their Africanisms—explaining their Creole. But not us.

We were people of the land—the southwestern Creoles—Creoles of the Bayou Country. Azaka's children. We felt no need to explain ourselves to any damn body because not many had been in the territory longer than us, save the Native Americans. We kept to ourselves and our land and our language and our traditions. We created zydeco and didn't know what the hell was a "second line" until we visited our bourgeois couzains in Seventh Ward of New Orleans during Carnival.

The vast majority of us grew up believing in the Holy Trinity and the Catholic Church, yet most everybody from Lake Charles to Baton Rouge knew somebody who was a *traiteur,* versed in the right hand practice. Yet very few knew anyone who was familiar with the left hand, and most spoke of those practitioners as evildoers. What Father told me on that horse ride was plain and simple. I am a Boudreaux man—a natural-born *traiteur* and *sorcier* born with two heads—whose *ti bon anj* (or little guardian spirit) could access the other side.

Oh great, I thought, now I'm a fuckin' witch. What else, Lord? But I tempered my cyncism and listened.

The practice required adeptness in hand signs, drawing, and a working knowledge of basic Creole, Latin, Haitian Kreyol, and various phrases from the Native American and Dahomey tribes, particularly the Kongo. Hand movements and drawings were the methods to communicate with and to summon old Nonc Sonnier. Petitions cost. Grievances are free. On the ground for the left. Off the ground for the right. In the air for emergencies. A well-intended whisper is the loudest. The left hand strikes. The right hand soothes.

I can't tell you exactly what Father told me because it's a secret and Nonc would get mad, but I can say that the sky is a notebook. A notebook with no lines or numbers. One big page. Just one page for petition or grievance. The ground is another page. One big brown page for requests. Please gimme gimme gimme. One page for gratitude. *Merçi beaucoup,* Bondyè. With both pages, I began a correspondence with the stars. It wasn't being Catholic or even religious. It was about knowing that I belonged to something bigger than myself. More alive. More powerful. It was about knowing that some special thing was actually looking out for me. And I knew its name. Not a grand, sweeping name like Jesus, God, Buddha, Allah, Obatala, Muhammad, Krishna, or the like. I knew there was someone specifically assigned to my case. And I could ask him for shit. His name, of course, was Jules Saint-Pierre Sonnier, FMC.

Movies and TV shows will have you think that such things, such interactions, are mere fictions, fanciful follies dreamt up by professionals to give humanity up to two hours of detachment from reality. As a result, we become desensitized, and not in a callous way, but in a handicapped, short bus way. We sincerely believe, most of us when being rational, that we can't physically experience "otherworldly" phenomena. But I knew who he was because Father kept the newspaper obituary clipping of M. Jules Saint-Pierre Sonnier, FMC, underneath his St. Peter prayer card in his wallet. He showed it to me. That nigga been dead since 1953 and still had the nerve to show up, as if I didn't have enough going on already, I thought. And how the hell do you explain this to anybody? You can't. No one would believe you and you'd get carted off to Ben Taub Hospital psych ward in straps.

Nobody ever tells you that it's okay if you start seeing shit. They'll say you're crazy or touched in the head or on drugs. Old-timers in Louisiana might say you have a *cauchemar*. Spiritualists might say you have a guardian angel or a spirit guide. Truth be told, I had all of that shit and his name was Nonc Sonnier. I should've been scared of him because, when I first met him, he had been dead for at least thirty years. But then again, we were related by blood. Fuckin' family.

By dusk, we'd reached Buffalo Bayou, where Father got off the horse. He squatted over the dirt, then looked up at me.

"What we do is secret, Sonny. You can't tell nobody, not even your momma. Do you understand? Tu comprends?"

"Huh?"

"Tu comprends? That means 'do you understand' in our language, in Creole. Tu comprends?" he asked again.

"Yeah, Daddy."

"Unh-hunh. Say 'wee.' That's how we say 'yes.' Tu comprends?" he asked again.

"Oui."

He stood slowly, legs still aching from his failed rodeo appearance, then held his hand out to help me off the horse.

"Descends de ce cheval-là," he said softly.

I climbed down from the horse.

Father took off his cowboy hat, extended a swollen foot forward, and bowed at the waist. I followed, then asked, "Why we bowin'? Nonc do that too."

He straightened up and looked at me like an adult and said—

"Respect."

I felt like his equal. Like he had picked me for his kickball team. Picked me first.

He grabbed my hands.

"These are your tools, Ti' John. Don't ever forget that," Father said, then he continued showing me the practice of Nonc Sonnier, both the right and the left. It was my birthright. When we finished that day's lesson, he told me one last rule—

Dice Rule 6: Never trick or manipulate the dice in the company of those who also understand unless you are working in concert with such a practitioner. (I wouldn't learn the wisdom of this rule until years later, when I was in my early twenties studying medicine in New Orleans and making an unwise but regular habit of fuckin' women born with the veil.)

"Where's God?" I asked.

Father stared through me with red veins of indignation webbing his discolored pupils. "God's right here, Son. Right here with us."

Later that night in the bathroom, I searched my chin for hairs. *Rien.* Sonnier stood behind me examining my chin from the mirror too. I looked at him. He was tall and thin. His skin had unnatural discolorations that showed on his face and neck. God must've taken him in and out of the oven a few times. The undertone of his skin was a tan olive with darker patches scattered about. His hair was like Father's—straight and long but tangled and unkempt. His eyes were small like those of a possum, beady, framed by long bushy eyebrows and dark circles underneath, sunken to the brain, where the lwa dwell.

He looked sinister until he smiled, and then I knew. It was his smile, which he did while I checked my chin, that told me he would never bring me any harm, but I knew he had the capacity for Shakespearean tragedy at the snap of a finger. To operate with Sonnier meant a very close and considerate adherence to his rules, because Sonnier had no problem taking out a family member who lost his way. The Boudreaux tragedies over the past century were almost always attributed to ole Sonnier, and most times those accursations were accurate. Fire and the gun. *Fais attention!*

"I know who you are," I said with as much bravado as I could muster, voice still in the final stages of cracking.

"That doesn't change anything, kinfolk," he responded.

Now I was completely freaking out. My heart was racing out of my rib cage and my neck was on fire. Sonnier leaned over the toilet and cupped a handful of toilet water, then slurped it.

"Why you hangin' around me?" I asked a little more politely.

He placed his hands on my shoulders. They were hot.

"I want you to remember everything your daddy taught you. Then I want you to forget it, every bit of it," he said.

"Why?"

" 'Cause a man without a knife don't get into too much trouble. But a man with a knife gotta keep it sharp."

"My daddy know that?"

"Yep."

"Then why he taught me that stuff about you?"

Sonnier smiled and leaned his head onto my shoulder.

"Three knives are better than two, Nephew. Your daddy and that priest told you about God. I'm gonna show you God," he said with authority and obligation.

The scent of burned wood hung in the air.

I wasn't scared of him now. In fact, I wasn't scared of shit. For the first time, for the very first time, I knew I had something. Power. And I liked it.

We walked outside into the woods. Despite my initial fear of him, Nonc Sonnier was a thoughtful, caring man, or so I thought. I was still making my mind up about him and this strange gift that somehow was connected to him. He knew I was curious.

"How did I, I mean, you end up?" I started but didn't quite know how to ask. Father had told me about his arrival in Basile and his eventual lynching in 1953.

"You're wondering how real this all is, right?" he asked.

"Oui," I responded.

"Most magic starts from love. Not power. Love is stronger, more personal, more intense than anger or hate. The feeling of love brings us closest to God. And with this closeness, we learn who we really are. And what we are truly capable of doing," he said calmly.

I didn't understand, so he elaborated . . .

twenty-four

sweet evangeline

Basile, Louisiana, c. 1881

On May 14, 1881, on a farm near Basile, Ameline Richard gave birth to a fair-haired baby boy whom she named Leon. It was an easy birth for the young Ameline, despite the fact that nobody wanted her to carry the child to term. Nobody except me. Ameline Marie Richard of the Richards from L'Anse des Rougeau—part Cajun farmers, part redneck scoundrels—was the very personification of the virgin Cajun belle, saved from sin and judgment and coloreds. Her father, Jean-Louis Richard, was one of Duson's speculator-thugs charged with ripping off *les gens du couleur libres* of their land in the name of Americanization and the almighty Southern Pacific Rail. For six months Jean-Louis had managed to sequester Mlle. Richard within the curtilage of their small cabin on the banks of Bayou des Cannes. However, M. Richard's floor plan betrayed his noble attempt to preserve his daughter's virtue. Her room was located at the rear of the house with a large window that opened to the listless bayou, which hosted bullfrogs and bewhiskered catfish. Occasionally, a hyper bigmouth bass would spring from the water with eyes set on tempting dragonflies that hovered above, dancing and gallivanting for the honey-haloed ingénue who watched by her window. Sweeter than any spring rain.

On summer evenings she found herself drawn to the open window in her bedroom as *loup-garous* and bayou owls moaned to her delight. Every evening after supper and a Rosary, young Ameline walked past her rag dolls from New Orleans (the ones she petitioned Papa Noël for with extra-special prayer and crudely written letters in passable French) to the window. Bayou des Cannes called to her.

Soon she began waking up with the first rooster to witness the quiet of dawn on the bayou, when even insects are still asleep or drunk or dead. The air stands still at summer's dawn in La Louisiane, still and static to the point of being downright thick. Thick air. Thick bayou air that can intoxicate. And mornings and evenings found Ameline Richard becoming a dedicated toper of the thick air of Bayou des Cannes. I watched her many mornings from afar. Watched her sleep, enthused over the gentle moment her eyes opened to see the morn. And after months of watching her, I was well aware that I was falling in love.

Her father told relatives she was fond of the bayou, which would make any good Cajun proud. Her mother encouraged her, believing that bayou air was healthy for a young girl who was developing into a fine young woman only four harvests since she first bled. Eventually she begged her father to build a daybed that she might put under the window. Of course, he obliged.

The bayou of brown murky murk provided quiet and quick transportation from Mamou to Evangeline Parish on late nights when my work required more time. Squirrel, who owned a durable Indian canoe, ferried passengers up and down the river for coin and had worked out an arrangement with me. I first saw her while transporting Dixie Boy whiskey along the bayou.

So one summer's night in 1880, I worked up the courage to reveal myself. It was the fireflies that carried the invitation that lured her from her daybed like the *feu follet*. She followed, easing carefully out of her window in her nightgown down to the banks of the bayou. I waited for her in my best clothes. And when she saw me at the bayou, she wasn't alarmed.

She smiled and said, "I wondered how long you would watch me."

"Sometimes waiting is more important," I responded as fireflies wrapped us in divine light.

She had heard of me and the colorful monikers—"witch," "bastard," "witch bastard"—but she chose to call me a name I had almost forgotten—Jules.

The following morning at dawn we kissed good-bye. In my haste, I left my medicine satchel on her new daybed, maybe intentionally. Watching me paddle away in Squirrel's canoe, she held my satchel to her chest with hopes that I would return for it. I believe she was in love.

Sweet Evangeline. *A prête moi ton mouchoir.**

A Year Later . . .

My plan was simple: set the Richards' sugarcane field on fire and wait for the men to rush toward the fire with buckets of water. This distraction would allow me the opportunity to steal the newborn before the vengeful Cajun *traiteurs* disposed of him. However, after the flame was set and I had made it across the bayou, I could hear Ameline crying uncontrollably. I was too late. The vigilantes had taken the infant away only hours ago and reportedly buried the child alive, since it was taboo to kill a being with powerful witch blood by hand. Moreover, I learned where the child was buried. By the burning sugarcane field near the cypress tree. My tree.

Some would say that I jumped over the bayou and dashed for the burning cane field. Others would argue that I took flight and jettisoned toward the field in midair. What is true is that I knew exactly where my child was buried. I could feel it. Near the outskirts of the burning field, under my tree, I

---

*Means "Loan me your handkerchief," which derives from a Creole tradition in the 1800s where a young man would hold out his handkerchief to a young woman, inviting her to dance at one of the old-time country dances usually held at homes. If the woman took the handkerchief, they would dance.

feverishly pawed the loose dirt until I found my son, naked and bloody but motionless. I could hear the Richard men desperately barking orders to put out the fire. Other white men, including the Cajuns who'd buried the child, had now joined the firefighting effort. No one noticed me near the cypress tree with my hands stretched to the sky begging for Bondyè's mercy. The infant was not breathing nor did he have a heartbeat. I meticulously used my pinkie finger to remove dirt from his nose and mouth.

Give my breath to him. Take my breath. Give it to him. Let him live with my breath. Let him live. And take my soul, Bawon. Do not dig the grave.

Then I sang from the bottom of my soul. I didn't know what else to do.

> *O kwa, o jibile*
> *Ou pa we m'inosan?*

Don't you see I'm innocent?

I bent down and placed my lips over his nose and mouth, then emitted a soft, focused breath of love and continuance.

"Eh! Come see! The nigger witch is eating its young!" yelled a half-drunk Cajun.

I looked up to find rifles pointed at me, but I ignored them and leaned my ear toward the child's mouth. Nothing. Then I leaned closer to the ground and whispered in the child's ear.

"Grab him!"

The vengeful Cajuns grabbed me. I didn't put up a fight. The child was still. I was defeated. The gods of Saint-Domingue had turned their backs on me, I thought, even after I'd offered my soul. At that moment, I gave up. They held me down spreadeagle and castrated me. Yet I didn't scream or murmur, which gave the Cajuns an uneasy feeling. The fire roared. A defeated man. A ruined crop. A dead infant with the lwa's secrets.

Jean-Louis Richard pushed through the crowd with a rope.

"Hang him, then set his heathen ass on fire," Jean-Louis ordered.

"Fais pas ça!" Nonc Emmanuel barked as he and thirty or so of his kinsmen emerged from the woods with rifles and buckets. Both families had arrived, the Guillorys and the Fontenots—the stewards of Basile. The Cajuns were outnumbered.

"He ruined my daughter!" Jean-Louis protested.

"And you have ruined him. So we should turn our attention to saving what's left of your crop to prevent further ruin to your household," Emmanuel reasoned as twenty of the Boudreaux men arrived with cane knives and guns.

"We have no quarrel with you and your people, 'Manuel. This nigger is a witch, you know that," Jean-Louis said while scanning the crowd of angry Creole men who could either save his crop or cut his neck.

Heavy steps on the forest floor competed with the roaring flames of the burning cane field, yet the Creole faction did not turn their backs to investigate the noise approaching from the dark forest. The white men's astonishment confirmed the noise and the new allegiance. About one hundred freedmen came to the forest edge carrying buckets and knives, not-too-distant flames shimmering off their sweaty bodies, some still carrying scars from slavery, scars they'd received from some of the men present, both white and Creole. But their eyes spoke of their new allegiance, and in their hands they carried the choice. Help or hurt. Bucket or knife.

While the competing factions had their standoff, I had managed to bury my severed penis in the ground and slowly climbed to my feet.

"Mon bébé!" Ameline cried as she ran toward the scene. She screamed when she saw little Leon on the ground. I averted my eyes and threw my hands over my bloody area. I was embarrassed.

Then, in the midst of the night air, among silent men and to the chorus of burning flames, my son screamed.

Ameline threw herself over the infant, and I ran into the burning field, never to be seen again during the lifetime of all present that hot night except for the crying infant, whose mother quickly carried him away through the thick, intoxicating bayou air.

Into the fire I ran, past orange and red gusts, with the burden of knowing that I had broken my bargain with Nonc Emmanuel and others—the bargain I'd agreed to the night of La Grande Promesse. I had caused a commotion, burnt a cane crop, and left a child. I would not be able to return to the community again. As when I first arrived in Basile, I was to return—alone.

PART III

confirmation
and its burdens

To whom shall I hire myself out?
What beast must I adore?
What holy image is attacked?
What hearts must I break?
What lie must I maintain?
In what blood tread?

—Arthur Rimbaud, public domain,
published in 1873, "A Season in Hell"

twenty-five

them your people

*Part Two: Incident at a Catholic
Church Teen Dance*

Black Jesus Ridin' Slab as Seen from Park Bleachers in 1987

A pearl white 1975 Chevy Monte Carlo glided down MLK, clean and glowing like E.T.'s muthafuckin' fingertip, bumpin' Darrell Scott's "14" out of sixteen-inch Fosgates and an Alpine deck. Two light-skinned girls from Missouri City both sat in the front sharing a wing dinner from Timmy Chan's with French fries showered in ketchup, Season-All, and Tabasco. In between nibbles, they smiled and primped with chicken grease glossing their lips. Pretty girls and fried chicken riding in a nice car on a sunny South Park Sunday afternoon, have mercy.

The Chevy was sitting on shiny Tru-spoke wheels with three-point spinners and Vogue tires dripping with bubble gum–scented silicon dressing that left wet candy oil trails in its wake. The immaculately lustrous chrome-spoked rims gleamed from the worn gray cement. God must've shined those rims personally with His very own spit and a white lamb rag. The roof was cut out on both sides for the custom T-top. That's how he liked it. Chop top pulled back so his daddy could see him shining. Ain't he looking good? Ain't he sharp?

"Black Jesus? 'Sup, nigga!" I yelled.

It was Black Jesus behind the wood-grain steering wheel running a soul brother afro pick through his TCB-moisturized shag, other hand on the wheel, leaning hard against the driver's-side door. He honked his police siren car horn and chunked up the deuce 'cause Black Jesus was all about peace, baby, and riding slab.

"Man, who you wavin' at?" asked Raymond Earl as Black Jesus continued down MLK headed to MacGregor Park, probably coming from the Village apartments.

"The nigga that bought the jube," I answered as Raymond Earl passed me a warm bottle of MD 20/20 Orange Jubilee wine wrapped in a brown bag. I took a deep swig.

"You better quit talkin' 'bout Jesus like that, Johnny. You gonna get struck down."

"You ain't see that white Monte Carlo with them redbones in it that just passed by?"

"I ain't see shit. I'm on that jube," he said as I passed the bottle back to him.

By now everybody called me Johnny since a bit of peach fuzz had started collecting under my nose. It had been two years since I saw Sonnier, even though I had made several requests to him. I guess he wasn't going to show up for dumb, childish shit, particularly around Christmas or my birthday. But Black Jesus was everywhere, and he was kinda ghetto. I never told anybody who he was. Some things are best kept secret. But he was around. Two years earlier, when my cousin in Louisiana escaped from jail and picked me up from Little League practice, it was Black Jesus who called Harris County Sheriff's Department. But this same Jesus would buy me beer and wine at the convenience store as long as I had half of the money. I was certain that Black Jesus wasn't "real," but this idea of "real" had begun to change during the past two years. I was beginning to see things.

Father and I regularly treated the ill on Saturday mornings throughout Harris County. As I moved into my second year, he began to let me treat alone while he waited in his truck. The patients were primarily old-timers who were acquainted with our ancient art and placed full trust in me. Sometimes Black Jesus would watch me heal. I think he may have been jealous.

But Black Jesus was never hard to find. MacGregor Park on Sundays. Rainbow Skating Rink on Friday nights. Saturday nights in the parking lot at the Rhinestone Wrangler or The Rock, leaning. Always leaning. Black Jesus always found something to lean on, and when he'd see me, he'd nod and say in a long Texas drawl, "What's happening, dawg?"

He kept everything at arm's length and never once said anything about being holy or tricking miracles or coming back from the dead. To be fair, it's not like I asked him, but I knew because he told me. You see, that was his only problem—he was a tattletale, which meant I had to be careful what I said and did around him unless he was participating too, such as buying my underage ass bottles of cheap wine and cold malt liquor.

I thought about Black Jesus and chuckled a little bit, more drunk than amused. We were sitting at the top of the bleachers by the ball field at Sims Bayou Park waiting on some girls. We'd promised them Bartles & Jaymes but decided to just save them a half bottle of warm Orange Jubilee.

I laid down on the metal bleachers with "Wake me up when them girls get here."

(Orange Jubilee)

"I made room in the icebox 'cause Pa-June bringin' me a whole bunch of ponies," Father announced like he'd just changed Baby Jesus' diaper.

Fuck, he's loud, I thought, while laying down my drunk in my bedroom.

Pony cans, as they were affectionately called, were the beer industry's cute venture in small six-ounce containers that only achieved further alcoholism. That little small can won't hurt you. Father was almost more excited about the arrival of small ale than about his sister's arrival in Houston.

Tante Doralise the Infamous had avoided warrants and lack of funds to find a moment of sobriety to escort her over the Sabine River. She and her motley offspring—all seven of them. There was no occasion for the visit. She'd barge into the lives of her siblings (four in Houston) for food, gossip, and, if she was lucky, a zydeco dance at the parish hall. But her arrival was always treated as a holiday. Dinners were planned, previous plans were canceled, and I was told I would be receiving my cousins—the Augustine boys from Lafayette (Alvin and Michael), Bad-Ass Billy Boudreaux from Grand Coteau, Rodney Boudreaux from Ville Platte, and Satan incarnate himself, Peter "Poon" Boudreaux from New Orleans.

The exact amount of theft and damage to property was incalculable. Various misdemeanors and felonies had been collected in seven parishes to the extent that Fathers James, Guillory, LeBlanche, Malveaux, and Cisneros would no longer hear any of the boys' confessions. Each had earned his own criminal celebrity, and by the time they crossed the state line into Texas, the oldest had only recently turned sixteen.

Of course I was the good cousin, the modern cousin, not relegated to rural rules of mischief. Their accents were heavy, their movements seemed abrupt and rash, responding to needs and wants quickly—brute-like. Honestly, they were embarrassing and simple. I was looking no more forward to their visit than Jesus was looking forward to Pontius Pilate. And Mother felt the same way.

By the time Father got all the particulars from the phone call, Mother had already said three Hail Marys under her breath. She knocked on my door and entered. I pretended I was asleep.

She announced, "Your cousins are coming today." And she wasn't the least bit pleased.

❖   ❖   ❖

"Man, that's fucked-up how you doin' your cousins," Mike said while I was two levels away from the high score on Galaxian at the arcade by my house.

I ignored him. I knew it was fucked-up. We had been at the arcade for two hours. This allowed me the opportunity to avoid calls from my visiting cousins, who wanted to hang out with me. Mike had taken his grandmother's Caddy out for a quick trip to Walgreens and ended up at my house. We had plans to go to a teen dance at St. Francis Parish Hall later, and there was no way I was going to that dance with my cousins. Mother knew what I was up to.

Booger was right over my shoulder, scarfing down a bag of Funyuns.

"Damn, dawg. Back up a bit with them Funyuns," I complained, but he didn't go anywhere.

Raymond Earl was pop-locking by the entrance. Run-D.M.C.'s "Peter Piper" rang, the song's famous chimes marking time with the buzz and bleeps of the arcade.

"Say, Johnny. You heard 'bout Joe Boy?" Raymond Earl asked while doing the tick.

"Nawh."

"Maan, he got in a fight at Videocity and got his ass thrown in jail."

"No shit?"

Videocity was a nightclub for teens at AstroWorld that was located right next to an arcade. It was the perfect spot to meet girls after hours of walking around the amusement park in dizzying rotations looking for familiar faces and females. By dusk, the teen girls collected at Videocity and the arcade, engaging in games of chance that cost not a case quarter but rather a phone number on a napkin or necking in the dark corners of the park. Of course, this cattle call increased the teen pressure already prevalent the minute they pushed through the turnstile entrance with a Coke can or a season pass. Who's he? Who's she? She's cute. He's fine. He runs track for Worthing. She's a cheerleader at Booker T. Questions. Inquiries. Where's your boyfriend at? Can I talk to your friend? Lemme holla at you. Hours of the flirting merry-go-round of AstroWorld culminating in the main event—Videocity. And it's that very pressure, that need to make a connection with the opposite sex with very little experience, that almost always prompted fights among the boys.

But that was AstroWorld. This was South Park. Fighting was a matter of personal politics and predilections. Hooking up with girls was stripped down to whether the girl would give you some. That simple.

Julius, Booger's daddy, appeared out of nowhere, as crack-heads were known to do, and commenced to begging with vaudeville theatrics. Today's performance? Michael Jackson's "Thriller"—move for move. He'd perform the entire video without missing a step. Booger pretended he didn't see him. Raymond Earl and I honored his decision.

"Shit!" I yelled. My flashy Space Defender died a horrible and tragic death to swarming, vicious electronic blinking lights. I looked around as Julius moonwalked out the front door and almost got run over by a white Rolls-Royce. The Rolls belonged to the biggest drug dealer in Houston—Champ Lewis. A black Mazda B2000 pickup pulled up behind him. Raymond Earl's older brother, Andre, got out of the pickup, followed by a tall guy with red hair. They spoke with Champ from the back window of his Rolls. Then the window rolled up and the Rolls drove off—

An empty forty-ounce bottle spiraled toward the redhead.

"I'ma kill you, nigga!"

The lit announcement sign by the parking lot read: "Teen Dance 7 P.M.–11 P.M., DJ Victor Bass, $3." In the upper right corner of the sign was a brown cross, I guess to remind teens that God was charging them three dollars to shake their asses. Sodas were fifty cents. Frito pies, a dollar. Chips, twenty-five cents. Malt liquor around the corner, ninety-nine cents on sale and cold as a witch's titty.

St. Francis Xavier was an upscale alternative to St. Philip's, and barely a mile separated the two parishes. It boasted a much larger congregation, which meant more girls. The teen dances held at St. Francis were more community events rather than social communion for believers. Sterling, Worthing, and Jones high schools were well represented, as well as Thomas and Cullen middle schools. Eighth-grade girls eyed high school boys. Middle school boys watched from afar, trying to decipher high school politics. Folding chairs lined the wall. A dim red light glowed near the DJ booth and, but for the bright light at the entrance, the place was fairly dark, which was perfect for grinding to UTFO's "Fairytale Lover" without being detected. That's what I was doing around 10:00 P.M. Her name? I forgot her name, but she smelled good and let me grind. Patrick was watching from the wall with Raymond Earl and Booger.

By the middle of the song, she'd started sucking on my earlobe. I noticed a few girls watching and pointing. Yeah, I was a real player with it.

"Damn."

"What?"

"My boyfriend just showed up."

At the well-lit entrance, he stood with his boys—the tall redhead guy with a bandage on his head. Ah, *cher bon Dieu.*

(Hot thick bayou air in an air-conditioned parish hall.)

Patrick and I stood near the wall watching. Booger came over.

"Maan. Ole boy say he gonna whip your ass, Johnny," he reported.

"I ain't know she had a boyfriend," I answered.

"I told him that, but he don't give a shit. That nigga crazy too."

"Ain't that Andre's boy?"

"Yeah, but Raymond Earl say he ain't in that shit. You better try to get up outta here 'cause he got like ten niggas from Worthing with him and that girl's in the bathroom crying 'cause he done already put hands on her. You next."

"Maan, yawl ain't gonna help me out?"

And with that, Booger joined the rest of the guys in my neighborhood by the DJ booth. Joe Boy was pointing and laughing. Everyone else just shook their heads. Fuckin' assholes. There was no way I could beat this guy. He had to be at least seventeen and I had a few months to go before I'd turn fifteen.

Nothing's worse than knowing you're about to get your ass kicked. The redhead guy just stared at me across the room while other boys whispered in his ear and pointed at me, instigating shit.

Whatsoever you do to the least of my brothers, that you do unto me—

(Hot thick Houston bayou air interrupts the cool, refreshing air-conditioned parish hall when the entrance door is opened.)

I felt it as I rushed to the bathroom with Patrick in tow.

"Stay by the door and don't let nobody in," I told Patrick.

"Maan, I can't stay out here. Dey gonna whip my ass," Patrick said.

"I ain't gonna be long. Just stay here."

I rushed into the bathroom. I spotted a small window over a toilet stall. Small enough to fit through. I went into the stall and stood on the commode. I pulled the lock latch and gave the window a tug with purchase. Nothing. The damn thing must've been glued shut. *There must be air without interruption or obstacle.* Think quickly. Patrick can't fight. I jumped off the commode and yanked loose the toilet seat, then back up. Eyes closed, I slammed the seat and the window shattered. Perfect. Now stop. Remember. Look. There. There it was, hiding between aluminum eaves and the top of a pinecone tree—the sky.

Make the request in the cupped palm of the right hand three times. Extend the right index finger above the head. Draw the opening to the East. Draw the required lwa or ancestor to the North.

Write the request West of the opening. Recite the Act of Contrition in Latin. Wash the right hand. Three revolutions to the West. Three revolutions to the East. Sign of the cross.

Desperate eyes stared back at me from the looking glass. Was this against God's will? I was scared. Maybe I should have said a Rosary. No time for a Rosary. Shit, God hates me. I'm gonna get possessed by the Devil like Linda Blair. Oh shit. Help.

Patrick banged on the door.

"Johnny! Hurry up, dawg," he yelled.

My damp right hand trembled.

Young Arthur pulled the sword from the stone. Moses split the Red Sea. The Evans family got out of the projects. Black Jesus turned Houston tap into Wild Irish Rose. Linus saw the Great Pumpkin with his own eyes. Perseus killed Medusa and the Kraken. Miracles happen every gotdamn day, right?

I stepped out of the bathroom expecting God to strike me down with His hottest lightning bolt. This was the first time I used the left hand.

(Hot thick air rushes through the air-conditioned parish hall as several enter.)

"Li' John! Boy, where you been?"

At the entrance, the whole rambunctious crew had arrived just in time—drunk, country, and anxious—ladies and gentlemen, back from a statewide tour of terrorizing southwest Louisiana, let's have a round of applause for the Boudreaux boys with special guests, the Augustine Brothers.

They were more than excited to see me. Hugs and hand slaps went around with every other statement—"Johnny, who's that girl?" Everyone in the hall took notice, especially the vengeful redhead guy. Oh, the odds were even, all right. In fact, any oddsmaker or sporting man would wager that I now had a slight edge. The truth is that I actually had a complete advantage. My cousins enjoyed fighting, the same way I enjoyed Galaxian, maybe more. All they needed was a reason, and it didn't take long for them to find one.

"Eh, Ti' John. That girl say them boys over there gonna beat your ass. For true?" Poon Boudreaux asked. I nodded.

"Look right here," Poon said, then pulled his pants leg up to reveal a chrome revolver tucked away in his snakeskin boot.

"Don't shoot nobody in here, Poon," I requested.

He just smiled. He didn't need the gun. He lived in New Orleans in the St. Thomas projects.

"How yawl got up here?" I asked.

"Uncle Coon let us hold his truck," Alvin Augustine answered, "as long as we don't wreck it and fill it up."

Patrick leaned into my ear. "Let's get the fuck outta here."

"Alvin, can you give us a ride home right now?" I asked.

Poon interrupted. "What? We just got here. You ain't gotta worry 'bout that nigga."

"Poon, I just wanna go home. Yawl can stay, just don't shoot nobody."

Ten minutes later, Patrick and I were sitting on my roof passing a bottle of "Ricky's" (Wild Irish Rose wine). No one said a word except "Pass the Off!" I guess the mosquitoes were in league with the redhead guy.

"Funny how you spent the whole day trying to avoid them and they just saved your ass," Patrick said.

No need to respond. Of course I felt foolish. I was so busy trying not to act like family, but I had no idea how deep family went for each other, particularly among the Boudreauxs. I'd learn soon.

And after all that hoopla, it finally hit me. The petition worked!

The next day I sat at a long picnic table covered in newspaper and loaded with boiled crawfish and family. My cousins knew that I had been trying to avoid them, but they never mentioned it. Father knew too, which is why he loaned them his truck and told them where I was hiding. Mother had argued, but Father said that what I was doing wasn't right. Them your people, whether you like it or not, whether they like you or not. Them your people. It didn't matter if I had more or less of anything than them—them your people. It didn't matter if I had better grades in school or thought that I was better than them—them your people. Opinions didn't matter. The fact was—them your people. I looked at Poon and Alvin at the other end of the table. They laughed and joked, forgetful of all the negative things people said about them in Louisiana, forgetful of the warrant out for Poon's arrest in Orleans Parish, forgetful only for this moment, when crawfish brought family together.

"Eh, Ti' John. What was that girl's name last night?" Poon asked.

"I don't know," I responded.

Everyone broke out in laughter.

"We went through all of that and you don't know her name. Couillon," Poon chided and the conversation changed.

My entire life had been one endless pursuit to fit in with South Park and the guys in my neighborhood. Yet when the chips were down it was my cousins who came to my aid. They loved me even though they knew I carried some bias toward them. Poon glanced at me with a rotten-tooth grin. I was ashamed. After Patrick and I left that dance, so I heard, Poon and the guys waited for the redhead guy outside the parish hall and beat him within an inch of his life. Not Booger. Not Raymond Earl. But family.

I looked at the tree near the fence, the tree that I would climb when I was younger when things didn't go my way, and there sat Nonc Sonnier drinking a beer. I placed my right hand over my heart, then extended it out. Sonnier did the same, then disappeared. I turned to see Father watching. He nodded stolid approval.

My wandering ear could hear the noise and commotion and music and laughter on Ricky Street, but I was no longer intrigued. They turned their backs on me and left me with only one opinion—fuck them. They didn't matter anyway because now I had proof. I was a gotdamn witch.

twenty-six

couche-couche et caillé*
for skeptics

Grease. Burning grease in the air. Hog skin. Wild hog skin. Wild hog skin burning in grease. I can smell it. Am I at St. Andrew's trekking along the tree line? No. I hear a fiddle. Scratchy. Buoyant. Delightful. An old fiddle. An up-tempo waltz accompanied by a heavy stomp. I'm facing a forest. The beginning of the forest. I turn around as an anxious hawk falls upon a smelly cottonmouth, grapples with claws. Up they go. Up to that Great Albino in the sky for cottonmouth court bouillon. Behind me I see a large, dried-out field littered with dug-out holes, pockmarked.

People are in the forest. I hear their voices. Familiar voices. I think they know me. It feels that way.

The hawk is a dot in the sky.

I take a step toward the familiar.

I'm in the woods. I'm sure of it. But I'm not in the woods behind my house. I'm somewhere else. It smells different. Burning grease. The fiddle plays, calls. I'm moving through the forest and I haven't taken a step. Hickory nut. Fig. Cypress. Oak. Pine. Pine needles. There's a creek with tadpoles that glow. I drink the

---

* *Couche-couche et caillé*: similar to curds and whey or corn bread and milk. It's cooked cornmeal and curdled or clabber milk.

water from the creek. Sweet water. Over the creek. The voices are louder. *This ain't no dream, my boy.* Someone is singing along with the fiddle. A man is singing in Creole. Past the creek there is a house with a tin roof. The house is made of cypress planks and sits on two-foot wooden blocks. In the yard, several men are gutting a huge hog. The back door is open. On a stump, a tall man with big hands and broad shoulders plays the fiddle with closed eyes. He is my grandfather, Paul Boudreaux. I never met him and have only seen one picture of him, but I know it's him.

I'm in the kitchen now. Several women are cooking and chatting. I listen. Creole. I'm managing. Amédé Ardoin died in an asylum in Pineville. Timothé Fontenot was still missing. The women are stuffing boudin. The Klan are burning down black-owned grain silos. Pa-June got thrown in jail in Elton. Emile Victorian is still courting that Laurent girl. Coon spotted Nonc Sonnier by the creek. *What?*

I'm in the woods again near the house. A little boy sits on the ground digging a hole next to a sweet potato kiln. He puts a clay crock jar in the hole and covers it. I remember what Father said—

"Back in the country when I was small, we'd have a *boucherie* ever so often. We'd kill a couple of hogs, maybe a cow, then carve up the meat and give it out to everybody in the area. With the hog skin, we'd fry it for cracklins. We'd salt the meat, put a veil on it, then bury it in the ground to keep it fresh. In those days, everbody was poor, so we'd have a *boucherie* to share the meat 'cause it was important that we all had something to eat. We took care of ourselves."

"Mon Neg!"

The little boy turns quickly toward the voice.

"Venez ici!"

He looks around a bit frightened. It's the voice. He knows that voice and it scares him. I'm near. I look down at my bare feet. I take a step, then another, and walk closer to him.

"Qui ce que toi?"* he says, voice gently trembling. He's no more than three years old. His little face is dirty, as are his hands and clothes. His cotton shirt is too big for him. He wants to run away, but he sees that I am bigger and I can catch him.

"Fais pas epouvanté,"† I say as calmly as possible.

He doesn't believe me. He looks familiar, more than familiar. His dark, fine hair is pulled back into a ponytail tied together with a worn shoestring. He's poor. He's been poor for some time. *Ghetto.* It's in his eyes, his big chestnut eyes. I know him. I hold out a hand to him. He holds out an open palm. Something is in his palm. Something stares at me from his palm. A red cicada. Quiet. Still. Winged ruby of God. It stares at me. It's hot. I feel it. The child smiles.

"I'm not going to hurt you," I say, but he's circumspect. The fiddle changes tune and tempo, more spirited, more intense. The women laugh in the kitchen. He doesn't understand English. I remember. I slowly place my right hand over my heart, then extend that hand to him, palm to the sky. He understands and smiles with the innocence of a newborn. He places the red cicada atop his head and takes my hand as he rises. *Lève-toi.* He's peed on himself, but he's not embarrassed. He's too young to be vain.

"Qui ce que toi?" he asks again, but how can I tell him he's my father?

"Ton ami," I say.

He smiles and takes the red insect from his crown with precious reverence.

"Baisse-toi," he says.

I bend over, and he places the red bug atop my head. It's heavy, very heavy and hot. Hot coal. But it doesn't burn; rather, it belongs. I don't sense this belonging. I know it like old thoughts. I don't know why. I straighten up. It's heavier but it's

---

* "Who are you?"
† "Don't be scared."

not heavy anymore. It's hotter but it's no longer hot. The child smiles proudly as the red bug on/in my head begins to sing. God watches, doesn't watch. Time passes, doesn't pass.

The child runs behind a shed, then returns with a tattered white baby doll. He holds it out proudly with a bigger smile.

"Qui ce ça?" I ask.

"Bébé Blanc. Ça mon couzain," he says with certainty.

"Eh, Coon! Come see!"

He runs into the house with wet pants and a white baby doll in his hand.

The singing red cicada takes flight through an opening in the sylvan ceiling toward the sun. I'm riding the red cicada—Icarus reborn as a light-skinned nigga boy making good luck with the assistance of the gods, wings melded to the body magnificent with sugarcane juice and wet prayers. The red cicada insists that we won't fall nor burn but shine in the mighty red circle that Jesus secretly scorned for forty days. I look below and see them pointing at me—the dead—all standing in a pockmarked field of burnt cane stalk.

The red cicada stops singing, but its song becomes my heart-beat. My feet are on the ground electric. I don't wince. I don't itch. I just feel the thoughts and prayers of those before me. I am not alone.

Burning grease is in the air. More people are arriving by horse and wagon for meat. Bois Sec Ardoin arrives with an accordion and joins Paul in a tribute to his late cousin Amédé.

I am in a field of tall sugarcane. Muddy ground. The cane looks down on me.

"Bon soir, Couzaine," they say.

The night sky is hot orange. Fire everywhere. Closer.

"Don't run, Ti' John."

"Daddy?"

Dark faces between the stalks. Eyes moving closer.

"Don't run, Nephew."

"Nonc?"

Five. I'ma 'bout to roll a five.

Orange walls of flame surround me. *Breathe it in.* "Take that boy to church." I close my eyes. The cicadas scream.

Then, silence.

. . . *And on the third day, He rose again, in fulfillment of the Scriptures* . . .

twenty-seven

the first noelle

Houston, Texas, c. 1989

Seven in the A.M. by Bellfort and Scott. Crack rock with toast.
Twelve P.M. riding by Yates for second lunch, eat at Frenchy's with
a red bone. Three P.M. for the re-up, the afternoon crowd. Six P.M.
at the car wash on MLK by Jones. Forty ounces so cold that
malt liquor taste sweet. Buy a pack of Kools, a MoonPie, and a
Big Red. Ten P.M. re-up. The late-hour desperate walks like a Star
Wars action figure—stiff, blank, removed. $6,425. Not a bad
day. Hard selling. Soft on slow motion. HPD patrolling. Don't
run, might drop something. And it wouldn't matter nohow
'cause I'm getting slow.

Sitting at the light on the corner of Bellfort and MLK, I
imagine that's what he thought, following the hours like ants up
the evergreen, avoiding obstacles and flying to the moon. I wondered if he ever thought about our childhood, if he reflected. If
he remembered that he was the one whom we all wanted to be.

I hadn't seen any of them in about a year. After a full season
of toiling in the food-services section of AstroWorld, I had managed to purchase my first car—a Volkswagen Rabbit—but at the
cost of AstroWorld losing its fanciful charm. Once enchanted by
its lights and sounds, I now despised the place, knew its secrets,
had soiled its mainstay status in my childhood memories.

I turned to see the Median Man run forward as the light
changed to generous green and I moved along.

He must have thought this, I considered, having a temporary obsession with the presumed thoughts of my old friend. We never talked much after the night of that dance at St. Francis. And somewhere between that night in the old world, the old way of seeing things, and the winter of 1989, my beloved Raymond Earl had become a stone-cold dope man—midlevel, eighties style with all the accoutrements.

Before I reached Reed Road, I saw what looked like Cookie Green and little Anthony Turner setting up Christmas decorations in somebody's yard. Black angels made of cardboard with a plywood backing, mouths open in song, on display for all of South Park to see. They weren't there, the dead—I confirmed from the rearview mirror. But the black angels held their note. *The first Noël* . . .

The angels did sing. I heard them, all of them, even the one that was a little flat. It sounded glorious nonetheless.

I had been sixteen years old for exactly one month and I still hadn't gotten any pussy. The opportunities were there, but I just didn't do it—a lot of heavy petting, though, whatever the fuck that meant. Mike and Russell teased me for admitting to cunnilingus, yet I was the only one of my friends who hadn't taken the glorious journey. It wasn't by design, I promise. Some moments in life require poetry—a sequence of defined opportunity, happenstance, and a bit of magic that fall in place with eerie precision. You never know it's supposed to be like that until it happens and then you know. But you have to be open to magic for those poetic moments to take shape. That's what Sonnier told me. Oh yeah, he came back but in an advisory capacity—sometimes as an annoyance, other times as a savior. It didn't feel weird anymore.

Father and I spent less time treating the ill on Saturday mornings. In fact, we spent less time doing anything together. Neither of us really seemed interested. Besides, people in Houston were more likely to turn to health insurance than to my secret prayers. I didn't much mind anyhow.

"Remember when you stepped on that nail?" I said, breaking the silence in the car.

Mike and I were headed to Wheeler Avenue Baptist Church in Third Ward for his father's campaign event. By now, I had firmly put myself on a trajectory of what I believed would be a successful high school career. My friendship with Mike had thoroughly exposed me to the Jack and Jill crowd, the crowd of the haves, and there was one common denominator among all of their parents—a solid education at a reputable university. So I began aping the behavior of my Jack and Jill friends—the clothes, the conversation, the activities, et cetera. And although I never got into that group, I made sure I was involved in every leadership-developing activity at school with the belief that it would improve my profile when I'd apply to college next year. Young Professionals of Houston, NAACP, National Honor Society, Student Council, and the like. My dress was based on the preppy Kappa fraternity guys I saw at the University of Houston—khaki pants, button-down shirts, and penny loafers. Everything about my manner suggested I was older and ambitious. That was my intention. I had the grades, I just needed to polish off the South Park, purge the ghetto, and let go of Sonnier's archaic practices.

Thirty minutes later in the back of the church, as I was listening to Big Mike make pledges from the pulpit, Sonnier walked in wearing a police uniform.

"Nice outfit," I whispered to him.

"You're the one getting fancy, 'tit négrite," he said while staring straight ahead.

He meant to insult me, so I walked outside, and that's where I found her sitting on the curb smoking a cigarette with a holder and gloves, legs crossed and looking around like she was at an imaginary parade and she didn't have a reason to stand up and watch.

"Not in the mood for politics?" I asked.

"Not really. I'm here with my mom."

"At least you're dressed for the occasion."

"Trying to be funny?"

"Not really. I'm just saying, you have a nice outfit."

"I'm a movie star, darling. Couldn't you tell?" she said while whipping her long dark hair off her shoulders in dramatic fashion. She was wearing a strapless black dress, matching pumps, and long white gloves. She was beautiful.

She stood up and did a few spins, then posed—

"How was that?"

"Exceptional."

"Thank you, darling. You're too kind."

Enjoying her playful theatrics, I approached ceremoniously and bowed—

"Johnny Boudreaux at your service."

She giggled, then held out a gloved hand for me to kiss.

"Enchanted, darling. Simply enchanted. Noelle Auzenne, darling of the silver screen," she replied.

Auzenne. A Creole girl.

"Parlez-vous français, mademoiselle? Ou Creole?"

"Aah, français seulement."

"Formidable."

"A gentleman. Well, I declare," she said, then walked off into the streets. She wasn't waiting on her mother. Noelle Auzenne didn't wait on anybody. It wasn't in her constitution.

Noelle Auzenne was a few years older than me. Her mother was a beautiful artist from Caracas, Venezuela, eclectic by Houston standards. Her father was a black 'Nam vet from Dallas, by way of Breaux Bridge, Louisiana, who sold life insurance door-to-door. Together they were postmodern hippies with huge personalities, competing with each other for God's attention and anyone who happened to be around. Their daughter, Noelle, was an absolute by-product, a tragic fabrication. She was beautiful and witty. The sun always shone on her even when she was sad. She wasn't bourgeois. She was artsy. When girls her age were being introduced to Judy Blume, she was finishing Simone de Beauvoir.

"You know she's crazy. You can see it. That look on her face.

Cookin' crazy vittles in that little kitchenette in her head," Mike offered as I drove him home.

"Crazy or not, she's fine and weird."

"You like that, don't you?"

"Of course I do."

"You probably'll fuck. She fucked a whole bunch of guys."

"Why you gotta rain on my parade, Mike?"

"I'm just letting you know."

"Man, I don't care."

"You get her number?"

"Nawh."

"She lives by my house. You want me to hook it up?" Mike asked.

"Yeah. Do that."

I didn't care what Mike said, she couldn't have been crazier than me. I was the one who had an active relationship with a dead cousin and a ghettoized messiah. Who was I to call anybody crazy?

Later that night, headed back home, I stopped by Timmy Chan's for a wing dinner. I pulled into the little parking lot that reeked of spoiled chicken and grease. Local rap favorite K-Rino was selling tapes from the back of a Regal. He had come a long way from that lanky kid at the St. Philip's bazaar. From rap battles at St. Philip's bazaars to the talent shows at Sterling High School, K-Rino had earned the title of South Park's greatest, and he treated anybody he ran into in the hood as family. Guys would see him on the street and say, "My man K-Rino, that's a trill-ass* nigga," and they meant it.

---

* *Trill:* a South Park term that meant "true" and "real," referring to a stand-up guy. *Trill* was a serious word, a power word, that carried responsibility and purpose, bestowed on those who exhibited the highest virtue of street ethics and honor. It wasn't found in a dictionary (although in later years it would be thrown around like dice), but it was ingrained in the South Park idiom, eventually branching deeper into the greater Gulf Coast black street vernacular, harkening back to a time when a fight was with fists, all pussy was good pussy, and you didn't have a car stereo if your license plate frame wasn't rattling. It wasn't a New York word or a West Coast word. It was our word, our term for validating ourselves—a Southern black Declaration of Relevance.

"Say, Johnny. Check out the new album," he offered, hand gripping his notebook of rhymes. That was his calling card no matter where you saw him, notebook in hand—a testament to his dedication as a Southern rhyme sayer. I walked over to the car and looked in the trunk filled with cassettes.

"I'm performing at Spud's tonight, you should come through, Johnny," said K-Rino.

"Man, I don't get paid until next Friday. I can either buy a wing dinner or your tape, and I can't eat the tape."

"It's cool, Johnny. Go 'head and take it and get me the next time," he said, then offered his album.

I entered the wing joint and approached the dirty counter.

"Wing dinner, rice with gravy, please," I said.

"Two seventy-five!"

The cashier handed back five nickels, so much for the Dig Dug game in the corner, then I noticed him. It was hard to make him out at first because his face lay on a dirty booth table. He was asleep—Booger.

"Wake up, we're going to the rodeo in McBeth," I said, shaking his shoulder, but he was knocked out. In the past year he had become a dedicated primo smoker, joining his late father in the ranks of South Park's addicted. He smelled awful, more awful than when we were younger. He smelled adult awful. I threw his arm over my shoulder and carried him to my car.

In the car he finally opened his eyes.

"Hey, Johnny."

" 'Sup, Booger. You aight?"

"Whatta you think?"

"I got you a wing dinner with fries."

"Yeah, dawg, with fries. Don't know what they puttin' in that gravy."

Then he went back to sleep.

I pulled into his driveway. The house looked abandoned and the front door was wide open. I carried him into the house.

There was no electricity, and the place was a mess. A streetlight cast a piece of light through a busted window. I spotted a couch, where I laid him carefully. He came to again.

"Ain't got no lights, Johnny, but light one of those candles."

I found several seven-day votives strategically placed throughout the house, along with drawing after drawing on every imaginable medium—cereal boxes, cardboard, construction paper, soiled bedsheets, wood, the walls, and the floor.

He propped himself up when I handed him the food and ate ravenously.

"When was the last time you ate?"

"What's today?"

"Saturday."

"Holiday."

"Yeah."

He stopped eating, then looked at me. His big eyes were red with dark circles fencing off everything that meant to harm the remnants of his soul. The redhead guy had killed his father a few months after the incident at the teen dance at St. Francis and his mother was living comfortably in a Harris County psychiatric facility selling encyclopedias and subscriptions to *Jet* magazine. Nobody remembered that Booger was still at home. Ms. Bunky had passed a year after that, and with his mother in the nuthouse, the checks stopped coming in. Booger was alone, forgotten. I had to do something.

"You want me to help you? You know, with my thing I do?" I offered.

"You can't help me, Johnny, 'less you gonna conjure up some dope," he answered, then returned to his food.

He was right. There really wasn't anything I could do for him. I couldn't get his momma out of the nuthouse, clear her mind, and make her a good mother. And I couldn't bring his father back from the dead and beat down his drug demons so he could be the father that Booger deserved. I couldn't. And if I happened to work up some money for Booger, he'd smoke it up by the end of the week. He had already dug up all the money he hid from his father in pickle jars. And if I did help him with his drug demon, then what? He couldn't even read. That's it!

"How about I help you with your reading?" I asked.

" 'Tha fuck I wanna read for, Johnny? Huh? What tha fuck did anybody ever write down that meant anything to me? You tell me. I can count, add, subtract, divide a lil', and multiply by two, five, and ten. Besides that, I draw. You know me, nigga," he said.

He wasn't embarrassed. He was honest.

"That reminds me. I got something for you, Johnny," he said suddenly with a hint of excitement. He rushed to the floor and milled through drawing after drawing. I examined the room more closely, discerning the fanciful drawings. This was all he had left.

"Here it is," he said, then handed me a drawing on manila paper—three little boys throwing rocks at a dragon.

"That's me, you, and Raymond Earl having a rock fight with a water dragon, and see here, we have gun holsters but we got rocks in the slots for bullets. See?" he said.

"We winning?" I asked.

He put his hand over the drawing and stared directly at me with extreme gravitas—

"We never win, Johnny. Never. Even when we think we winnin', we ain't," he said.

"It ain't all that bad, dawg. I mean, we try."

"Gotta keep trying, Johnny. Some of us, at least. Gotta keep trying. You gotta keep trying. Aight? Promise me that. Promise me you gonna keep trying. Try for me," he asked.

"Nawh, dawg, don't say that. You can do anything if you put your mind to it," I offered.

"That's what the grown folks say to people like me. They say that shit to keep people like me from robbing their ass or hittin' 'em upside their head, but it ain't true. They wish I was dead."

"Don't say that, dawg."

"Nawh, maan. Even out here when I be walkin' around, I see people and they don't say nuthin'. They just look past me like I'm invisible, like I got invisible powers and shit. I ain't do nuthin' to them. When we was little, they would speak, let you drink out their water hose and tell you not to get hit by a car. But now, shit, when I see them same people, the same muthafuckin' people, it be like I know they wishin' I just get hit by a car and die so they won't have to look at me. What I do to them, Johnny?"

"You ain't do nuthin', dawg. People just fucked-up, that's all."

He looked at the drawings on the floor, then looked up—

"I'm sorry about your bike back in the day, Johnny. Remember?"

"I ain't trippin'."

"Nawh. I shouldna' done that. I just figured you and your daddy would build another one."

He started collecting all the drawings into a pile. "I worry 'bout dying, Johnny."

"Don't say that."

"Nawh, dawg, I worry 'bout that shit. I don't think God want a nigga like me up there, you know?"

"Quit talkin' crazy."

"I'm serious, Johnny. Think about it. Look at how my life done played out. I didn't want any of this shit to happen and look what happened. And then they say God controls all this shit and I'm like 'Damn, God. What the fuck?' Man, what I do to God?"

"You ain't do nuthin' to Him, Booger."

"Damn right I didn't do nuthin' to 'im. So how I'm supposed to believe He gonna look out for me up there? I don't wanna be no ghost."

Amen to that, I thought.

"I'm going away, Johnny, 'cause I'm tired of these muthafuckas lookin' at me crazy."

"Where you gonna go?"

"You know where I'm going."

"You can't go out there, Booger. Ain't no food."

"All kinda food out there, Johnny. You know I used to hunt out there."

"Don't do that, Booger. For real."

He stood up and walked toward the door. He was waiting for me to leave.

"Thanks for the wings, Johnny. You my nigga."

I didn't want to leave, but I left.

The next morning I went to Booger's house with breakfast but he was gone—as were all of his drawings.

The angels did sing. They sounded like an electric bass and a Moog synthesizer tuned to the key of the Isley Brothers with only a rim tap to pump the blood. Bad-boy bass slow-dragging with a drowsy Moog with too much to drink. The license plate rattled like a squeaky bed frame during an afternoon romp—the Isley Brothers as angels, angels as the band. And maybe she's the only one in the concert hall, alone, wearing a corsage on her bra strap. A gloved hand resting on the empty chair to her left, waiting for her mister. Noelle. All of this was going on in my head as I finished wiping down my car, bumping to "For the Love of You." Damn, there was something about her—something grown, something risky, something ghetto. But there was also something fresh about her, invigorating—cut grass in the morning. Wet and green and new. Actually, she didn't smell like cut grass but Chanel No. 5, and she knew how to wear it. I could tell.

That little brief encounter felt like it had history behind it and in front of it. It hung in the air after she left sashaying down Scott Street. You could almost touch it, but I was reluctant. Who was she? What was she? A taunting tease or a delectable gamine?

Father walked out of the house carrying an ice chest.

"They ropin' in Hitchcock, wanna go?" he said perfunctorily; he knew the answer.

"Nawh, I got plans."

He didn't stop or turn but rather continued to his truck. He'd stopped giving a damn whether I went to the rodeos with him almost two years earlier. I think we both were hurt by this development, both realizing that hero worship was dead.

An hour later, I drove past the Shrine of the Black Madonna church heading into Third Ward. I felt better. My plan was working. Today's extracurricular activity was a docent internship at the Museum of Fine Arts—a nice addition to the activities section of any college application—but I was also trying to get a closer look at the good life.

Five minutes into my museum tour a hand was raised in the back of the crowd. I couldn't make out the face.

"Yes, the person in the back."

"What time will we start the finger painting?"

It was Noelle in short cutoff jeans, shell-toe Adidas with neon fat laces, and a tight-fitting Houston Oilers T-shirt. Some in the crowd chuckled while she held deadpan, then winked. I wanted her.

The others on the tour pretended not to see, and that was a lot of pretending. Even in cutoffs and sneakers she carried an air of quirky elegance—Audrey Hepburn as the Creole ingénue in *Brunch at Brennan's* (the director's cut). Directly behind her on the wall hung a massive Monet—a picnic scene of sorts—pixilated pigments so delicate the gentle lady's skin appeared ripe as the peach Noelle slowly nibbled on after the laughter settled and more than a few wandering-eyed husbands nursed sharp pinches from their wives. And who wouldn't look? Peach juice dripped off her hand, down her forearm, and onto the floor, by design, of course. It was downright pornographic.

"No finger painting today, sorry," I responded.

"What a tragedy." She smirked and continued with her peach.

As I guided the tour from room to room, she drifted in the rear, entertaining herself. Sometimes she'd skip or waltz, but not for my attention or anyone else's; rather, she was entertaining herself. By the time we reached the African exhibit, she had begun a full conversation with herself. A few tourists noticed, probably figuring her performance was part of their museum admission, considering her discussions that afternoon were all related to the artists on exhibit and the work—silly anecdotes, rumors, unknown facts, minute details, all manner of bizarre almanac shit. And the funny thing was the level of detail she'd proffer: Picasso's personal physician inspired some pieces after a torrid tryst with a blind pantomime from the Basque Country who only spoke in Latin, or Diego Rivera once urinated for over four minutes. By the end of the tour, the inner wall of my mouth was bite-laden after two hours trying to maintain the astute composure of a studious and informed junior docent for the Museum of Fine Arts. What brashness! What ridiculousness! Seems Noelle was as hilarious as she was beautiful.

By 5:00 P.M., we sat atop Hippo Hill in Hermann Park, adjacent to the museum, eating ice cream sandwiches. I wanted to hold her hand. Other couples in the park were doing it. Walking up the hill, I had moved closer, brushing her elbow, then playfully held her waist from behind as she made exaggerated steps up the grassy hill that faced Miller Outdoor Theatre.

"Whatcha doin' there, Captain Schoolboy?" she asked with her back to me.

"Playin' caboose," I answered, a bit coy.

"How come you get to be the caboose? What about what I want?" she spat, although I had no idea whether she was serious. Her constant shifting of characters made it difficult to determine when I was dealing with *her,* and I had parsed that much even though I hardly knew her.

She stopped and turned to face me. A children's theater troupe was rehearsing *Le Petit Chaperon Rouge* on the stage behind me. She narrowed her eyes and pursed her lips. It was cute.

"Answer me! Answer me, Rhett, or I'll never get any sleep," she protested with a careful Scarlett O'Hara as she closed her eyes and threw her forearm to her brow with "Catch me, Rhett. I confess I do feel a spell coming upon me."

She fell into my arms.

What big hands you have.

The young thespians applauded along with damn near everybody in earshot.

Head in my arms, she slowly peeked, then stuck out her tongue.

"If you're gonna play with me, you're gonna have to give me what I want. Can you handle that?" she asked.

"Depends on what you want."

"Just say yes. It don't cost nuthin'."

I looked around. Most everyone still watched our hillside soap opera.

"Are we still in command of an audience, Rhett?" she asked with a slight grin.

"Appears that way."

"Then say yes, silly goose, and kiss me."

I looked into her deep brown eyes—she was dead serious. And crying.

"If you kiss a girl while she cries for want of love, you're granted one wish if your heart is pure," she said while managing a desperate smile.

Cher Catin.

"First, tell me what you want," I said, attempting to regain control of the moment.

"An ice cream sandwich."

We kissed. Just like in the movies. Our audience applauded.

On that sunny Saturday afternoon on the side of Hippo Hill, I fell in love or what I believed to be love at the time.

My, what big teeth you have.

The better to eat you with, my dear.

Now an hour later, as we sat eating ice cream sandwiches,

counting clouds, and watching children's theater, Noelle gave me a hand job and told me she knew.

"You know what?" I asked.

She took her time. I waited, naturally.

Finally, while cleaning her left hand with a hand wipe from Church's Chicken and not even glancing my way, she responded, "I know you're a witch."

A prête moi ton mouchoir.

twenty-eight

les haricots sont
pas salés

L'Anse aux Vaches, Louisiana, c. 1928

Rice go down
Liquor go up
Corn stay the same,
Fish and bread keep a po' man fed,
Rev'nue man keep a-comin'.
Rice go up
Liquor stay the same
Corn aplenty,
Black snake hidin' under dem caps,
Rev'nue man keep a-comin'.

Paul Boudreaux had more on his mind than the cases of whiskey hidden under the sacks of rice in his wagon as he watched Emory Lafleur and Pitre Benoit figurin' with fingers on Benoit's porch in L'Anse aux Vaches. Paul sat in the wagon some thirty yards off the porch on account that Pitre Benoit didn't 'low na're nigger twenty feet from his front do', business or no business. Paul could've been amused by his leery Cajun customers attempting to appear as though they were negotiating the price of shine, but he knew that it wasn't really a negotiation if'n they negotiatin' by theyself. But the figurin' on the porch was only performance—Dixie Boy whiskey price was nonnegotiable. And how the hell that nigger Boudreaux keep gettin' his hands on that stuff? most white folks in Acadia and Evangeline Parishes wondered.

Dixie Boy whiskey was mighty powerful shine, sold from Mobile, Alabama, all the way to Fort Worth, Texas. It was a flavorful, smooth sipping whiskey with a distinctive label that hosted a proud Confederate flag waving in the upper left corner and a cornfield in the background with a few black figures scattered in the field, probably working for free. In the foreground, an elderly white man in a white suit with a black shoestring tie leans against a wooden barrel with a big grin. The image harkened to the antebellum days and naturally was a big hit with white folks throughout the South. Not a respectable white home in the former Cotton Belt that didn't have a bottle of the famed elixir tucked away somewhere. And despite the Prohibition Act, law enforcement throughout the South turned a blind eye to Dixie Boy whiskey, including most Southern-born revenue agents.

Yet despite its widespread notoriety and loyal patronage, the maker of the whiskey had remained a mystery. Many believed that the whiskey was manufactured by the Ku Klux Klan with proceeds funding the rogue outfit's terrorist activities until the Grand Dragon publicly denounced the allegation since liquor was illegal in the eyes of God (the Protestant version) and man—Mr. Grand Dragon was also a pastor, hallelujah. Others theorized that Dixie Boy was being distributed by shifty Italian mafia guys in New Orleans from stills operated by Florida crackers, although experienced palates insisted that the taste clearly indicated local birth. Either way, no one really knew who made Dixie Boy whiskey or the resulting profit (which had to be massive), at least nobody white.

Pitre Benoit spat on the ground, then turned to Paul and nodded, signaling that the deal was complete.

Paul yanked the reins against the hinds of his old mule, King Arthur (a name he remembered when Clarice LaChapelle read

fairy tales to his young boys, Simon and Arnaud). The two moseyed over to a grain silo at the edge of the field. He squinted at
the sea of green before him—green beans. A few brown hands
waved at him above the green sea—brown butterflies hovering
over the green sea looking for a branch to rest their wings. He
didn't wave back.

Tommy Lastrape, the field foreman, approached Paul with a
generous smile but not because of the Dixie Boy in the wagon
(Pitre Benoit wasn't partial to sharing firewater with niggers and
Injuns); rather because of the gunnysack resting next to Paul.

"Eh toi, Boudreaux. Ça va?" Lastrape asked while motioning
two field hands to unload the wagon.

"Ça va bien."

"T'paré?"*

Paul nodded from a distance still removed, burdens on his
mind. He delicately grabbed the gunnysack as Tommy placed a
worn bullhorn to his lips and blew a low, guttural note. The field
hands in the green sea stopped working and looked at Tommy.
They recognized King Arthur and double-timed toward the silo.

Paul watched the green sea. A hot breeze blew.

Sixty or so field hands gathered around a low-hanging tree.
Tommy placed a wooden crate in the center. Paul wouldn't look
at them, too burdened. He stared at the gunnysack in his hand,
then raised his sullen eyes to the waiting crowd. He slowly sat on
the crate and removed an object from the sack—a fiddle.

"Joue la danse de vieille temps!"† Tommy yelled as he started
with solid hand claps separated by heavy foot stomps, yet Paul
didn't respond to the cadence, rather remained preoccupied
with the fiddle in his lap.

"Chanse, Boudreaux!"

He closed his eyes, remembering. He raised his hand and
Tommy stopped. Paul took off his straw hat and placed it over

---

* "Are you ready?"
† "Play the old-time songs!"

his heart, then began a blues lament in Creole. But he couldn't finish the song. Sometimes the sorrow weighs too much. The only way out is joy. He started clapping and foot stomping, then belted into an energized a cappella of the famed *juré* song *"J'ai Fait Tout le Tour du Pays."*

An hour later he traveled a back road along a bayou toward Basile, rejuvenated by the midday performance. His spirits were up until he noticed somebody coming out of the woods into the middle of the narrow road. He slowed King Arthur to a halt.

"What you want?" he asked.

"That's no way to talk to your people," the figure said, "particularly when you know I been calling on you."

"You know where I live."

"I ain't goin' 'round there."

Paul pulled out a cigar, bit off the end, and lit it, all the while eyeing the rude obstruction in the road.

"You gonna move? I gotta get home," said Paul.

"Gimme that smoke."

Paul took the cigar from his mouth and threw it at the requester. It fell on the ground.

"You know I can help you with your problem," said Sonnier as he bent down and picked up the cigar.

"I ain't weak for Satan, Nonc. And I ain't no hoodoo," said Paul. "And you better stay away from my family."

"I made a promise, Nephew. You know that," Sonnier responded.

Paul quickly pulled out a double-barreled shotgun and trained it on Sonnier, who wasn't a bit bothered.

"You ain't the first of my kin to threaten my life, Nephew, but pulling that trigger ain't gonna make a damn bit of difference. So I reckon we gonna have to make a deal," Sonnier said calmly, but Paul didn't lower the gun nor dismiss Sonnier. He listened.

"That woman of yours ain't right, ain't never gonna be right. But I get one of your boys," Sonnier said.

"Ain't got but two boys, Nonc, and I need them for farming."

"Ain't talkin' 'bout them," Sonnier answered. "Talkin' 'bout down the line."

Paul stared at his uncle for long seconds, then lowered the shotgun and spat on the ground. Sonnier moseyed back into the woods with a trail of smoke in his wake. Paul made a sign of the cross, then yanked the reins so King Arthur could return to Camelot.

Cher Catin

When they first married, he'd wash her hair in the front yard. She, sitting in a pine chair that he had constructed from the same tree that he built their wedding bed from, slumped over a tin tub resting on the dirt ground between her legs. A *jogue* of sweet well water poured from his hands above her—young Mme. Marie Boudreaux—his new wife. The sweet water carefully trickled off each delicate strand of her silky auburn tresses, dampening the muddy floor below, her soft beige bare feet mired in forgiving Basile soil. The wet gown clung to her bounteous breasts as he stroked her hair with gentle wet fingers. He separated the locks into two parts and carefully braided her hair into plaits, never too tight. And they'd talk the way old married couples do—about everything and nothing. *Tout les choses et rein.*

A month after Simon, the youngest, was born, she stopped talking, doing. She stared at the ground when he plaited her hair—silent.

A curious dragonfly watched from a tree branch—

When evening comes, he picks her up and places her in the pine-framed bed. He ties twine to her foot and secures it to the bedpost with a small bell so she doesn't wander.

In the mornings, while the babies are still asleep, he takes her out of bed and places her in a chair covered in burlap while he changes the sheets she's soiled during the night. He takes her outside at dawn and washes her while she stands in a tin tub, then dresses her in a clean cotton gown. Next, he washes the soiled sheets and hangs them to dry. Afterward he takes her back to bed and places one end of a string of worn Rosary beads in her hand. She grips them. The other end he holds as he recites the Rosary to her. She hasn't spoken in fourteen months. But he's never left her side nor their pine marriage bed, which he continues to share with her despite her incontinence. He is her husband. And she is his wife.

As the cock crows, Clarice LaChapelle, a petite young woman from Lafayette who lives in Elton, arrives to tend the babies, Arnaud and Simon, and Marie. Clarice will never see Mme. Boudreaux's soiled sheets, gowns, nor body, even though she's offered to assist. Paul is her husband. Marie is his wife.

Month after month, he watches her deteriorate to a shell of flesh and bone. In the early stages, he found life in her eyes, but now that life has reduced to vacant orbs. His wife is gone.

Paul could see the white truck in front of the house as King Arthur trod along the muddy lane to their home. She had been to doctors in Opelousas, Lafayette, and even Baton Rouge, but there was no hope for her and a decision was made.

Joe Guillory, Edmund's son, told him to consult with Sonnier, but Paul steadfastly refused. He was ashamed of the wily heretic Sonnier.

"I'm a devout Catholic, Joe. I cain't be foolin' 'round wit' Nonc. I got children ta raise and dey gonna believe in God the Father and go to Mass. If dey need somethin' I cain't provide or dey cain't provide for theyself, then dey gonna ask God, not Nonc," Paul argued, yet knowing that wasn't altogether true.

Clarice held both babies as two uniformed orderlies helped Marie out of the house—the house Paul began building with pine the day after he talked with Marie's pa. The babies didn't cry. They didn't know their mother's voice, hadn't grown acquainted with her touch. But they knew Clarice's warm tone, her precise, melodic French that caused them to giggle when she humored them after *dîner*. They knew her small, soft hands that changed their cotton diapers and bathed their bottoms and held their little lives to her bosom under the Evangeline sky and deep green Acadian forest of the little home fifty yards from the bayou.

No, they did not cry, nor did she, Marie Boudreaux, who lost her sense of self, space, and time the minute Paul strummed a note on his beloved fiddle. By the time he realized that the fiddle was driving her crazy, it was too late. He figured she was just being ornery about his fiddling—a complaint that he believed wasn't anything but a show for attention from a new wife. Other married men told him to expect that from her once they made the sacrament at St. Augustine's. But when she stopped talking, doing, he knew something was wrong.

Paul jumped out of the wagon and ran to his wife. The orderlies stopped.

"Cher catin. Mwa regrette, ma catin," he said slowly as he caressed her shallow cheeks and kissed her lips for the last time.

They took her to the asylum in Pineville, where she died months later.

But that night, as he sat on the porch smoking his pipe, he pulled out the fiddle that he wasn't allowed to play around her and stroked a heartfelt lament while Clarice rocked the babies to sleep.

Clarice LaChapelle never left.

twenty-nine

saint lo

Houston, Texas, c. 1990

I was starting to feel a detachment from South Park that was growing day by day, but it was difficult to break free without feeling some sense of betrayal. No more school days in better parts of town. My high school, Jesse H. Jones Senior High School, was ten minutes away from my house on St. Lo Road. St. Lo—Capital of Ruins. The high school was no exception. However, the school district planted an accelerated program at the site amid the ruins, calling it "Vanguard." And somehow, I was in this program. Smart kids were bused in from all over town for small classes taught by those same highbrow white folks who taught at St. Andrew's. Many, though definitely not all, were liberally educated rednecks who got hip and high at Bryn Mawr, Wellesley, Yale, Barnard, and the like, then returned to Texas in the 1970s with long hair and doctorates, versed in Ginsberg, Rimbaud, TM, granola bars, Acapulco gold, yoga, and muthafuckin' cowboy boots. Just like the folks who taught at St. Andrew's, sans the New Testament Christian proselytizing. Don't get me wrong, they were well-meaning teachers and administrators, but many carried an air about them that they passed down to many of the Vanguard students, mostly white kids who had never been to South Park. Sure, we were the smartest kids in school and kept the overall GPA pretty high at Jones, but we (all of us, regular and Vanguard) were there to get an education on equal footing. And because some of these teachers were promoting a pejorative view of the kids in the "regular" program, kids from South Park, I began to detest those teachers although they would never know it. There was no reason for them to know. I mean, fuck, they were deciding my grades and I was on a mission.

Despite certain Vanguard teachers' efforts to segregate Vanguard students from the regular students, at least in spirit, their attempts were futile and a bit of a farce. Architecture was the equalizer. We, the Vanguard program, were not sequestered off in some random annex building sitting on cinder blocks. No. We were right in the main building with the rest of the students, sharing the same hallways, water fountains, cafeteria, restrooms, and locker rooms. These coveted Vanguard students were forced to mingle, which worried those certain teachers and administrators in the Vanguard program, not to mention more than a few white Vanguard parents who didn't want their golden savants mixing with the natives. The irony was hilarious.

But for me, it made school days at Jones feel like some strange musical theater of the absurd. Mr. Boret, my history teacher of pure Cajun breeding, constantly blasted classical music from his room with the door open before school, after school, in between classes, and during lunch, which turned the entire black inner-city public high school, at least on the north wing of the first floor, into an insistent cinema verité with illuminated nigga moments that would have brought James Evans back from the dead to electric-slide to Wagner's Ride of the Valkyries. In fact, it made everything at school kind of strange. Troubled students who had problems with each other usually planned their fights around the stairwell across from Mr. Boret's classroom for the musical accompaniment of whatever type of drama was scheduled. Fight over a stolen chain—Chopin's Nocturne Op. 9, No. 2, in E flat major. Talking shit after shooting dice in the bathroom—Verdi's "L'onore! Ladri!" from *Falstaff*. Boy breaks up with girl—Orff's "O Fortuna" from *Carmina Burana*. Girl breaks up with boy—

Bach's Suite for Orchestra No. 3 in D major. Good grades after cheating on a test—Vivaldi's Concerto for Violin in E major, RV 269, Op. 8, No. 1, "Spring": I (Allegro) from *The Four Seasons*. And a well-publicized fight practically required *Peer Gynt*'s Suite No. 1, Op. 46: IV, "In the Hall of the Mountain King." It didn't take long for Mr. Boret to figure this out. By the time I matriculated in his homeroom, I'd learned that he occasionally looked out the small window in his door to check the stairwell so that the right song was playing. I mean, he'd been at Jones for over twenty years, back when it was white, so he had the program list. I mean, those songs listed above weren't random. Sure, he'd hit the intercom and call campus security if things were getting messy, but he was never in a rush, even that time when Peanut shot that gun in the air. Beethoven's Symphony No. 5 in C minor, Op. 67—"Fate": I (Allegro con Brio). I mean really, who's gonna turn that off once it gets going. Certainly not Mr. Boret, even when the police were trying to take a statement minutes later.

Inside the classroom, though, I was somewhere different with different people, a foreign land with foreign people all around me, including the beautiful dark-haired girl of Venezuelan origin with gorgeous brown eyes that were making me think of Noelle as a righteous boner arrived in the middle of Dr. Levy's lecture on Richard Wright's *Native Son*. A car passed by on St. Lo blasting Mantronix's "Fresh Is the Word"—all bass—vibrating the windows. Fluorescent lights hummed above. The Mexican American kid sitting behind me wore too much cologne—eyes melted on the Venezuelan girl, probably. Meanwhile, the class was trying to figure out why Bigger killed that white girl, the Venezuelan girl was blushing because she knew I was looking at her, and I couldn't stop thinking that something was probably not kosher about getting a hand job in public while watching children's repertory theater.

"Aah. Mr. Boudreaux, would you care to add?" asked Dr. Levy, with his heavy Woody Allen New Yorker accent. Boy, he must've been lost, I thought when I first met him, until, that's right, somehow by the grace of the Almighty Albino in the sky, Dr. Sol Levy had a connection with somebody in my family. Naturally, he took a special interest in me. I played it cool, but I didn't read the CliffsNotes.

"Just 'cause you poor don't mean you just gonna kill a white woman," I spouted with a hint of good ole Public Enemy–inspired black nationalism. And he read right through it.

"What does that have to do with what we're talking about?" he asked.

"I'm just sayin', white folks treated black folks bad back in the day," I continued.

Some of the white kids in class tensed a bit, then squinted their eyes slightly to appear compassionate and interested in the black struggle, bless their hearts. Hell, they were surrounded. Miss Venezuela smiled again. Fuck, I should've worn the beret. Me and La Morena. Sitting in a tree. K-I-S-S-

"Mr. Boudreaux, while I'm sure we're all interested in your recitation on race relations back in the day, I assure you my times in Mississippi during the sixties with your cousin were . . ." he drifted.

Who? Nonc? Hell no, it couldn't be, I thought as Levy explained that as a student he'd marched with one of Mother's cousins. I, of course, had to bring in a full book report on the entire ridiculous episode of the fine Mr. Bigger Thomas. But I didn't care. I couldn't stop thinking about Noelle.

I loved kissing her. It was intense immediately, and I knew that I was going to fuck. We never talked about it on the phone like I'd done with girls before, slow-jam tape playing in the background waiting to see who would fall asleep first. No. We talked about art. She knew way more than me and I was the docent. We talked about jazz (particularly Miles Davis's *Bitches Brew*) and being free and Thomas Meloncon's stage plays with "How Do You Love a Black Woman?" and Nikki Giovanni poems and finger painting and Paris and Rome and

Diana Ross's *Mahogany*, and, of course, the ballads of the artist then known as Prince. Oh yeah, I knew I was gonna fuck. I could smell it like July Fourth barbeque in someone's backyard when you pull up in the front driveway and take a whiff. *Cher bon Dieu!*

We started going everywhere together. I was happy to follow. My heart was open for the first time. A young flower blooming, petals tasting life's sweetness with gentle, virgin lips still fresh off life's titty milk. The only thing was that I didn't know when or how to get it, waiting on the man with the green flag or a whistle or something. I asked Sonnier for advice over a game of dominoes. He stopped.

"Leave her alone," he said.

"Why?" I asked.

"I said leave her alone. And that's all I'm going to say. Don't play with me, Ti' John."

"Johnny. They call me Johnny."

He grabbed my throat.

"Don't make me hurt you, Nephew," he said. "This ends with blood. Real blood. Are you prepared for that? Huh? You got an *envie** for blood?"

"I ain't scared of shit," I answered.

He released me and stepped back to examine me.

"Don't you hear what they're saying about her? Aren't you listening?" he asked.

"You know as well as I do that they lie a lot. Always with that bullshit. Most of them. I'm not gonna jump just because they're trying to fuck with me," I answered.

"You done got cocky. And ain't even done shit yet," he said, then backed up and took a deep bow. "There may be hope for you yet."

"That's all you got to say? Huh?" I asked.

"You're still clean, Ti' John. Remember this time. Hold it

---

*A hankering or desire.

tight in your secret place, 'cause it's not gonna be that way for long," Sonnier said.

"I play by the rules, Nonc."

"That's what you think? You 'play by the rules'? Shit, Nephew, you don't play at all."

thirty

repast road

A month later after studying all night at the downtown library, I drove Noelle home. We pulled over at Hermann Park for a makeout session.

I got deflowered. *Cher bon Dieu.*

It felt better than the time I kissed Royal. The whole world suddenly made sense and I felt like a man, but that feeling wouldn't last long.

She killed herself a few weeks later after her mother discovered she was fucking her dad too. I was shattered.

We are not promised angels. We are not promised jubilee. The first Noël, the angels did sing but not for me. No, we are not promised angels, only fortunate to catch a glimpse of their fluttering wings.

Red Nigga Witch

A roach is such a brave, stubborn creature. Reckless but committed. Maybe too committed. Crawls the inches, pulled by a desire to know, to gain. Sometimes they die. Other times they live. But not the one skittering across my kitchen floor. Crunch. That's what it sounds like when you step on a big, fat, dark brown Houston roach. Crunch . . . like the muthafucka got bones or something.

She was dead but her mother never said anything to anyone about what she discovered. Noelle overdosed on her mother's Nembutal—Marilyn style. My little darling went out like a movie star. And now I had an *envie* for blood. Mr. Auzenne's blood.

Lil' Ant was the first to tell me, but I ignored him. Then Cookie and Adelai Green. Lying, all of them, I thought. I was too busy being in love with her to accept it even though she gave me a few signs. Your first love is always blind because the emotion is so new. Nonc did tell me that the dead don't lie, and I told him to stop sounding so cliché. But Boudreaux men have to learn things for themselves, that's what Father always said.

Now I sat at the dining room table staring at the dead roach on the kitchen floor, contemplating my next move. Father came home.

"Ain't you supposed to be at school?" he asked.

I ignored his question and told him what I knew. He listened, then I asked—

"Can you do this for me?"

He stared at me for a bit, probably feeling sympathetic, then answered—

"Son. I've given you everything I know and now you're gonna have to work with what you got. But I can't do this for you and I advise that you leave well enough alone. That business right there don't concern you."

Then he left.

I couldn't ask Nonc because he'd already warned me. Mother was no help either, too consumed with comforting my grief with Rosaries. I hadn't spoken to hardly anybody since the funeral except for Father.

I remembered the first person I treated by myself. It was an old man with eye disease who was going blind. I cured him in thirty minutes. And I was so proud. But Father told me to never take pride in the work because it was Bondyè's doing, not mine. "God works through us, Ti' John. It ain't you," he said.

But Nonc said that the left hand was our personal doing, but not to mention it to others lest we be burned at the stake. I figured if God let Noelle die because of her father's actions, then . . .

I went to the dirt for her father. He killed himself three days later. I hoped God wasn't watching. Black Jesus quit talking to me for about two weeks.

Noelle came and went like Joe Turner, but now her story would be my story, transferred to my psyche—a new employee of my personality. I hurt.

Kinda pitch-black.

Aramis cologne.

"Bless me, Father, for I have sinned."

Olde English 800.

"Ti' John. You been drinkin'?"

"Yeah."

"Ti' John, I'm really sorry for your loss but drinking isn't the answer."

"You should talk."

"I've been prayin' for you, Johnny."

"Oh yeah. Prayin' to who?"

"Who do you think?"

"I don't know."

"Well, who do you pray to?"

"I pray to my gotdamn self, Father Jerome. Me. Johnny-muthafuckin'-Boudreaux. And guess what? I answer my prayers. How 'bout you, Father Jerome? Huh? The big man answers your prayers? Your horse ever come in?"

"You've lost your way, Ti' John."

"Fuck you, man."

Pitch-black.

I never considered myself a tough guy, let alone a killer. But that's what I became in the spring of 1990. It wasn't difficult,

merely suggestion placed in a troubled mind—a slight push
over the cliff—but I felt like a monster nonetheless. The stench,
I could smell. My hands, heavy with blood. It happened in the
woods behind my house. I hadn't been back there since Booger
and I scoured the trees for the red cicada years ago. We found
the rare insect that afternoon. It called to me.

Who are you?

"I'm John Paul Boudreaux the Second," I said aloud.

"Who you talking to?" Booger asked.

I pointed at a branch on a sickly oak. Quiet. Static. Regal. A
red cicada. Booger moved closer, but he didn't want to catch it,
but, rather, witness its beauty, hold the memory against uglier
thoughts for balance.

Am I in danger?

"No," I answered.

Near a creek I found a low bush planted in moist dirt. No
weeds or grass. Three fifteen in the morning. I cut off the flash-
light and felt the soft forest floor. I trembled. *God's watching
you, boy,* Paul Boudreaux chided. I smelled burning wood,
intensely.

"Nonc! That you?" I yelled.

Silence but for the hum of the train on Mykawa Road. I was
still here in the woods. I still smelled him, burning wood.

"Nonc, where you at?" I yelled but no response.

Thou Shalt Not Kill.

I made the first mark on the moist ground, then traced it
with Mother's cornmeal.

What we do is secret.

A fiddle sang "Blues de Basile."

"Pépère! Is that you?" I yelled. He doesn't know my voice.

*My children gonna believe in God the Father and the Holy
Trinity.*

I smelled his pipe.

*Whatsoever you do to the least of my brothers, that you do
unto me.*

"I'm dead, Ti' John," his voice wailed.

"No, you're not, Nonc. You're here with me," I answered.

Tithonus's lament for love. We don't die. My hands were hot. The gun and the fire. No burning bush saying don't do it. No appearance from Nonc explaining the repercussions. I thought of her on that particular morning when we skipped school to watch dragonflies in Adair Park. We waited until the park closed and walked hand in hand through the woods until we saw small dancing lights.

We sat on the ground and watched them until we fell asleep. At dawn, she arose and put her head on my chest. The first thing I saw was my reflection in her deep pools of black-brown eyes. We listened to each other breathe until our breath whistled in unison, feeling out heartbeats until they were one.

"If things were different, I'd have your baby, Johnny. I want you to know that," she said as gently as words can pass through lips.

"What kinda things?" I asked.

"Fucked-up things, Johnny, so don't ask. Don't ruin the morning," she responded.

We stared at each other for five more minutes with pauses for the occasional blink—nothing lost, still locked on to each other, heart, breath.

"I've made up my mind. I'm gonna love you forever. Whether you like it or not," she offered.

I believed her.

I was too angry to cry in the dark. I asked and they told me. Noelle's father would die soon.

As I walked back home from the woods, cold drizzle fell. I would never be a farmer. The ground doesn't yield for the mark of Cain. I listened for the red cicada but heard nothing.

When I returned to bed I wanted to pray, but I knew nobody would listen. Cain. Untouchable. Unforgiven. Walks alone.

The next morning I began to see them more frequently—the dead.

* * *

I was driving down MLK. Black Jesus riding shotgun. Sonnier was passed out drunk in the backseat. Black Jesus leaned against the door, talking to himself about ninety-nine-cent tacos at Jack in the Box and Spike Lee's *School Daze*.

"Hold tight. I ain't seen it yet. You be talkin' too damn much," I blurted.

"That shit's good, dawg. Make a nigga wanna go to college," he responded.

At Old Spanish Trail Road the traffic started. Sunday afternoon at MacGregor Park. I was angry that day. Angry and uptight and lost. School was recall and dice games. Social was talking on the phone and dates, petty dates, talking about nothing, not really selling myself but reminding myself that something better was going to happen if I let it. If I got out of my own way. If I didn't use the magic. Something was wrong with it.

"You need to go to church, Johnny," Black Jesus asserted. I ignored him—didn't want to mismanage my expectations.

"You sittin' in the car right now so let's have church," I said, "You know what I mean."

We edged on in traffic surrounded by competing car stereos—a thousand angry bands marching slowly to the majestic pines of Third Ward. A thousand black faces encased in depreciating glass and steel, marching to fellowship, marching to communion. The Median Man jogged by wearing a shirt reading: "Reparations Now!" An old black man sold barbeque out of his wayworn pickup hauling a huge, black, bellowing pit in the parking lot of the Shrine of the Black Madonna. Faces in cars yelling at one another like rowdy inmates in a crowded cellblock waiting on rec time. Waiting to get out of the cell, the car, the hood. Anxious to see and be seen. I turned up the radio, looked around for the cops, then took a long swig from a forty-ounce.

I could've saved her, Noelle. She should've told me. Why

didn't she tell me? Sonnier said I could've saved her. Black Jesus said it wasn't really cool to kill yourself. It didn't matter anymore. Noelle was dead.

You never recover when your first commits suicide. You blame yourself for imaginary reasons, knowing that those reasons are fiction but wanting to believe something. Maybe it's Catholic guilt. Maybe I was her swan song.

Socially, the incident had a life of its own, caught in the rumor mill. Some girls were scared of me, whispering that I literally drove the girl crazy. Creole girls learned of my grandfather's first wife from their grandmothers. He drove that po' girl crazy with that fiddle, chère. Don't mess with him. Dem Boudreauxs are crazy, dey witches. They were right.

Noelle and I never talked about that witch business after that day on Hippo Hill, but I knew she was drawn to it. She wanted it for herself. Why else would we fuck when she was on her period? It wasn't about pregnancy. It was about power and the perception of power. A young woman's foolish fantasy after too many love-magic poems and baths for Ochun's blessings and Betty Wright–laced all-night spades games with her strange empowered ghetto-ass girlfriends who smoked joints in feathered roach clips and sucked off bourgeois Bellaire High School boys to Edith Piaf and incense (never strawberry).

If you know what that means, then you've met one of her kind or you're part of the tribe. They come in all shapes, races, languages, and lifetimes—la belle femme extraordinaire. Adventurous. Distant yet intimate. The smartest woman you've ever met even though you know damn well she's probably diagnosed or she's so fuckin' gorgeous that everyone simply ignores the fact that she's a gotdamn lunatic. Usually unacknowledged parental defiance is the undertone, but that's nothing. She'll make you actually believe she's the first woman you've ever met in your life. You might believe it. She wants you to believe it, and it has absolutely nothing to do with your momma. She wants you to believe in her. And by your believing in her, she will, if she's really part of the tribe, convince you that you believe in yourself. This is her gift. La belle femme extraordinaire. Without surgery or séance, she becomes part of you and you never notice. She only asserts one thing with a smile—lips rounded, curved—

"You never needed me, Johnny. Remember that. You never ever needed me. I know about you, darling. When you touch me, when you're inside me, I know. I know that you're the one that's fucked-up in the head. You think it's me, but nawh, lover, it's you. And you know it too. You one of them voodoo niggas. You don't need me."

That's what she said after I came in her and she told me she'd "jump off the Transco Tower before she'd bring," and I quote, "my red nigger witch baby into this world if black folks ain't got no power." She wasn't sad or angry. She was serious. And while I helped her douche out my little red nigger witch sperms while she sat on the commode, she offered plaintively—

"He ain't gonna let me have no baby, Johnny, so don't worry."

I was too relieved to ask *who*. I should've asked at that moment. Learned what hid behind her eyes. But that particular night there was a Jones Gents' party at the U of H student rec center, and I had plans to meet my boys there. I should've asked.

Now, after the funeral and the rumors, I was alone again in the tree, listening to the train and the mouse, listening to them whisper about me. *Them*. The dead. They whispered in Creole and the tongue of the Dahomey. They were noisy.

I was drunk at MacGregor Park, sitting in my car parked at a gas station on Calhoun Road. Music blasted. "Hey, Johnny!" The faces spoke but I didn't hear them. The train roared from the ground, screaming. But I tuned it out—numb—all of it. My seat was dropped, but I kept my head up, looking around for her, knowing she'd never show. I wasn't present or tardy. I was absent, floating in a flood of brown faces, and I still couldn't swim. I had nothing to ask for, prayer.

Cassette deck tuned to Funkadelic with the bass ramped up,

Garry Shider crooned slowly about *water signs*. Noelle was an Aquarius.

By the middle of the song, Raymond Earl had come out of nowhere to my car door holding out a handbill, saying something about Donnie Carter. I was so fucked-up on lost and alcohol, I said, "Who?"

I took the handbill. Donnie Carter looked back at me. The handbills were everywhere—

"Donnie Carter—Missing."

In black and white, his face was up and down MLK, stapled between posters for the Fresh Fest at the Summit and posters for an Angleton rodeo with special guest championship bull rider Arthur Duncan, who'd be signing autographs. I had seen the flyer all over the place, but I never really stopped to look at it.

Donnie Carter was last seen at the Greyhound bus station in Downtown Houston. He was wearing black parachute pants and an orange OP. Donnie liked orange.

We blamed Pork Chop for Donnie's disappearance later at the car wash by MLK and Bellfort. Everybody was there and everybody was quiet. Niggas don't say much when they're feeling guilty. Shoulda tuffined him up. Shoulda showed him how to fight. Man, not after some muthafucka done tow' your booty hole open. Raymond Earl glared at Pork Chop.

"Why yawl lookin' at me?" Pork Chop pleaded.

But Raymond Earl didn't care. Nobody ever talked about Lil' Ant. Nobody could admit it because nobody saw it. Pork Chop tripped the little dude, causing him to fall into traffic and die. And Pork Chop never answered for that and this enraged Raymond Earl. They were gonna fight. We could see it. Raymond Earl had that look—he was gonna swing on Pork Chop in the name of Lil' Ant and Donnie Carter. I got in my car and left just as Raymond Earl started taking off his shirt.

thirty-one

dirty polaroids

On the brochure for the University of Pennsylvania, a nice multicultural collection of college students stand around a bronze bench where a bronze Ben Franklin sits, one arm atop the back, bespectacled, reading bronze notes. The students smile. He grins too. In the background, a stone building hides behind serpentine ivies. The cobblestone pathway is aged but clean. The bronze is polished. The smiles appear genuine. I looked closer, studying the pigment on the glossy card stock, fingers tracing the running ivies upward. Upward. Upward. *Wake up.*

The voices were louder now. And they were not in agreement. The only voice I recognized was Sonnier's. Clear as a bell. Grouchy. Vulgar. I wanted to believe that I'd played no part in Noelle's death or her father's. I needed to believe that.

It was after two o'clock in the morning. I was drunk again, parked on North MacGregor Drive looking at houses that I always wanted to grow up in. Mike was in one of these massive homes gambling with bourgeois boys—the kind with BMWs, big allowances, and not a care in the world. And I was drunk because I hurt, the world frightening me, taunting—both Polaroids—flipping back and forth like butterfly wings. I was seeing things that I shouldn't see. And why not? Violence was an intimate friend, an old friend.

I glanced at the brochure again. The bronze smile everlasting. Father knew what I was going through, though we never spoke of it. He was one of us—Those-That-Know. I was one of him and he, one of me, connected to Sonnier, bound by blood and profane DNA. Why me, God? Don't you see I'm innocent?

I placed my hands on the steering wheel and examined them. All they had done, ruined, held, built, caressed—pointing with cosmic authority and designing a new truth with intentions. This can't be right.

The forty-ounce was empty. Damn! Can't buy it after 1:00 A.M. He whispered. I listened.

"Ti' John! Ti' John, wake up!" Mother yelled while banging on my bedroom door.

Ten minutes later, I pulled onto the dirty road of South Park nothing. The barn had burnt to the ground, killing all thirty-six horses—burnt alive like witches.

Father sat on the ground crying as the fire inspector surveyed the damage.

"Hey. You all right?" I asked Father as I slowly walked toward him. But he was distracted, drawing on the dirt. I moved closer and passed a foot over his grievance. He stopped. I took a knee.

"Don't do that," I told him.

He wouldn't look at me.

On that day, John Frenchy gave up drugs, alcohol, and the gift. The Trinity was broken.

thirty-two

johnny boudreaux's complaint

Houston, Texas, c. 1991

Booger's body had been found by Taub's hunting dogs a few weeks back. No one was sure exactly how long he had been living in the woods or what he'd managed to eat because his body did not appear malnourished. In fact, the exact cause of death was a mystery. They found him lying on his stomach in a field of dandelions with a large, flattened refrigerator box below him as a canvas. Crayons and pencils were scattered everywhere. He was drawing when he passed, and the coroner's report said that he had a huge smile on his face even though his body was badly decomposed. There was no funeral—nobody to claim the body—so Father Jerome agreed to say a Mass in his memory.

His final picture was that of a horse, and signed at the bottom right corner was—

"Delano Tiberius Jackson."

Thud, thud, thud, thud.

My license plate frame shuddered with each punctuated bass drop emitted from the soundbox of four six-by-nine-inch Sherwood speakers safely sitting in the small hatch of my gray '84 Volkswagen Rabbit. Seven in the morning and headed to school. Senior year. College applications were mailed, addressed far away from Harris County and the mighty Gulf with its wicked ways.

MLK Boulevard was teeming with low-wage workers headed to the grind, little black schoolchildren collected at bus stops, winos uncorked for the morning's first taste—the same collage of dirty Polaroids. I rolled up the block bumping the Geto Boys, hoping that the line at the Jack in the Box drive-thru wouldn't be long. It was time for breakfast. Two tacos for ninety-nine cents and a Coke. Breakfast of champions. Still exhausted from folding towels at T.J.Maxx until eleven the night before, I wiped the sleep out of my eyes and settled my focus on the passing collage. Tired. Tired of it all, seeing dirty strange things lying atop each other, demanding to be seen, demanding to be understood. Passing St. Philip's, I saw Lil' Ant playing helicopter. I waved. Why not? Despite my less than enthusiastic drive to school, the day held some promise—an announcement would be made today. Today I would have a moment of glory.

I finished my breakfast with a burp as I careened into the student parking lot. Several clusters of students loitered around, waiting for the first period bell. Nineteen minutes. More than enough time to increase my meager minimum-wage earnings.

Scooby, Leon, and the rest of the varsity defensive line were already congregated by Country's Regal, shaking the ivories. I parked and walked over with seven dollars in hand. The shooters knelt around a small towel lying on the concrete—ghetto felt. I could smell the undeniable stench of cheap wine and malt liquor from a few teen breaths. Perfect. Coupled with the early hour, alcohol was sure to affect their alertness. I might only need five minutes. The key to shooting craps in the streets is conversation, getting your opponent to double up on his bet by command. It requires a very delicate application of shit talking, coaxing your opponent to bet more than he intended. Now the delicacy of the coaxing was dependent upon who was being coaxed. One wrong word to the wrong person could result in a shooting or stabbing, so attention to psychology was critical.

By the time I stood up with most of their money, a few had blurted several threats as sweat collected in their vacant hands. But nobody was going to touch me. I was the senior class president.

First period.

I strolled down the hallway like a peacock and not because of my winnings. Word had spread quickly that I was on the front page of *The Houston Post*. And not because I had shot anybody or caught a football or signed a record contract. I had made it to the cover of the newspaper because I was intelligent.

Despite the low graduation rate in South Park and the glaring statistics predicting my doom, I had been accepted to every college I had applied to, including three Ivy Leagues. Teachers cheered. Students whispered and smiled. I was a beacon for all the potential that South Park held in its grimy hands. I was hope and everybody knew it.

Mr. Davenport, the guidance counselor, approached with pride, as though he had something to do with it.

"Well, John, looks like you're on your way to the big time."

"Yeah, it looks that way."

And I kept on strolling. He didn't lift one finger to help me during the application process. I was graduating on time, so his job was done. I had already learned that God helps those who help themselves. And if anybody was responsible for my newfound celebrity, it was Mother. After twenty years of her answering the phones at the school district administration office, word got around that her son was something special. In no time a reporter called my house for an interview, saying that he was looking for an emotional story of hope. The reporter wanted to show those rednecks that good things could happen in South Park. I was to be the poster child.

My schoolmates offered a mix of snide remarks and praise for the accomplishment. None of our sports teams ever made it to the play-offs, so the mere mention of our high school on the front page was exciting. I couldn't wait until homeroom announcements, when the principal would surely offer me praise in front of the whole school.

Dazed, daydreaming about the future, the riches, the fame. How far could I go? And what would it be like on the other side? The bronze smile and cobblestone. I hadn't yet stepped foot past Texas or Louisiana, but I was certain that exotic lands awaited me. Lands I had read about or seen on TV. Lands where nobody knew me or where I came from. Lands where I could start over, free from assumptions, free from burdensome context, free from Sonnier and South Park. I would leave this place soon. South Park. It would become a memory tucked away in the abyss. And as much as South Park was a part of me, I longed for the moment to be free from its drunken stupor, unleashed into verdant pastures of optimism, to walk in fields where daisies bloomed promise.

Homeroom.

For the senior class president, homeroom was the prescribed "roam freely" period, although I took such liberties throughout the day. The duties were minimal, visit senior homerooms and make announcements. Senior Prom was on autopilot, senior T-shirts were ordered, and the senior class gift was determined. There really wasn't anything for me to announce, but I made my rounds anyway, still gloating and anxiously awaiting the principal's voice echoing my name in the empty corridors. I wanted to hear that echo, so I kept my visits brief, mere pass-throughs. My last stop was in the music wing adjunct building with one senior homeroom in the band room. I approached the building, opened the door, then I heard it—

"Aah, teachers and students, I'm sure some of you may have heard but one of our students is featured on the front page of *The Houston Post* for academic excellence. Our very own Johnny Boudreaux. Students, John is a great example of that Jones spirit and I hope his accomplishments encourage all of you to strive for excellence. John, I'm sure I speak for all of us when I say we're all very proud of you, son. That's all."

The bell yelled.

End of homeroom.

Students poured into the corridor as I entered. I took a few steps toward the band room as students filed past with pats on the back. A bewildered boy walked past me, brushing my shoulder and offering no excuses. I turned to him, then—

"She got a knife!"

The bewildered boy turned quickly and our eyes met. His expression was vacant, the face of one who had given up a long time ago. And for two of the longest seconds in the history of Time, we stood three feet apart in a private moment of forgiveness. I sought an apology and he knew it, but his sullen, brown eyes told me that he was out of apologies, so engulfed in dread that he was beyond reproach. And the last second (or second number two) he acknowledged that I understood and that an apology would not be necessary. And in that last, quick second, relieved from the burden of apologizing or confrontation, he offered a slight smile in appreciation. This would be his last smile.

It was a fourteen-inch kitchen knife, the kind used to carve a Thanksgiving turkey. It entered from his back, between the shoulder blades, and pushed out from his left breast, severing arteries to his heart. She kept a firm grip on the handle as two boys grabbed her. Peanut pulled her off as she still held the knife. Deep red blood flowed from the boy's chest as students screamed and kept their distance. He looked at me again, searching for understanding, needing help but not knowing why. He was confused, and when he saw the girl struggling with Peanut, he panicked and ran.

The girl attempted one more swipe at him, only to catch Peanut's hand with the blade. And I was frozen, standing in a puddle of fruit punch syrup. As though a switch clicked in the young girl's head, she dropped the knife and calmly walked to the principal's office. But the boy continued to run, leaving a trail of warm fruit punch syrup in his wake. A few students chased after him, but he ran and ran and ran, then collapsed at the doors of the cafeteria. Mr. Douglass, the vice principal, rushed toward the boy and took him by bended knee. The boy's glazed eyes stared through Mr. Douglass as his fading heart pumped out the last and final quart. Students gathered around, and with a soft murmur he spoke—

"That bitch was talkin' 'bout my momma."

His body slumped on Mr. Douglass's knee as he joined his mother, who had died two months earlier. His name was Bruce Watkins and he was fifteen years old.

Students rushed past me to get to the boy, but I walked away in the opposite direction. I didn't want to see blood anymore. And if you listened with discriminating ears, you could hear Bizet's *"Je dis que rien ne m'épouvante"* from *Carmen*. God had a twisted sense of humor, I thought.

Paramedics, HPD, news vans, and the coroner fell upon Jesse H. Jones High School. We watched it from the park across the street, passing forties and blunts with quiet reverence. Country set it out for everybody, and no one said a word. We just watched and drank and smoked. Nobody really knew the kid and nobody ever would. And I brooded over my Olde English, mad as hell. A fucking dead sophomore stole my thunder.

Thud, thud, thud, thud.

It took almost an hour to get my car out of the student parking lot, but when I did break free, I rolled back the sunroof, leaned against the door, and let Guy serenade me to my new girlfriend, Donna Fontenot, in Third Ward.

Donna was a cute little cheerleader at Jack Yates Senior High School, and she probably was my cousin, considering I first met her at a family reunion. We had been going out for the past few months, mostly a movie, a bottle of Boone's Farm Strawberry Hill, and a late-night make-out session at The Lakes of 610. After the day's tragedy, I needed some sex to settle my nerves in a way that Olde English couldn't provide. It was a quarter to five and Donna's cheerleading practice would be wrapping up, so I headed to Third Ward.

I could see the red and gold pom-poms from Scott Street as I headed toward Yates. Fine black legs and thighs jumping to and fro in soulful, syncopated movement reminded me that Frenchy's Fried Chicken was having a sale—two legs and two thighs for $1.99. I knew Donna would be hungry.

Thud, thud, thud, thud.

She spotted me and smiled, her envious cheermates leering. She ran over and gave me a dramatic kiss, all tongue, for her girls to see. She tasted like red Now and Laters. Pretty little vanilla thing with dark brown hair down to her ass because Creole girls didn't cut their hair. I played it cool like Denzel in *Mo' Better Blues,* accentuating her performance with a loving embrace, opening my eyes to witness her girls snickering for want of passion. And there in Donna's arms, lips locked in red Now and Later madness, I saw her. Charity Alexander. Captain of the cheerleading team and definitely the finest high school girl in Third Ward or South Park. Green eyes, big titties and thighs. This girl was a testament to staying out past curfew, buying gold charms and trinkets, and not using a condom. Her caramel skin glistened with afternoon sweat, taunting me with treasures I did not know. And despite the fact that almost the entire cheerleading squad had their eyes on me, she could care less, choosing to busy herself with her sneakers. But I wanted her attention. I wanted to know what the boys would so easily fight about. I wanted to know what hid behind those emerald eyes and underneath that skintight uniform. I wanted a distraction.

"You ready?" asked Donna, interrupting my fantasy with hopeful eyes. She had shown the newspaper article to everybody, so my arrival carried more weight than usual. Girls were always more open to discussing academic matters, but these Third Ward ingénues restricted their comments to "You gonna go to one of them white schools?" And I had never really thought of it like that.

Donna was prouder than me about the news coverage, only

briefly asking about the stabbing that had already hit the wire. I was quiet, watching the road and her hairy legs, feeling my subtle malt liquor drunk fade into perspiration. Slowly, I was returning back to awareness with jolts of the bewildered boy's face nagging me. That haunting face asking me to help was becoming my nemesis. I was falling back into that moment of stillness in action; orbiting around my numb pole were the faces and sounds of that terror, yelling in unison—"Help a brother out." And then it stopped. *Thud, thud, thud, thud.* And a thousand torches of truth alit in my head, scorching my better self. *Thud, thud, thud, thud.* I had failed him, that bewildered son of South Park. I had failed him.

"The light's green," Donna reminded me.

I was stuck at the corner of Blodgett and Dowling, stuck at the corner of bad memories and promising aspirations. I needed a distraction to continue, so I slid my right hand between Donna's legs.

Nothing mattered more than the moment to be released from the day's burden. She hadn't showered, I hadn't brushed my teeth or popped a mint. Neither of us really cared. Her mother would be home in forty-five minutes. Hairy legs around my waist, firmly clasped hands, soft daybed, tender moans, hurried thrusts, the odor, the fear of detection, the knowing, the mischief, the damp hair—for a brief moment, I was free. I came. I left. Returning to the streets that bore me, returning to the dark crevice where fruit punch syrup stained dirty linoleum, unclean and unforgiving.

Mike was waiting for me when I got home. He'd heard about the killing and wanted a firsthand account. I gave him every detail. Mother watched from the window, staring expressionless, attempting to ascertain my mental condition, worried that I had been psychologically scarred by the tragedy. She wouldn't come out, respecting my need to confer with a friend. But it had already happened and the damage was done.

"That's fucked-up," Mike said.

"The crazy thing is, he had just walked right by me. And the girl ran right by me."

"You didn't stop her?" he asked.

"It happened too fast. But guess who I saw at Yates?"

"Charity?"

"You gotdamn right."

"Man, you need to leave her alone; three dudes done already went to jail behind her."

"I ain't gonna holla at her, Mike. I got five months. Five months and I'm gone," I said. And I meant that shit.

thirty-three

the beatification of jules saint-pierre sonnier, fmc

Eunice, Louisiana, January 5, 1953

On the day Nonc Sonnier was to be hung, the entire city of Eunice, Louisiana, shut down, and not out of respect for Nonc but fear. Cautious white men extracted him from his cell and led him to a mule that waited in front of the jail. It was Sonnier's request to be taken to the gallows by mule—Sonnier loved performance. For his last meal, he requested a bowl of couche-couche et caillé prepared by his relations. When asked if he'd like to see a priest for final rites, he laughed and sang—

> O kwa, o jibile
> Ou pa we m'inosan?

The priest made prayer for the heathen nonetheless.

They led the mule all the way to the Boudreaux rice fields. Had to teach that nigger witch a lesson, they reasoned. They knew the spot—right by that tree. Nonc looked around and let off a haughty laugh that scared everybody, including the mayor of Eunice, who'd prosecuted his hanging—Leon Richard, Nonc's son. Now Leon was in effect *passé blanche* in Evangeline

Parish, but the Boudreauxs knew the truth, as did Leon himself. He was ashamed of his witch negra blood, so when he learned that it was Sonnier who'd cast a powerful spell to rid him of fits and fevers, he took it upon himself to prosecute Sonnier for attempted murder by use of black magic, although Sonnier actually saved his life. Yet Sonnier didn't raise a fuss, particularly when he noticed they were going to hang him from an old cypress tree. The joke would be on them.

He looked at his son and winked, which unnerved the mayor. They placed the noose around his neck and gave him a moment to say his last words—

"Tell them when they ask, tell them that wasn't no nigger hanging from that tree. Tell them it was a Frenchman, a free man of color. Tell them it was Marguerite's kin that they hung on his own gotdamn property. Tell them. And if you don't, then ta hell with all y'all."

The mule's rear was slapped. The animal took off. The rope tightened. Nonc Sonnier dangled from the cypress.

thirty-four

the gun and the fire

Houston, Texas, c. May 1991

The next day at school buzzed with the makeshift eulogy of the boy nobody knew. Speculation and fact were the day's soap opera sponsored by a school that was officially in mourning. School psychologists held small assemblies to assess the student body, to ensure that this wouldn't happen again, but the students were generally nonchalant, more concerned with winning tickets for the Superfest concert from Majic 102.1. And I among them had let the event pass into the Yearbook of Things-to-Be-Forgotten with Bruce Watkins's autograph signed in blood. He would never know that of the entire eighty-six-page picture book of students, there was not one photo of him. He had skipped Picture Day to attend his mother's funeral.

Fortunately, I had other things on my mind. The closing of the school year marked the parade of scholarship interviews and ceremonies.

For a ghetto child scholarship recipient, it was a chance to show articulateness, presentation, and poise. Countless hours of television mimicking and Mother's constant correction of my speech had developed an even and succinct "white talk" into my vernacular that could easily be summoned at the turn of a phrase or the shift of a conjunction. The ability to express oneself well when presumably inarticulate is sometimes rewarded, and the articulate ghetto child takes advantage of that myth.

Scholarships (or rewards) were handed out by one of three kinds of people: (1) those who recognize achievement on its face and reward it; (2) those who have an obligation and would be negligent to ignore it; and (3) those who either feel guilty or have a God complex (i.e., white folks). That was the lineup, and first at bat was No. 2—an old black fraternity later that evening.

Mother was to meet me at Wyatt's Cafeteria at six sharp. I was receiving a thousand-dollar scholarship from an old historic black fraternity. I arrived early and sat in my car drinking, waiting on Sonnier to show and give me an explanation, tell my future, which he never did.

"Why you wanna know that, Nephew?" he said once. "It's more fun when you don't know."

One by one, I watched suited, obese black men waddle into the crude eatery, some holding the newspaper article. They greeted each other with a hug and secret handshake, at least that's what I had gathered from *School Daze*. They belonged to each other and they were proud of it, following each other into old age with familiarity. They would never be alone. I thought that was cool, probably like that gang that my cousin Alfred ran with in Los Angeles.

I drained the bottle as Mother drove into the parking lot. My head felt lighter and I swayed. I popped a mint and greeted her. Her face turned from the malt liquor aroma, her eyes asking, "How could you?" I shrugged off her glare and entered my reception to find that the fine fraternity men had already turned my award banquet into happy hour. Half gallons of every known spirit were collected at a busy ad hoc bar. Loud, deep laughter accompanied long cocktail gulps, and the Main Guy offered me a soda while leering at Mother. These niggas were just looking for an excuse to get drunk. I was seated on a dais and waited through a few half-drunk speeches about the fraternity with not-too-subtle suggestions that I sign up when I get to campus. Yeah, right. Mother was annoyed but maintained a congenial smile. She was still proud of me. And finally I was brought up to the podium to accept my scholarship by the Main Guy, and my drunk was official. We met at the microphone and he hugged me (pretending to give me their secret handshake for laughs), but he pulled back with a questionable expression. He smelled Olde English. I smelled Chivas Regal. We both were drunk and we both knew it. I grinned, took the check, and tried to steady myself at the podium. Normally, I would've given an elaborate speech, but I knew these fat, greasy men were anxious to return to drinking, so—

"Thank you."

However, Mother gave a tearful, hour-long speech in the parking lot as I dozed in and out in the driver's seat. Frustrated, she took my keys and left me with instructions to call her when I sobered up. So I slept.

THUD, THUD, THUD, THUD.

Dammit! I had a hangover. I turned the volume down.

Thud, thud, thud, thud.

Much better. The same boulevard. The same faces. The same intersections with bloodshot eyes teasing me by design, shifting to emerald eyes, Charity's eyes. Familiarity breeds contempt, and I was angry. Too familiar. The damn dirty Polaroid. I envied the birds and jet planes that flew over my sprawl with barely a glance, never to know Bruce Watkins or Timmy Chan's Chinese food, only splashes of color canvassed on the earth below, waiting to be shit on, waiting to be speckles in the far-off horizon. Waiting to be nothing, nothing that mattered.

I parked in front of the school and watched. It was Friday, a day filled with promotions of the after-school boxing matches, dates kept and broken, quizzes given back for a parent's signature, relief, celebration, and escape. The drab brick building stood attentively, probably as anxious for the weekend as its occupants.

First period. But not for me.

thirty-five

bad gris-gris

Saturday night, Mike and I headed to a scholarship benefit teen dance at the Texas Southern University student rec center. Three dollars at the door ushered us in to Lagerfeld cologne, conspicuous fake gold earrings, Contempo dresses, Tommy Hilfiger button-downs, Girbaud jeans, Timberlands, audacious rayon shirts, proud fake-leather Africa medallions, flavored lip gloss, alcohol breath, whispers, sneers, laughter, pretentious arrogance, teenage fear, nervousness, infatuation, and a whole lotta ass shaking. Yes indeed, the party was jumping. These were good kids from good schools who were going somewhere, doing something positive with their lives. Patrick, Ricky, and Russell joined us.

"Say, man. What's wrong with you? You still trippin' on Noelle, 'cause that ain't your fault," Mike asked.

"Mike, if I told you, I promise, I mean I promise, you wouldn't believe me. And it's probably a good thing if you don't," I answered and zoned out.

"Man, you can tell me."

"Okay. Do you believe in God?" I asked.

"Yeah, of course."

"Why?"

" 'Cause I do, why you askin' why?" he queried.

"Why do you believe in God? Have you seen God?"

"No."

"Have you felt God, like something touching you?"

"Dawg, you trippin'."

"Am I? I mean, really. Am I?"

"Do you believe in God?" he asked.

"Oh yeah. I believe."

"You don't even go to church anymore."

"So?"

"So how you gonna say you believe in God and you don't even go to church?" he asked.

"Nigga, we havin' church right now."

"You crazy, Johnny."

"You know what, Mike. You're absolutely right. I'm crazier than a muthafucka."

After eighteen years in South Park, I had chosen my circle of friends from greener pastures. Gone were the days of Booger and Raymond Earl. So long to Charles Henry and Pork Chop. Most of them were in jail or dead or just blurry images that I nodded to while passing in and out of Clearway Drive like the postman, on the move, headed elsewhere with purpose. I even chose a different school than my former playmates, who, at some point or another, showed up at Sterling Senior High School. The St. Andrew's crowd was safer.

With Donna babysitting half a mile away and half a case of beer quaffed between Mike and I, the night was wide open for the girls. There were always one or two "cute, new faces," a cousin from the other side of town, the new girl from Louisiana, or the pretty little thing whose momma let her out of the house for the first time.

Then there were the "hard-to-get" girls, fine-looking debutantes who practiced a "better than you" role, most likely inherited and encouraged by their parents, assuming a prim, condescending manner that pleased no one but themselves.

And last, but certainly not least, were the "fo' sho' " girls. If you had something to drink and your own car, you could win. They were the final call, giving new meaning to the DJ's rant—"Last dance!" This was our playground. And just like maneuvering through monkey bars, we dangled from girl to girl with guile and intent. Phone numbers written on napkins, kissed with cherry red lip gloss, scented with her momma's second-best perfume, were passed out and collected like Uno cards. There wasn't a wild card in the bunch, given my recent celebrity status. Even the "hard-to-get" girls looked on me with favor and cautiously offered congratulations and praise. I was now somebody they could bring home or attend the cotillion with or Sweet Sixteen. I was becoming somebody—somebody who wasn't from South Park.

The crowd paused as the lights dimmed, decisions were made, offers were rejected or accepted, and the couplings were determined by the third bar of Bobby Brown's "Roni." The grinding commenced.

Her hair smelled like apricots, her breath like mints, and her ass was soft as Charmin. I had a hard-on and I didn't know her name. But I lost myself with her on that dance floor, grinding like there was no tomorrow, groping like nobody was looking. I could feel her lips haphazardly caress my neck, then she wantonly swabbed her tongue in my ear. It felt great as long as nobody was looking. But they were looking. Mike, Russell, Ricky, Patrick, and Donna. Donna? It seemed her babysitting gig was canceled. And there she was, hairy legs and all, petrified with quiet tears as her friends whispered and pointed. There really wasn't much I could do, so I kept dancing and looked elsewhere, following the domino effect of whispering girls and glares. Oh, I was a scoundrel, but they already knew I was a cad. And Donna held her ground the way women wait for their man to come to his senses, to come home, to come back to them. But I kept grinding with my nameless tenderoni, half drunk and avoiding Donna's silent siren song.

As our song came to an end, I noticed a coy girl standing far off in her best skirt. She went to my school but I didn't know her. In fact, she was the only person at the dance from my school. She glanced nervously at the faces; she didn't know anybody there. Could she be attempting a social exodus? Had she grown as weary of South Park's morose social fabric as I? She found my familiar face with a hint of relief and a grin. She wanted me to come to her, acknowledge her among her friends, confirm her upward mobility by the acquaintance with I, El Social Butterfly. And I saw that need and I felt compassion, even more. I felt oneness with her, my South Park sister. Us. We. We were at this party, spiritually together as countrymen fight in foreign lands, unified by origin and language. Ours was the language of South Park. The knowing of its secrets that bind us eternally. I had to speak with her. I must. My existence depended upon it, as the hand connects to the arm or the foot to the leg. I was she. I promised my nameless tenderoni another dance in a few and was making my way toward my sister until—

"Them niggas shootin' outside!"

The curious rushed to the door. The cautious huddled close together near the rear of the center. But it was no use. A group of twenty or so Third Ward knuckleheads burst through the front door, knocking down the admission table and stealing the scholarship money. They were met by some resistance, a few guys from private school varsity football. But they were no match against this wild group of street kids who didn't play varsity nor win scholarships. Three private school guys were knocked out before the last of the scholarship money was swiped from the floor. A large crowd of angry partygoers managed to push the invaders back, past the broken doors and outside, creating a passageway for flight. Mike was right behind me. This wasn't our fight. We didn't start it and we damn sure weren't going to finish it. Mike's eyes agreed. We skirted along the wall for our exit. Yet when we got outside the real hell broke loose.

Beer bottles flew, gunshots rang, girls screamed, boys were targeted and jumped, car windows were shattered. The panicked partygoers realized that this attack was planned and quickly shifted from defense to offense. An all-out brawl. We moved through the crowd, avoiding hostiles, headed for my gray '84

Volkswagen Rabbit. I had just unlocked my door when the gunfire heightened. It seemed some of the enraged partygoers had reached their vehicles to retrieve their weapons. *Ghetto. Bourgeoisie.* This was now a gunfight.

The tight parking lot was congested with cars attempting to exit onto Blodgett Street, a narrow, asphalt two-lane sided by four-foot-deep ditches. But the mass exodus created a snail crawl on the two-lane. Invaders lined Blodgett and pelted rocks at cars stuck in traffic; we turned left into the procession.

Thud, thud, thud, thud.

My heart was racing; couldn't this traffic move faster? Yellow Adidas warm-up suit flashing pearly whites, black skin. *Thud, thud, thud.* Giant Wasp rushing to my car. My car. Toward Mike and I. *Thud, thud.* Toward I. Me. *Thud, thud.* The Wasp holds a black object, holds it heavily. *Thud, thud, thud.* The Wasp is certain. The Wasp is closer. *Thud, thud.* The black object is a gun. *Thud, thud.* The black object is a gun. The gun is coming closer to me. The gun is coming for me. I've seen this before and not on TV. This is real. *Thud.* This is now. *Thud, thud.* I must respond. Mike is scared and so am I. *Thud, thud, thud, thud.* The Wasp with the gun is getting closer, getting certain, aiming the black object.

Sonnier leaned into my ear, into my head, and said firmly—

"*Tirez ça nèg!*"

Shoot that nigga!

Under the floor mat of the driver's seat—

> *Deus meus, ex toto corde paenitet me omnium meorum*
>   *peccatorum,*
> *eaque detestor, quia peccando,*
> *non solum poenas a te iuste statutas promeritus sum,*
> *sed praesertim quia offendi te,*
> *summum bonum, ac dignum qi super omnia diligaris.*
> *Ideo firmiter propono,*
> *adiuvante gratia tua,*

*de cetero me non peccaturum peccandique occasiones
proximas fugiturum.*
*Amen.**

Don't you see I'm innocent?
THUD, THUD, THUD, THUD.
Ninety-eight miles an hour down 288 south, turn west
onto 610. We were moving, fleeing the scene with anger and
fear. My hands gripped the steering wheel tightly to restrain
the trembling. Dry mouth, fluttering heart. I wanted to vomit
but I had to get away, get to safety. Mike's adrenaline was in
overdrive, arguing with me to go back and get him. I told him
that we were out of bullets, but he couldn't hear my words,
shrouded in outrage, gasping over the cliff's edge and not falling
but walking over the cliff, daring God to let him fall. His fear
had turned into fierce rage, ignited by the scream of the gun and
the aroma of gunpowder, warrior's incense. He was now a lion;
only minutes ago he was a lamb. Mike, incensed by the threat
yet encouraged by my response to the Wasp's stinger. A chrome
.380 semiautomatic.

Pushing down Main Street with headlights attacking and
passing on to their next target, a neon sign hovered afar like
a finish line. Two Pesos Mexican food, a late-night hangout. I
desperately piloted the vehicle to a parking spot. *Thud, thud.* Silence but for my heartbeat, which was anxious to rest but still in
flight. Hands still gripping the steering wheel, I turned to look
at Mike, who scowled out the window. It was over.

"Say, Johnny! Whatcha get when you mix red and yella? A
nigga on the ground."

I hadn't noticed the brown Seville following me from the
battle. It was Broderick and his boys from Fifth Ward. They
jumped out of the Caddy whooping and congregated around
my car. I slowly let go of the steering wheel and my hands

---

* Act of Contrition in Latin.

shook violently. I eased out of the car. Mike didn't move. They cheered and gave me every detail. The Wasp had been maimed. One shot above the knee. One shot from a nickel-plated .380 semiautomatic. *Oh, no.*

A hot fog settled over me, percolating into every pore and follicle, suffocating my being in one long, hot flash. Nigga hot. I couldn't tell if I was breathing, certain that for two of the longest seconds in time, I was dead. Broderick handed me a bottle of Orange Jubilee. I drank deeply, searching for the prize at the bottom. I had achieved a status that none of us had before. I was officially a gunfighter, and I didn't like it.

Broderick and his boys continued congratulations and comments, then left for a nacho plate. I still leaned against the car in a daze, clutching the cheap wine for dear life.

"If you gonna drink that, you better get in your car before you get busted."

And there she stood. An angel cut from the clouds. A demon escaped from Hell. Lilith reborn. Charity Alexander. For the first time she looked directly into my eyes, staring at my naked truth with a grin. I thought of Noelle.

Somehow her expression revealed a new development, interest. She approached me with certainty and asked for a sip. I obliged. She didn't need a cup; she went straight from the bottle, and that turned me on. Hallelujah! What a sweet distraction. With Fate dealing and Fortune at my right, I was dealt a pair of deuces for the evening, yet as she lowered the bottle, warmed by the libation, it occurred to me that a pair of deuces just might win. I opened the backseat door and we climbed in. Mike was still stoic, frozen in anger. She took another sip, then passed the bottle.

"Why'd you shoot that boy?"

" 'Cause he was gonna shoot me."

And now I had said it, offering my defense that might someday be heard in court. I focused on the open sunroof, watching the bright neon sign announcing "24 Hour Mexican Food." She stared more intensely, more closely. I met her eyes, she took my trembling right hand, then offered, "Is there anything I can do?"

My head fell back against the seat, loaded with guilt. How could I let this happen? I must be. I have to be. I gotta be. I am. I am the dumbest nigga in the world. I had hoped better for myself. I raised the bottle to my lips, hoping for sweet orange salvation fermented with the promise of a better moment. Better than now. But no amount of alcohol could hide the truth—I fucked up. I pondered my next move with dread. Yet Charity saw a hero, a bad boy, a gunfighter. She saw a reason, so she went down on me. And I? I finished the bottle of jube with Charity giving me head and cried.

I rolled down the window and pointed a shaky finger toward the night sky to write my petition. Mike noticed in the rearview.

"Man, what you doin'?" Mike asked.

"I'm pointing at God."

"Why?"

" 'Cause He's pointing at me."

thirty-six

pointin' at god

Since I was old enough to sneak onto Ricky Street, I was aware of everything that was wrong with South Park, and not just its lack of noticeable glamour. Compared to the rest of Houston, or the world for that matter, South Park represented the stereotypical blight of Black America, a true ghetto, heart and soul. And I tried at every opportunity to distance myself from it, to not fall prey to its depressed trap. I had reprogrammed my machine to counter its effects. But when I awoke that next morning and considered the events of the week, I knew that I was a South Park nigga. And my survival would depend on my knowledge of being a South Park nigga. I had shot someone. Inquiries would be made. And the Wasp was somewhere thinking of revenge. He had a gun too, and certainly he had every reason to use it.

Mother entered my room with a strong, proud smile and a letter in her hand. University of Pennsylvania had offered to pay my tuition. She had hoped better for me and her prayers were answered. My ticket out of South Park was confirmed. Now, the only thing I had to do was survive.

Monday morning I pulled into the student parking lot and prepared for the morning dice session. Country stood near the guys and motioned for me. He walked away from the crowd, and he wasn't smiling.

" 'Sup, Country?"

"Man, what the fuck you think you doin'? Shootin' at niggas and shit."

"Man, that fool was coming for me."

Country paused and stared at me. He was the school drug dealer, a transplant from Dallas who had to graduate as part of his parole. Flashy and clownish, Country earned his rep for using his head and staying under the radar. Buffoonery was his veneer, a clever ruse to keep rivals and cops off his back.

"You still got the gun?"

"Nawh," I lied. It was in my backpack.

"Good. I don't think you gonna have to worry 'bout ole boy, tryin' to work something out now. I need your keys."

"Wassup?"

Then I saw a few guys approaching. It was Raymond Earl and Joe Boy. But they didn't go to my school. They didn't even go to school. And I hadn't spoken with them in years, just nods and waves as I traveled in and out of Clearway Drive trying to be somebody. Somebody else. My abandoned childhood friends had conferred with Country and come to my assistance. They had a plan and an objective. Under no circumstances was I to go to jail or be harmed. They greeted me as though no time had passed between us. They made no inquiries and requested no explanations for my absence from their lives.

In the movies the car would be dumped in a river off the beaten path, but who could afford a new car? They were going to get my car painted to avoid identification. They only had one question. Which color? And before I could swallow my embarrassment and guilt, Raymond Earl, el Comandante, chimed in, "Black."

After school I took a bus to the better side of town for a scholarship interview with Houston's prominent white leaders. The interview was held at the posh Waldorf-Astoria hotel. The black doorman tipped his hat—it was Sonnier.

"Don't fuck this up for me, Nonc," I asked.

He grinned and snapped his heels together.

I entered, greeted by a barrage of the affluent who smiled and commented. The newspaper article had been distributed like handbills announcing the circus or cheap auto insurance. I was the event. This wasn't the first time I had participated in such spectacles, seeking to wrangle favor from the privileged, assuming the role of the brash stripling with a flair for sharp repartee.

Three individual interviews with pillars of the community sans South Park, Third Ward, Fifth Ward, Acres Homes, Sunnyside, and anywhere else black folks huddled in Houston. These were representatives of the "other" community, the community of the "haves." I performed my routine tongue-in-cheek "white talk" with ease, reassuring my benevolent patrons that, indeed, I was a good investment. Then, the final interview.

He was the district attorney for the city of Houston, responsible for putting niggas in jail five days a week. He was short, cocky, and wore a well-tailored suit. We sat five feet apart from each other, and he didn't have that cheesy grin that the other interviewers had had before. He was accustomed to questioning young black men. He was discerning, intent on finding a flaw. Why? Because on paper, I was perfect. So his questions started, one after another, some relevant, some trivial. My school record. My dating preferences. My school choices. My favorite TV show. Current events. The person I admired. He wouldn't stop, then started floating arcane *Jeopardy!* questions. Unnecessary questions meant to catch me slipping. But I had all the answers, and I could tell this was really pissing him off. This small man with the well-tailored suit who put niggers like me in jail. South Park niggas. And only arm's distance away was a chrome .380 semiautomatic in my backpack. I didn't have any bullets, but I was ready to pistol-whip him if I had to.

Then he stopped. I'd won and he knew it. The conversation shifted to my car as I rose to leave. We shook hands, then he threw one last jab—

"Volkswagen, huh?"

"Yep, 'eighty-four."

"You know what Volkswagen means?"

That had to be the stupidest question I'd ever been asked.

What in the hell did that have to do with anything? He mustn't have known, couldn't have known. I am John Paul Boudreaux, Jr., Free Man of Color. Somebody better tell him.

At the half-open door, I paused. He waited for an answer that he assumed I didn't have. The cicadas screamed. Nonc Sonnier screamed. Booger screamed. Charles Henry screamed. Raymond Earl screamed. Country screamed. The Wasp screamed. Arthur Duncan screamed. Pork Chop screamed. The Median Man screamed. Father Jerome screamed. Mike Braddock, Jr., screamed. Johnny Watson screamed. Edmund Guillory screamed. Herman Malveaux screamed. Joe Boy screamed. Paul Boudreaux screamed. Donnie Carter screamed. Paul Gagnier screamed. Squirrel screamed. Harold screamed. Coon screamed. Bruce Watkins screamed. Even Black Jesus screamed. EVERY NIGGA BOY SCREAMED—

"TELL THAT MUTHAFUCKA, TI' JOHN!"

I shifted my backpack on my shoulder, feeling the weight of the empty chrome .380 semiautomatic resting above my kidney. The small man felt big, triumphant, another nigger going to jail. I heard whispers competing for my ear, but I tuned them out.

"The people's car."

And I left.

I walked out of the Waldorf-Astoria and nodded to the white doorman with a bounce in my step. A lightness of heel.

"Have a good evening, young man. Ya might need an umbrella tonight if you're ridin' the bus," he offered.

"Nawh, I'm good. I think I'm gonna walk tonight. Rain ain't never hurt nobody," I countered.

He tipped his hat with "Sounds like a mighty fine idea, young man."

Mighty fine, indeed.

A nice set of hedges hugged the pearly white building. I looked around, then unzipped my fly. A few drops of drizzle hit my penis. I laughed while zipping up my pants and headed into the wet streets.

Walking down Main Street near Hermann Park, I could see Hippo Hill. That's where he was waiting for me.

I climbed up Hippo Hill and approached him with a deep bow. He returned the salutation. We sat down on the grass. He was eating a piece of sugarcane.

"I'm gonna be leaving soon," I said, waiting for a response. None.

"And I ain't gonna be doing none of this anymore. Tu comprends?" I continued.

Sonnier shrugged, then held out his hand. I gave him the gun.

"And I ain't making no deals with you either. You ain't even supposed to be alive," I continued.

Sonnier put the gun on the ground and continued chewing on the cane, taking his sweet time if you will, then without looking at me he managed—

"Who said I was alive?"

I let that sit in the air, waiting for him to turn to smoke or vanish like he'd normally do, but this time he just stayed put chewing on cane, so I left.

I headed down Hippo Hill, leaving Nonc Sonnier with his sugarcane and the gun. I'd never see him again until years later in New Orleans, and then he acted as though he didn't know me. Fuckin' family.

I promised myself I wouldn't tell anybody about Nonc Sonnier, but I figured nobody would believe me anyway. I mean, you don't have to believe me. You can believe in crying statues or Bigfoot or something. But if you don't believe me, then ta hell with all y'all.

(Hot, humid air settles on pinecones above. Quiet. Still. A red cicada watches from a branch. A police siren moans far off. Hot, sticky bayou air lingers.)

Still walking as an olive fog greeted me in MacGregor Park, I wasn't fatigued.

The green street sign read: "Martin Luther King Jr. Blvd."

Almost home. Keep walking.

Nigga hot. Humidity left a greasy film on my face as I emerged from the olive mist and tall pines of Third Ward, headed to the forgotten, abandoned battlefield of South Park. Headed home. Walking under the 610 Loop overpass, I reflected on Father carrying me through the brown murky murk on that precarious night; a night wet with death, life, hope, struggle, surrender, and the low voice of a stranger—all mixed into a big stockpot, heated and stirred until it smelled familiar and tasted appropriate. There are no apologies in this pot, no explanations or laments—only the soft whisper of Those-That-Know saying, *"Lâche pas la patate, mon cher."**

We don't get to determine how we're born or to whom. We play the cards we're dealt. Sometimes we trick the dice for advantage, other times we accept Fate without question. Either way, we continue into the unknown with delusions of certainty as a safety blanket and a hope that the next day will be kinder than the last. And if you have red nigger witch blood in your veins, well . . .

I continued walking as a light rain fell on the oil-slick, potholed streets of MLK. And like the Median Man, I continued down this boulevard that promised nothing but life continuum. One step after the other, I made my way home. Walking toward the woods.

---

*"Don't let go of the potato, my dear"—colloquial Creole saying that means "Keep the faith."

Acknowledgments

I am deeply grateful to my editor, Malaika Adero; my agent, Charlotte Sheedy; my parents, John Oran Guillory and Lois Marie Carmouche Guillory; Kelly Carmouche; Joseph M. Carmouche; Helen Mouton; Roselia Guillory; Evelyn LeBlanche; Louis Guillory; Roy Guillory; Wanda Kennedy; Quincy Troupe; Dr. Marvin Hoffman; Wolf; Sostan Lemelle; Maurice Williams; Dr. Eric Perkins; Bill Summers; Father Joseph Bell; Louis Benjamin; Anthony Hall; Craig Kennedy; Rey Alton; Brian Simmons; Angelbert Metoyer; Roger Pliakas, Esq.; Rob Walker; Sister Eva Regina; St. James Episcopal School; St. Philip Neri Catholic Church and School; Jesse H. Jones Senior High School; Timmy Chan's Chicken & Rice; Paul Deo; Tish Benson; Shelli Harris-Blackshear; Faith Gibson; Dr. Barry Ancelet; Joe Teisan; Christophe Landry; Garth Trinidad; Mateo Senolia; Kim Alston; Osunlade (Yoruba Records); Dr. YBamur Flores-Peña; Michelle Moore; Yusef Davis; Ava K. Jones; Jonathan Mannion; Les Brun; Wood Harris; Taz Arnold (TI$A); Emily Etling; S.H.A.P.E. Community Center; the city of Houston, Texas; the city of Opelousas, Louisiana; the city of Basile, Louisiana; the city of New Orleans, Louisiana—my estranged mistress; Love 94 FM; Majic 102.1 FM; KTSU; AstroWorld; the Guillory family; the Donato family (Opelousas, Louisiana); the Fontenot family; the Carmouche family; the Alexander family (Breaux Bridge, Louisiana); my boys from South Park—Llyarron "Muscle" Greer, Brian Smith, Lil' James, Booger John, Ronnie, Joe Boy, Calvin, Boobie,

Rodney, Maurice, Charles Henry, Scooby, Dwayne, Eddie and Haywood Dean, Tim, Benjamin "Frank" Leviston, Xavier Williams, K-Rino, Ganksta N-I-P, Lil' Fry, B-Rock, Sean DeVaughn, Doug, Paul Brown, and all the little black boys off MLK Boulevard—you have a voice; anyone I failed to mention, believe it was not intentional, much love.

Printed in the United States
By Bookmasters